Praise for *Secrets of th*

"Professor McKenna needs to get away. Taking a step out of her ordinary life, she accepts a house-sitting job in the idyllic setting of Lake Como, Italy, where she becomes concierge to a group of high-spirited American women on holiday. It is here she experiences a whole new taste and aroma of life. *Secrets of the Italian Villa* is a perfect romance novel!"
—Liz Connors, actor and director

"Deeply sensual and haunting. I adored it!"
—Linda Stunell, author and filmmaker

"An intriguing story of healing and forgiveness, and lots of romance. A heartfelt love story in an exotic location."
—Babe Gurr, musician

"*Secrets of the Italian Villa* is a romantic, sensual novel that exquisitely engages you on Gerri McKenna's journey of loss, exploration, awakening, self-discovery and passion."
—Joan A. Harris, music promoter

Secrets of the Italian Villa

M. J. Milne

Author of *12 Golden Keys for a New World*,
and, *Universal Tides*

Love happens when you forget to hesitate.

Blue Heron Productions
B.C., Canada

Paperback ISBN: 978-0-9739654-5-2
Electronic Book ISBN: 978-0-9739654-2-1

Cover Designer: Jerry Leonard
Author Photo: Michael O'Shea
Interior Formatter: Sweet 'N Spicy Designs

First Edition: 2024
Publisher: M. J. Milne/Blue Heron Productions
Website: www.mjmilne.com

Dedication

To my family.

And to the OWLs—Outrageous Wiser Ladies.

*I am not now
That which I have been.*
—Lord Byron

*When you write the story of two
happy lovers, let the story be set
on the banks of Lake Como.*
—Franz Liszt

*If love is the answer, could you
rephrase the question?*
—Lily Tomlin

Contents

1. Pandora's Secret 1
2. Mother Teresa and Mozzarella 8
3. A Haunting Vision 24
4. What'll I Do with Thirteen Lesbians? 37
5. The Bell Over the Door 49
6. An Artist's Gaze 65
7. *Bizarro* Bellagio 72
8. The Owl of Varenna 88
9. *Tête-à-Tête* 98
10. Rousing the Huntress 101
11. The Talking Wall 118
12. Wildflowers and Headstones 125
13. *Oh, Madonna Mia!* 138
14. Breaking Rules 145
15. To Market We Go 150
16. Lust on the Menu 162
17. Daring To Be Bold 176
18. Initiation into the Mysteries 181
19. The Olive Grove Lovers 189
20. *Bellezza, Bella Mia* 198
21. Milan's Last Supper 208
22. Awakening Allegra 223
23. Tunnel of Tears 233
24. Full Moon Festival 238
25. The Pirate's Secrets 253
26. Slamming Doors 265
27. The Shift 270
28. Surfacing 277
Author's Note & Acknowledgements 284
About the Author 285

CHAPTER 1
Pandora's Secret

*Writing a journal makes me realize how afraid I am
to take risks. There's not much time left. I need to
learn to step across the lines drawn in the sand.*

—G. A. McKenna, journal entry

A year had passed since my husband Paul's fatal accident. Morning sunlight peeked in as I sat in my kitchen nook—in shock, my hand shaking as I held his phone.

"Unbelievable!" I said aloud to myself, frantically scrolling back and forth.

The dates indicated their phone *sexting* began months before his death and continued until a few days before he died. Just the other day, my grief counselor had encouraged me to begin letting go of his possessions, keeping a few mementos. Today, being the first day of summer break at the Vancouver college where I teach, and the anniversary of Paul's death, I felt ready to tackle it, renewed with a sense of purpose to begin a new chapter.

I started with his work phone, having found it hidden in his dresser drawer along with the charger. And this is what I find! Frontal nudes and selfies of them together with Paul's hands all over her body. That woman! Practically my opposite, she stared back at me: thirty-something, plump with long dark hair and weathered skin; compared to my fifty-something fit body with light brown hair and purposely nourished skin.

"God, why didn't I listen to my intuition? It shouted at me."

Woman's intuition—my dire *Gift*, as I've come to call it—made me hesitate to open what turned out to be a Pandora's box. Like Pandora, my curiosity had made me open the photo gallery on his phone, expecting to find family photographs. Instead, out swarmed far more than I had bargained for and, like the Greek myth, "hope" wasn't one of them.

"Damn you Paul!" I hit the kitchen bench with my fist—"Shit! That hurt."

Living alone since he died, grieving deeply, surrounded by all his stuff, I'd been talking out loud to him and even to myself quite a lot. Furious, I marched upstairs and threw his clothes into garbage bags, all the while obsessing about Paul and *that woman*. I figured she had to be in the Merchant Marines. Paul had worked as a water-taxi driver for a marine transportation company. He and our twenty-three-year-old son, Thomas, drove freighter personnel back and forth into town off the foreign freighters that streamed in and out of Vancouver's busy port. From the photos, she obviously worked on a freighter, so I dubbed her "Miss Freighter Girl," and also, "She-Who-Will-Never-Be-Named." I didn't know her name anyway and liked it that way.

"Married twenty-five frickin' years. Paul, you schmuck. I hope you can hear me," I yelled, dragging the garbage bags downstairs into the kitchen. I wanted to immediately kick all his belongings to the curb for pickup but threw them beside some empty boxes.

In defiance, I opened his booze cupboard, grabbed his best Canadian Club whisky, and proceeded to pour some into his cherished, expensive crystal glass. Raising the glass high, I stared at one of the framed photographs on the kitchen bookshelf, the one of Paul and me in Hawaii, laughing and happy.

"Cheers, you *arsehole!*—Wait a minute."

Still holding the glass in mid-air, I had a light bulb moment. "No wonder we had no sex for years. You had a sex buddy!" Poking at his face in the photograph, I shouted, "Hey, here's to *me!*" and took a large swig that burned my throat. Not used to drinking, I coughed and choked, my face scrunching up. "It needs ice."

Digging some out from the freezer tray, I read a note I'd posted on the fridge door weeks before: "Face the lion. Don't run from it." The anger switched to grief, I closed my eyes and my chest heaved with deep sobs as gut-wrenching images crashed through.

I see the curl of the wave first, then the ripples and how Paul's limp body cuts the surface. It bobs face down. Seconds pass like minutes. Another wave curls from the boat's wake and turns him over, his eyes stare up at me, wide-open. I hear a blood-curdling scream, then realize it's mine.

A noise brought me back into the present moment; a familiar sound that called me to the kitchen window. Through the glimmer of dusk, I looked into the backyard. Yup, there he was, that old barn owl, perched on the back fence, where he'd been visiting every night since late May, sheltered under an umbrella of wet evergreen branches. My Spirit Animal, that wise owl, looked back at me knowingly.

"To you, Mister Owl," I said, raising my glass. Mister Owl winked at me, and I laughed, then took a swig. We stared at each other for the longest time.

"What's next, Miss McKenna?" I heard myself ask. I had no idea. I just stared out the window, in silence, sipping on his whisky, seeking bravery, and wondering whether to tell my son and daughter.

I jumped when my mobile on the counter beeped, wondering if the "Universe" had heard my question. A text from Rosie, my oldest living friend.

The text read: "Gerri, call me!"

My BFF from age twelve. In sixth grade, she had decided our futures: I'd grow up to be a teacher; she'd become a flight attendant, which is exactly what happened. Years later, it broke my heart when Rosie moved away to Devon, England, with her second husband, Bill. Sadly, I'd never gone overseas to visit. But, thanks to cell phones and email, we'd kept in touch. I would have shrivelled up and died without her constant calls over the last year, along with visits from my children, friends, and neighbours who dropped in and kept me fed and conscious in the physical world. Rosie kept me sane.

A few seconds later: *Brrr-ring!* Rosie Campbell calling.

I answered and clicked the speakerphone. Rosie's voice boomed out, desperate-sounding: "Gerri, I need your help!" The voice faded, then, "For God's sake, are you there?"

"Hello! Yes, I'm here. What's up?"

"Thank goodness." Rosie blew her nose. "We're in London's emergency room. Bill needs an operation. Appendicitis."

"Oh, no, I'm so sorry to hear—"

"Gerri, I hate to ask, but I need a favor. I mean, isn't it the anniversary of Paul's death?"

"Please, never mind that," clearly not the time to tell her of Paul's treachery, "How can I help?"

"Hold on a minute. It's, ah, the surgeon." Rosie muffled the receiver.

Waiting for Rosie, I fussed about, straightening framed photographs on the bookshelf: a black and white photo of myself as a newborn baby in a crib; an older one of Paul in army fatigues with our children, Thomas and Julie, now grown. Right then I decided not to tell them of their father's adultery, wanting them to have only happy memories of him. And my favorite photo of Paul and me in Hawaii, when we were our happiest. I wondered, if he were still alive, and knowing that fifty-five percent of people who cheat do it again, would I forgive him?

I raised the glass to the photo. Thinking of my cooking school students, I warned them, "Don't do this at home, kids." I took a gulp of the drink, holding it in my mouth, gargling.

"I'm back. Geraldine, you there?"

Choking, I spit the whisky into the sink. "I'm here for you. How can I help? Anything, as always. You called me Geraldine, must be serious."

"We've got a job, house-sitting for a month. We're with a new agency, new clients, important clients. Obviously, we can't go with Bill in hospital. And, well…" She paused.

"You need a house-sitter? Is that all?" I said, pulling nervously at my bangs. "Don't worry, I'll help you find someone."

While listening to Rosie, I opened a kitchen cupboard, looking for things to discard that reminded me of Paul. Seeing his "Best Husband" mug, I tossed it and his personalized barbeque set into an empty box. Clang!

I got an unmistakable whiff of Paul's aftershave, a recurring sign of Paul's ghostly presence over the last year. I sipped the whisky, this time allowing the warm amber liquid to slide down my throat, then tossed a "Dad's Are Great" metal beer stein into the box, hearing a loud clang as it landed.

"Bonehead moron," escaped my lips.

"Say what?" Rosie said on the phone.

"What? It's nothing. Just talking to myself. Nothing new. Go on."

As I listened to Rosie's pleas, I hiccupped. Now slightly intoxicated—it doesn't take me much—I stomped over to the bookshelf beside the fridge and grabbed the photo of Paul and me. The floodgates opened; tears streamed down my cheeks. Staring into his eyes, I whispered, "You make me feel ashamed even though I did nothing wrong." Biting my lower lip, I threw the picture, just missing the potted plant, and heard the frame's glass shattering inside the box. "Score!" I mouthed the word with a fist pump.

Rosie rambled on, something about travel healing a broken heart. Rosie's lyrical voice always comforted me, but now it sounded frantic. "I'll *pay* you for the month. Maybe two months, or—"

"Wait, you mean *me*?"

"Yes, *you*, fraidy-cat. I've told you for months how fantastic it is, being international house-sitters. We get paid to travel the world and live like the rich. And you've always wanted to—"

"Hold on," I said, wiping my tears, "You want *me* to house-sit—for a month? When?"

"Right now! It's an emergency. It's your summer break, right? Your passport's current, right? I've booked your flight. You have two days to pack and will arrive June 1st, and start Saturday."

"What? In two days? No way. Where?"

"Lake Como."

"Lake Como, *Italy*?"

"No, Alaska! Come on, Professor McKenna, you need a holiday, and you've always wanted to go to Italy."

"Are you crazy, Rosie? I can't traipse halfway across the world. Besides, I'm in the middle of grief therapy. Ask my daughter, I still need it."

"Don't go to therapy. Go to Italy. That's your therapy! And a surprise awaits—"

"Oh no, I can't *wait* to hear."

"Well, so, um, guests are coming, an eight-day rental—I'll tell you later. You can do this. And everyone will love you in Italy, what with your culinary skills. You remember some Italian from your parents. Right?"

"Yes, some. We spoke Italian at home, with my parents and especially with my grandmother." I fell silent, pondering Rosie's offer.

In a gentle tone, she whispered, "Time you got back into life, Gerri. It's summer, school's out, take a holiday. Or retire early. *Il e dolce far niente*—the sweetness of doing nothing."

"Nice. But *me* retire? No way, maybe in a few years...." I quickly thought about how much Rosie needed my help and, truth is, I needed a holiday, the run-away-as-far-as-you-can kind.

"Come on, Gerri. Grief therapy or an Italian holiday?" she said.

"The sweetness of doing nothing, eh? Pronounced *eel-eh doll-chay far nee-entay*, huh, close enough?" I said, slurring. I shut my eyes and whispered, "Okay, I'll go."

"Both your children would want you to go."

"Rosie, I said I'm in."

"What? Excellent!" Rosie squealed. "You're a life saver." Then, without skipping a beat, she was all business: "All right, listen up. Time is short and I want to tell you one more itty-bitty."

"Oh no, here we go," I said, recalling that phrase from our school days. "All right, Rosie. What's the itty-bitty this time?"

"The villa rents out its rooms to tourist groups, right? There's a group coming. Thirteen people, and, ah, well, they're..."

"Here comes the kicker at the end of an itty-bitty."

"...the guests are all...well...lesbians."

"LESBIANS!"

"Thirteen American lesbians, from California."

"*Thirteen*? That's an odd number. What do I do with thirteen American lesbians from California?"

"Well, if I remember from our university days, you were a little bit partial to a bit of—"

"Stop it! Don't open that Pandora's box. That's not fair. You know that was just an experiment."

Rosie laughed while saying, "Look, all you do is welcome

them an' whatnot. You won't need to cook or care for them, you just need to watch over the villa, and act as concierge. There's even a maid to clean house and a handyman."

I heard Rosie take a breath before asking in a more serious tone, "Are you okay, Gerri? I know you well. Is there something else going on? You seem out-of-sorts."

Not wanting to tell her about Paul and Miss Freighter Girl, I said, "You're right, Rosie. I need a holiday, and I've never been to Italy. Plus, all the grief books say to be grateful. I'm grateful for your friendship, I'm grateful my children grew up with no diseases or drugs and grateful I worked hard to own my own home." I tried not to cry. "I'm grateful my students love me, and I love them. I've got a fantastic career. But, shit, I feel empty inside, I'm stuck. I don't want to just follow the headlights. Not anymore. I want to veer off the road, start a new adventure before it's too late. And thanks to you, well…. Everybody needs somebody to kick their butt. So, thank you. I will try to be the best concierge ever."

"You're welcome, Gerri. Please be all right. Read the emails I sent. *Rocambolesco! Rock-am-bow-lets-go!*" Rosie cheered. "Italian, it means: 'It's time to go on an incredible, fantastical adventure.' You won't regret it, I promise. Gotta go. Talk to you in a bit. Bye, honey."

She hung up and click went my life in one outrageous, life-defining moment. I held up the whisky glass, this time with a solemn, heartfelt toast: "Gerri McKenna, your new life begins now!"

CHAPTER 2
Mother Teresa and Mozzarella

If Sophia Loren looked that good on a spaghetti diet, there's hope for me yet.

—G. A. McKenna, journal entry

"W hat in the world am I doing here?" I asked under my breath, tripping off the airplane onto the ramp at Milan's airport.

"Lighten up, McKenna. Breathe."

The two flights, Vancouver to Paris and Paris to Milan, felt like one long blur. Walking down that ramp into the airport, my thoughts were racing: Why have I come here? For Rosie, of course, but deep down I knew there was more. "Why am I *really* here?" Italy was my parent's long ago homeland, not mine. We often talked of visiting there together, but never did. And here I am, venturing away from my safe, comfortable home in Canada— the only home I've known—into the wilds of Italian life, solo. Yes, solo. No mama, no papa, no Paul, no kids. The fear of solo travel finally hit me.

Rosie's words were ringing in my ears, "You won't regret it, *I promise.*" Why do people say that? They say it in the movies: "It'll be all right. The monster won't break down the door. I promise." But monsters always do, and my personal monsters were certainly traveling with me.

Dazed and disoriented, I followed the other passengers into Milan's airport terminal. Taking a deep breath, I felt more present than in a long time, as though sitting on the precipice of change. Looking around, it slowly sunk in, "Holy cow! I'm in Italy."

I followed international stick-figure signs to the sleek, modern train that took us into Milano Centrale. Barely noticing the impressive Art Deco architecture, I wandered around the terminal looking for the Lake Como train until two nuns offered their help. The downloaded translator voice-to-text app on my phone came in handy. Soon I was on the train with a handsome porter helping me stow my way-too-large suitcase into the compartment's baggage rack, and he pointed to a place for my daypack on a shelf above my designated seat. Exhausted, I collapsed into the comfy train seat just as the train began to move out of the station.

I caught sight of a reflection on the window glass. There she is again, that anxious-looking woman who really needs to brush her hair. Yup, it *is* me. Suddenly, I felt scared. Traveling abroad, alone, for the first time in my life made me feel as fragile as a lost child. Loneliness crept in to ravage my fearful heart.

"Buck up, McKenna! Don't go there," I heard my inner voice admonishing me. "Listen to the train. Watch the city of Milan fade into the distance and see how the green landscape hugs the train tracks. Be happy to be in Italy."

Leaning back into the seat, feeling better, I caught my reflection in the window again. It confirmed my wide bright blue eyes and my shoulder-length light brunette hair, shimmering with highlights. Not bad for fifty an' a bit. People told me I looked ten years younger than my age. Except now, a stress sign showed itself with a red "V" on my forehead. I could make out red blotches on my neck, which also happened when I get sexually aroused—so rare these days. Must be the Italian air!

I felt the heat rising through my pores as I started to perspire, or was it a hot flash? Undoing a shirt button, I watched the bright moving landscape, trying to acclimatize to the heat. I'd planned to spend this time writing in the new travel journal that my daughter had given me as a going-away gift, but I just wasn't in the mood, so returned it to my daypack; along with the Italian phrasebook I'd tried to study on the airplane to refresh my stale Italian, and a guidebook of Italy that I had bought at the

Vancouver airport. Sitting up straight, I opened my purse and turned on my now-unlocked mobile, thanks to my son, Thomas, who had helped me get ready on short notice, along with my daughter Julie. Then I noticed a telephone message from Rosie and put on earbuds to listen.

"*Ciao*, honey," said Rosie's cheery voice. "Hope you arrived safe and sound and made it to the train. I'm hoping a driver will meet you in Como town, but don't count on it. Take the ferry. You did remember to print out the instructions I emailed you?"

"Instructions? More like a doorstopper," I mumbled and yet, knowing the last forty-eight hours had been a tornado of activity, I was grateful for her itemized lists.

"Did you make copies of your passport, debit and credit cards, and return flight ticket? Keep the originals in the money belt Julie gave you, including your cards and cash," Rosie advised.

"How did she know Julie gave me a money belt? They must be in touch."

"Yes, *wear* your money belt. Yes, *under* your clothes. Don't keep valuables in your purse."

"Now who's being psychic?" I took the jam-packed money belt out of my purse and, hoping the other passengers wouldn't notice, I fastened it around my waist and stuffed it in my pants. Now I looked pregnant.

"I need to tell you one more itty-bitty…" Rosie's message continued.

"Shit! Now what—?" Oops! I'd said that a little too loud. The lady across the aisle averted her eyes, smiling.

Rosie asked, "Remember I said thirteen American lesbians are coming?"

Feeling flushed, I undid another button, muttering, "And the itty-bitty is…?"

"Yes, well, your lesbians will arrive tomorrow, no set time, so get some sleep tonight."

I tore off my cardigan as the hot flash hit full force.

Rosie's message went on, "Read your notes. And stop worrying. Lesbians don't bite. Although you might still like that. Sorry, had to go there."

Of course, she meant that girl in university—the biter—the one Rosie won't let me forget. I've always called that dalliance "my experiment" and kept that particular door sealed shut after I got pregnant by mistake, acquired a husband and a full-time job, and found no key to unlock the door.

"Oh, wait, I almost forgot to tell you," Rosie's message continued, "If you need anything, a buddy of mine, Davide, lives up the lake in Bellagio, owns a hotel, *Casa di Sognatori*. He's a good ol' sport. He'll make sure you're all right, among other things," she chuckled.

I caught the end of Rosie's voicemail. "*Ciao bella!* Text me when you arrive at the villa." She paused, then added, "Dear Gerri, it's time to say yes to life. *Ami la vita*—Love life."

Sighing, I said, "Why does everyone want me to say yes to life? Bless their hearts. They're lucky I'm still breathing."

That lady across the aisle and a few other passengers looked at me quizzically again. "It's all right," I said in English, "talking with angels is all right. Mother Teresa talked to angels." They nodded out of politeness.

Feeling suffocated, I grappled with the upper window. A breeze sifted into the train compartment and, strange, but I thought of my parents. My mother, who believed in angels, always said I had a guardian angel, and she also believed I was a bit psychic. "You have the Gift," she'd say. After Papa passed, I refused to let Mama wither away, and now she lives happily in a retirement community, with Papa as her guardian angel. She likes to joke that she's not interested in a new relationship because she's "romantically retired." Like mother, like daughter, I guess.

While visiting her on my way to the airport, she reminded me again to use my special gift. "Your intuition is a gift, Geraldine, and that connection is always right there within," she said, pointing to my heart and then one gentle tap on my forehead between my eyebrows. "Remember to trust your inner guidance, dear, as it will guide you on your journey."

"Yes, Mama, I know. You've told me many times."

"But do you listen?" she asked with a smile. "That ol' universe speaks to all of us in different ways, but only you can decide its true meaning for you. Listen to it. Believe it. It'll keep you safe on your *pellegrinaggio*."

I chuckled at the idea of this being my "pilgrimage" and leaned back into the seat as the train took off again after a quick stop. The chug-chug-chug of the train comforted my soul as I gazed out the window and breathed in the rolling hills and vineyards, feeling amazed that I'm here in Italy, of all places, on my way to my future, whatever that might be. Ah, yes, to babysit thirteen American lesbians from California. What has Rosie got me into?

Another handsome porter in a dark, tailored uniform marched down the aisle shouting something in fast Italian. And passengers scurried about in the aisle, grabbing their gear. An American hippie with long sun-bleached hair and surfer patches on his backpack got waylaid in the aisle and stopped in front of me.

I tugged his sleeve, "Excuse me, what did he say?"

Before he could answer, we pulled into another train station. "*Stazione Como Nord Lago*," the porter yelled. I spotted the large sign on the station's platform: "Como."

"Como, that's my stop!"

I grabbed my daypack and scrambled out of my seat toward the door, forgetting to breathe. Noticing that I looked disorientated, the young American backpacker took pity on me and lifted my heavy suitcase out from the rack.

"Catching a ferry, like me?" he asked. I nodded, deciding to follow him. But, as I stepped off the train, my borrowed wheelie suitcase fell hard onto the platform, causing the zipper to split open with a pop! Everything fell out, including my underwear on full display.

Mortified, I scuffled about to grab my belongings. Out of nowhere, a glamorous late-30s Italian woman stopped to purvey my strewn underwear, setting down her *haute couture* shopping bags from Milan. I looked up at her, embarrassed. Dripping in gold jewelry, she resembled a young Sophia Loren Lookalike, aka "SLL."

"*Sta scherzando.*"—You've got to be kidding, she said, reaching down to pick up something. "It is a dead fish," she announced, holding up my grey sports bra by its tail for everyone to see. "Love of self is *hee-den* underneath, *si?*" she said, frowning.

Red-faced, I snatched it from her. "*Grazie.* I wear it jogging," and stuffed it into my suitcase, tugging the zipper closed.

I'd lost sight of the American hippie as he all but ran toward the train station's exit.

"*Scusa, signora*," I asked the SLL, "which way to the ferry?" Using one long, painted fingernail at the end of a long, dangerous-looking finger, she pointed, "*Lago di Como* is to where the water is." She turned on her heel and, with her shiny brunette hair bouncing and voluptuous figure swaying, elite shopping bags swinging, she marched on ahead, hard to do on those shiny four-inch heels.

As we all emerged from the station, she headed straight toward a black Mercedes limousine parked at the curb. An Asian chauffeur, wearing a dark suit, dark chopper sunglasses, and a jazzy porkpie hat, stood beside the car. He spotted her and hurried to open the side door.

"Signora Lazzaro," he said with great respect. Out popped three little girls, ranging in age from about four to nine, all dressed in frilly little dresses. Each of them had long, black shiny hair and a black unibrow. They ran to "*Mammina!*" who dropped her bags to open her arms and hug all three, smothering them with kisses.

Out of the limo's other door stepped a short square-shouldered man, cooing, "Carmela, darling," as the SLL put her face coolly forward for him to kiss one cheek then busied herself with her daughters. I saw where the girls got their unibrow; his thick eyebrow matched his full head of wavy black hair. At first, I thought he had a moustache and a goatee; on second glance, I saw that his jaw had a thick shadow of prickly black hair. He wore a tailored multicolored track suit, not your average gym apparel, probably by Versace.

I'd read that, to make a good impression in Italy, it's more than just having beautiful clothes or a beautiful figure. *La Bella Figura*, a form of proper decorum, is part of their obsession with having everything in life be as beautiful as possible. This philosophy of life, almost an unapologetic self-love, is so alluring. We Canadians are taught to be polite, not to take undo pleasure in ourselves. Nevertheless, wearing black stretchy jeans, striped top, and runners, I felt like a Second-Class traveler next to the First-Class Carmela Lazzaro.

I spotted the young American hippie hurrying on ahead with other train travelers and kept my eyes on him, not even stopping to glance at the lake across the road until we reached a wide-open town square. *Piazza Cavour*, I overheard someone say. In the center of the *piazza*, I stopped in my tracks, letting the others hurry onward without me. Positioned at the southernmost point of the lake, Como town's church steeples, low-rise buildings, and narrow streets invited me in.

The smell of fresh oxygenated water became overwhelming, along with the aroma of eucalyptus and oleander, with a hint of basil, olive oil, and garlic from the baked mozzarella pizza in the pizzeria across the square. I raised my chin to the heavenly smells and, only then, did I take in my first look at the lake across the road. Sparkling. Iridescent. The rolling hills, melted into the long open lake. All along the boardwalk, boats and yachts of all sizes and shapes shifted in the gentle waves, and a breeze filtered the sound of halyards clanging the sailboat masts, signposts of the lake's omnipresence.

My heart thumped, "Yup, I'm here. Lake Como. *Mozzafiato*— breathtaking."

Enchanted, I pivoted on one foot, taking it all in. The sights, the sounds, the many scents, all generated an enigmatic feeling. Standing there, I began smelling lavender and suddenly felt someone push me from behind. I felt my world kick in and start to revolve in orbit again. Turning around, I saw no one but got hit with another wave of lavender. Very odd, because looking around at the flower beds, there were no lavender plants.

Then I noticed, in the distance, the sun-kissed Alps shone in the soft orange-purplish light as the sun threatened to sink behind them. "Oh no, it'll be dark soon." I ran across the street and along a promenade to the ferry ticket kiosk, where the American hippie dude from the train waited to buy a ticket. He watched me pull out my notes for a quick scan; then, next in line, he turned to the woman inside the kiosk.

"Isabella, good to see you again."

The young ticket woman lit up with a smile as the handsome American bought his ticket. Then he turned back to me and asked: "Where you headed?"

"Ah, the town, it has a weird name."

"*Attenzione*! Next," yelled Isabella, staring right at me.

As I flipped through my notes, the American waited, smiling, while Isabella drummed her fingers on the counter. A snicker sputtered out of the side of her lipsticked mouth, the same color as her fake reddish-orange hair.

Finally, the name came to me: "Are-EGG-no?"

"You mean Are-JANE-yoh?" The pretty ticket girl's gum-chewing jaw dropped open; she raised an eyebrow, her interest piqued. "*Signora*, are you sure?" Isabella rolled her amber brown eyes at the American while sliding words out the side of her mouth, "*Non questa essere lei.*"—That can't be her.

I wondered what she meant and handed her some Euros for my ticket.

The passenger ferry slipped into Como's dock. A young deckhand swung the heavy rope to lasso the cleats onshore. Passengers scrambled toward the ferry as the crew waved us on. Coming to the gangplank I stopped, frozen. People bumped into me from behind. Terrified, I couldn't move forward. I ventured a look over the edge, down into the bottomless gap between land and ferry, a dark, watery sinkhole into the unknown. I hadn't been on a boat since my husband's drowning a year ago. Discussing my PTSD, post-traumatic stress disorder, with my grief counsellor had obviously not cured this fear of deep bodies of water.

Another deckhand, in a Greek fisherman's cap, yelled from the other side of the ramp: "My beauty, do you go, or do you stay?"

"Is it safe?"

He clomped down the wiggling ramp and jumped on it, making it swish from side to side. "See? She's safe." Before I knew it, he had me by the elbow, but my feet still wouldn't move. "Please, *signora*, make up your mind. My wife, she waits," he implored. The other deckhands made whistling sounds at him, but suddenly another sound overtook their camaraderie.

The loud call of a bird echoed overhead. Everyone within earshot watched the huge owl circling above us. It's unusual for a nocturnal owl to be flying about in daylight, even though the sun was setting.

"Is that a good sign or a bad sign?" I asked aloud.

"*Madonna, Madonna!*" the Greek-capped ferryman said, scratching his bushy moustache and scruffy beard. He took a fleeting glance at the owl, "Is a good sign. Go, go," he insisted, trying to tug me, suitcase and all, onto the ferry's ramp. The owl, my spirit animal, landed on the upper deck's railing. I took this as a sign and lurched onto the ferry—onto the lake. Once onboard, I turned to look at the owl, but it had flown away.

"*Bravissima!*" yelled the deckhand, also jumping aboard as the ferry took off.

Minutes later, I made my way to the upper ferry deck and stood beside the American hippie, sailing into the winds of sunset. Isabella, the ticket girl, leaned on the railing next to the lifeboat. Smoking a cigarette, grocery bags at her feet, she eyed me with what I interpreted as suspicion.

I leaned my head back and breathed consciously, filling my lungs with the cool alpine air. I'm actually here, on an Italian lake, with its lush green hillsides, pale cumin and ochre villas along the shoreline, and no concrete high-rises. Paul would be proud of me. A memory flooded in.

I married him at five months pregnant; 'twas a shotgun wedding, or so my parents had joked. Even though Paul Lang was seven years older, we both loved similar activities such as cycling and hiking. That old saying became our motto: Couples who play together stay together. Sometimes. He never gave me any indication of deceit, which meant I must have been turning a blind eye to the telltale signs. Looking back, I had to admit to myself that, for years, the bloom was definitely off the rose and I had been living an illusion.

Looking up, I caught my first "sunset dipping" in Italy and held it in my heart, breathing it all in—until the alone feeling bubbled up to the surface. My heart, the lake, the blue sky got darker. A tear rolled down my cheek. I gripped the ferry's railing. The lake's surface glowed with light as the sun slowly dipped behind the mountains, the water turning gloomy, along with my mood. No matter where I go, it's there, surfacing…

The day had seemed perfect. For our anniversary, Paul and I spent the weekend with family, at our waterfront cottage up inlet. In the afternoon, Paul grabbed his fishing gear, "Well, I'm off to catch dinner," he announced.

"What, no stopping at the yacht club to buy the biggest fish?" He pretended to be shocked and shook his head. "In that case, I'll

be your frontierswoman and forage for fiddlehead greens, and you catch, or bring the fish. Candlelight dinner tonight, just the two of us?"

"Can't wait," Paul said and kissed my cheek. "You're the hottest chef on the coast, honey. And your male students know it. Oversexed little bastards."

Laughing at his little running joke, Paul hurried down the dock to where Thomas waited and jumped into the motorboat. I waved and watched the boat disappear up the inlet.

Later, I sat at the picnic table near shoreline, marking student papers. I looked up to watch the shimmering ocean in front of me, an inlet as calm as a lake. A ripple of water swept toward shore like a dark harbinger. I felt a premonition shudder along my spine. Reacting, it made me press too hard on the paper, breaking the red lead in my pencil with a snap.

A boat's motor echoed over the water, and I watched its approach. Paul and Thomas looked sunburnt and happy; Thomas slowed the motorboat as they cruised toward our cottage dock.

I walked down the dock and helped them tie up. Paul ran to me, picking me up in a twirl of exuberance, his arms and bare chest all wet.

"Honey, you're all sweaty. Time for a shower," I suggested.

"I've got a better idea." His arms let go of me, setting me down as he turned, ran to the end of the pier, and dove into the water.

We waited for Paul to come up for air. Thomas yelled for Paul to stop kidding around. It wasn't unusual for us to jump, but not dive, off the pier. We waited longer. When he didn't surface, I began to panic.

Finally, minutes later, in the tiny dark ripples tipped with golden sunlight, Paul's body cut the surface and it bobbed up, face down. A wave curled, turning the body over—Paul's dead eyes stared back at me. I heard a blood-curdling scream, then realized it was mine.

A loon's long, mournful warble across the darkening inlet felt strangely but decidedly as though Paul were saying goodbye: "I'm over here, it's all right, I'm safe. I promise." I felt his spiritual presence so strongly, but the shock closed my vision. Sirens, and the voices of neighbors as they ran over to help. I held onto Thomas, both of us crying. The beach swarmed with

paramedics and police. I fainted into my son's arms.
The next morning, I found myself at the end of the dock, staring
down into the clear water. The police figured Paul dove in and
broke his neck instantly on a large rock below the water a little
way from the pier. What made him dive instead of jump? We'll
never know.
I haven't been back to our cottage since.

A loud voice shot me back into my body—on the ferry, on
Lake Como, staring down at the dark ripples tipped with golden
sunlight.

"Yo! Your hands are shaking," said the wide-eyed American.

"Yeah, it's been a long journey. To here, I mean." I tried to be
present. "I'm Gerri. What's your name?"

"Shaun Slater. You okay?"

Several feet away, the ticket lady glanced over again, still
watching me.

"I'm fine, thanks, Shaun. It's so unreal, being here in Italy.
What does that even mean?" I took a deep breath, my hands still
shaking.

I heard a ringing sound. It wouldn't go away. "Oh, no, my
phone," I cried out.

Fumbling for it in my daypack, I grasped the phone and pulled
it out with my shaking hand. In that moment, the boat lurched to
one side, and I lost my balance. Like a slippery fish, the phone
sailed out of my hand, overboard into the dark lake, the ringing
sound drifting away.

"NOOOOOO!" I screamed. "My phone! My entire life's in
that phone."

"Bummer," Shaun sympathized, "But it's okay. Your life's all
in the Cloud, all your info. You just buy another phone. It'll be
cool, I promise."

"Yes, yes, it's all in cloud storage. Thanks for reminding me."

Isabella yelled: "Ay, is too bad, but, it is fate," Isabella
announced, making the sign of the cross as she approached me.
She flicked her cigarette into the black lake. She smiled at me with
a remorseful frown, which meant either she thinks I'm a crazy
lady, or she feels sorry for me. "*Quello che sarà sarà*—What will
be, will be. So sorry." She patted my shoulder.

Wiping away tears, I muttered, "I got this. It's just a phone. No one died. I can handle this."

The ferry floated closer toward a village dock. "Time to go, *sì*." Isabella said to me, then snapped up her grocery bags and hurried toward the staircase that led to the lower deck, eyeing me one more time as she walked away.

Following her, Shaun said to me, "Gotta cruise. I'm the stop after. Maybe see ya' around, I hope. Good luck." With knapsack in tow, he flipped back his long surfer hair and helped Isabella down the metal steps to the disembarking level.

Argegno, that's my stop too, but, still shaking, I stayed on the top deck to watch our approach. Argegno glittered with lights as dusk settled over the lake, making it resemble a fairy village with a few pointed steeples and house lights on the hillside.

I rummaged in my day pack, digging deep to get Paul's phone. "Why couldn't I have lost *his phone*?" At the last minute before leaving home, for no rational reason, I had stuck it in my bag, perhaps to hang on to some shred of Paul, who knows the reason? I should have smashed it with a hammer into a million pieces by now! But in this moment, I was relieved I'd brought it. I pressed "Power" to see if it worked and waited.

After a few moments, as the ferry was nearing the dock, the signal icon registered. Shocked, I shut it off. Knowing his two-year phone plan from his job was still active, I hadn't expected it to work here. Then it hit me: of course, Paul would have a World SIM card for international freighters. The last call for passengers to disembark came over the loudspeaker, and I hurried to the lower deck where my large suitcase waited.

This being their last trip up the lake, the ferry crew quickly secured the ramp, but the sudden rocky waves shifted the ferry, creating a moving, bottomless gap to step over. A disembarking passenger crossed the gap while hanging onto the ramp's railing. My body shuddered just watching him.

Obviously, Isabella knew all the dock workers and received special treatment and help with her groceries. She glowed. Tanned and buxom, even a little plump, she was stunning. Our cheeky Greek-capped deckhand even gave her a kiss on either cheek.

A deckhand tossed my suitcase over to a dockworker, and I was supposed to follow suit. Hell-bent that anywhere my suitcase goes, I go, and feeling another odd push from behind me, I took a leap of faith across the moving ramp and the gap, landing with a little hop-step. As the ferry pulled away from the dock, the friendly dockhand grinned and waved to me.

My suitcase had popped open a bit, so I zipped it up, putting Humpty Dumpty back together again. The lakefront village of Argegno welcomed me with laughter spilling out from a nearby bar and *trattoria*—an Italian restaurant. I wheeled my luggage to the curb, not knowing where to go. Instead of panic, a surprisingly sweet calm came over me. My body relaxed. I plopped down on top of my suitcase and filled my lungs deeply.

Argegno lay in purple shadow, birds roosted on treetops, cafe lights infused the street with inviting warmth, the fabulous scent of something cooking wafted past me, and my stomach gurgled. I had, indeed, arrived at my destination. I felt total relief, happy I'd made it this far. But which way to the villa?

Sudden, loud, squealing of car brakes broke my trance. Glancing over my shoulder, I saw two blinding headlamps zooming toward me as if to run me down and realized I sat in a parking zone. Then came a torrent of Italian swear words, the loud barking of dogs, the slamming of a car door and, under the headlights, two feet in western boots stomping toward me. I struggled to stand.

"Sorry, sorry." I raised my hands like a polite Canadian, feeling the angry-yet-scared vibrations of the dark-haired man in front of me.

"*Sono qui!*"—I'm here, he shouted into his mobile. Even grumbling, he was a handsome young man. Mid-twenties, dressed in a misshapen hand-knit sweater and blue jeans, which had been stuffed into wildly colored leather cowboy boots. Wide-eyed, the pseudo-cowboy sputtered a stream of Italian too fast for me to understand.

People poured out of the tavern across the road to see what had happened, including Isabella who yelled into her phone, "Alex, stop it! It must be *her*—Dr. McKenna," or so I translated, wondering how the ticket lady knew my name.

"Are you sure?" Alex answered.

"Who else English-speaking to be here at late hour?" Isabella insisted, switching to English, perhaps for my benefit.

Alex, the cowboy wannabe, shutoff his phone, took off his scrunched fedora hat and practically prostrated himself before me in apology. "*Scusa, per favore. Signora.* You are so late, we thought coming tomorrow now."

It struck me that Alex must be the driver Rosie had mentioned would pick me up. With anger abated, he helped me up gently, then grabbed my suitcase and ran to open the back of the old Fiat Doblò van. Its white color did not hide its many dents and scratches. Two wildly barking dogs greeted us as he hoisted my bags into the back.

"I, Alex, at your service. Meet Pucci and Goldie, your wards, *si*?" he introduced the small terrier cross and the golden retriever now wagging their tails at me. His grin showed a set of rotten front teeth, ruining an otherwise charming smile.

"Am I to look after the dogs, too?"

"*Sì*, Dr. McKenna," he nodded, opening the passenger door. Feeling exhausted, I got in. At this moment, I would have followed anyone anywhere.

"*Grazie.* But drop the doctor." He didn't understand. "I'm not a doctor, I'm a teacher," I yelled, thinking he'd understand better.

"Please for you to meet Isabella," he pointed across the road.

"Yes, we've met, sort of."

"Isabella, you will come with us?" he yelled at her in his strange, non-Italian accent.

"In that? Never again," she retorted, then explained to me, "No brakes."

"I fixed it," he implored, using the well-known, shaking pinched finger gesture that means, "What do you mean?"

"Aleksandar Pandev, you are not mechanic. You are gardener. I walk home." And she went back into the trattoria's bar.

Driving fast along the dark winding road out of the village, Alex kept looking at me and talking with his hands. Apparently, he knew the road so well he didn't have to look at it.

"I need to practice English, Miss *Americano*."

"I'm Canadian. And you? Your accent is not Italian."

"I am kinda Italian, from Macedonia."

Suppressing a chuckle, I said, "So, you're Greek-Italian? Or perhaps Syrian?" I said deadpan, figuring his dark handsome features were more akin to Middle Eastern.

"No, no, *signora*, I am Macedonian. Aleksandar Pandev. Like Goran Pandev the soccer player. And a little bit Italian, *si*? I am Alex, handyman and mechanic, at your service."

His attempt at covering his tracks exposed his immaturity, reminding me of students who burned their dishes during a culinary exam because of "the oven's fault."

"Where is Signora Rosie Campbell? She comes tomorrow?"

"Rosie Campbell is delayed. I'm her temporary replacement. My name's Gerri."

"Ah? You have boy's name, Miss Gerri. You're too pretty for a boy. Cool wild hair. Canadians are wild."

"Eh, what?" In the van's side mirror, I caught a glimpse of my unruly shoulder-length hair.

Alex was quiet for the rest of the way, although I caught him watching me. After negotiating two switchbacks on the steep hill, he swerved off the main asphalt road onto an entranceway between two gate columns. The dark road led up to a villa perched on a gently sloping hill that overlooked the lake and the town below.

My first view of the expansive villa took my breath away. A small tree at the entrance twinkled with tiny lights and reflected onto the light-colored exterior of a tall double-storey mansion; other than that, the villa was shrouded in darkness. Alex drove up the stone-paved driveway along one side of the villa and stopped the van, saying, "We are here."

He shut off the motor. Stepping out of the van, we invaded the silence surrounding a monolithic structure, or so it seemed. When my ears adjusted, I heard the eerie sound of wind through the hillside olive grove and the underscore of loud chirping of cicadas. I felt estranged in the present moment. Where the heck am I? From the parking area, I stared up at the front entrance of a large stone villa hidden in darkness and caught sight of a swimming pool surrounded by ghostly white marble statues.

The playful dogs barked in the back of the van as Alex grabbed my luggage, but he didn't let them out. Carrying the bags under one arm, he gently guided me up three driveway steps and around to the side of the villa. He placed my suitcase and packsack at an unlit door, unlocked and opened it, and switched on an interior wall light, revealing a small kitchen area.

"I welcome you to Villa della Cantante, m' lady." He smiled. "This *pensione,* a guesthouse, is for you. It connects to the main villa."

"Um, well, thanks for driving me…"

Holding out a set of keys, he said, "Here, the caretaker keys. I go now," and he turned to go. The five metal keys held together with a string felt hard, real, in my hand. I had finally arrived.

"Wait! Don't leave," but then I reconsidered, "Sorry, just a little edgy."

"It's good. I take the dogs for tonight. You are tired. Tomorrow you will feel settled. *Ciao.*" And with the dogs still barking in the van, he drove off out the front gate.

Standing there, in the villa's entrance, a peculiar feeling came over me. Alone again.

CHAPTER 3
A Haunting Vision

A large oil painting hung on the bedroom wall, a portrait of a beautiful woman with long brunette hair. A noise startled me. I sat up in bed. There, at the end of my bed, stood the woman from the portrait, her gaze riveted on me. Her image wavered with light and I could see right through her. And then, seconds later, she melted back into the painting.

—G. A. McKenna, journal entry

Barking dogs woke me with a start. A distant radio blared a Taylor Swift song.

"Where am I?" Slowly opening my eyes, squinting at the bright sunlight pouring through the windows, I remembered. "Lake Como." The song ended abruptly with the slam of a vehicle's door. Rattling as it drove off, the sound reminded me of last night's van. "Must be that Alex."

The alarm clock read: 8:30 a.m., Italian time. In a jet-lagged fog, I remembered a maze of haunting images, mirrors, long hallways, and a large looming portrait of a woman on the bedroom wall. I sat up in bed, squinting in the bright morning sunlight and looked around the room for the painting, almost expecting the woman to step out it, but no such painting was on the wall.

"Must have been a dream." And then, I got hit with a whiff of lavender. With eyes half shut, I stumbled around in my silky nightie, shutting the floor-to-ceiling draperies to keep out the blinding sunlight.

A loud vacuum cleaner turned ON.

"What the—?"

Grabbing my blue silk dressing gown from my open suitcase, I figured the sound came from behind the door. Last night, I had discovered the door led to an upstairs hallway that connected to my two-storey guesthouse. Opening the door, I squinted in the sunlight to see a woman vacuuming.

"*Buongiorno*, Signora McKenna," she yelled. "Did you sleep well?"

I pressed my hands dramatically over my ears and she got the idea, flicking off the vacuum.

"*Mi dispiace*, sorry."

As my eyes adjusted to the light, I recognized her. "Aren't you the ticket lady, Isabella?"

"*Scusa*? My manners. It is Isabella. Signorina Isabella Maria Magdalen de Barclaino." As she smiled, her happy face lit up as bright as her hair. "I am named after two fighting grand mamas from Barclaino in the mountains, my two *nonnas*." Isabella crossed herself, talking fast. "I am so pleased to be here, Signora McKenna. Pleased to do work for the owners and for you."

"You're the cleaning lady, here? *Piacere*—pleased to see you, again, Isabella. Call me Gerri." I surmised she might be wearing one of her grandmother's dresses, rather dowdy and ill-fitting, but crisply ironed.

I heard the pitter-patter-clickety-click of many feet running and slipping on the shiny wooden staircase. "Are the rental guests here?" They turned out to be paws, not feet. The two dogs from last night bounded towards us at a full gallop along the long hallway, then stopped to bark at me.

Isabella yelled, "*Basta*! Stop it." and they settled down to sniff my ankles.

"Pookey and Goldie, right?"

"The little one is *poo-chi*. The owners leave them here to go on vacation."

Pucci, the Terrier cross, a cute, fluffy mix of white and brown fur, looked older. Goldie, the friendlier Golden Retriever thumped his tail against my leg, knocking me further off balance. "What a good puppy," I said in my most cheery voice. The sound made him wiggle and waggle, quite happy.

Isabella resumed her vacuuming. I followed, feeling like a barefoot Contessa walking along on the cool wooden flooring, my jaw agape trying to take it all in. I peeked into each of the six upstairs bedrooms, decorated in a blur of upscale grandeur: elegant, canopied beds with hand-carved headboards and deluxe marble-tiled bathrooms.

"The owners, whoever they are, have expensive taste."

"*Sì*, as you do. You have expensive silk dressing gown. You are lovely lady."

"Sweet of you to say."

"I brought you pastries for breakfast, you eat now? Or…" Isabella asked, stuffing the vacuum into a hall closet. I sensed she wanted to tell me something,

"*Sì, grazie.* And espresso?"

The rambunctious dogs and I followed Isabella back along the upstairs hallway and into the second floor of my guesthouse, located in a separate wing of the villa.

"Rosie Campbell, she telephone early this morning. I no wanted to disturb-ed you."

Entering my bedroom, I stubbed my bare toe on the addition's uneven flooring, "Shoot!—Please disturb me next time."

"Okey-doke. You're here for one month, etcetera. *Sì?*" Without waiting for an answer, the energetic Isabella tested the lock on my bedroom door from the inside, instructing me firmly: "After the guests arrive, lock this door, unless you want the guests to be visitors. For now, let the air in." She left the door open.

Isabella opened all the draperies that I had just closed on purpose. "You no like the view?" With arms akimbo, she stood between the two double windows: one with a lake view, and one overlooking the lush olive-treed hillside. She opened a door that led onto a vine-covered portico, where she drew in a deep noisy sniff of the fresh air. Smiling, she explained, "The lake air is good. Your kitchenette and living space downstairs also have *grandioso* lake views. *Sì?*"

But instead of taking the bedroom stairs down to my private kitchenette on the first floor, Isabella opened a second closet door, revealing an enclosed stairwell.

"Goes to the villa's main kitchen. This secret. Never use secret staircase when we have guests. Only emergencies. Please to remember."

While wondering about other hidden doorways, if any, I grabbed my slip-on thongs from my suitcase and followed, careful of my footing on the narrow winding staircase. I felt like Alice entering Wonderland. At the bottom, Isabella opened another closet door, and we stepped out.

"Wow, it's beautiful."

In my jet-lagged stupor, the villa's large kitchen became my first fully conscious image of the main villa. I squinted in the sunlight that poured in from the tall bare windows and gawked at the modern accoutrements and the stone and terracotta flooring.

"You've never seen a proper kitchen, Miss Gerri?" Clearly, she didn't know my chef's background.

"I'm a culinary arts teacher, and I know this particular deluxe gas range is bloody expensive," I said, running my fingers along the top of the magnificent sixty-inch gas stove.

"Here, sit." Isabella pulled out a wooden chair at the long, unusually wide table with seating for fourteen guests. She unbuttoned her dowdy cleaner's housedress, removing it to expose a cute outfit more befitting her age.

I shivered in my seat, unprepared for no central heating. At the other end of the table was the main working area, complete with a marble countertop and two huge sinks below the windows that overlooked a grove of cypress and olive trees.

"One shot is good, *si?*" she asked, sounding like a chirpy schoolgirl, while warming up a Moka espresso maker on the stovetop. "Here, fresh-baked from Carlo the local baker."

She placed an array of homemade pastries in front of me. Starving, I devoured one and wrapped two in a napkin to stuff into my pocket for later.

"You hungry woman," she winked with a smile. "Eat, please, what you want, today is your first day, it's good. After, you get supplies, then you're on your own, as the saying is. But Isabella is here now. I like to help. The owners, they pay me well."

"Thanks, Isabella. By the way, who are the owners?"

She gave me a sideways glance while pouring the espresso, commenting, "Hoopte-doopte. They no tell you?"

Just then, before she could say more, we heard the front doorbell clang several times. "You go, I busy," Isabella said.

"But I'm not dressed."

"Nonsense. You lovely. Go, go!"

Being a jogger, I sprinted out of the kitchen to the foyer. Still in my nightie and robe, I unlocked the grand entrance door and jumped back onto the staircase to make room as four women came in like a storm with screeches, screams, laughter, and shrieks. "It" was alive! Whatever "It" was, hopefully, they were friendly.

Upon seeing me, the four women froze, their excited voices silenced. Gulp. With my dressing gown halfway down my shoulder exposing my nightie, my hair all a-dither—no wonder they stared at me.

"Well, hello, gorgeous," said the rather masculine tall one in her best Barbra Streisand impersonation.

"Ouch!" The woman beside her had slapped her arm.

Were these some of the rental guests? All four of them dressed in casual but trendy clothes, a gaggle of gorgeous women, primed and ready for a feast of fun and frolic.

The tall masculine one with a multi-layered haircut, long on top but similar to rocker Pink's undercut, and Clark Kent-type eyeglasses, extended her hand toward me. She stepped forward, moving in closer to catch my hand to shake it, staring at my exposed negligee. "Sorry if we woke you. I'm Erin. And these crazy ladies are ready for *merry* gaiety. Whoever Mary is. Oops! And this is my girlfriend, CJ."

"Nice to meet you. I'm Gerri, your, um…I'll, ah, go get some clothes on."

"Not on our account," said CJ, the cheeky, athletic Black woman dressed in stylish comfy sports clothes.

"Um, are we all here?"

The feminine, strawberry blonde answered, deadpan: "They're coming. Except the Indian's missing."

"Indian?"

The bombshell stepped forward, "Skip it, private joke. You must be the replacement. I'm Dana, the travel agent. I spoke with Rosie Campbell on the phone—your associate?" We shook hands; hers felt cold.

"My associate, ah, yes."

A broad-shouldered woman, wearing a tailored jacket and jeans said, "Right-oh, I'm Vera." Her deep voice with a slight British accent complimented her English boy's haircut; she also shook my hand while gazing at me, smiling.

Feeling flushed, I said, "Have a look around, I'll be right back." Remembering Isabella had left my bedroom door open, I backed up the foyer's winding staircase, then ran along the villa's upper hallway into my bedroom and locked the door.

Hurrying to get dressed, I listened to their joyful voices as they toured the place. My secret closet door had been left open and their voices sailed up the narrow spiral staircase. I heard them enter into the kitchen to meet Isabella.

"Oh dear, not exactly private for them." I shut the closet door as quietly as possible and latched it to remind myself to keep it closed.

No time for a bath, *dammit*. Quickly, I chose a tight black skirt, white silky blouse, and black heels—befitting my image of a caretaker. Adding a string of pearls for effect, I checked in the mirror for self-approval: Yes, elegant, yet, prim and proper. Too prim. I fluffed my hair into chic messy curls, creating a sexy style, applied a little blush and lipstick, and paused for another look in the mirror, "Maybe even a *little* gorgeous," I said, parodying Erin. Ready to go.

Walking across the connecting hallway, I looked down onto the foyer, listening to Isabella talk to the guests—my lesbians. Here we go. I waltzed down the main villa's grand staircase as if I owned the joint. I did trip a bit but recovered gracefully. They turned to watch me, a few with raised eyebrows and smiles.

At the bottom, Isabella handed me my espresso and a pastry, then continued, "I tell you all a story and show you in the other room. I show you all." Leading the way, she smiled as I ravenously ate the pastry with the fragrant *caffè*.

"Villa della Cantante, she built in 1790 by wealthy persons. After many owners, the rich Ferrario family from *Milano* bought it, industrialists, who fixed her up." Her spiel sounded well-rehearsed.

The athletic CJ with her curly bob, asked, "Villa della Cantante, it means Villa of the Singer?"

"*Sì-sì, La Cantante*—the beautiful, exceptional singer. In

1930, Max Ferrario the rich Milanese businessman gave the villa to his young wife as a wedding gift." She nattered on as she led us through the exquisite dining room. Lowering her voice, she told me privately, "My *nonna*, ay, my grandmother, was the maid here who told me the story. My mother, well, she went to school, became a teacher. As did you Miss Gerri. I too, one day. I study but am not so good."

"I can help you study," I suggested. Isabella lit up.

We entered the spacious living room, with its elegant furnishings and high ceiling. The focal point of the entire room was a life-sized oil painting of a stunning woman wearing a strapless operatic ball gown; the crystal beaded, lace bodice showed off her lovely *decolletage*. The portrait hung above an intricately carved marble fireplace. For me, it was a mic-drop moment. Nothing else mattered in the room; the breathtaking painting took precedence.

It's her!

As the four women guests busied themselves roaming around the room, commenting on the ambiance, flopping down on the couches, testing them out, I stared up at the portrait. The haunting, blue-eyed Italian temptress stared back at me. Yes, she was the woman—the vision—who had visited me at the end of my bed. Her wild brunette hair lingered on bare shoulders, winding across her lace-covered right breast and purple satin gown.

I stood in awe: she was holding a sprig of lavender.

Isabella noticed my stare and came up behind me. "*La Cantante bellissima*. Our beautiful singer yearned to be a famous opera diva."

"An Italian with blue eyes. The Nordic influence?" Isabella gave me a quizzical look, so I explained, "I've read that the further north you go in Italy, the more you'll see Italians with blue eyes."

"*Sì*, as your eyes. You have the look of her," Isabella said, as she scrutinized me and then the portrait.

"Do I? I don't see it."

"Killed by a Nazi General in 1945. Days before the war ended," Isabella announced, her jaw clenched.

Shocked, I couldn't remove my gaze from the elegant woman in the portrait.

"He murdered our beautiful La Cantante. Right where you

stand." She pointed to my feet.

"How atrocious," Dana the travel agent said. "That's not on the villa's website. No ghosts, I hope."

Murdered here, in this room—it felt so chilling and macabre. Enraptured by the story, I entered a sort of dream state. Her bright blue eyes in the painting followed me as I moved about the room, glancing back at her.

Isabella, right at my side, whispered, "Alex, he say she was a spy. But *neh-neh*," she wagged her finger. "She saved lives."

"What was her name?" I asked, and all the women turned to hear her name.

"Signora Angelina Lucia Merosi-Ferrario," Isabella's voice cracked, remorseful while whispering the name in a hushed prayerful tone. "My mother say, that Signora Angelina was psychic, *sensitiva*. She saw things, divine, like a saint."

"Let's hope her psychic powers warned her," Dana said. Isabella frowned, cocking her head to one side. "You know, like, she got a premonition of being killed."

"Aye, she did. Some villagers say her daughter has the visions, too," she said to me.

Vera, the British one who slouched, opened the living room's patio doors to take a look, "Blimey, checkout the pool," she screeched, breaking the moment, and her three friends followed her outside.

"Students of life are easily distracted," I chuckled.

"Miss Gerri, come with me. I need to show you." Isabella turned away and her full hips swayed from side to side as she walked into an adjacent room. At the library's doorway, I stopped and turned for one more glimpse at the painting. Her bright blue gaze reached deep into my soul and extracted a surprising, unknown longing. I sensed a *déjà vu* as Signora Angelina's ghostly presence filled the room with the scent of lavender and a haunting familiarity. It sent a shiver down my spine.

I moved into the villa's library, scattered with comfy wingback chairs and lined with floor-to-ceiling bookshelves. The small fireplace looked too clean and too shallow to be of any real use. In the corner stood an antique walnut-veneered writing cabinet that had finely designed marquetry panels. A chiming clock crowned the tall cabinet.

"Sixteenth century? I've seen similar writing desks but can't think where. Perhaps my grandmother, before she died? How does this one open?"

"No open, it's for show."

"Oh, but these old cabinets usually have secret compartments, in fact—"

"Is private. Not our concern." Isabella shrugged.

Instead, she pointed toward one side of the fireplace at the black and white, framed photographs located in a recessed niche of a bookshelf.

"Here, I show you. Happier times before the Second World War. As a famous opera singer in northern *Italia* and *La Scala* in *Milano*."

The photos hung on fake masonry bricks. Photos of picnics on the villa's manicured lawns under a huge oak tree; a yacht party with everyone wearing white, mid-1930s attire; and later, the opera singer with her husband and a newborn baby.

"Her daughter was born during the war. In 1944. They had tried many years to have a child." Isabella pointed to another photo, "Here, in this photo is Signor Max Ferrario, her husband. And here, the opera diva herself," Isabella said and touched the photo of a performance-ready Angelina, giving it a kiss with her fingers. "She was murdered too young, before world fame, a sad tale. The baker in the village knows the story all too well. Village gossip says they were great friends."

Her eyebrows rose, as if she wanted to say more but intentionally clammed up. My ears perked. The baker either knew the story or knew *her* intimately. I wanted to know more. I leaned in to see the photo but then noticed a mark on the brick beside it. A shape had been carved into a masonry brick. I ran my fingers over its design, trying to decipher it.

"A mason's mark, by the builder of the library," Isabella said. "A different builder who, how you say, *ad-edited*."

"Built an addition?" I said, and she nodded.

With my fingers still on the wall's brick, I leaned in further for a closer look at the mark, accidently pressing on the brick. It clicked, and the entire brick popped open similar to a small wooden drawer. Isabella sprinted to my side, making me jump. She pushed on the fake brick, and it locked back into place.

"Faulty builder. The place, she falls apart." Isabella herded me out of the library.

Passing a ground floor master bedroom, "La Cantante's bedroom," explained Isabella. I peeked inside. Right out of an architectural magazine, the master bedroom had an elegant, canopied bed, high ceilings and marble floors. But the plastered walls were bare.

I caught up to Isabella outside, and we walked along a path of small white rocks toward the backyard pool area where the four guests sat on deck chairs or dipped their bare feet into the pool.

"Who are the present owners?" I asked again, blinded by the bright sunlight.

Isabella lit a cigarette, took a drag, making me wait. She waved her lit cigarette around while pronouncing the name: "The present owner, Signora Marcella Ferrario-Eaton, La Cantante's daughter. She, the one who redo the villa." Isabella smiled at me. "Now you know her name."

"Angelina's daughter still owns it. Wonderful. I mean, to keep it in the family."

"Sì, she lives here with her husband."

"Signora Marcella must be, what, in her seventies?"

"Mid-seventy, but active." A quick change of subject, "Here, they redid the pool last year. There's a new steam room around that corner, toward the back. It's good to go. You are allowed."

In front of us, the reflecting swimming pool sparkled with morning sunlight; three steps led underwater into the turquoise-blue bottom. On the lawn loomed the huge oak tree shown in the photograph I'd just seen in the library. Much larger after seventy years, its wide trunk, leaves, and branches now shaded most of the garden.

Isabella tried to interrupt the nattering guests but they only half-listened to her as she explained, "There's a path downhill to the village. Lots of trails in the hills. There," Isabella pointed toward the bushy verdant hills. "But not go to the olive grove."

Even with my hand shielding my eyes from the sun, I had to squint at the olive-treed hillside, small vineyard, and the misty shadows of the surrounding hills.

No one was listening to Isabella's low voice as they chatted and laughed together. I whispered to her, "First rule of being a teacher: incite their curiosity. Like this…" Turning to the four, who were still busy chattering away, I exclaimed: "Oh, dear, how frightful! Don't go into the olive grove? That's a fascinating story, Isabella. Tell them."

Their ears perked up; she took her cue. "On the hill, the owners have a working olive grove and small vineyard," she said, pointing to the hillside. "There are olive and grape pickers, but they're not allowed near the house. Refugees, migrant workers, gypsies, some Syrians. Not go into olive grove, understand?"

Everyone nodded, including me. Dana, the travel agent, asked, "Are they dangerous?"

"They are poor. They sleep in the hills. Stay away from the olive grove, *si*?"

"Got it."

By the look of everyone's wide eyes, she did a good job of frightening them.

Now that she had their attention, Isabella moved on to telling them about the area, pointing every which way, "From here, the ferry stops at all the towns of the Golden Triangle: Bellagio, Varenna, and Menaggio. To the north, up one ferry stop is Lenno, it has a supermarket, a big one. The mini-market in Argegno costs too much. But the bakery, it is excellent, *favoloso*."

To me she whispered, "You will go."

As we walked around the pool, I noticed Erin ran her hand over the top of a resplendent stainless-steel barbeque in an alcove beside the pool. Another great cooking area.

"Are we allowed to use the barbeque?" the tall butch Erin asked.

"Of course. Anything here is for you. Come, I show you one thing you must do. It's tradition."

Squinting at the pool area, several life-sized female Roman statues stood like sentinels. Venus, known in Greece as Aphrodite, stood a little distance from a replica of Michelangelo's David, much smaller than the original but life-size. We followed Isabella around David's perfect buttocks to a frontal view. Dear David's usually resting penis had a hard-on, yet he stood politely turned away from the lady statues.

"Blimey, how the boy has grown," Vera said. "Not like the one in Florence."

Isabella rubbed the protrusion with a respectful laying-on of hands. "*Amor tutti fa uguali*—Love makes all men equal," she said, rubbing vigorously.

I laughed, a loud guffaw.

Isabella frowned at me, serious. "You do not believe in true love? You will need to rub hard." She rubbed the erect penis a little harder to show me, in particular.

CJ said, "I'd rather rub Aphrodite's breast," and she proceeded to do just that.

"Thanks, I'll pass for now." I blushed, saying, "I'll leave you to it," and hurried away while the women kibitzed, having fun.

I heard Isabella tell them, "Enjoy the pool area. Signora McKenna will meet you in the foyer when the others arrive." She caught up to me, walking alongside. "Something wrong?" Then she noticed I stared down the hill from the villa toward a small church with a bell tower and a graveyard.

"*Chiesa di San Sisinnio*. Winston Churchill painted it when he stayed here. This way, Miss Gerri, come, I need to…"

Isabella led me through the gardens and around the side toward the gardener's shed, near my entrance. The overhanging bougainvillea, the grassy knolls' cypress trees, various perfectly carved hedges, and blooming June flowers delighted my senses. Nearby, two red sports cars were parked in an old garage.

Isabella noticed my interest. "A 1920s and 1960s Alfa Romeo, there is history here," she commented, her eyes downcast. "The owner, Signora Marcella, drives the newer one, the one her first husband, the card shark Giorgio Romano, died in. Murdered. Hit and run. We think by the *Camorra* mafia, from Napoli. Everyone knows. It's no secret, except what's secret. Ask your friend, Rosie."

"Why would Rosie know?" Listening intently, I bumped into a deck chair.

Instead of answering, she continued, "The newer car, see, still has the dent where it ran into Giorgio. Killed by his own car. You have keys to both cars and the van. Except no one uses the Alfa Romeos, *capisci*? You understand?"

I nodded. "Where is Angelina's daughter, Marcella, now?" I inquired.

I followed her as she spoke. "After Giorgio, she married again, much later, to a Mister Eaton. Signora Marcella and Mister Eaton live here but spend one or two summer months at his estate in Devon, England."

"Devon?" I caught my breath, then, "Where my friend Rosie Campbell lives?"

"*Correctomundo.* Next door. You didn't know?"

"So that's how Rosie got the house-sitting gig."

"Now you know. Later, I suspect you go into town for supplies. The village of Argegno is about a ten-minute's walk. Follow the pathway downhill, past the cemetery and the church." She jerked her head toward the lake, "There's a small motorboat. Downhill, at the dock, she is tied up. If you want, you can use. A boat key is on your key ring. *Bene,* it's time for my other job."

"You have yet another job?"

"I am an entre-pren-eur woman," she said in her best English. "Alex, he calls me a mover an' shaker," she shimmied her shoulders, making the dogs run around her legs. "Aye, aye, not to forget, Pucci and Goldie need a long walk everyday; otherwise, this one," she patted Goldie, "he gets antsy-pantsy. Dog's leash hangs in your kitchen. Don't let them growl at you."

"The dogs growl?"

"Not the dogs, the villagers," she laughed. "I go now. Signora Marcella left all the paperwork in your kitchen. You will greet them and give them door keys. I am honoured to meet you. You are now the boss—*il capo.*"

Oh, shit.

CHAPTER 4
What'll I Do with Thirteen Lesbians?

My heart had hidden secrets—until
she unleashed them like a storm and swept me away.
I'd never met anyone like her. How did it start?

—G. A. McKenna, journal entry

Entering my suite off the pathway into the airy kitchen and living quarters, I noticed Paul's phone on the counter where I'd plugged it in next to the toaster and my tablet. Quickly, I texted both children, my mama, and Rosie about my phone sinking into the lake and to use Paul's mobile number— hoping it wouldn't cost me a fortune, knowing his monthly phone bill had always been on auto payment.

Immediately, a text came back from my daughter Julie: "Thank God, you're safe. We called and texted all night to the wrong phone. Love you, Mom."

At precisely high noon, I heard cars outside and peeked out the kitchen window, watching as the parking area filled with a white Alfa Romeo sedan, two Fiats, one a convertible, alongside a Citroen with an open sunroof. Amongst the suitcases on the villa's white gravel driveway, I counted twelve joyful women greeting one another. Where's the thirteenth? Perhaps the missing "Indian"?

I went looking for the paperwork Isabella had left for me in the kitchen. There it was, on the table, a manila envelope with the villa's logo. Skimming the detailed instructions inside, I found just what I needed: a list with names and descriptions of the guests and the room keys.

"Time to put on my big girl pants and be *il capo*, the boss," I muttered to myself. "I am *il capo di casa*, head of the house."

It felt right to use my own separate entry door from now on, exiting onto the side of the villa and walking around toward the grand front entrance.

As I hurried around the corner, a taxicab pulled into the front driveway and out stepped the thirteenth, final guest. The cab driver collected luggage from the trunk while an argument ensued.

"You shyster! I gave you a twenty-euro bill. Now you say I handed you a fiver and owe you more? Hey, I lived in L.A., it's the oldest trick in the book. Check your back pocket. Or I'll do it for you."

The driver swore in Italian, jumped in the cab and drove away, the tires spraying rocks.

"*Hasta la* bye-bye, prick," she said, then noticed me. "Oh. Hiya!"

"Hiya? Um, welcome to the villa." I suppressed a giggle, feeling an instant kinship with a duped tourist.

Forty-something, the thirteenth guest looked naturally tanned with a healthy glow and wore her medium-length brunette hair in a layered bob, now tied into a short ponytail with unkempt strands. I watched as she tore off her tailored jacket. She tossed it carelessly onto her suitcase; obviously feeling the heat, her brow sweating. She wore a low-cut T-shirt the color of red wine, ripped stretchy jeans, a bright scarf, and high heel ankle boots. The low-cut tee, one size too small, clung to her curvaceous body, showing off the top of her lace-rimmed bra and delicate cleavage. A straw fedora hat hung off her travel backpack, the final touch of her artistic flair.

Nervous, I relayed the in-joke, hoping I wasn't overstepping: "Are you the Indian?"

"Ha! Dana must be here. Ignore her."

She dragged her wheelie suitcase over the tiny rocks to where I stood on the first step, stopping about two feet away. From the step, I gazed over the top of her sunglasses down into a pair of stunning hazel eyes, which at the moment had red swollen eyelids. *Had she been crying?* It ignited my curiosity.

"The name's Kate Bradshaw. And you're Geraldine McKenna, right?"

Without waiting for me to reply and using both her hands, she shook mine in a firm grip. Strong, dry hands. Kate's eyes canvassed the villa's vine-covered entrance as she announced, "Hell-oh! So, this is the villa of the murdered opera singer." Glancing at me she murmured kindly, "By the way, sorry to hear about your husband's tragic accident last year."

My mouth dropped open. "How did you—"

"I researched you. You're all over the Internet, Miss Culinary Arts Professor, awards and all. Quite impressive. But the photos don't show how alluring you are."

"Interesting. And what does it say about you? Let's see..." I skimmed over the rental instructions, "Says, ah, you're from Indian Canyons, California. Thus, your Indian nickname?"

She stepped closer to scan the paper, "My mother's birthplace, not mine. She's half Cahuilla Indian." Kate scrutinized me with a raised eyebrow as she stepped even closer to me. I felt the heat radiate off her body. "My family and I live in Sonoma Valley, on our vineyard, the Owl's Gate Winery." Her dimples brought out a naughty lasciviousness in her smile.

"Interesting. I have an affinity with owls."

"Then it must be fate, Professor McKenna," she said, stepping even closer. I got a whiff of alcohol.

She took off her sunglasses as she examined me. "Love your hair. Hard to know if you're a natural blonde or a brunette?"

"It's a *balayage*, the French coloring technique. It makes me look blonder. In case you're interested. Not that you are, I mean..."

"Oh, I'm interested." Her eyes dropped to my lips. I felt the blush on my cheeks and neck, and she watched it happen. "Sweet." She melted into a half smile. The blush moved down to my chest.

With one hand, she pursed my lips and gave me a quick kiss. Surprising myself, I didn't pull away and my lips parted for just a second. But then I turned my head. She stepped back.

"You kissed me!"

"You kissed me back."

"I did not. And you smell like scotch. Bloody rude. I should slap your face."

"Slap me anywhere," she muttered with a smile and a tiny burp.

"Unbelievable. My students have better manners than you."

I turned to walk inside. Kate dragged her wheelie up the steps, following me into the foyer. Not much intimidated me, but it had been a long time since a woman flirted with me, even a cheeky flirtation. I'd forgotten how soft women's lips are, and no beard stubble.

She greeted her friends with a "*Ciao, ragazze!*"—Hello, girls!

Everyone greeted Kate with shrieks and hugs. As they touched Kate's shoulders or hugged her, they had sad expressions. Something had happened to her. Curious, I felt drawn to her.

Feeling a little nervous, I slipped into the background, waiting for them to settle in. They had all arrived safe and sound, including their suitcases. All were exceptionally dressed in stylish clothes, and all good friends. I counted six light-haired and seven dark-haired, with varying lengths of hair, and varying ages, a few looked mid-thirties, but mostly forty-something, even late-forties. Hard to guess.

"Come on, gather round. Check-in time," Dana ordered, as she moved to stand next to Kate. Placing her hand on Kate's shoulder, I overheard her say, "Glad you could make it."

Kate shrugged it off, saying, "I'm fine everyone. She's long gone, months ago. Let's move on. I have."

The women came closer and lounged around the circular rosewood table in the center of the foyer, some in spoon position, others side by side, hugging one another.

"Check out this conga," said the one with the perfect plastic L.A. face and black straightened hair. The hourglass-shaped djembe drum stood on the bottom shelf of a glass cabinet that also held a woodwind flute. She read aloud: "Africa, sixteenth century. Whoa!"

"Hannah, don't touch," Dana barked.

This awoke everyone and brought about a barrage of voices that challenged me to listen:

"Hey, how was your flight?" "I'm jet lagged." "You should have come to Rome first. Exhausting, but amazing." "Please, no *shoulds.*" "Crap, I'm thirsty. Who's got wine?" "I'm famished." "We need to go shopping." "Yes, figures you'd want to go shopping." "Are there tennis courts?" "Good thing you brought your racket, it'll keep away mosquitoes." "MOSQUITOES? I hate mosquitoes." "Jamie, great choice of villa. Love it." "Where are our rooms, Dana? I want the one I chose." "I need a nap, where's my bed?"

Dana yelled, "Shut up and let her speak."

Smiling, I waited for them to quiet down. All eyes turned toward me, waiting for me to say something. I put on my teacher persona like a uniform and stepped forward, taking charge. For the moment, they were quiet. As a teacher it told me one thing: they wanted structure. Here in a foreign country, not knowing the lay of the land, even students of life need structure. Interesting.

"Welcome to *Villa della Cantante*, where a famous opera singer lived. You've no doubt read all about her on the villa's website." I was aware of Kate glancing at me over her sunglasses. "You'll find Lake Como is an amazing place."

"Lake *Homo* is a trip of a lifetime."

"Good one, Bibi," said one of them.

Everyone laughed at the cute, plump Bibi. Some couples held hands or put their arms around one another's waists, a few kissed a quick peck. I felt the warm blush on my cheeks get hotter, trying not to watch them but I couldn't help myself.

Bibi said, "Oops, sorry, not sorry. Carry on. And you are?"

"I'm Miss McKenna, your, um, your personal concierge," I said, realizing what Rosie had meant: I am a property manager for the owner, plus house-sitting, plus an adviser or *consigliere*, providing help and information to the people staying here, thus, a concierge. I regretted introducing myself as Miss—a momentary lapse into teacher mode. I felt Kate's eyes watching me.

"Oh, by the way, Miss McKenna," Dana said to me. "We're staying for the strawberry festival. Hope that's all right. Saturday to Saturday, but leaving Sunday. I did call."

"Yes, that's fine. It's in the notes, here," I pointed to the paperwork. "And please, call me Gerri. Let's do a quick roll call as I hand out your keys," I announced. "I'm told you've already chosen your rooms, so, um, you'll find them upstairs. Except one downstairs, through the living room. Who's the lucky couple to get the master bedroom?"

"That's us. We drew it from the hat, right CJ?" Erin said, giving her girlfriend, the sweet-faced Black woman, the high five. Aware of them watching me fumble with the key envelope, I heard a few snickers. I kept thinking, geez, you're a teacher, Gerri, used to standing in front of college students. What's the matter with you?

"Um, so…" I opened the sealed envelope of keys, and watched, perplexed, as the metal antique keys slid out hitting the marble floor with several TINGING sounds.

Kate crouched down under the foyer table to help me retrieve them. Bending over, her low-cut tee revealed more of her cleavage, soft, lovely. I fumbled the keys, noticing that each antique metal key was engraved with a room number and a nametag.

She whispered to me, "Hey, don't worry, we're easy." She smiled at me, but then looked serious. "Sorry about, um, you know—the kiss thing."

Kate's sunglasses slid down her nose as she looked at me, wide-eyed. I nodded, blushing, and then knocked my head on the table as we both stood at the same time.

"Ha. Excuse the interruption," I said to the others, trying to focus on the list of names. I chose a sheet with no surnames, just the facts; then cleared my throat.

"The owner Marcella Ferrario-Eaton wants to welcome you. Signora Marcella has included your names and individual professions. This'll help me get to know you." Glancing down the list, I said, "Looks as if most of you live in California: Los Angeles, Manhattan Beach, Palm Springs, except one of you lives in London, England." I took a breath. "Now for the keys. You'll notice your key has an engraved room number. Most of the rooms are upstairs." I reached into the envelope and pulled out a key, reading the nametag: "First, Renee and Tracy?"

Tracy, the one who slouched, shifted forward to take the key, a red and white Lamborghini leather bag slung over her shoulder. Renee and Tracy were attractive androgynous women, both tall and slim, both with short choppy hairdos. Beside Renee and

Tracy's names, their career info had been handwritten: "IT Computer Specialist" and "Real Estate Agent."

"I get the window side. You know I need fresh air." Renee grabbed the room key.

"Dr. Wanda and Dr. Brittany?" A loud laugh announced both women present; both the epitome of health. On the list, Signora Marcella had written just "MD and ND" for Medical Doctor and Naturopathic Doctor, respectively.

"The Puerto Rican beauty!" one of the gals exclaimed.

So I assumed Dr. Wanda was Puerto Rican. Her thick, medium-length hair had a slight burgundy tinge. The beautiful Wanda wore horn-rimmed eyeglasses, she had perfect white teeth, and she spoke fluent Spanish.

I'd heard of Dr. Brittany, a Hollywood psychic and medical intuitive; feminine looking, with long flaxen hair, one of the youngest at age thirty-five. She had a calming presence and a wide smile with brilliant white teeth. I hoped she wouldn't read my uptight mind.

Comments swarmed around the foyer, but I kept my focus.

"CJ and Erin?" I'd met them earlier. CJ the "Tennis Pro"—the one with a tennis racket in her hand luggage—looked super-fit and super-athletic with a sweet face, but my notes said CJ was also a financial analyst. Her partner, Erin, the tall lean one, was as stylish as the other women but more handsome than pretty, and nonbinary; an "Ex-Army Veteran"; the oldest of the bunch and much older than the thirty-something CJ, to whom she seemed overly attentive.

"Where's the nearest tennis court?" asked CJ.

"Um, I'll find out for you," I fudged, handing over their keys.

"Next, Bibi and Luciana?" In brackets beside Bibi's name it said, "Corporate Accountant, L.A., age 32", the youngest of the group. Bibi was quite plump, and showed it off, dressed in a sexy outfit that purposely showcased her voluptuous figure. Bibi's girlfriend Luciana had short dark hair, olive skin and brown eyes; she was, perhaps, Mexican-American. Her body was muscular, befitting a "Santa Monica Police Officer." Together, an accountant and a cop. Interesting.

"Next, Jamie and Hannah?" Listed respectively, as "TV Newsroom Researcher, Hollywood," and "Medical Examiner's

Assistant, L.A." I read the word "birthday" next to one of their names.

"Which one of you is the birthday girl?"

Jamie raised her hand as if a shy student. "It's the big four-O."

Jamie was cute, petite, possibly Asian-American with her dark hair cut into a bob; all blended together to create an adorable young woman.

"A fortieth birthday. Congratulations. Great way to celebrate."

Next down the list: "Vera and Dana." We'd already met. The words "single beds" written beside their names told me they weren't a couple, or else they disliked sleeping together. Both early forties. Beside Vera's name Marcella had written "London Lawyer (litigation paralegal)," and for Dana the clipboard-wielding strawberry blonde, "Travel Agent." Not as tall as Erin, Vera looked robust and healthy; in fact, all the women did.

"And last but not least, Kate." The word "Artist" with a capital *A* had been written beside her name; and another name had been scratched out, which meant one thing: her ex-partner was not coming.

"You're an artist?"

Cheeky Bibi, the accountant, piped in, "A freakin' brilliant artist."

Kate Bradshaw, wearing a solemn expression, reached between two couples for her key. "*Grazie.*" She didn't look at me. Her mood had changed; a light had shut off.

Putting her arm around Kate's waist, Dana said, "Kate, honey, how about bunking with me? We'll put Vera in her own room to snore all night by herself."

"Nah, thanks, *foo*. No offence, but I need my own room."

Clearly they were all close, and everyone had a compassionate expression for Kate. Whatever had happened to her or to her companion, I wanted to comfort her but thought it inappropriate at the moment. Instead, desperately needing fresh air and an escape route, I hurried to open the front door.

"All right, then, if you need anything please let me know. I'm located next door in the, ah, guesthouse," I stuttered, realizing our close quarters might present a privacy issue. "Enjoy Lake *Homo*." They laughed as I eased my way out the entrance. I wanted to escape and hoped I'd left my suite unlocked because I couldn't remember past Kate's "Hiya!"

I paused outside on the front step to overhear Tracy, the realtor, yell, "All right ladies, stop drooling, our hot chaperone has left the building. Crack open the wine."

"What wine? We've got to go shopping. Quick, ask her, ask her," yelled Jamie, the birthday girl.

Bounding into my quarters, I locked the door behind me and flattened my body against it. I'd escaped. I walked around my small open living quarters. My heart was racing. "Why am I so nervous?" Pucci and Goldie wagged their tails and stared at me as I paced back and forth. I undid two buttons and fanned myself. "Must be the Italian heat?"

But the answer came as a complete shock, "No way, can't be. I am *not* attracted to her."

My tablet rang on the kitchen counter next to my phone, breaking my thought. The video chat app automatically answered the call and Rosie's face appeared; she sat in an English garden with greenery behind her. Her naturally curly short hair looked all askew, and her transition rose-colored eyeglasses had darkened in the sunlight.

"I'm in the middle of thirteen lesbians! What have you done to me?"

Rosie laughed. "Good, you've introduced yourself." Her friendly face grew larger on screen as she came closer, a frown embedded on her forehead. "What's wrong?"

"Thirteen lesbians!"

"Why?"

"You did this to me on purpose, didn't you? Because I had one little affair with a woman in university, you think I'm a closeted dyke. And yes, well, they're all very attractive. A nice group of butch, femme, non-binary. Who's the handy one?"

Rosie guffawed. "The handy one? As in, hand job? You tosser. Wait 'til they start rocking those antique beds. Don't you remember what it was like? Va-va-voom!" she said, chortling. "What was her name, your university girlfriend?"

"Oh, stop! I was young and adventurous. Her name was Louise, if you must know. We spent two semesters together. I helped her graduate with a master's by helping to write her papers. Then bye-bye, off she went. And that was it." Saying her name brought all the memories to the foreground. Feeling the warmth again, I undid two more shirt buttons.

"I haven't thought about her for years."

"Liar," Rosie snapped. "I know damn well you're secretly attracted to women. Admit it."

I had a sudden memory from way back in grade school, playing Truth or Dare with a girl in my class. We ended up kissing, my first kiss ever. I had never decided if I liked kissing, or if I liked kissing a girl. I frowned at the thought.

"This isn't easy for me, Rosie. I haven't peeked behind that door in years."

"Fine, stay in the closet, you stubborn goofball," she laughed, her pink cheeks shining onscreen.

"That's right, laugh it up. Obviously, Bill's operation went well. Can I go home now?"

"My dear Gerri—"

"Yes or no?" Waiting, I brushed a strand of hair off my forehead.

"It's a no. Bill's still recuperating. Anything I can do, besides be there?" My best friend turned serious, so I calmed down. Rosie smiled at me onscreen, adding, "I'd never let anything bad happen to you."

"What does that mean?" I could see the concern on Rosie's face. "I'm sorry. You don't need the extra worry. I can handle this." She felt so far away.

There was a knock on my Dutch door.

"If you need anything, ask the *handy one!*" Rosie bellowed.

"Shhh! I love you, Rosie. Gotta go." And I hung up.

Immediately, beside the tablet, Paul's mobile phone rang. "Shit. Might be my daughter." I pressed the video answer button. A woman with long black hair appeared.

"Paul, I'm in town. It's been ages. Are you there?" said the woman.

She froze. I froze. She couldn't see me because the phone's video function was off. I pressed "Cancel" and Miss Freighter Girl disappeared. It had to be *that woman*. Right there in front of me on my dead husband's phone. My body shook in a cold sweat.

"This phone is toast."

Another knock. "Coming!" Still angry, I flung open the top

part of the Dutch door, "Yesss?" Kate stood outside. "Oh, hi. It's you." Her presence softened me.

Kate Bradshaw, the Artist with a capital *A*, leaned her fit and shapely body against the door frame. "They sent me to ask you something." She looked sheepish.

"Why you?" I said, imitating a snotty headmistress.

"My lucky day," she said with a chuckle. "Except I offered, and I wanted to apologize again, formally. Sorry, I was a bit rude earlier."

"Okay, thanks. Yeah, me too. Sorry. Apology accepted." Compelled by her sweet demeanor, I asked, "What's the question?"

"Question?" Her eyes lowered onto my chest. "Right, yes, ahhh," she paused. "Did you know your shirt's open?"

I looked down to see my buttons undone exposing my basic schoolmarm bra and my cleavage. "Shit, sorry. It's hot, in here. Your question?" I blushed and fumbled with the buttons.

"Right, um…" She smirked with a raised eyebrow, watching me do the buttons up all the way to my chin. "Yes, ah, we need to do a wine run, grocery shopping. Do you know—"

"In Lenno, there's a supermarket, I'm told. One ferry up. I mean, take the ferry up to the first stop." I had trouble forming my words. "Or Argegno has a grocery mini-mart but it's expensive. And there's a fabulous bakery."

"A bakery, well, I'll be going there."

"Yeah, me too. Later today. I'm ravished—I mean, famished."

I watched the quiver at the edge of her mouth, her beguiling hazel eyes softened. The air felt swollen between us.

"*Grah-tsee-ay.* Thanks. By the way, you're okay, right, with *us*?"

"Of course." I felt hot and flushed again.

"This is our first time to Lake Como. We'll try not to bother you."

"Hey, it's fine. Disturb me any time, I'm here for you." I could've kicked myself for that innocent innuendo. "By the way, don't go into the olive grove, in the hills, it's, well…lots of migrant workers."

"Yeah, right, more like secret trysts in the olive grove with the village girls. Like at our vineyard in California."

"Good to know. Is that where you hang out?"

"Ha! Funny lady. It's the grape pickers, they sneak into the vineyard at night with their dates. Anyway, perhaps later you could give us a *rub*down, ah, *run*down, on the area." Kate took her leave, backing away. "Not that we need it. Lesbians are quite...*handy*."

I took in a breath through my open mouth.

Trying not to smirk, Kate hurried around the corner, saying, "*Namaste.*"

"Fff..." Feeling intoxicated from her energy, I leaned on the door. "Handy? Oh, my god, she overheard Rosie. Shit, I'm a knucklehead." But then I heard loud screams: "She's in trouble."

I gathered my *il capo* persona and ran outside, around the corner to the backyard and got accosted by the sight of—Oh no, a naked body in the pool, skinny dipping, and Bibi stripping off her clothes and jumping in, and—I scrambled away.

"Time to get the hell outta Dodge."

CHAPTER 5
The Bell Over the Door

New experiences lie outside my window,
awaiting my attention. I wish to surface to the
completeness of being here, opening a space to
release the past for change to occur. Take the road
that whispers my name. Don't look back, Gerri!

—G. A. McKenna, journal entry

In the afternoon, the time had come to venture outside on my own for an exploratory walkabout. The thought of being out, on my own, in Italy, finally excited me. Besides, I needed food, and the dogs and I needed a jog. As I changed quickly into shorts and a top, the pups kept whining at the happy sounds of the guests enjoying themselves next door. The women's voices echoed through our adjoining kitchen wall.

The minute I opened my door, the dogs bounded outside, and I jogged beside them down the gentle slope toward the orange-tiled rooftops of Argegno below. The Italian summer hugged me in a sweet embrace. Ancient olive trees alongside the cobblestone path resembled crooked, gnarly old men. Pucci and Goldie loved jumping in the long grass and chasing one another in circles, so free. At the bottom of the ancient path, a busy road, *La Strada Provinciale*, ended our delightful romp.

"Pucci! Goldie!" I yelled. The terror in my voice made them run to me, and I put them on their leashes.

Isabella had said about ten minutes to the village; jogging there took much less time. We crossed the road to a medieval stone footbridge over the narrow River Telo, or so I read on the tattered sign. Before the bridge, an abandoned section of old houses clung precariously to the sides of the river's crumbling ravine.

On the other side of the bridge, I found myself entering the village through its back door, similar to a servant's entrance into a dilapidated estate and not at all a typical tourist hotspot. The three-storey buildings leaned inward and over me as if vultures. I had read that most Europeans rented these rundown apartments, as opposed to owning them.

Both dogs pulled me along the cobblestone alleyways. I sidestepped falling dust from a balcony above me, where a woman in a flowery dress swatted a rug. Her eyes widened when she saw me, and she hastily shut her door and closed the lace curtains. Nice friendly folk. Given the weirdness about the place, I couldn't wait to see what lay around the next corner.

I hurried along a covered alleyway into the full sunshine of an open *piazza* or square, and found a cluster of small shops, bars, and places to eat. In the center of the circular square stood a simple fountain, past it was the roadway with a row of parked cars and motorcycles, and across the road was the ferry dock and the lake; all empty. From where I stood, the tree-lined lakeside promenade ran the entire length of the small town, and the vacant *piazza* must be at its heart. Having arrived late last night, I recognized only the dock and the tavern across the street.

"Where is everyone? Must be siesta time."

I tied the dogs' leashes to a bench and ducked into the *farmacia*. Once inside, I felt as though I'd entered a seventeenth-century apothecary with its many jars of dried herbs and brown bottles of tinctures lining the walls. A balding pharmacist, possibly mid-seventies, in a white smock busied himself behind the counter.

Waiting for service, there stood a tall policeman, blowing his runny nose into a cloth handkerchief. He wore a black hat fitted with a visor, a light-blue regulation summer shirt and black pants, tall black leather boots, and a holstered gun strapped to his waist.

The unshaven *Carabiniere* turned to me, "*Buongiorno, signorina,*" he grinned, "Or shall I say *good morning* in English?"

I felt flattered. "*Signorina* is for young women, thanks for the compliment. Do I look English?"

"You look, how I say, new here." The policeman tipped his hat, showing his light brown curly hair, "I am Police Chief Niklaus Koehl, in case you ever need anything," he said, studying me.

The balding pharmacist turned and handed the uniformed policeman a small glass bottle, saying, "Ciao, Niklaus." As the policeman left, the pharmacist said to me, "*Buongiorno,* how can I help you?"

"I have a prescription…"

While I rummaged through my purse, I glanced at his name tag that read, "Johan – Farmacista & Erborista," I asked, "You're also an herbalist, Johan?"

"Ya. My family is trained in German Herbal Medicine, you see there," he said, pointing to his certificates and a few framed photographs. One black and white photo showed a young couple in neat but threadbare clothing holding a newborn in an olive grove. Beside them stood a well-dressed young woman, her face blurry.

"It is Signora Angelina Ferrario, with my parents, and me at three-years-old."

"Really? La Cantante."

"Ya. The famous La Cantante. My parents worked in her olive grove."

"Fascinating," I said, but thinking to myself, there's a story here I need to explore.

I found my prescription for sleeping pills and handed it to him, having meant to fill it at home. He nodded with a slight smile.

He read my name: "*Frau* McKenna, a pleasure to meet you. But your prescription is not good for you, Madame. Valerian Root Extract is better. It's a plant that makes you sleep like a baby."

I agreed with him and paid for the Valerian. Johan walked me outside, and Pucci and Goldie greeted him with wagging tails. His eyes widened as he stepped back. "Those are the villa dogs. You must be… Forgive me, I have to go, I'm busy." He shut down suddenly and went back inside his shop. Another strange reaction.

The dogs yanked me away to the other side of the square's fountain where a teenage boy stood at a cart selling lemons and small sealed bottles. Near him a white-haired woman tended her flower cart.

"Please sit?" the teenager said, while making something using crushed ice and a lemon-colored liquid. The lemon seller nudged me to sit down on the concrete bench in front of the fountain. "Here, for you," he said, handing me a lemon slushie drink. I gulped it down, grateful to quench my thirst in the hot sun.

"Thanks. How much?"

"*Attenta*, be careful!" he yelled, as I began to lean back against the bench. "You see," and he pointed to a white chalk mark on the bench, now half smudged. He made a sign with his hand in the shape of a scrunched "C" symbol.

I recognised the ancient Germanic-Nordic Rune symbol and knew it represented a secret matter or hidden things, and also, a game.

"Are you playing a game?" I asked, curiously watching him repair the smudged symbol.

"Not allowed to tell, *signora*."

"Oh, I see. That usually means a secret rendezvous," I said, half-kidding him.

"You want more? Three euros," said the unshaven teenager, attempting to divert my attention.

Paying him, I said, "I'll pass. It made me feel woozy."

"You no want *limoncello*?" he asked.

"*Limoncello*? Isn't that with vodka? A lemon liqueur? Oh dear."

Not waiting for an answer, I followed the dogs as they pulled me toward a row of storefronts. They ran up to *Rocco's Ristorante la Piazzetta*, "The Restaurant on the Little Square" with outside seating and yellow umbrellas. Both dogs sat at the door, barking.

"Pucci, Goldie," called a girl's singsong voice from inside Rocco's. The dogs sat stubbornly, not budging, and I had to abide. A young female server with bright purple highlights in her otherwise brunette hair emerged from the shop, carrying two small gelato dishes for the dogs, who held back and waited until she set them down. "*Sì-sì*, eat-eat," she cried, and they went crazy, lapping up the ice cream. She stared at me with an inquisitive frown.

"Signora Marcella has returned already?" asked the Gelato

Girl.

A booming voice yelled, "Lia!" from inside. Behind the counter, a dark, muscular man with black bushy eyebrows, waved and jerked his head, meaning "get inside."

"Rocco, mind your manners," Lia scolded the big-bellied man behind the counter. "Sorry about my boss. Must go," and she stepped back inside. Standing there, they both looked at me as though they'd seen a ghost. All quite curious.

The dogs wanted to continue their set routine, and pulled me to the bakery next door, the *Panificio Vacchini*. Police Chief Niklaus Koehl, whom I'd met in the pharmacy, exited the shop with a loaf of bread similar to a baguette under his arm, and held the door open for me.

"We meet again, *signora*."

"Now I'm a *signora*, a middle-aged woman. My, I age fast," I joked, making him laugh. He tipped his hat again and left, still eyeing me.

The bell over the door tinkled as the dogs and I entered. "Are dogs allowed inside shops?"

The aroma of fresh bread called forth a ravenous appetite. From the outside, the bakery looked tiny, but once inside it unfolded like a rose with each petal a separate area, including a sitting area parallel to the glass counters. Although the hand-printed sign announced a bakery, it sold other eclectic products. One shelf, labeled "Made in Switzerland," displayed Swiss army knives, casual watches, chocolates, but nothing too expensive. The town of Lugano lay across the Swiss border, not far away. Over the top of the counter, I could see into a back room that had ovens and kneading tables characteristic of the baker's trade.

"Yes, yes. *Ciao cuccioli!*"—Hello puppies, sang an elderly man behind the counter as he hung up the phone, his back to us. A full head of white hair and a hunched back were the first things I noticed about the old baker, his slight figure held together by bulky shoulders and strong arms. He wore a white baker's smock. When he turned toward me, both of his massive hands carried a slice of *crostini* with jam slathered on top.

"My famous fig jam, dogs love it," he explained, feeding the dogs. As they licked off the fig jam, the old baker eyed me from behind his wire-rimmed spectacles.

"Good morning, *signora*. I am Carlo Vacchini." He smiled the most sincere smile I'd seen directed toward me since I arrived.

"Good morning, Signor Vacchini," I replied, then asked, "I detect an accent, but what?"

"Swiss-Italian. Still, I have an accent to you?" he said with boyish glee.

"*Piccolo*, a little. But your English is excellent." He must be the old baker Isabella spoke about, so I asked, "I'm staying at Villa della Cantante. I believe you knew the owner, Angelina, the famous opera singer?"

"Eh?" He cupped a hand around his ear, or was he pretending not to hear me? He had a strange smile on his face, his brow furrowed with deep lines and, with his head cocked to one side, he seemed to be studying me, although he kept glancing past me to outside.

"She keeps watch," he said, unexpectedly.

"Beg your pardon?"

"My ex-wife, there," he deflected, pointing to the old flower-cart lady in the piazza. "She refuses to speak to me. We're both stubborn old goats," he said, then chuckled. In a more serious tone, he asked, "How can I help you? You are the *vedova* at the Villa della Cantante? Signora Marcella's *vedova?*"

"*Vedova?*"

"*Sì*, the widow."

"Excuse me, what? How did you…"

I didn't expect the word *widow*. I'd gone from *signorini*, to a *signora*, to now a *vedova*. Crazy, but I'd never called myself a widow. I must have turned ghost-white, either from the shock, or from the limoncello. I felt even more woozy.

"Signora, are you not well? Here, sit down." I watched as he moved in slow motion toward me. His strong arms held me upright as I fell onto a wooden chair.

He brought a pitcher of water and poured a glass for me. The bell tinkled and a customer came and went. I stared out the doorway, trying to gather my thoughts. Signor Vacchini left me to attend his customer and I contemplated to myself, feeling dazed:

I don't feel so good. What am I doing here? I want to go home. I want to lie on my couch and watch television, to bleed away my life in useless passages of time. To be numb. But I am numb, damn it. *Wake up, Gerri!*

Another customer came and went, and the now-soothing sound of the bell over the door tinkled again. I gazed at the reflections in my water glass in a drowsy trance of melancholia, aware the baker kept watch over me as he went about his business.

The bell over the door jingled again and Kate Bradshaw walked in.

"*Buona,* um, *giornata?*"—Good day, she tried to say in Italian to the baker, and then noticed me sitting at the table. "Gerri, hiya! I was hoping to run into you." Kate hesitated, then said, "Are you all right? You look a bit pale."

"I thought she would faint," Carlo the baker said.

Kate touched my shoulder, and I whispered, "I'm happy to see you." I looked up at her too fast and the room spun.

Kate sat on the chair next to me and leaned in, "What's up, Professor? Jet-lagged like me?" Gently, she touched my arm and smiled at me. The gesture warmed my heart. The energy between us embraced silent words. I started to feel better by focusing on her radiant face.

Carlo crept by us, shut the door, and flipped the sign to "Closed."

"What's he doing? Should we make a run for it?" Kate joked quietly.

Carlo poured me another glass of water, his hands trembling, then sat across from us at the next table. "What do you want, *signora?*" he asked me.

"A baguette, *signor.* Or, I mean, *un pagnotta.*" I pointed to the fresh loaf of peasant bread in the basket, shorter than a French baguette. "I'm going to make my own *crostini,* or rather, um, *bruschetta.*"

He laughed, his tobacco-stained dentures clicking in his mouth. He handed me the bread.

"And a jar of your homemade fig jam, *per favore,*" I replied, hoping "fig jam" wasn't an espionage code between two agents. Where does my mind get this stuff?

Kate must have felt the uneasiness and interjected, "And I'll take thirteen croissants, thanks, or if that's bad luck, then a dozen and one on the side."

He kept his gaze on me and provoked me more: "No-no, what do you *really* want?"

Looking steadily at Carlo, "I don't understand, I…" I paused, remembering what Isabella had intimated to me, ask the baker about La Cantante, so I just blurted out: "Were you in love with La Cantante?"

"What the heck?" Kate gawked at me. "The opera singer in the villa's portrait?"

His joviality disappeared. His hands shook again as he grabbed metal tongs to put the croissants into a paper bag. "We all loved her. She was *bellissima*. But, yes, I fell in love for Signora Angelina Ferrario at first glance. I was sixteen. She, barely thirty, and a divine opera diva." His honesty surprised me. He continued, "*Amor regge senza legge*—Love rules without laws. I'm in my nineties, no one cares now. She is the reason I married late in life, with my broken heart. Ah, but when I was young…" he trailed off momentarily. Then, staring out the window, continued, "We lived in Germany. My father, Italian; my mother, Swiss. To escape persecution by the Nazis, my family escaped to my mother's homeland of Switzerland." He paused.

"In the 1940s?" Kate asked, paying him for the bag of croissants.

"1939, before the Nazi death camps went into full operation to murder Jews and many others."

"Yes, even homosexuals," Kate said, frowning.

"*Sì*," Carlo nodded. "My family is not Jewish, you understand." Carlo explained. "I come from a family of gilders, architects, stonemasons. Under the Nazi regime Freemasons were persecuted. This is odd because Hitler needed stonemasons to build his monuments. My father was a famous stonemason."

"That explains the Masonic emblem hanging on your wall," I said, pointing over his shoulder to the familiar symbol. "It's a Masonic square and compass, with the letter G inside. For Freemasonry?"

Carlo placed a finger onto his lower lip, "*Sì*, the Freemason emblem."

Kate said, "With a *G* as in Gerri. Odd place for a Masonic symbol, in a baker's shop?" Kate leaned in closer to him, "And your gold pin?"

He touched the gold pin on the lapel of his baker's smock as if clutching his heart. The pin resembled a lapis-blue, five-petal Forget-Me-Not. He said, "Both family souvenirs."

"Don't tell me, a Freemasonry symbol, right?" He nodded in agreement. "Hey, I'm not just a pretty face," Kate said.

Carlo smiled at her, then became serious again. "Because Hitler wanted a famous Master Mason, he sent Gestapo spies to hunt for my father. The Swiss villagers forced us to go across Lake Lugano into northern Italy. To conceal my father's identity from Mussolini's pro-Nazi army, the underground changed our papers to say "baker" and not masons. Our family became known as the Swiss bakers, even though my father was Italian. Funny, we were not bakers. Why bakers? *Stupido*." Carlo coughed through his chortling.

"When we arrived in Argegno, we hid in the hills, and in Signora Angelina's olive grove with other war refugees. Because of her, we survived."

He touched his heart, and then said, "With the last of his money, my father bought a bakery and a rundown hotel, at a cheap price back then. I stayed working in the bakery because I loved it. My son now works at the hotel, *Casa di Sognatori* in beautiful Bellagio."

I recognized the hotel's name. The same hotel Rosie's "good old sport" owned.

Kate said, "Bellagio, oh yeah, it's on my list of places to visit."

"You will love it. That is a promise. You will go together?" Carlo asked.

"Ah, perhaps tomorrow," Kate said, glancing at me.

I smiled and shrugged, not knowing.

Signor Vacchini stood up and walked slowly behind the counter.

I leaned closer to Kate, asking, "I wonder, why is he telling us his story in such detail?"

"Yeah, but what a fascinating family history," she said, placing her hand on mine in a friendly gesture, "Have you two met before? I get the sense he knows you," she whispered.

I shook my head and touched the top of her hand, feeling her soft skin. "Thanks for staying. I'm sure you've got better things to do."

When she smiled at me, so did her eyes. We paused in silence; then we both removed our hand. Needing to change my focus, I called out, "Signor Vacchini, what's—"

"Call me Carlo."

"Thanks. So, Carlo, stonemasons had individual marks, correct? What's with the Mason or Rune mark on the bench outside, by the fountain?"

He froze behind the counter, then shrugged. "Never noticed. But I will now."

Carlo returned with a bottle of clear white liquid and three shot glasses. The homemade label read *Grappa Bianca*. He then brought over a plate of pastries and an open jar of fig jam, making my stomach grumble. "Eat, eat," he ordered. Watching me, he sat down carefully, like a dowager with arthritic knees, and then poured the chilled grappa liqueur. He wet his finger with the grappa to draw a mark on the tabletop.

"That's the one I saw," I said.

Kate snapped a quick photo of the mark before it dried.

"How odd, why is it on the bench?" he wondered. "It's our family's Mason mark, for each generation of stone masons. *Perthro*, the protector."

"The symbol also means a secret game is afoot," I smiled, helping myself to a pastry.

"You know the Runes?" Kate asked. "You're full of surprises, Professor," Kate said, then lathered fig jam onto a pastry.

"I memorized them during my university days, made extra money by charging for Rune readings."

Carlo's smile dropped momentarily. He frowned at me, his eyes two slits, as if he thought I knew something I wasn't supposed to know, something forbidden. His fingers threaded through his white hair and thick strands stood upended. I heard the wall clock ticking.

"Please go on. We won't tell anyone, right, Kate?"

"Mum's the word."

"Everyone knows. *Piccoli segreti, a poco a poco.*"—The little secrets, little by little. He pushed full shot glasses toward us.

"You became friends with La Cantante. How did you meet?" Kate asked.

"After we opened the bakery I delivered baked goods to their estate. She was older than me and married to Signor Max Ferrario, a rich businessman from Milano. Max knew Mussolini. He called him, *il mostro*—the monster." Carlo's fingers curled into two closed fists. "In a way, Max's acquaintance with *Il Duce* protected her, for a while. At such a young age, my heart had wings only for her. *Salute!*" he shouted, holding up his shot glass, waiting for us.

"Oh, gawd, down the hatch. *Cin-cin!*" I toasted.

We downed the grappa together. The cold liquid hit the back of my throat and slid down with an icy, crisp taste. He stared at me, waiting for a reaction.

"A little burning, but not too bad."

"*Bravissima!*"

Kate on the other hand, had a coughing fit, "Yikes. Strong shit."

I patted her back, which seemed to help. I left my hand there, rubbing the base of her neck as I would a baby's or dare I say it, as I would a lover's? Kate and I gazed at one another for a few warm seconds. I felt butterflies and smoothed my hand along the nape of her neck, very bold of me; must be the alcohol, especially the grappa that knocked me out of my comfort zone.

Carlo seemed to drift off into his memories. But then, his eyes turned dark.

"Then *they* came. By 1941 Mussolini was little more than Hitler's puppet. Nazi soldiers and SS officers cropped up everywhere, helping themselves to our villas and our art, and even our Freemason antiquities. Among those of the German Reich, the one-star *Gruppenfuhrer* was Otto Weber, the group leader. Barely twenty, he rose through the ranks quickly by following orders without question. Weber would visit our bakery often, boasting of his job escorting Mussolini and his mistress when they stayed in the Villa Belmonte. Soon after his arrival, Weber met and fell in love with Angelina at her opera recital. That night in Como's piazza..." he closed his eyes, pausing.

I removed my hand from Kate's back and watched Carlo carefully. As he continued, I realized he spoke of Piazza Cavour, the large square in Como town. I'd forgotten about my experience there, when I had felt as though someone pushed me from behind, and my feet had lifted off the ground for a brief second. I saw it clearly in my mind's eye:

On a warm summer evening in 1943, the young Angelina Ferrario stood center stage at Piazza Cavour in a magical halo of light. In the audience sat village locals, area dignitaries, and a row of black-uniformed Nazi SS. The hushed crowd felt a premonition, breathless, awaiting the flower to open and show her blossoms. Resplendent in her gown, Angelina waited, motionless. The conductor's baton sparked the air. The music filled the area. Her voice spun a silken thread connecting everyone's hearts. A powerful lirico-spinto soprano, La Cantante's exquisite artistry surged and trilled freely over more than four and a half octaves. No one present that night would ever forget her, and SS Major-General Otto Weber fell in love. And so began the downfall of one of the most beautiful voices in Italy.

Beads of sweat formed on Carlo's forehead, "After La Cantante's recital, a few villagers and I, we see Commandant Otto Weber kiss her hand. He fawned over her. She had to be careful of his advances for everyone's safety. She put herself in danger. He adored her, and he fell for the ruse."

The young general in his black Nazi uniform leaned forward to kiss her hand, bewitched by her loveliness, her bare shoulders soft and inviting in the night's breeze.

"The next year, in October of 1944, Angelina gave birth to a daughter, Marcella, a blessing Angelina's husband Max had longed for. Six months later, the family's happiness ended abruptly. I'll never forget the sixth of April 1945. The Allied Operation Grapeshot began in Lombardy. On that day, our beautiful La Cantante was murdered by Otto Weber. His Nazi superior forced him to kill her..." Carlo started to shake, the color draining out of his face. "He murdered her for love, a deranged love. And because..." He stopped to stare at me.

"Because they discovered what? That she helped refugees?" Kate suggested.

"Yes," I agreed.

"Forgive me," then, oddly, he said, "You will want to know."

He composed himself, closing his eyes for a moment, in preparation. "After killing her, Otto Weber shot himself. There was a witness, one of the house servants." Carlo filled our shot glasses. "I hated the Nazi commandant more than Mussolini, who was shot by partisans just north of here in Mezzegra. The Allied attack took one month to force the Germans in Italy to surrender. Argegno rejoiced along with the rest of Italy. Except me, I mourned for *la mia meravigliosa bellezza*—my wonderful beauty. Angelina, you are the love of my life. I am to be with you forever," he intoned, singsong, as if quoting a love sonnet.

He stood unexpectedly, yelling, "*Salute!*" He shot back one more grappa, hobbled to the door, and flipped the sign to "Open."

Amazed he had opened up to us without hesitation, I wanted to ask more questions, but I respected his cue. I felt the grappa take effect. Kate and I paid for our baked goods. I left more money than necessary on the table. Kate thanked him and the bell jingled as she opened the door and took the dogs outside. I turned back.

"It's been a pleasure, Signor Vacchini, our meeting."

He approached me, "Wait, I wish to give you this." He unfastened the gold Forget-Me-Not pin from his smock.

"That's kind of you, but I can't accept it."

"I insist." We were eye to eye, he and I, and my affection for him grew; his thick fingers deftly fixed the pin on my lapel.

"Thank you, I'll treasure it always," I said.

"*Signora*, may I hear your name?" he asked with a tilt of his head.

"It's pronounced Gerri McKenna." He tilted his head to the other side, and I explained, "Gerri stands for Geraldine."

He straightened his head, in fact, his entire body straightened, and he leaned back: "*Sì, grazie.* You are *realigned.*"

Realigned? I felt a question pop into my head as if a sharp stabbing pain but decided not to give it breath. I put it down to not understanding his Swiss-German to Italian to English translation, thinking he might have meant a different word.

As Signor Vacchini held the door open for me, he said, "We will talk again." It was not a question.

The word "realigned" nagged at me as I left the bakery and joined Kate outside in the sunshine. We finished our grocery shopping together at the expensive mini-mart. Feeling tipsy, I found myself wishing I had brought the van instead of lugging my groceries uphill all the way back to the villa. Kate helped by carrying one of my bags in her strong arms, walking alongside me. She grew excited talking about what Carlo Vacchini had said. Between the alcohol, the dogs, and my new cloth bags full of food, my pace lagged. Determined, I forged ahead like a centenarian pilgrim, relaying to Kate a story Rosie told me of an old Greek man she once met on her travels. Going up the steep hill to the pilgrim's church of Monolithos on the island of Rhodes, he took it slow and easy, one step at a time. It doesn't get you anywhere fast, but it gets you there. Young tourists raced up the long steep climb and by halfway up they felt too exhausted to continue. The old Greek man passed them, akin to the tortoise and the hare. Not unlike the slow unravelling of the truth about Angelina and her husband, their daughter Marcella, and Carlo the baker—the little secrets, little by little.

An excitement grew inside me. On the entire walk uphill, both Kate and I talked about the old baker and his unrequited love for Angelina Ferrario. And wondered, was it truly unrequited? As in, a secret love story?

I enjoyed Kate's company. We arrived at the villa, bubbling with lively enthusiasm. When she said goodnight, she quickly squeezed my hand and then ran off with a little skip in her step. It felt like part of me went with her. I packed away the groceries and busied myself making a fresh vegetable soup for dinner. Later in the evening, all was quiet. All the guests had left the villa in their rental cars for an evening excursion. Isabella had left, riding off on Alex's red Vespa scooter, its metallic-sounding motor zzzzinging past like a frantic wasp. The villa became all mine.

The dogs were restless, so I brought them upstairs to my bedroom, just in case…in case of what? Burglars? Ghosts? The ghost of Angelina? She'd been murdered inside her own villa. What a story!

Chilled, I hugged the dogs, "Good puppies." I got into bed and both dogs snuggled up to me taking most of the bed. But tossing and turning I couldn't sleep. My new leather journal beckoned me.

When I left the Vancouver airport, my daughter Julie had handed me a lined travel journal, along with adhesive tape and plastic scissors, saying, "When I travel, I collect one thing each day. I cut and paste memorabilia into my journal to remind me of the people or places. You know, pictures from travel brochures, business cards from shops or cafes you visit along the way. You'll love it. Journaling is a souvenir that lasts a lifetime. The thing is, you've got to promise to do it every night. Otherwise, it gets away from you." Hugging her tight, I had agreed to write in it daily.

Wanting to keep my promise to my daughter, I pulled out the leather-bound travel journal and sat at the intricately carved desk that overlooked the lake. I peered out the window at the dark lake that sparkled in the distance, misty and foreboding. I pressed down the journal's first page and took hold of my inexpensive but favorite fountain pen, the one I'd used for many years, loving the free flow of real ink on paper.

"What's the title?" I asked aloud, hoping the ghosts of famous memoir writers would answer: "Anaïs Nin, Virginia Woolf, Maya Angelou, anyone available?" Silence. "How about, My Italian Journal, or, Surfacing on Lake Como?" No reply, except a dog's tired moan. "Right, let's leave it blank."

Turning to the second page, I wrote the date, June 2nd, in the year of my rebirth; then wrote, "She arrived like a storm and swept me away…" I stopped. Wait, is that too clichéd? Still, I had never met anyone like her. "Oh, gosh, I can't write that, my daughter might read it," and scratched it out.

Instead, I wrote, quite unconsciously, "I am blind to the present until my eyes open onto the real journey. Covet curiosity to see again. Here in my own room, closed off, the space holds no ghosts except for the ones I choose to contact. Therefore, this is a room to fill with new phantom memories."

I heard a few car doors slam and looked out the window, hoping I might see Kate. I felt the memory of her gentle hand on my arm. One of the rental cars had returned to the small parking area, but I didn't see anyone.

Writing in my journal again, scribbling fast and furious whatever came to me, stream of consciousness writing, and then I stopped to read it:

*New experiences lie outside my window, awaiting my attention.
I wish to surface to the completeness of being here, opening a
space to release the past for change to occur, and take the road
that whispers my name.*
Don't look back, Gerri!

"Not bad for a cook," I said, chuckling, knowing the phrase
"new experiences" was a subterfuge reference to my developing
feelings for Kate.

When I jumped up to get my purse, I glanced out the other
window, the one overlooking the lush hillside olive grove and
spotted a light. And then another light. "Hmm, what is that?" I
figured the olive pickers must be using flashlights.

"Picking olives at night? Weird. Or secret trysts?" I remembered Kate had mentioned they do that in her California vineyard.

I retrieved a small, square, napkin out of my purse and taped it
in the journal. Imprinted on the white napkin was a little red ink
drawing of the bakery. Julie was right, little snippets of travel
memories are revived by the small items we collect. Signor
Vacchini's words came flooding in, and I resumed writing. It
came out more like a spy story, about Angelina helping refugees
escape persecution. A good movie premise.

I focused on one of the last things Carlo said to me: "You are
realigned," I said aloud, hearing the words reverberate into the
silence.

"Yes, of course…"

A secret magical drawer in my mind opened. If I rearranged
the letters in my name Geraldine, it spelled *realigned*. Why
choose the anagram *realigned* for Geraldine when he had other
choices? Was he telling me something using Masonic Code? The
mystery eluded me.

CHAPTER 6
An Artist's Gaze

I want to say to her, *"Look within my soul for a moment's darkness before letting in your light."*

—G. A. McKenna, journal entry

The next morning at sunrise, I awoke with a start. Downstairs, Pucci and Goldie barked at something they heard outside. Not wanting them to awaken the guests, I grabbed my long silk dressing gown, going downstairs to my kitchenette to give them some food to eat.

As both dogs wolfed down their meal, I made myself a cup of coffee and then opened the door for fresh air. They pushed past me and bounded outside. *"Stupido,"* I scolded myself and was forced to follow them, tiptoeing outside in my bare feet. Thank goodness none of the guests seemed to be awake yet.

I heard them whining, along with something like an owl's deep *HUU.* I followed the sound and rounded the corner of the villa. There, in her pyjama shorts and a low-cut T-shirt, sat Kate. I froze. Both dogs sat alongside her with their tails wagging happily. Sitting on a chair under the small flowering arbor, she faced a grand view and held a sketch pad and pencil.

While drawing, Kate sang a long, drawn-out tonal sound, similar to OM: *"HUuuuu…"*

In my bare feet, I quietly approached her. "Hiya!"

She jumped—her pencil scratched across the paper, ruining the sketch.

"Damn!"

"Sorry."

Kate looked up at me, then laughed, saying, "Doesn't matter, it was crap anyway."

"By the way, what were you singing? It's beautiful."

"Doing my morning contemplation. It focuses me when I'm drawing or trying to draw."

With an apologetic grin, I sat on the narrow railing along the hillside in front of her. Private and shady, the arbor overflowed with bougainvillea, magnolia, and climbing rose plants. The viewpoint jutted out and gave a beautiful view of the town and lake below.

"You're up early," I said, smiling at Kate's sleepyhead appearance; her hair looked delightfully ruffled and as messy as mine.

"I prefer to get the morning light, with the play of light and shadow."

"May I see your drawings?"

"All right, but this one's ruined." She ripped it out of her sketchbook.

"Sorry, again."

She didn't hold it up, so I stood and looked over her shoulder as she flipped each page. Just then, my robe slipped off my shoulder.

"Great view, isn't it?" Kate said, turning her head to look up at me. "Yup, liking *that* view," she said, eyeing me by leaning her head back toward me.

Embarrassed, I pulled my robe back up and inspected her drawings. I was amazed by her skill and perspective, but murmured an indifferent "They're good," and returned to the railing, questioning why I said that?

"Thanks, Professor. Didn't know you were an art critic."

"Well, I know what I like." I looked away to continue fussing with my silk robe. "You're a painter, right? Will you be doing any painting while you're here?"

"Not into painting these days." She looked at me, unsmiling, serious.

"Oh, but it's so inspiring here, especially for an artist."

Kate stared at my slippery silk gown; the flap had opened to expose my legs. "Your legs are inspiring, I mean, um, drawable. May I draw you?" She flipped to a blank page in her sketch pad.

I went to cover my legs, but Kate said, "No, don't touch. Please. Come, sit here." She positioned a chair for me.

"Gosh, no, I look terrible. I haven't brushed my hair. I'm not wearing makeup—"

"I don't want you in makeup. Your natural beauty will do." Kate's gaze wafted across my entire body.

The dogs milled around my legs, "Shoo, lie down," I said, and being good pups they slumped down around my feet.

"Sit a little sideways. May I?"

Kate reached out and touched my shoulders to move my body slightly. She draped the silk dressing gown loosely around my shoulders and opened it to expose my legs which I thought went a little too far, making me squirm.

"Excuse me," I said in a prudish manner.

"Sorry, needed to expose a leg." She fiddled with my robe, arranging the bottom around my feet. "You've got awfully cute feet, you know."

"I do?" She made me chuckle.

She moved the collar of my silk gown, draping it seductively off one shoulder. Her hands smoothed over my skin with a slow, gentle touch. With a rush of butterfly tingles on my lower spine, I got goose bumps. She adjusted my gold chain, positioning its pendant to fall between my breasts. I felt my lungs drawing in a deep breath, and my nipples rubbing against the silk material, growing erect; I hoped Kate didn't notice.

"It won't take long."

What won't take long? The drawing, or the seduction of one Professor Gerri McKenna?

Without asking, Kate snapped a few photos of me with her phone and even a few of the dogs sleeping at my feet.

"Hey, no photos," I insisted.

"Too late." She smiled, holding her sketch pad. She chose a drawing pencil from her case and started to draw with fast, loose movements.

While she drew, Kate said, "Are you comfortable? Don't move your head but look at me. If you're uncomfortable looking at me, look past me, over my shoulder."

"You don't make me uncomfortable."

"Good." She smiled, watching me, looking quickly back and forth as she translated me onto a flat white page. While drawing, she stopped everything to look at *me*, the woman, the flesh. Every time our eyes met, I felt an electrical connection. I sat perfectly still, watching her watch me. She glanced at me and then sketched; and while she sketched I took her all in. Her hazel-brown eyes glowed, her full lips parted, and her tongue wetted her lips, an unconscious gesture while obsessed with drawing. She was stunning.

I felt a little embarrassed when she caught me enjoying the view of her pyjama short-shorts. Wanting to elude the feeling, I asked, "Um, where are you and your friends going today?"

"Tracy and Renee want to see Bellagio. The place the baker mentioned."

"Hey, me too. Later." Still feeling exposed sitting half-naked in front of her, I asked, "I'm curious, do you teach art?"

"I studied at UCLA, and, on occasion, they invite me to teach. I could teach a lot more, but I find it interferes with my painting, when I'm painting, that is." Her tongue got busy, once again involved in drawing.

I watched her quick looks at me. Only once did she hesitate, caught somewhere looking at my body. She blushed at something but deflected and kept drawing. Ten or fifteen minutes must have passed, and I enjoyed every moment, watching her.

"Let me know when I can breathe?" She didn't seem to hear me.

Finally, as though her presence had re-entered her physical body, while her drawing hand moved across the page, she said, "You can breathe now." Looking up and smiling, she changed the subject. "At the bakery, you seemed to know Italian. Did you take lessons?"

"Um, my parents are Italian-Canadian. They talked about taking me to the old country but never did. So, yes, I speak it a little."

"Then you understood Carlo the baker whenever he spoke Italian? A fascinating story, I mean, I couldn't stop thinking about it last night and wanted to see you, to talk about it."

"Me, too."

She glanced up at me in *that way*, her head bowed, her eyes at half-mast. I stopped breathing again, until I said, "I have a little translation book with me. Last night I came across the word *sprezzatura*. It means *effortless grace*. Just like the way you draw."

Silence filled the space between us while we gazed at one another. Until…

Her cell phone buzzed. "*Hella* loud, who's calling me this early?" She glanced at the caller's number, "My art agent in L.A., excuse me—Hello? … Yes, I can hear you. Yes, I'm at the villa, why?" Kate listened to the response. "They what? Are you kidding me, they want one more? Damn right, that's awesome. Oh shit, I don't have one more, not to sell."

Kate covered the phone and said to me, "Sorry, Gerri, I'll just be a moment." As she listened to the caller, Kate kept looking at me; her eyes scanned me from head to toe, until she said into the phone, "Leave it with me," and she clicked off.

"Must be good news, your face is all lit up."

"My agent got me into the Venice Biennale at the Peggy Guggenheim. To exhibit one painting, but—"

"*La Biennale di Venezia*? The Guggenheim is modern art."

"Yes, I paint a form of modern art. Not like Picasso, Dali, or O'Keefe. More Raphael with a Frida Kahlo twist. Or, Renoir nudes in a modern Renaissance landscape. I call it *romantic surrealism*. Anyway, the exhibit has one painting already, now my agent tells me they want another one, but I don't have one more. You see, I haven't been painting, not since, well, just can't get back into it."

"The ex-girlfriend? Give it time. Your muse is resting, healing; it'll come back to you. I had no idea you were such a popular artist. Congratulations, Kate."

Unable to contain her excitement, Kate said, "Thanks for sharing this moment."

She moved her chair closer and leaned forward, then cupped my face in both her hands and kissed me, an all-too-brief yet sensuous kiss, meant to be a simple thank-you. After the kiss, neither of us moved, enjoying a moment of silence.

"I'd better go," I heard myself whisper, looking into her eyes.

Does the rest of the world exist?

"Don't go." Kate glanced at my bare shoulder and lower to my breast's cleavage, and then said, "I think you'd better go."

"That's what I just said."

"Right, so you did."

"Are you going to let me go?" I said, smiling.

"Only if I have to." Kate slowly removed her hands that had slipped down to my bare neck.

My heart was racing. I couldn't stop smiling as I turned to waltz away toward the villa.

"A smile is the most beautiful curve on a woman's body," Kate said, watching me walk away. "This drawing of you, it reminds me of someone—Wait!" Carrying her sketchpad, she ran up to me, grabbed my hand and pulled me toward the villa's entrance, "You've got to see this, if I'm right."

"I can't go inside while guests are here."

"They'll sleep for hours, jet-lagged and hungover from last night. Come, please. This is too uncanny."

Kate snuck us into the villa's living room, and we stood below the huge portrait of La Cantante, Angelina Ferrario.

Kate held up the drawing to view both it and the portrait that hung over the fireplace mantle. "Look at that. Uncanny, isn't it? The same eyes. Same mouth. Shape of the face. Even the neck, look at the nape of the neck. Don't you think it's interesting?" Kate touched the indentation at my neck, meaning to show me.

Playfully, I swatted her hand away, "I see an unfinished drawing."

Kate's roughed-in sketch had a similar posture to the portrait of Angelina, whose long satiny silk opera gown showed her bare shoulders. She'd spent most of her time sketching the details of my face and eyes.

"Check out her eyes. Angelina's eyes, right?"

I stared at Angelina's blue eyes, then the black and white sketch, but said nothing.

"Similar, right? Even the lips. The nose not much."

"I don't see it. You've drawn Angelina, from memory. You haven't drawn me."

"Did not. I drew *you*. I wonder who painted it? There's no signature."

"What, really?" I took a closer look. "You're right."

"No doubt an Italian artist, before the Second World War, or even during the Nazi occupation. I'll check some art history sites." Kate held up her sketchbook again, comparing the two. "The neck needs fixing, right here," and she touched me again, running her fingers along my erotically sensitive neck toward my collarbone. Kate leaned in to take a closer look. "How do I paint such radiant skin?"

"Do you, ah, tell that to all your art models?"

"You're far too inspiring to be just…" her voice trailed off. She touched my bare shoulder with her soft hand. "There's something about you, Professor." Kate moved in closer.

"I'd better go," I said calmly, and edged the dressing gown up around my neck.

"Yes, you'd better. Let me kiss you on the cheek like the Italians do?" She kissed me on my cheeks. Lingering lips on one cheek and, then, a slow movement across my front to the other cheek, and a third kiss that felt like a raindrop, with slightly wet lips. When do I begin to breathe?

I stepped away and, feeling light-headed, hurried out the front entrance, my long silk gown whipping the sides of my bare legs.

CHAPTER 7
Bizarro Bellagio

When do I begin to breathe?
You kissed my cheeks. It felt like tiny raindrops,
warm, wet, lingering. I opened my lips, hopeful.
Instead, a beautiful distance bore you away.

—G. A. McKenna, journal entry

Restless, after walking and feeding the dogs, unable to settle down or even eat breakfast, I jumped into the shower, then got dressed, including my gold pendant, remembering Kate's gentle fingers had touched it. Then, touching my cheek, I remembered the gentlest kisses I'd ever experienced.

I grabbed my purse and sunglasses and sneaked out of my suite, leaving the dogs inside. Although I smelled coffee and heard a few plates rattling in the guests' kitchen, I saw no one.

Walking briskly down the path, over the ancient stone bridge, before I knew it, I stood at the dock waiting for the ferry, a bit nervous at water's edge. But stepping up to the ticket booth, a familiar face comforted me.

"Isabella? You work *here*, too?"

Her face beamed. "Here, there, all over the lake. Only the early shift today. You want a ticket, Miss Gerri?"

"*Sì, uno* ticket, *per favore.* How's my Italian?"

"Is that Italian?" Isabella grinned. "Everything good at villa?"

"So so. *Così così.*"

"Okey-doke, better than not good." Isabella waved me along to serve the next in line.

Turning towards the ferry, I heard, "Miss Gerri, Miss Gerri!" It was Isabella, her chubby finger beckoning me to come back to the wicket. She leaned out and whispered with great urgency, "Tell guests not to go into olive grove at night. The pickers, they migrate. You understand?" I nodded but still did not understand why this was so important.

"Doesn't olive and grape harvesting take place in September?"

I imagined Italy had the same migrant worker practices as the Okanagan Valley in British Columbia. The pickers worked in the vineyards and went from one property to the next, picking a swath across the entire valley.

"You sure it's not lovers in the olive grove?" I laughed, but Isabella's eyes widened. "You and Alex perhaps?"

Isabella blushed, "Miss Gerri, shush. Mamma no like him."

I made the sign of zipping my mouth, and she understood.

"Traghetto, ferry!" someone in the crowd yelled.

The passenger ferry arrived with a whoosh and a slap to the side of the dock and a deckhand tied up. With a clang, he moved the metal ramp across the gap and secured it. I recognized him in his Greek fisherman's cap. Embarrassed, I shielded my face, blending into the wave of passengers rushing on board until—my feet wouldn't move beyond the crack, the freaky gap between land and boat. The metal ramp had small open holes and, once again, I stared down the deep chasm into the dark water and shivered.

My nervousness turned into a shaking. "Come on Gerri. Move past the fear."

"Signora, you are still undecided?" he acknowledged me with a tip of his cap and a handsome grin, his dark eyes sparkling. With that pinched-finger hand gesture, he pleaded, "Please, *signora!* You make us late."

How many ferries had I been on since I was kid, going from Vancouver to the outer islands? How many times had I watched ferry boats dock into a ferry slip? And how many ramps had I walked across? But the memory of Paul dying in water, surfaced again. Pushing it back down into the deep, I tried not to think about his dead body floating toward shore. Then I remembered the face of his mistress on his phone.

"Get it up, McKenna," I whispered and bit my lower lip, taking shallow breaths, determined to forge right past the ferryman. With wobbly land legs, I stepped onto the ramp, over the gap, and onto the boat.

"Brava!" he bellowed, his playful humour making me stronger.

I felt him watching me until I hid inside the passenger cabin. Finding it way too claustrophobic, I climbed the metal steps up to the airy top deck, hugging a spot by the railing beside a lifebuoy. Standing near a group of happy tourists and their guide, I felt safe and protected, letting the sunshine warm my soul.

My guidebook showed a map of the lake. I read the small blurb on each ferry stop as we glided through the calm, glistening waters. After a few stops, the ferry passed a wooded promontory on which a spectacular grand villa perched in the reflecting golden sunlight; it had statue-lined balustrades and green, terraced gardens. I overheard the group's tour guide call it La Villa del Balbianello.

We ferried beyond the promontory and across the lake to Bellagio, the professed jewel of Lake Como. On the map, Bellagio is located on the lake's inverted "Y" between the two legs of the lake, right where a woman's vulva lay. Or so it seemed to me from the map. My thirteen guests came to mind.

In my journal, I had decided to call them the *Villa Galz* or *Villa Girls* for easy reference—meant in a playful way. Should I have stayed and helped them? Every student of life needs reassurance; but Rosie had said no, not unless they ask for my assistance. Perhaps I should have given Kate my mobile number in case she needed me. Why? Why would she need me?

Pulling into the Bellagio dock, the town enticed me with its tree-lined promenade along the waterfront and the row of hotels, trattorias, and shops. I noticed how the steep incline of stone steps led up to a Romanesque church and beyond it lay a lush, green hillside speckled with grand villas.

Once again, the deckhand spotted me in the crowd of passengers. He waited for me to cross the precarious gangplank and dark water below. It had become a game to see if I'd panic. This time I crossed without even flinching.

The deckhand yelled after me, *"Ciao, Carina!"*—Goodbye,

Pretty One! He tipped his cap again. Nice fella; wearing a wedding ring but still flirtatious. I waved at him and kept walking. Following the tour group to Bellagio's information kiosk, I snapped up a tennis and golfing brochure for CJ, one of my Villa Galz.

I passed a *tabacchi* shop, a few bars, leather and silk shops, then paused at one of the promenade's cafes when I spotted Shaun, the blond American hippie dude I'd met on the train. He lolled about in the sun, chatting up two giggling younger women at the next table. I waved to him, but he didn't see me; he was too busy being a young man on the hunt.

Continuing along the waterfront promenade to *Il Giardini di Villa Melzi*, I strolled through the villa's manicured gardens and sat on a bench in the marble gazebo watching the lake sparkle with sunlight. Here, I felt an overwhelming sadness engulf me, feeling lonely with no one to share this new experience. I felt the gazebo's white marble statues watching me watch them: Venus, Athena, the Egyptian Goddess Pakhet, and then, Apollo. Inexplicably, Apollo's marble bust morphed into the face of my dead husband, and I felt Paul's presence, his face looking down on me for just a flash. When I blinked, Apollo had returned.

Sitting on the bench, unable to think of Paul without thinking of his deception and *her*, She-Who-Will-Never-Be-Named, I spent a few tears. Then I immediately felt guilty for feeling sorry for myself and angry for playing the victim. The first anniversary of his death had passed like a tsunami clawing over the water's surface, and now the destructive aftermath lingered.

"I've got to find a way to move on," I whispered. "I'll never get over what happened, but I have the right to move on."

I gazed at the statue of Venus, the Goddess of Love, whose face looked a little like Kate Bradshaw. For the first time in a long time, I found myself asking, "Would I dare risk falling in love again?" It made me think of C. S. Lewis's quote: "To love at all is to be vulnerable." The idea of exposing my underbelly filled me with terror. Being vulnerable means, someone can get inside and mess me up.

One day I would be brave enough to love again. Thinking of Kate's hazel-brown eyes, her plump lips, her warm hands, her breasts…"Okay, enough!"

By the time I walked along the lakeside's sunny promenade back toward the main center of Bellagio, I felt uplifted. Once on the road near the shops, I ducked into a crowded bar to freshen up. No one noticed me as I went straight for the *Toilette* sign at the back.

On the way out, I bumped into Kate and two other Villa Galz. I went beet red, flashing on the thoughts I'd had in the gazebo. Tracy and Renee greeted me cheerfully as they headed to the bar. I heard them order *soda al caffè ghiacciata*, iced coffee sodas. I got caught in the wide doorway with Kate, unable to move. My attraction to her made me incredibly awkward.

"Small world, seeing you here. Synchronistic."

"Yup, it's a small lake. We tried to go to the grocery store in Lenno but missed our stop. And you?"

"Tootling about."

Her closeness in the doorway made my stomach flutter. My mind flashed on her short-short pyjamas earlier this morning.

Kate tapped the top of my nose, "Forgot your sunblock, I see."

"Oh, no. Is it burnt?"

"Here, ah, I've got some," she pulled out a tube from her waist pack, "Shall I?" and she squeezed some into her hand.

Gently, Kate smeared the cream across my nose and cheeks with her fingers. We were eye-to-eye, and the closeness made the crowded pub disappear; there was only Kate and me, gazing into one another's eyes.

"You're welcome to join us," she smiled, and I felt my heart race.

"Um, no, don't want to impose."

A short, burly man squeezed between us in the doorway, pushing us apart and making my world spin back into normalcy.

"It's not an imposition, by any means." She slid closer again and I lost my brain.

Hurriedly I left, still rubbing in the sunblock, "Thanks. Bye. See ya later." I slipped out, regretting it. My arm rubbed against her as I left, feeling the electricity between us.

Minutes later, kicking myself for not staying, I forged up the narrow cobblestone steps. I heard someone on the steps behind me and turned around. I laughed when I saw Kate.

"Are you following me?"

"Yes, I am. Hope that's all right," she caught up to me, stopping one step below.

"It's a free country," I said, then chuckled. "But you might not like where I'm going."

"Sounds intriguing, Professor."

She followed me further up to a little hotel sign, and we went through the arched gateway. *Casa di Sognatori*—House of Dreamers, a three-story hotel, had a warm Tuscan-yellow exterior that stood out from most lakeside villas painted in muted cream, peach, or terracotta. A stone footpath led us past a glass-enclosed breakfast veranda, and we entered into the lobby. I found it to be a simple 3-star hotel, not fancy, yet everything was clean and freshly painted, furnished with handsome antiques, most likely family heirlooms. Room keys with large, cumbersome key chains hung in cubbyholes behind the reception desk, easily accessible.

"So, this is a European hotel. My first."

"Are you booking a hotel room? For a secret affair or something?" Kate asked me.

"Ha! Not. A friend asked me to say hello to the owner."

In the hallway stood a large glass display case filled with black and white photos with names on chits of paper.

Coming close enough to examine the photos, I recognized a much younger Carlo Vacchini among a group of people; his family, I assumed.

"Gerri, take a look at this photo. Is that who I think it is? I recognize her eyes," Kate said, pointing.

My breath sucked in when I saw a photo of La Cantante, circa 1944. Signora Angelina Ferrario held a swaddled newborn. The label identified her with Carlo and her husband Max. All three stood shoulder to shoulder, and both men had an arm around her waist.

"Do you find it revealing how the younger Carlo is gazing at Angelina and not into the camera, or am I imagining things?"

"Interesting deduction, Sherlock."

Another photo, taken some years later, showed Carlo with Max and his daughter, Marcella, a pouty girl about age nine or ten, her hair sun-bleached and in disarray. As Carlo had told us, her mother Angelina had died years before.

As Kate clicked photos of the display, I watched a young

brunette, late-thirties, with a shapely figure, go behind the lobby reception desk to hang a key. As the hotel's Front Desk Clerk, she turned to greet two men, both wearing expensive suits and serious expressions. The bald bruiser with a goatee shadowed the other man, possibly his boss, whose facial plastic surgery and black hair dye looked too obvious. "*Consigliere* Rossetti, you are early," she said. Rossetti carried what resembled rolled up architectural drawings. I hid beside the display case and snapped their photos. Kate came over to me. "What are you doing?"

"Get behind me." I shooed her to stand out of sight with me as we both peeked around the cabinet.

The clerk escorted them to a conference room and knocked on the door. It opened to reveal a second bodyguard. Astonished, I recognised him as the Asian chauffeur wearing the porkpie hat. Another businessman in a smart, copper-colored linen suit came forward to greet them, none other than the husband of Carmela Lazzaro, the SLL or Sophia Loren Lookalike, whom I had met in Como town. His five o'clock shadow and jug-like build were unmistakable.

As they shook hands, I overheard his first name: "Vincenzo."

"Mayor Rossetti, please, come in," Vincenzo said with a slight bow, as if greeting royalty.

Something about this felt secretive, even furtive, or so my intuition told me—that tiny, insightful, interior voice. It also told me not to be seen and to erase his name from memory: Mayor or *Consigliere* Rossetti.

Before the bald bodyguard hustled them inside, Vincenzo Lazzaro flirted with the brunette hotel clerk, giving her a cheap "tit-tit" sound through his clenched teeth. He tapped her butt with a firm hand and whispered something into her ear. She looked embarrassed. I wondered if his wife knew of his crude ways.

A dark-haired, handsome man in a crisp white shirt and beige trousers, exited the conference room with an empty water jug and spoke to the brunette clerk; he then hurried down another hallway. I wondered if he was the owner, the man Rosie had sent me to meet, i.e., Carlo's son.

I pulled Kate across the hallway onto an outdoor terrace. The inviting vine-covered sunny terrace, perched above the ever-present lake, had metal tables and chairs scattered haphazardly.

"Why so secretive, Sherlock?" Kate chuckled.

"I'm not sure, but…do you ever get premonitions, sort of, as if you're having an inner conversation with a secret part of yourself?"

"Yeah, sometimes. Like a *déjà vu* or an intuition. Why, what's up?"

A breeze whistled past and I heard my name, "Signora McKenna?" and turned, startled.

Sitting at the far end of the terrace, Carlo Vacchini waved us over. Our shoes crunched into the little white pebbles as we walked toward him.

"And your friend Kate, *buona giornata.*" A gentleman, he stumbled to stand. Grabbing both my shoulders, he kissed me on both cheeks and a third kiss for good measure, letting me know we were now friends; otherwise, he would have shaken my hand, as he did Kate's.

"Please, please to join me for a drink. It's not often I sit with two beautiful women. They will say, that Carlo, he knows everyone." Carlo's full head of white hair looked neatly combed, his beige suit perfectly pressed; but nothing impressed me more than his gentlemanly charm.

"*Grazie*, Signor Vacchini. Your bakery in Argegno is closed today?"

"Sunday is my day off. I try to spend it with my son, but he is preoccupied."

Kate dragged two chairs closer, and we sat down at his table.

"You have a lovely hotel." My inquisitive Professor McKenna persona kicked in, and I asked, "Those two men inside, Signori Rossetti and Lazzaro, it must be a business meeting."

"You know Franco Rossetti?" Carlo glanced at his gold watch and frowned.

"I overheard their names. Friends of yours?"

"No friends. It's business. They want to build a casino and hotel in Argegno."

"In little Argegno?" Kate said with raised eyebrows.

"Like the casino they built in Menaggio," he said, frowning, and grumbled a curse. "My son meets with them to talk them out of it. He represents the people in the village who hate the idea."

"I can see why," Kate said.

Carlo raised his arm, signaling a male server who looked to be in his late teens or early twenties. With two fingers up, he ordered drinks without asking what we wanted, and he made a circular signal in the air. "Roberto is my grandson from my daughter, a good boy. We open for lunch soon. I hope you like Prosecco. This particular sparkling wine comes from the Veneto region, north of Venice. You like, *si?*"

"If you do, we will," Kate spoke for us both. "I wouldn't mind a snack."

"Does your hotel have a kitchen?" I asked.

"*Sì,* yes. Ah, but the chef, too many temper tantrums," he chortled. "But still, life is good."

From somewhere deep inside of me, I replied, "Life is good, yes, so long as I don't mind change too much. Seems I've had a lot of it lately. And I can tell you, change is humbling, especially when life kicks you down. But I've learned to be willing to get up again and again."

Kate said, "Well said, Professor. I feel a dissertation coming on."

Carlo raised his trim white eyebrows to view me with either appreciation or apprehension, I couldn't decide. "You don't like to waste time, Gerri McKenna. How can I help you?"

"*La Casa di Sognatori,* the House of the Dreamers, is your son's hotel. I'm here to meet him, he knows Rosie, a good friend of mine."

"*Sì,* I'll introduce you to him. Later. He's busy now."

Carlo watched me carefully as young Roberto presented the bubbly Prosecco wine and a platter of prosciutto, olives, and cheeses with toasted chunks of olive-oil-soaked peasant bread.

"Yup, I really am hungry," Kate said, eyeing the snack.

As Roberto poured the wine, Carlo said, "*Cicchetti*"—Chee-KETT-ee, Carlo pronounced it. "Appetizers. Eat, eat."

He took a piece of peasant bread and thin slices of prosciutto and cheese, then dribbled more olive oil on top. "This is your villa's famous olive oil. Please, try."

The olive oil, infused with basil, blushed with a deep golden color. It glowed in the sunlight, a delicious wet river. The Organic Extra Virgin Olive Oil in a dark bottle had a logo with a cameo image of Angelina. The label read: "La Cantante, Product of

Argegno, Lake Como, Italy."

Kate and I helped ourselves to the food, copying Carlo's ritual. He raised his glass into the sunlight and, squinting at the tiny sparkling bubbles, said, "*Essere innamorato della vita*—Be in love with life. My beautiful *vedova*."

Perturbed, I didn't pick up my glass. He frowned.

"You do not like being called a widow? Here, in Italy, we honour you. Please to drink."

I sipped from the special tulip-shaped wine glass with its wide rim. The bubbles popped up my nose. Served cold, it tasted dry, yet sweet. It felt wonderful to be sitting on a sunny terrace, gazing out onto the lake with an elegant, true Italian gentleman and with Kate sitting beside me.

Carlo asked, "Now, can I help you?"

"In that case, um…" I paused, surprised by what I wanted to ask. First, I leaned over to Kate, "Hope you don't mind, but I'm following a golden thread." And then I turned to Carlo, "The first time we met, you told us the story of Signora Angelina Ferrario. Can you tell us about the present owners of Villa della Cantante? Kate and I saw the photographs in the hotel lobby. The one of Angelina with her husband and a young girl. I presume the young girl is their daughter Marcella, the present owner. Your families must be quite close." I watched him over my glass, then asked bluntly, "Is Angelina's daughter, Signora Marcella, related to you?"

Kate choked on her Prosecco and I felt her kick me under the table. Yes, it was a rude question. Isabella had mentioned to me that the village gossips thought their relationship had become closer than friends.

Carlo gulped his Prosecco, raising his eyebrows at the same time, then said, "Signora Marcella Angelina Ferrario-Romano-Eaton, but we drop the Romano, her first husband Giorgio had a tragic death."

His recitation of her long name made me chuckle.

"Why do you want to know about her, *signora*?" he asked, raising one bushy eyebrow.

Kate pretended to cough into her wine glass, mumbling "Segue," meaning he did a smooth pivot away from answering. Or did she want *me* to segue away from the question?

"I'm living in her home. I'm curious. And you know everything about everyone. Please?" I tried to persuade him. He eyed me enigmatically over the rim of his glass while taking a sip of wine. "After Angelina died, Marcella became a wild teenager. Her father, Max, traveled a lot to Milan, for business. He was not equipped to be a single parent. My wife and I tried to help, whenever we could, to raise her like a daughter."

I felt another tap from Kate under the table, more like punctuation.

"In those days, Marcella was a handful. Still now, even in her seventies." Carlo chuckled. "Signorina Marcella got pregnant in her late teens—you couldn't control her—some olive picker in the field most likely. No one knows, and Marcella would never say. The baby died after birth; it's secretly buried in the cemetery close to the villa."

"How tragic," I said. I glanced at Kate whose eyes looked sad.

Carlo touched the rim of his glass and said, "*È vero*. It is true. Then one day Marcella left; she travelled around Italy and stopped to work in Rome. She used to write my wife and me letters. While holidaying in the south on the Amalfi Coast, she met a rich gambler from Naples who drove a red Alfa Romeo. The one parked at your villa."

"In the garage, yes. Giorgio, the Mafia man."

"We do not like to use that word. He swept her off her feet. They married in a flash before we could stop her. A few months later, his fortunes turned cold, and the Camorra organization of Naples tried to kill him over gambling debts. Disgraced and afraid, they fled north to Argegno. The Mafia has a long memory, but I believe after Giorgio died, they decided to spare Marcella."

"Should you be telling us this?"

"There are no secrets on the lake, unless you swim below the surface, to the bottom," he winked.

"What the heck does that mean?" Kate asked. "Sunken bodies killed by the mob?"

Carlo chuckled and gestured for Roberto to refill our glasses. "To hideout, Marcella and Giorgio lived for a time in Portovenere, a small coastal town near Lerici and the Cinque Terre. I remember her letters from the time. She fell in love with the poetry of Lord Byron, the Englishman who lived there in the 1800s." Carlo smiled with an enigmatic side grin, and then said, "You can see Byron's poetry books in her library. One book in particular." With his eyes intent on me, he recited one of Byron's poems:

> "There be none of Beauty's daughters
> With a magic like Thee;
> And like music on the waters
> Is thy sweet voice to me…"

Once again, Signor Vacchini had charmed us.

He raised his glass, "To Beauty's daughters," he said, watching me, toasting the invisible Marcella, or perhaps her mother Angelina. "*The Poetical Works of Lord Byron*, a First Edition, look for it in the villa's library."

"Thank you, I will."

Kate's phone rang. "Excuse me," she said as she walked away to answer it. A moment later she returned to the table. "Sorry, must run. My friends are waiting at the ferry. It's been lovely." She took a 20-euro bill out of her wallet, but Carlo wagged his finger. Instead, they shook hands. "Thank you, Signor Vacchini."

"I'll walk you out." I excused myself for a few minutes from Carlo's company and walked Kate into the lobby hallway.

She said, "Tomorrow we're going on a tour of that *Star Wars* villa, Balbianello. Join us?"

"Ah, thanks but, um, I shouldn't."

"I hope you change your mind, would love to see you."

We hugged and exchanged friendly cheek kisses.

"I like this Italian tradition, kissing cheeks," she said, her lips near my ear.

She held my hand, our fingers entwined. In that moment I caught her essence: a mingling of sunshine and sweet oranges. Then she left. As if in a dream state, I moved my body slowly back toward the terrace. The empty chair held Kate's presence as I rejoined Carlo.

As he refreshed his plate with more antipasti, I wanted to continue my line of questioning: "What happened to Marcella after Giorgio died in the hit and run?"

"You mean, after Rossetti had him rundown for the mafia? But you not hear it from me."

"Rossetti, the man in your hotel?"

Carlo ate his open sandwich, taking tiny bites in order to keep talking. "No proof. Ignore me. I say nothing." While he whirled his hand in the air, tiny droplets of olive oil fell on the napkin in his lap. "Marcella changed her name back to Ferrario in honour of her mother. Several years later, in 1980, Marcella met and married her second husband. Nowadays, they live two months of the summer at his English estate in Devon, where they met your Rosie Campbell."

"Yes, Isabella said they live next door to one another."

He raised his glass, "*Innamorarsi*," he toasted.

"What does it mean?"

"*To fall in love*. I fell in love with Angelina, Marcella's mother, from the first moment I breathed in her space." His deep gray eyes glazed over, but then, he shook his head. "Until now. When I sit across from the loveliest of women. I fall in love with you, Geraldine McKenna, in a fatherly way, of course." He smiled at me over the glass rim while taking a sip of his wine.

Noting that Carlo excelled in changing the subject, I then realized that he had not answered my original, discourteous, question: Was Signora Marcella related to him? Meaning, was she secretly his daughter? Kate had also noticed, commenting on his segue.

Looking into the hotel, Carlo's face lit up, "Ah, Davide! Roberto, bring my son to me."

Roberto stopped setting the tables for lunch and ran into the hotel's hallway to speak to the same handsome man who had filled a glass pitcher for the "suits." Within moments, the handsome man walked onto the terrace.

His lean stature topped with a full head of wavy dark-chestnut hair and sophisticated, graying temples, his dark eyes, and large hands were my first impressions. Suffice it to say, he had a mix of George Clooney and an early-1950s Marcello Mastroianni. Over his crisp white shirt and beige trousers, he now wore a navy-blue suit jacket with a white silk handkerchief in the breast pocket. Tanned. Did I say tanned?

"Davide Flavio Vacchini, my son the hotel owner, has an economic degree from London. This is Signora Geraldine McKenna from Canada. She is Marcella's—"

"The *vedova* at Marcella's, yes, you've told me." He frowned at his father, then said to me, "But he never told me how beautiful you were." My eyebrows lifted but I remained seated. He glanced at my clothes, or perhaps my figure. "Do you wear black because you are a widow?"

"I, ah, no, not at all." I'd taken off my blue cardigan, being too hot, and I was indeed dressed in all black: a black V-neck tee and black jeans.

"I am honoured to meet you, finally."

"Finally? What do you mean?" I questioned. I decided to stand to gain an equal footing and realized Davide was a mere two inches taller. "Then you must know I'm Rosie Campbell's friend. I wanted to say hello, that's all."

"Yes, of course. Rosie, how is Rosie?" He glanced over at Carlo, then turned toward the hallway, anxious.

"You're distracted. It can wait," I said.

He stared at me, finally seeing me. "I have waited a long time to meet you. That is, because of Rosie. Please, I apologize. You're right, I am distracted. I hope we will get to know one another," he said, then became preoccupied by a ping on his phone. He glanced at it and frowned. Flustered, Davide turned to Carlo and muttered something in quick Italian.

He noticed my interest, and changed the subject, holding up his phone: "The chef, he is a nuisance, he's a madman, he asks too much of me. I'd fire him but there is no one else. It's been a pleasure to meet you." He took hold of my hand, intending to shake it.

I said, "Chefs are narcissistic children. They need constant admiration. Feed their ego and they feed you brilliance."

He froze for a few seconds, caught. He continued shaking my hand longer than necessary, "I forgot, Rosie said you are a chef."

"I'm a teacher of chefs," I corrected.

"Even better. Can I call you, for a ride around the lake?" He lifted my hand to his lips and kissed the top of it. "You are too beautiful to be a widow, signora."

At that moment, we heard the cry of a bird. It flew overhead and circled high above us. My hand still in his, we watched it together. I turned to view Davide, sensing a fleeting connection that vanished as soon as he spoke.

"It's the falcon from Varenna, La Castello di Vezio has a falconry. Have you been?"

Our eyes met then. Jittery, he let go of my hand.

"No, I haven't. Where's the castle?" I squinted at him, sunlight in my eyes.

Davide touched my upper back to turn me to where he pointed across the lake, "Varenna is over there, the small town with a church steeple. The castle ruins are on a hill above the town." I could feel his breath on the side of my cheek. "You must go today. The falconer is exercising his birds. I'll call you at the villa, is all right?"

"Yes, a ride around the lake would be, well, fine." I figured an afternoon with a dashing Casanova was something to write on a postcard to my daughter.

"*Sei bellissima*—you're very beautiful. Good day, Signora McKenna." With barely a nod at his father, Davide rushed inside.

The entire time, Carlo had sat watching us. "My son, he can be, how do you say, a rascal. But he's good at business."

"Funny business?" I chuckled. He laughed with me.

Standing beside Carlo's chair, gazing down at the top of his white head of hair, I felt like a schoolteacher as I asked, "Do you have something more to tell me before I go?" I don't know what made me ask, except I'd picked up an anticipatory feeling from both of them.

"For now, no." This time Carlo managed to stand, and he put his arm through mine, escorting me to a set of stairs that led to a terraced garden. "Say hello to the owl for me."

"The owl?"

"At the falconry above Varenna. There are several birds. The most prized is Artù, the owl. Good day to you, Signora." Carlo also kissed the top of my hand, but more genuinely, the two men as different as immature and ripe fruit.

"They don't make gentlemen like you often. *Arrivederci*— Until we meet again, Carlo." I smiled in farewell and went down the stone steps.

I followed a narrow passageway of hedges, hoping the pathway led to the waterside promenade. Stopping at a balustrade overlooking a secluded terrace, I heard a sound which made me look back. Vincenzo Lazzaro stepped out onto the terrace with a shapely brunette, but when she turned around I realized that it wasn't his wife. In fact, it was the hotel's desk clerk. This woman had the Sophia Loren Thing going, too, but she clearly put more effort into pleasing Signor Lazzaro. He pulled her close, whispering in her ear as he dropped something down into her cleavage. She squealed and rubbed against him as she pulled the sparkling necklace out of her lacy bra. Vincenzo's beard stubble had grown in the hour since I had seen him, making his white teeth stand out in a wolfish grin as his mistress put on the new necklace and posed for him. I heard them laughing, brassy, lustful, as she ran away gleefully, and he hurried back into the hotel.

"The bastard's screwing around on his wife. No surprise there."

I stormed away, feeling insulted, all my pain at Paul's adultery brought up and thrown right smack in my face by this tacky, unshaven stranger.

"I need to get the hell outta here. Bye-bye, *bizarro* Bellagio!"

CHAPTER 8
The Owl of Varenna

*Even when we're together, we're alone,
especially after a deception.*

—G. A. McKenna, journal entry

Buying a ticket and jumping on the ferry without even thinking about it—propelled by my anger—and the Greek-capped ferryman nowhere in sight, I rode over to Varenna in a silent fume, the wine going to my head in the hot sunshine.

Alighting onto Varenna's quaint promenade, I bought a bottle of water from a *tabbacchi* shop. A sign pointed to the Castle of Vezio and I stormed past dozens of young, fit tourists. I powered up the steep pathway to the top of a craggy hill, past the tiny hamlet of Vezio, and into the castle ruins where I collapsed at the entrance. The young adults passed me as I rested, my heart pounding, my face beet red. I gulped down the water.

Beside me, at the entrance where I sat, stood a white plaster cast of a hooded ghost carved out of chalk. Once inside the stone walls, more ghost sculptures sat scattered about for a special art display. Unsurprisingly, I found the castle fortress spooky. The other tourists had disappeared somewhere. Drawn to a stone archway, I climbed a flight of stony steps and crossed over a drawbridge leading to the top of an ancient tower. I stepped up to look over the edge, gasping in delight.

From this height I had a 360-degree view of the long, narrow lake. A colorful, painted map gave a "You Are Here" description of what I was looking at: to the south, Lenno, the Villa del Balbianello, and the Villa Carlotta; to the north, Tremezzo, Cadenabbio, Menaggio; and other towns. I felt entranced by the views of sparkling lake water, blue sky, and mountains. All those vibrant colors, as though God had taken a brush of many colors and washed it across my vision. The beauty opened to me all at once. Breathtaking. So much beauty in the world. So much. Too much. Completely overwhelmed, I started to cry.

I felt so lost. Where was my "You Are Here" map? How had I been so blind: Paul and a younger woman? It seemed so unlike him, but I had undeniable proof. Did my son, Thomas, know her too? He worked with Paul; he must have known. I cried even harder, wishing I'd never turned on his damn phone.

"No, of course Thomas doesn't know," I reassured myself. "So, what now?" I yelled out into the vastness of space, into the wind. No answer, except a rumbling in my nauseous stomach.

"Geez, if I talk to myself, why can't I answer myself?"

The answer came as I wrapped my arms lovingly around myself.

I'm scared of growing old, I admitted, of transitioning into Elderhood. "Yup, I'm scared of being on my own." Yes, there it was. Facing a future of growing old on my own. I need to open the door to this new chapter in my life. I need to face that reality. Embrace it. You weren't expecting it, but here it is. On your own. The map says it so clearly—You Are Here: This is my ascension into middle age.

"Yes? No? What a thought. I'm not ready!" I cried out to the living, breathing lake. "Is this my midlife meltdown?"

Nothing stirred. Still no answer.

I felt sick. Stomach churning, I ran down some stone steps and hugged the first tree I came to, smelling magnolia and cypress, trying to stop the queasy feeling.

"I'm still young! Barely fifty." I cried into a stand of cypress trees.

The tall trees swayed and suddenly, a familiar sound—the hooting of an Owl, my Spirit Animal. It was so soothing to hear, as if it was welcoming me home.

"OOHU-OOHU-OOHU."

For a moment, I felt the sound came from somewhere inside of me.

"OOHU-OOHU-OOHU."

I followed the sound into the dry cypress forest, hurrying among the tall shadows and sunlight. Felt a silent WHOOSH nearby. Overhead? I heard the breathlike sweeping sound of a large owl's wings above me.

"Where are you, Owl? What do I do with this anger?" I asked it.

"OOHU-OOHU-OOHU."

Turning and spinning, I tried to see the owl. I felt the anger coiled up inside me like a snake wrapped around my sternum, solid, stiff, suffocating. "Oh, god, I have got to get rid of it." I held on to a tree trunk to steady myself. Tears streamed down my cheeks. I felt depleted, empty, and laid down on the earth's floor looking up at the sky.

"Damn you, Paul!" I screamed. My head spinning, I fell onto my knees. "You were a good man, before you were an asshole." All of my anger and rage was expelled from within in one sudden heave.

"OOHU-OOHU-OOHU..."

I rolled onto my back and laid there for a bit, gazing up into the treed canopy above me, it reached up to the sky with swaying treetops, fluttering birds, and a sunny blue hole punched through the dark clouds. "Is this what rebirth feels like?" My heart wants to open like that hole into the light. I want to regenerate, to be reborn. Or do I just need to get laid?

"God, let me get laid!"

Slowly, I pulled myself up, removed the twigs from my hair and clothes, and tossed a bunch of leaves over my wee vomit. Stumbling forward, I walked through the long, damp grass, following the Owl of Varenna's whooshing sound into a grove of olive trees.

Hot and sweaty, the skin under my bra's elastic support was itchy; I tried to wipe away the sweat under my breasts with my hand. Fumbling, I ripped off the ugly old bra, using the old "unhook it at the back and slip the shoulder straps out of your sleeves" trick, and voilà!

"Out, out, damned bra!" Laughing, feeling delirious, hysterical, I threw it to the ground, stomped on it, and kicked it under a pile of branches.

"Bra begone!" I shouted. "Watch out! Lady havin' a panic attack." I laughed even more at the stupidity, yet at the clarity of the moment. After all, here I was, a solitary figure standing in a misty orchard, braless, and talking to a hidden owl. "The oppression of breasts from age thirteen," I said to the trees. 'Twas like their gnarled faces stared back at me in agreement.

"OOHU-OOHU-OOHU."

Startled, I felt the WHOOSH of the great owl above me again and followed his tailwind, coming out of the woods—I stopped in my tracks. At the edge of the hill stood the falconer and several young European tourists. The view was open, wide, expansive: blue water, blue mountains, blue sky. The young falconer held out his arm and the great owl swooped down to land on his forearm, its claws digging into the gauntlet glove. That is the largest owl I've ever seen.

"Artù, where'd you go laddie? You took a detour," the falconer admonished, waving his finger. The tourists were delighted. The freckle-faced falconer spoke with a thick Scottish brogue. With his short red hair and leather tunic and pants he resembled a twelfth-century serf.

A wind rose out of nowhere. I shivered and looked up, caught the sun, and sneezed.

Artù heard me. Motionless, he stared at me with wide yellow and black eyes. His tuft-like horn feathers and the spotted plumage on his face fluttered about in the wind.

I understood why, as a spirit animal, the Owl was an ancient symbol, a keeper of higher wisdom. Seeing the "bird of Minerva" reminded me that I must heed the warning and listen to my inner guidance as my mother urged me. For her, acknowledging my innate ability to be guided by my inner voice meant for me to listen to the most secret part of myself, which she referred to as Soul. She taught me to believe in my intuition and to not be afraid. I'd lost touch with this part of me.

Suddenly I heard my inner voice speaking to me, as if Soul was giving me insights:

Time to awaken and be reborn.

I felt a part of me had died, here, in the forest, but I hadn't realized it might portend a rebirth. From inside myself, I heard more:

If you decide to live, you need to wake up the hidden part. Wake up Soul—the conscious you.

The magnificent owl stared deeply into me as though he knew me and had a direct connection into my heart. I stared back, transfixed, as the group of university-aged tourists admired the amazing creature. A young couple entwined their arms, like a marble statue of two lovers. I envied them. The others in the group, wearing backpacks and hiking boots, were attentive, curious, vibrant, ready to venture out in the world as I had been at their age. It made me think of my own time in university.

"Whatever happened to living my life as I'd planned? To live deep and see the world."

I recalled the time in university when my lover, Louise, and I had planned to run away to Europe together, to see the world. But after graduation, she left, and I was heartbroken.

She just left, and I met Paul, and it all changed. I closeted my dreams of travel and exploration in exchange for complacency. Deep down, I still yearned to drink the last bit of adventure out of my life. And, thanks to Paul and his phone, I can do anything now.

Yes, I knew, it's time to risk living again, to learn to be enough, to accept my authentic self, to create a new story. I am independently owned and operated. Time to cast off from the safe harbor, alone if necessary, and brave vulnerability again.

"Come on, Gerri. Stay curious. Reinvent yourself over and over until you find home. Find your Self. You got this."

From somewhere deep within I felt encouraging words like a gentle Soulspeak:

Brave the wilds of your journey. One doesn't need to travel far to be adventurous.

Be bold where you stand, I dare you. Why risk standing still?

Deep within my musings, I became acutely aware of my sexual attraction to Kate. The inner voice of Soul whispered once again:

Be brave enough to be vulnerable, to open yourself to love.

A dark thundercloud rose from behind me. Full of energy, it moved over the towering castle. With a cold wind on my shoulder, out of the corner of my eye, I glimpsed a ghostly shape sitting on a low wooden fence. I did a double take. Heat rose off one of the chalk sculptures, and another face wavered over the top of it. Paul's face. His image sparkled in the air with tiny atoms of refracted light. I sucked in my breath with a weird sound and yelled:

"Go! I forgive you. Now, leave me alone. You are no longer welcome." I watched triumphantly as that ghostly presence dissolved into thin air, for good.

Artù the Owl heard my yell and stared at me. I felt his nod of approval.

Feeling raindrops, the falconer hurried the tourists along the gravel path toward the raptor cages inside the castle. I followed them up to the turret just before the thundercloud opened with a ferocious downpour.

As the rain came down from the dark clouds in angled sheets, we spent our time inside, looking at the permanent fossil collection. Most interesting was a *Lariosaurus*, a water reptile with a long neck and head, bulging abdomen, two short legs like a lizard, but it resembled a one-meter-long slimy serpent. The plaque said the reptile species had been found in Lake Como and had recently surfaced in China. "Recently? What the heck does that mean?"

The wind howled over the high hilltop above Varenna. I wrapped my sweater around me as I stood at the turret's window. The lake had erupted into rocky white caps—the return ferry ride would not be pleasant. The rain had let up a bit. I decided to make a run for it with the others, down the gravel path. The downpour had washed away pieces of the chalk ghost sculptures, dissolving them into milky white rivers running down the walkway. Slipping and sliding on the chalky liquid, a few tourists and I created living art all the way to the bottom of the steep hill. Someone said the chalk was mixed with lime and potash to restore the hillside grass.

By the time we reached the bottom, the rain had stopped completely. My hair was a curly wet mop. My clothes felt damp against my skin, but the sun was out once again, beating down full strength. Three o'clock in the afternoon. I decided to return to the villa, but the ferry wouldn't come for another half hour.

Spotting a wooden bench in the sun, I sat beside an older Italian woman dressed in black from head to toe—a *vedova* like me. I could have ignored her, many would, but there's always a reason we meet strangers.

"Hello, *Buonasera, signora*," I said to the old *gattara* or cat lady who was feeding kibble to five stray cats. Her head bobbed a few times, inspecting me up and down. "Here we sit, two women dressed in black, on a bench in lovely Varenna."

The old widow smiled at me, showing one front tooth missing, then she sat with her eyes closed, her chin raised to the warmth of the sun. With her soft wrinkled face, white curly hair, and crooked fingers she appeared ageless and content. I felt a great thirst to drink up her story, to connect.

"You look so happy. But you're a *vedova* like me."

It felt as if an explosion had gone off, jolting the old gal awake. Our eyes met.

"English no good," she said in almost perfect English. She had smiling eyes, full of light. I yearned to hear from her.

I moved in closer and nodded, "*Italiano, no va bene*, no good."

She looked up at me with a slight smile, then threw a handful of kibble to the cats.

"I mean, *come donne vedova,* as widowed women, we are alone—*perché siamo soli.*"

She said nothing. I continued, "It seems we are having a relationship with ourselves, to embrace life on our own." My two hands hugged myself for emphasis. "You seem so happy. What's your secret?"

My toothless companion waved a figure eight in the air, the infinity symbol, or else one of those crazy Italian hand signals. I pulled back to squint at her, hopeful I might understand what has no ending and no beginning. My nose ran; and I wiped it with a shaking hand. She gave me a clean tissue from her pocket, and then scattered the entire bag of kibble to the hungry street cats, who scurried around her dangling feet.

Suddenly, I understood. "Got it," I said to her. "It's our time in eternity, *sì*? Barbara Marx Hubbard—she's an American author, she's in her eighties—she calls it *regenopause*, when a woman trusts her own intuition and gives birth to her most authentic self. Resuscitating, reviving, reawakening after menopause, we regenerate. It's a new beginning, not an ending." I made my own figure eight in the air, then paused in my professor-like dissertation. She nodded with a wink which made me think she did understand English a little.

"You're an OWL—an Outrageous Wiser Lady—like I call my friends in their seventies. Smart, classy, vibrant, and adventurous women, still trying new things, still curious. But that's not me. I'm frickin' dead. They're remaking themselves in regenopause. I've been on endless pause."

Then I called out with a fist pump in the air, "Not anymore!"

The old woman's hand shot up into the air, *"Certo!"* she exclaimed in a craggy voice. We were one, she and I. Her little black-shoed feet dangling off the bench began to wiggle and move, excitedly.

"I want to be like you—happy and content. A vibrant silver sister—*sorella d'argento.*" She seemed to understand me. I extended my hand, and she shook it in mutual agreement.

The old gal looked at me with a big, gappy smile, then with a fist in the air she cried out, *"Brava!"*

Together, this lovely crone and I fell into silence. My tenseness dissipated, and I slouched back against the bench seat in surrender, exhaling deeply.

"I'm spent. I'm done. The anger, it's gone. *He's* gone."

And then I wondered, where does Kate Bradshaw fit into my midlife design?

Once again, I heard, *Be bold where you stand, I dare you.*

Soon after my emotional exorcism, the ferry boat arrived. I said to her, "Thanks for listening. *Abi cura di te*—Take good care of yourself."

The old woman stood up, all five feet of her. With another big grin she grabbed both my shoulders and kissed my cheeks, saying in Italian, *"Piacere. Tutto è in ordine."*—Pleasure to meet you. All is in order.

I stuffed a ten-euro bill into her dress pocket, I couldn't think why, and said, *"Grazie mille."*—Thanks a million. I ran for the ferry, calling back, *"Arrivederci."*

Standing in line to buy my ticket, I saw another old widow in black sit down beside her on the bench. Both widows kissed cheeks, old friends. Seeing the bill poking out of her pocket, the friend showed it to her and pointed at me. My old *vedova* raised her hands and called to me in English, "My silver sister."

Just then, three old men toddled by in front of her, one lifted his hat in greeting, and my toothless *vedova* pinched his bum. The old man jumped. The two old women laughed.

The ferry gate opened. I jumped onto the ramp and hung onto a rain-drenched tourist as we crossed the gap. Because of the quickness of the storm, the huge whitecaps took longer to settle down. I stayed in the claustrophobic passenger cabin. Steam heat rose off our damp clothing. Inside the cramped cabin of tourists, workers, and residents, I squeezed in to sit between two young Italian women who smelled of flowery herbs and spices. I recognized the Gelato Girl from Rocco's cafe, the bright purple highlights in her hair.

"*Buonasera*, Lia, we meet again," I said, knowing she spoke English like most young Italians.

Lia pulled back against the seat. "Hi again. You're Signora Marcella's *vedova*. Please to meet my friend Nicole." Nicole nodded politely. Lia leaned forward to continue talking across me to her friend. They talked so fast, but I was able to pick out phrases. I overheard the word Argegno several times along with frowns and sad moans.

I asked, "*Scusami*, is Argegno not well?"

Lia's friend Nicole complained, "I lost my job. It's not good in Argegno. No tourists come. The area mayor is corrupt. Shopkeepers struggle to pay high rents. Right, Lia?"

"*Sì, kaput*," said Lia, with a slicing hand gesture to her chin. She leaned over in front of me to her friend and whispered, "Time to ask the baker?"

"Pardon me? Ask the baker what?"

"We want his son, Signor Davide Vacchini, to run for mayor."

The two girls gave a thumbs up and Lia said, "Davide will give those rich developers the boot. They want to tear down our homes and shops to build a casino complex."

"Won't it bring business and jobs?" I said, as a rolling wave hit and rocked the ferry.

"And corruption and high taxes. No, no, no, not our sweet Argegno," Nicole said.

Lia added, "We go bankrupt, the country goes bankrupt. But no one wants a casino in Argegno. Davide, he would stop it."

The loudspeaker announced, "Next stop, Argegno!"

We pulled into Argegno's ferry slip, bouncing through the high wake of a passing car ferry. Onshore, dockmen tied up the ferry. Clang went the ramp, and the girls bounded to the exit. Regrettably, I sat too long waiting for the ramp to clear of passengers. As a result, by the time I reached the ferry gate, the onshore apron ramp had closed. The loud noises of the boat hitting the ferry slip and the listing of the boat from the whitecaps made me hang onto the nearest ferryman for dear life.

"Let me off, please!" I yelled into his hairy ear. Of course, it had to be my Greek-capped buddy. My wild eyes, windblown hair, and panicked face alerted him to the seriousness.

"Okay, my friend," he reassured me. Then called out, "Lower the drawbridge. Open the gate!"

"Gianrico, you crazy?" the onshore dockhand balked but then lowered the drawbridge.

Gianrico reopened the gate, loud bells sounding, all the passengers watching. I ran across the ramp onto land.

"*Mamma mia*," he said, crossing himself, "You are beautiful woman. I want you, but you crazy."

"*Grazie*, Gianrico, I owe you a kiss," I yelled to him, finding my land legs.

A few ferrymen laughed and blew kisses to him, yelling, "Gianrico, come get your kiss."

As the boat pulled out, Gianrico with his dirty hand, took off his cap and waved, "I wait for it, Signora Vedova."

"*Vedova*? Oh, my gawd. Does everybody know?"

CHAPTER 9
Tête-à-Tête

She moves me but I can't move.
Be bold where you stand, I dare you.
Brave love! Why stand still?

—G. A. McKenna, journal entry

After dinner, I wrote in my journal at my desk. I wrote about being with Kate in Bellagio and with Carlo Vacchini at the hotel, and about my Varenna *vedova* with the gap-toothed grin. Then I recorded the words, *"Be bold where you stand, I dare you,"* and the story that Carlo told of Lord Byron's poem: "There be none of Beauty's daughters / With a magic like Thee."

I felt sweaty from the long day, not ready for sleep. Grabbing my silk dressing gown, I went outside into the colors of twilight. I hurried to the steam room Isabella had mentioned, around the corner to the backside of the villa. The door was unlocked on the circular concrete structure. Magical streams of light from tiny ceiling pot lights cut through a vaporous mist. I could see no one, so I stepped inside into the brightly glowing fog. Flimsy white cotton towels hung on wooden hooks. I hung up my night clothes and wrapped a towel around my torso, then stepped half-naked into the white billowy clouds of thick steam. It felt wonderful.

In the center of the circular room was a fountain with a statue of a nude woman, her pottery water jug pouring a stream of water into a basin. Instantly, feeling hot, I dropped my towel to splash water on my body, dripping it down my front, the rivers running between my breasts, down my belly, and between my legs.

A slight sound. A movement of air from behind. The steam shifted.

A voice behind me said, "How lovely."

Startled, I spun around. Kate stood behind me, wearing only a white towel.

"You scared me."

"Sorry, didn't mean to." She covered her eyes but pretended to peek unapologetically at my nakedness. As she handed me my towel, I snapped it from her and covered myself. Deflecting, Kate said, "The spa is designed like a Turkish *hammam*."

Her unfazed, confident air relaxed me—slightly butch in a feminine way. I bit my lower lip, feeling shy, as she uncovered her eyes.

"Do you realize this is the second time I've seen you half-naked? I could get used to this. Can I offer you some Turkish tea?"

Gently, she took hold of my hand and walked me over to a small bar. I let her.

"Let me show you a towel trick," she said.

She placed her hand possessively on the small of my back and kept it there while adjusting my flimsy towel. The moment she touched me, I wanted her strong hands all over my naked body, which excited me. Gobsmacked at my arousal, I pushed her hand away.

Without removing the towel, she put it horizontally around my body. I felt her brush past the side of my cheek. She rolled down the top edge. Her fingers gently touched my breasts when tucking-in the towel edges. I let her, with an ache between my thighs. I am now mesmerized by her, melting with each of her touches. She stepped back. And then she poured us tea.

Nervously, I fiddled with my necklace.

"Interesting pendant. I noticed it earlier," she said. "The All-Seeing Third Eye inside a double triangle."

Kate slipped in closer and held it between her fingers. Again, I let her. "Kind of a Goddess Isis thing, isn't it? Or Masonic, like the old baker talked about. Is it from someone special?" Her liquid hazel eyes pierced right through me; my heart palpitated, bringing up long-dormant passions.

"It's special to me. A family heirloom, of sorts," I managed. Her hand grazed the bareness of my chest. Slowly I started to glow red hot. Sweat ran down my body, my neck, my arms, between my legs. My erect nipples rose out of the now-wet, transparent towel.

"Have you ever been with a woman?" she asked nonchalantly, turning her head to sip tea.

"That's private. I'd rather not answer," I stuttered.

"Hmmm, there's more here than meets the *eye*. Sorry, bad pun," she said, letting go of my necklace. "May I kiss you?"

My mouth opened to protest, but no words came out. Kate took that as a yes. I didn't object. Unable to resist, she kissed my upper neck, under the ear. Aroused, I let her, not pulling away this time—which surprised me.

At that moment, Tracy and Renee in spa robes burst into the steam room with a cacophony of laughter, until they saw us and froze. Our closeness vanished into the mist.

I folded my arms over my breasts. "Welcome, ladies. You can have my spot at the tea bar. I've been cooked and simmered for long enough. Good night now."

Waltzing into the entrance change room, I overheard Renee ask Kate, "Oops. Did we intrude?"

"Is the Pope Catholic?"

CHAPTER 10
Rousing the Huntress

Hear me, Divine Goddess.
Speak to my woman soul.
Love's door has knocked.
And I have opened.

—G. A. McKenna, journal entry

Taking an early Monday morning walk with the dogs, I mentally planned my visit to the famous Villa del Balbianello, via Lenno. Upon my return, I dressed in a blue silky shirt, stretchy white capri pants, and a crushable straw hat—no more dark widow's clothing for me, thanks. I knew Isabella would arrive to clean the villa, so the dogs will have company.

Wanting to avoid meeting any villa guests, I snuck out and ran down the pathway to the ferry, wearing no bra and enjoying the sensation of my boobs jiggling all the way.

I felt calm getting on the ferry today. It glided along on the smooth lake and arrived in Lenno at about ten o'clock. The tourists had already descended; in fact, the trattorias and cafes were full of late-breakfast patrons. What a difference from quiet Argegno. I spotted Lenno's supermarket; the place to go for reasonable prices. I needed to stop there on my way back, before siesta or *riposo* started at 13:30 hours. During siesta, most businesses, shops, and museums close for a long lunch, and then they stay open until late, meaning until the tourists leave.

Strolling along the waterfront road, past the meticulous estates of Lenno, I came to an uphill trail that led into the woods. It became a hot climb even in the shaded forest. I took off my hat and tied my hair up into a bun to cool the back of my neck. As I dragged my feet, I reflected on what Lia, the Gelato Girl, had said on the ferry yesterday, "Time to ask the baker." I wondered whether Davide Vacchini was even interested in running for mayor.

About fifteen minutes on the trail, feeling the heat, I arrived at the tall iron gate of Villa del Balbianello. "Morning, *signora*, the free guided tour has started. You missed it," the elderly gateman informed me.

"Fine by me, I like to wander on my own."

The jolly man had a three-legged little dog who sniffed my shoes. The friendly wee dog ran inside the gate and sat waiting for me, its pink tongue hanging out of its mouth. How could I resist this lovely greeting, offering me a subtle sign to enter?

After buying the entrance ticket, I strolled the tree-lined pathway through the garden in the cool shade of swaying cypress trees. Having been raised in North Vancouver in an evergreen forest, I am drawn to trees of all types and variety. Here, on terraces that dropped straight into the lake, grew candelabra plane trees, tall dark green cypresses, bay laurels, and others, and even a gigantic Holm oak, an evergreen tree native to the Mediterranean.

A female tour guide dressed in a navy-blue Armani-like suit led her group out of a beautiful *loggia* onto the walkway toward the ivy-covered villa complex. I hurried to catch up. To my astonishment they turned out to be my Villa Galz. I remembered Kate had mentioned they were coming here today. Not wanting to intrude, I hid behind a bush.

I saw tall Erin with CJ, the tennis pro; the doctors, Wanda and Brittany; Hannah with Jamie, the birthday girl; buxom Bibi with Luciana, the cop; the lookalike models, Tracy and Renee; Vera, the lawyer, walking behind Dana, the travel agent; but where is—

"Hey, Gerri!"

Hearing my name, I swung around to the *loggia*—Kate Bradshaw stood at the carved marble balustrade of a covered outdoor porch or gallery, waving at me to join her. The other Villa

Galz had strolled ahead, and without seeing me, had entered the splendid mansion. I waved and ran to Kate.

Open on both sides with several marble columns and arches, the open-air rectangular *loggia* framed spectacular views. As I passed through the ivy-laden archway, blinding warm sunlight put a haze across my vision, giving me a rather odd, ethereal feeling. I continued walking toward Kate, now engulfed in cool shadows and windowless arches, as though I'd entered an imaginary cloister. Like walking through into a new life.

"We meet again. Must be fate," I said, reaching her.

"I like your hair up," Kate commented, tucking a fallen strand behind my ear. I swooned at her touch. It woke me.

"I must look a fright. It's a long hike."

"You're beautiful." Kate smiled at me, face to face, in close, yet keeping a respectful distance. The energy between us was electric.

In fact, we had a *beautiful distance*—I later described it in my journal as the feeling of energy between two people invisibly interconnected with a sense of familiarity and a sensuous yearning. This time she touched me without even using her hands. I blushed like a schoolgirl, embarrassed, and turned away to take in the view.

"Gardens underneath which rivers flow…" I murmured taking in the beauty.

"Yaas?"

"It describes paradise, from the Qur'an."

Kate nodded, then said, "Lovely image. Hey, listen, do I need to apologize again, for anything, like in the steam room, or anything else inappropriate? It's that, well…"

My cheeks burned, remembering her touch and her near-nakedness in the steam room. "No, not at all, it's fine," I said, glancing into her eyes. I blushed, again. Needing to change the subject, I glanced at the lake, rattling on, "Wonderful, isn't it? On one side, there in the distance, is the misty Comacina Island, the only island in Lake Como. And on the other side, the villa's garden. I love the *loggia's* tile flooring and yellow ceiling, it's perfect for—"

"Weddings. It's all they do here. Pity. Would make a great disco," Kate said, lighting a rolled cigarette. A familiar scent, straight out of my uni days, swirled around us.

"Where did you get that?"

"From the gardener, this morning," Kate announced.

"Alex the gardener? He came to the villa?"

"Yeah. He was looking for Isabella. Why? Something wrong?"

"No-no, I, why—he sold you pot?" I stood there like a schoolteacher, arms akimbo, shaking my head.

Kate stopped toking, "Shush. The place might be bugged," she said, smiling. "I never smoke. He asked me to try it, so what the hell. Anything to get over *her*, short of suicide." She held out the joint. "Wanna drag?"

Horrified, I glanced around, "We could get arrested, I mean— Oh, what the heck." I took the joint. Kate chuckled. I took a deep puff, too deep, and had a coughing spell. She patted my back. "It's quite strong," I noted.

Kate nodded, "It's homegrown, he said, from his private stash. I'll bet he grows it in the olive grove?"

"I hope not. You said *her*. Anything to get over *her*. You mean your ex-girlfriend, the one who didn't come to the villa?" Seeing Kate's smile fall into sadness, I apologized. "I'm sorry. It's none of my business."

"Five years we lived together. Her ego went fishing. She got hooked on a younger woman." Kate's large sunglasses slipped down her nose; and, for a fleeting moment, her hazel eyes welled with tears. "We should have broken up earlier, when it started to fall apart. I'd been sort of bracing for the breakup. Now that it's long gone, I'm doing okay, ready for a new start."

"At least your ex is still alive. You can have it out with her," I blurted out. Kate shot me a long steady look and leaned on the balustrade for a better view of my face.

"What're you saying?"

Could I say it aloud to a stranger, who knew no one else in my life? It came out all at once: "My husband screwed around, a younger woman, he died before I found out about the affair. Here, take a look." I opened my phone's photo gallery to show her.

Kate's mouth dropped open. She took off her sunglasses and leaned even further toward me. "And you're still breathing?"

One loud guffaw exploded from within, "Barely." We both erupted into laughter. She passed me the joint again.

"You know, straight couples don't have exclusivity on the younger woman scenario," Kate admitted. "On holiday at a Puerto Vallarta resort, I went down to the pool. After a while, like, what's taking her so long? I went back up to our room and caught my partner on a video call with her new little friend. While we were on vacation. Not nice. She looked shocked and embarrassed when I walked in." Kate took a quick puff. "And you know what? She got caught and then tried turning it around to make it my fault for disturbing her."

"Typical. Gaslighting."

"Honestly, I must have known. The writing was on the wall— things weren't good between us—but you still never expect it," Kate said. "I moved out months ago. I'm all right, you know. It feels good to be away from the toxicity. I'm myself again."

I touched Kate's hand, "Sorry you had to go through that." Reflecting as I took another deep puff and passed her the joint, "I never had a clue about my husband's affair. It's been a lonely road since he died, now this."

Kate touched my shoulder, a warm, gentle touch. "Some roads aren't meant to be travelled alone." Her hand slipped down my arm, and she gently squeezed my hand. "I like you, Gerri McKenna."

The touch felt warm, strong, inviting. But I pulled back a bit. Her beautiful eyes grew wider, noticing my panic, and she said, "Meaning, we're simpatico."

I felt myself relaxing.

Standing close together, leaning on the stone railing, our arms touching, the sun came out from behind a cloud and our entire outdoor room glowed golden. Even the twisted snake ivy around the portico columns seemed to spring to life, as did the hairs on my skin.

Intoxicated and made brave by the marijuana, I stared at Kate, enjoying the view. Her brunette hair shone with sunlight, making a halo around her mystifying green-and-gold cat's eyes. "You're stunning. How long have you been Gay?" I felt my cheeks blush. "Sorry, I don't mean to pry."

"It's okay. Since age fourteen. My first was much older than me. I love making love to a woman." The lull of Kate's soft poetical voice drew me in. "I love their soft bodies. Women are like the curl of a wave. The wave comes all the way toward shore, hardly noticeable, until it reaches the sand, and it crashes, exploding with life. And it goes on and on, keeps coming in until the final eruption. Sweet."

Was my mouth open?

Kate laughed and smiled at me, "Too much, huh? Back to the drawing board."

Her face was so radiant in the full sunshine. I had to look away. And then heard, once again, *I dare you.*

As if in a dream, I dared myself to look into her eyes, thinking, I want someone to love me fiercely; to rouse my sleeping soul. I felt a drawing together of the air. She squeezed my hand in response, as if knowing my thoughts.

We heard the happy voices of the others encroaching on us, although we couldn't see them.

"The tribe cometh," Kate said, taking a step away. She extinguished the marijuana joint under her sandal and stuck the end bit in her pocket. "Anyway, breakup or not, I'm glad I came to Italy, otherwise I'd be home drowning in chocolate and ice cream."

"Ha! I hear you," I said. "Can I share a secret that might help? When you're drowning, every minute becomes a choice, whether to use the razor blades or take the sleeping pills...." I felt a quiver. "But most of us get through it."

Kate froze, watching me. "That bad, huh?" A few moments passed. She didn't try to help me or fix me or explain it away; she took it in and listened. She made me feel *seen.* "I know what you mean. I was drowning. And you, Professor McKenna, are like coming up for a breath of air."

"Surfacing."

Caught up in the meeting of eyes, a few moments passed while Kate's sightline moved down and lingered on my lips. Is she going to kiss me? How do I feel about that, out here in public? My lips felt numb; stoned. No way she'd kiss me in public.

I remembered our closeness in the steam room...like slow, teasing foreplay. Recalling her half-naked, fit body, I impulsively placed my hands on both of Kate's cheeks, pulling her to me, and I kissed her. I kissed one cheek, then the other cheek, and then...I kissed her lips—warm, soft, wet, tender. All too brief, but I felt a

"Ping!" on my stone-cold heart as a crack opened to let a little light inside, and a tiny section of my defensive wall crumbled.

"Oh no, sorry," I made a pot-induced guffaw and stood back. "I shouldn't have kissed you."

"*Fay ce que voudras*—Do what you want. It's the motto of the Villa del Balbianello. Besides, now we're even."

"You're right. *Meravigliosa, bellissima*—Wonderful, beautiful."

I fell silent, questioning myself: Do I dare tell anyone I kissed you, or let it remain our secret, how you opened my heart with one touch? You probably didn't intend to and might never know.

"Kate!" We both jumped, turning toward the voice. Renee yelled, "Come on! The statues, you wanted to see them."

Having finished their tour of the villa, the rest of the jovial Villa Galz and Miss Armani Tour Guide filled the pathway like the murmuration of starlings moving gracefully in a pack. Normally, eighteenth century antique decors interest me, but at the moment, I cared less.

Had Renee seen us kiss? I knew my neck must be blotchy red. "You won't tell them, will you?"

"Tell them what, Professor? That you smoked pot, or that you kissed me?" Kate smiled.

"Oh, fuck." We both erupted into a fit of laughter.

"Quick, let's hide," she said.

Kate slipped over behind one of the wide marble columns. She disappeared. Being curious, I followed her. As I rounded the coiled vine on the column, she caught me, pressing her hands on my hips to hold me in place against the pillar. I wrapped my arms around her shoulders and pulled her to me, kissing her feverishly, unable to hold back.

"You are so hot," she whispered.

Her hands shifted to my waist, where she gripped me and lifted me a little higher on the column. She held me and braced her hip against my groin, pressing herself against me. I moaned. A twitch stronger than I'd felt in years shot between my thighs. The muscles in my legs trembled.

While sucking and kissing my lips, in a possessive move her knee spread my legs wider. We heard restless nattering from her friends. She hesitated, restraining herself, gazing into my eyes.

"We shouldn't."

"Not here." I pulled away, yet hungry for more.

"I'll catch you," she said, coming after me.

I laughed, "Nooo, stop it!"

We couldn't stop laughing.

Renee yelled, "Kate, we're waiting. Are you coming?"

"Not anymore," Kate muttered, and we burst out laughing again.

We stifled our stoned silliness by the time we reached the others.

Kate said to Renee, "Thanks for waiting. I bumped into Gerri. We got caught looking at the, um, the view."

"Right. Of course," Renee said, and then smiled mischievously at her girlfriend Tracy.

They investigated the marble statues on the balustrade and around the panoramic terraced gardens. I found myself somewhat out-of-body, watching them scurry about. I followed alongside Kate as closely as possible without drawing attention from the others. All I could think about was taking her somewhere private and ravishing her. I was on fire.

"Where is she?" Kate wondered, excited, investigating each statue.

Renee barked back, "We'll find her. I want you to paint her for me."

"Who?" Dana asked.

"*She*, the huntress," Kate said, then looked at me. "I've done paintings of her. Now I can see her in the flesh, so to speak."

Renee put her arm around Kate's shoulders, "Welcome back. I see your Muse has awoken. We've waited for you to start painting again. You've been so blocked. Don't let your crazy ex win. Paint up a storm."

"It's not my ex's fault. But I hear you." Kate stared at the ground, and she nodded. "Just lucky I had an older painting for the art show, painted it months ago." She turned around to find me looking at her. Her hair flew up in the lakeside breeze as the world seemed to pause. We shared a breath, a moment of our own.

"I'd love to see your paintings," I said, standing right behind her.

Kate touched my hand, a little squeeze, "I'd love to paint *you*."

Overhearing, both Renee and Tracy raised their eyebrows. Tracy quickly grabbed her phone from her Lamborghini bag to show me several photos of Kate's paintings. Women, writhing in sexual abandon in various degrees of intricate undress, but always tasteful, and in beautiful, surreal landscapes.

Tracy explained, "They're huge canvases. Massive. The brilliant colors pop."

"Yes, I see. It's like they emulate Renoir nudes in a contemporary Renaissance style, painted from a woman's gaze, not a man's. Amazing," I commented, which made Kate take notice. She looked at me, adoringly.

Tracy leaned into me, whispering, "She needs to paint. Appears you inspire her." She gave me a meaningful wink and quickly moved away.

I couldn't take my eyes off the paintings, walking blindly and staring at the phone. Kate touched my elbow, guiding me along the walkway. Heat rose between us. Beads of sweat formed on my chest. I felt hot, the sun was hot; she made me hot.

"By the way, did you find out who painted Angelina's portrait?" I asked Kate.

A little distracted she said, "Still a mystery. Might be the famous Italian portrait artist Felice Casorati, but it's not her style. Or Gino Boccasile from Bari, a well-known artist who did propaganda posters during the war. Could have been a local artist commissioned by Angelina's husband. Or even commissioned by the Nazi who was in love with her. Quite unlikely, huh?"

"Yikes, that's macabre."

Moments later, their tour guide pointed to the balustrade near the huge Holm oak, "The famous huntress, she's over there."

The life-size marble statue stood on top of the balustrade as did several other male statues. The guide said, "In Italy she is Diana the Roman Goddess. To the Greeks, she is Artemis. She's the great Goddess of fertility, the Moon Goddess, protector of wild animals and all girl children. The virgin huntress."

"And a lesbian icon," Bibi added, shutting off her phone, having read about it.

Bibi leaned over and spoke into Renee's ear while nodding toward Kate and me. Renee shrugged noncommittally. Had Bibi noticed my attraction to Kate?

I gave Tracy her phone back as I gazed at the Goddess of Virgins. I knew her as Artemis. She wore a flowing tunic and skirt, with her hair tied in a loose bun. Her strong athletic body stood erect, carrying her bow and arrows over her shoulder and resting her right hand on a dagger in its scabbard.

I bumped hips with Kate by accident, the sidewalk uneven.

"Why is this statue your favorite?"

"She's Artemis, the daring adventurer—Goddess of the Hunt." Kate turned to me and clicked a few shots as I strolled in front of the statue, "You look like her. Well, with your hair up." Click.

"No, stop, my hair's a mess." Click.

"You make me ravenously *sexcited*. I want to kiss you." Click.

"Will you kiss me, now, here?"

"Please, no, don't," I whispered so the others wouldn't hear. Luckily, most of them had moved on. "I kissed you, yes. I'm not used to pot," I said, feeling my taut nipples rub against my shirt; my mind turned off her, but my body didn't. "I don't want to lead you on or give you any ideas." I backed away, stumbling, knowing I lied. My body wanted her to take me right there, against the balustrade.

"As you wish, Professor, I will abide." Kate's eyes smiled. "Except you didn't answer my question: Will we ever kiss again?"

"I-I don't know."

"Hella good, at least you didn't say no."

"Hey, Kate!" called CJ, a living version of Artemis as she jumped onto the railing in one catlike leap. "Artemis is your type of woman, Kate." CJ balanced on the marble railing, hugging the Artemis statue.

Click, Kate took a photo of CJ, but her focus was still on me as I watched from under the huge umbrella-shaped oak tree, needing to cool down in the shade.

Bibi yelled, "Pull me up for a photo!" But her round belly and tush would not cooperate.

"No-no, get down!" Miss Armani Tour Guide waved her arms, frantic.

"It's not safe. You might fall."

The drop to the water and concrete boat launch looked two-storeys high. CJ got down but not before her girlfriend, Erin, snapped a few photos. Click. Click.

"*Grazie, grazie,*" the tour woman said, clutching her heart.

The others, with Renee and Tracy holding hands, moved on to the other statues. They followed the pathway of candelabra-pruned Plane trees that overlooked the gorgeous views of the Gulf of Diana and the Gulf of Venus. The women enjoyed themselves, in awe of the beautiful Balbianello gardens.

"I do apologize for their behaviour," I heard my Miss McKenna teacher alter ego say to the tour guide, and immediately regretted it.

Dana, CJ and Hannah flashed me a surprised look. I deserved it.

"Please excuse me," I said to them. "I have no right to discipline grown women. It's your holiday. A bad habit of mine—almost thirty years teaching school."

With a nod of acceptance, Dana announced, "Time to go, Sapphos!" Laughing and bantering, they thanked the tour guide and gave her a generous tip before making their way to the boat launch, a wild procession of excited goddesses.

"Bye all," I said, waving and heading away.

Tracy said, "Gerri, hitch a ride on our rental boat, it's faster."

I figured I might as well go with them instead of hiking the trail back to Lenno.

I joined Kate at the bow of the hired yacht, an open-concept Boston Whaler-type motorboat with a hired driver. The handsome young boat captain, busy steering, took his job seriously, never once cracking a smile. Beside him, Erin made her own gangly version of manspreading, sitting back with her long legs far apart.

Alongside Kate, I felt unafraid being on the water. No one spoke to me. Everyone stuck pretty much to themselves, each couple relaxing, holding hands or kissing, and enjoying the romantic view together, even Vera and Dana.

Kate snapped photos as we left the villa's elaborate launch; she also took everyone's photo in the boat. To steady her hand for snapping landscape photos, Kate lay back onto the bow's deck and rolled over onto her stomach. I took my hair down, letting it blow free in the wind, and joined her, lying on my stomach beside her. The side of my body touched hers. If we got any closer, we'd be on top of one another. She stopped taking photos long enough to look at me. It excited me to think I could easily lean in and kiss her.

Lingering on my eyes, Kate whispered, "Yes." The feeling was so intense, so incredibly sexy, that I did want her to kiss me.

Voices carry over water, even overtop of boat motors, and I overheard someone sitting behind us in the boat say, "What's happening there?" Sounded like Wanda.

"Yeah, Vera's been into Dana for a long time." Sounded like Jamie.

"Not those two—I meant Kate and Gerri."

Kate also overheard it. "Never mind them. Enjoy the ride."

I leaned in, saying, "I haven't decided to get rid of my training wheels."

Kate nodded. "Hope you find your balance soon." She gazed at me. "You have beautiful ice-blue eyes. Very sexy. It's hard not to reach out and…I can stop if it bothers you."

"No woman minds hearing she's sexy. But, let's slow down."

The boat was faster than walking along the road and several minutes later—way too soon—we alighted in Lenno and headed for the *supermercato*. I hadn't meant to tag along with them but needed to get groceries, too.

Before long, I lost all the Villa Galz as they disappeared into the enticing local shops along the promenade, which had reopened after siesta. Once they were out of sight I ducked into a lingerie boutique. I quickly pulled the plainest bra in my size off the rack, to the appalled chagrin of the full-figured Italian saleslady, who insisted I try it on. I gave in. She poked and prodded me and brought me several more specimens. According to her, the bra which fit me the best turned out to be a lacy orange number. Orange? Not my usual thirty-dollar, plain, schoolmarm bra. Comfortable yet sexy, this one fit like a glove and held "the girls" in place brilliantly. Created by a woman designer, it also cost a hundred Euros—almost $150 Canadian! I balked, threatening to leave the shop; I'd never paid so much for a bra in my life. The buxom proprietress offered me a 25% discount. Still I hesitated, remembering I had recently decided to go braless. So why was I buying one?

I was about to decline when the saleswoman, herself so chic and proudly curvy, leaned forward to murmur kindly, "Love of self is hidden underneath."

I gasped at hearing the exact same expression the elegant SLL—Carmela Lazzaro—had said at the train station days ago. I bought the damned bra. And the matching panties. For a couple hundred bucks I was jolly well going to wear them instead of carrying a shopping bag, and I felt pretty sexy as I stepped back out onto the street.

"'Sup, Gerri? No luck?" Black-haired, beautiful Hannah asked me as the others swarmed into a silk shop.

"Too pricey in there," I replied blandly, as I strolled alongside her. "Sorry about what I said at Balbianello. Schoolteacher habit popped out."

Hannah's face lit up, "A teacher of what?" We stopped in front of the scarf shop, watching her friends through the window. All types of silk scarves flew about like a swarm of birds.

"I teach a Culinary Arts program."

"You're a chef?" Hannah, forensic medical examiner that she was, asked me a lightning round of questions, "Like y'know, we're looking for a chef? We want an old-fashioned cooking class, Italian cooking—dah. Could you do it? We'll pay you," Hannah said, excited. "Is it a go? Please, come on," she pleaded.

She squired me inside the little silk shop, which seemed to bulge with six Villa Galz, plus me. The dumbfounded shopgirl edged toward the door, clearly tempted to flee.

"Hey, guess what?" Hannah yelled, "I found our chef." The entire room froze, hands and scarves in midair.

I broke the ice, "Well, yes, I teach cooking."

The others unfroze and cheered.

"How much do you charge?"

Uncertain how to answer, I said, "For groceries, I'll need to go shopping, and I suppose a teacher's fee. I'm not a fancy chef, delicious meals using local delicacies, it's my specialty."

Vera, the lawyer, confessed, "Blimey, I can make it when I get back to London. No more mushy peas out of the can."

"You're the takeout queen, you never cook, at least when I visit," Dana said.

"Any food allergies?" I enquired, not expecting a popcorn response.

"I'm allergic to onions." "I'm vegetarian." "I'm gluten-intolerant." They groaned at Dana. "Does that mean no pasta?" I shook my head, "Depends if you're celiac, Dana?" "No, not celiac." I assured them, "Good. Many Italians are gluten intolerant. We can use rice or quinoa pasta. Any vegans here?" They shook their heads.

Hannah tapped on my shoulder, "Is it a green light?"

I sighed, wondering if I could do it justice. "Give me a few days to organize, but yes, we're on." I heard a loud "Yesss!" Then they continued harvesting the silk goods.

The scarf bins did look inviting, and I tried on a few, knowing Kate was watching me.

"I can't decide," I said.

Kate squeezed between the narrow aisles to bring me a few samples. "Here, try this."

She wrapped a blue floral silk scarf around my shoulders. I looked in the mirror, and saw her standing behind me, so close. She watched me in the mirror.

"Guess I need help choosing."

"Choose or lose." Kate smiled and turned away, her innuendo blatant.

Pretending not to care, I played with a few scarves around my shoulders.

Doctors Wanda and Brittany huddled behind me. I overheard their playful banter. Wanda the Puerto Rican beauty asked her girlfriend, "What d'you think?"

Brittany the ND and Hollywood psychic said, "I like the blue one, it matches her incredible blue eyes."

Wanda rolled her eyes, whispering, *"¡Ay bendito!"*—Oh, my god! "Not the scarf, you goof. Do you think Gerri's a late bloomer? You're the psychic."

Both Wanda and Brittany examined me. Brittany said to her, "Leave it with me," and then winked at me in the mirror.

"Brittany, what if I don't want to be a late bloomer?" I whispered as politely as I could.

Brittany smiled, saying, "Whatever you resist, persists. Let go of things that have already let go of you."

My stubborn streak wanted to disagree. I paid for the blue scarf and hurried out the door, yelling, "Off to the supermarket, see ya."

Wanda said, "At the yacht, right? It's taking us back to Argegno."

I ignored her, thinking I'd take the ferry, feeling that enough is enough, I didn't want to play their guessing game anymore. I didn't really understand why I was fighting against opening that closet door. Kate blew me away at Balbianello—those kisses against the pillar—and here I was rejecting her. Was it too soon for both of us?

Out into the now-crowded streets of Lenno, I hurried to the supermarket and bought a few groceries. Spotting an art store across the street, I hoped Kate would see it and it sparks her artist's passion. At the water's edge, a ferry docked and loaded passengers, plus a tour group into an already crowded boat. I couldn't do it. I gave in and waited with my grocery bags by the Villa Gals' private yacht.

Vera arrived first. The likeable London-based lawyer, tall with lumberjack shoulders, carried two bags of clinking wine bottles. She sat on the bench next to me.

"I get to carry the booze. A very important job." Vera's ears stuck out of her short-cropped hair making her come across as a big friendly goof, which she probably used as a brilliant lawyer stratagem. But at present, she looked quite serious.

"Gerri, do you mind if I ask you something?"

"Go ahead."

"Do you swing both ways?"

I must have looked rather shocked; Vera sat back. When I didn't answer, Vera leaned over and said, "A little advice?" She waited until I nodded and leaned in closer, "If you're playing with Kate, she's already had a broken heart. It'd be a real cock-up. Best to leave it alone."

My heart sank. I felt wounded but knew Vera hadn't intended to hurt me. I felt impelled to respond. "You're wrong." I paused, then said, "Hearts don't break. They're strong and resilient. It's the ego that breaks. Trust me, I know."

Vera hadn't expected that. She thought for a moment, then said, "If Kate does open her heart after she's been hurt, then she's braver than I am." She stared at the ground.

Surprised, I saw Vera's mask drop away to reveal her pain.

Just then, our villa's van hurtled down the road. Alex paused at the stop sign, just long enough to see me when I waved at him. He drove over and I popped into the van.

"Please take me to the villa." It wasn't a question. Then, wanting to reach out to Vera, I asked, "Are you coming?"

A little startled, she said, "Thanks, but I'll wait for Dana and the others."

A disturbing thought then settled in my mind, that someone so hidden behind a mask could be suicidal. Vera's tough exterior hid a broken heart, and it might involve Dana.

The other twelve Villa Galz with their shopping bags and groceries came straggling toward their rented boat as Alex and I did a U-turn and headed for Argegno. Vera took all of Dana's shopping bags; Dana, too busy chirping with the others, missed the thoughtful gesture. I also knew Kate watched us drive away. She carried a rolled canvas, collapsible easel, and other supplies from the artist's shop.

The van rattled up the switchbacks like a tin can full of rocks. "Alex, please don't come to the villa without first checking with me, out of respect for the guests." He made a disgruntled face.

"The lesbian women," he puffed out his chest as if he was bragging, "You see Alex not so dumb," he gritted his rotten front teeth.

"Why don't you fix your teeth? Isn't there a dentist in Argegno?" His face crumbled in humiliation, and he sagged forward towards the wheel. "Sorry Alex, forgive me," I said. He said nothing. After a moment I pushed on, "About the van, I need to borrow it. I'm doing a cooking class for the Villa Girls—I mean, the guests."

His eyes widened, "You are chef?" I nodded but he wouldn't speak further. He drove from the main road into Argegno, stopping and jumping out in front of the busy bar that overflowed into the street with fun-loving locals. "You can take it now. I don't need. *Ciao.*"

"Aleksandar," I called to him and he stomped back to the van. I kept my voice low: "Please don't sell the villa guests marijuana. *Capisci?*"

His mouth dropped open as he frowned. He stormed toward the bar, cursing under his breath, "*Merda! Non mi rompere i coglioni, vedova.*" Roughly translated: "Don't bust my balls, widow." I would bet the entire bar would hear about the *vedova's* "clitzpah"—the gutsy widow.

I jumped into the driver's seat, flipped the van into gear and sped away, rocks flying. Even Alex turned to watch. Driving the Fiat van up the road, the stick shift ground as I changed gears. I hoped Alex didn't hear, but the sound echoed across the lake.

Five minutes later, I gunned it into the driveway and parked. The villa was quiet, no one about. I regretted telling Alex to fix his teeth; the poor boy had no money, and I realized it had been my own deflected anger.

"God, I'm a bitch," I admitted as I lugged my groceries into my suite and fell onto the bed, exhausted.

CHAPTER 11
The Talking Wall

We wear masks that never fit, that never make us feel who we are. Once you remove them, you choose to stand in your authenticity, coming home.

—G. A. McKenna, journal entry

Sunset blazed with purple and pink flashes reflected in the lake. Pretty, yes, but my stomach growled, as did Pucci and Goldie's.

"What's for dinner?" I asked the pups, opening a large can of *Golosi straccetti* dog food. I stirred in kibble and warm water; within two minutes, they had both gobbled it down.

My turn. Ravenous, yearning for "forbidden fruit," I settled for a pot of boiling water for pasta. For the sauce, I made fresh pesto in the blender using fresh basil, the villa's own extra virgin olive oil, pine nuts, a few drops of lemon juice, lots of garlic, and 1/4 chili pepper, deseeded. I used the rest of the *pagnotta* bread from Carlo's bakery and cut it into rounds to make a combo *crostini bruschetta*, depending on the thickness of the slices.

"I say *crostini*, you say *bruschetta*," I sang.

After brushing a little olive oil on top of the thin bread rounds and rubbing them with a garlic clove, I broiled them in the sparkling toaster oven in my wee kitchen. I happily anticipated adding on top of each slice some prosciutto, goat cheese, a basil leaf, and Carlo's homemade fig jam. I then chopped some fresh garden tomatoes, minced a garlic clove, chopped more fresh basil, then mixed in one tablespoon olive oil and a dash of balsamic vinegar to make a separate tomato topping for my toasted rounds. We couldn't wait to try it, meaning the dogs and me.

While taking out the tray of toasted *pagnotta* rounds and adding the toppings, I heard voices, many voices. Two taxi vans had arrived with the gaggle of Gals and their groceries. Soon afterward the guests started to prepare dinner. Our kitchens had one adjoining wall. Next door exploded with dialogue, laughter, the popping of wine bottles, the noise of kitchen pots and pans, plates and cutlery set onto the long table.

I could hear most everything they said. I dropped my gluten-free linguini into the boiling water, poured myself a glass of local Valtellina red wine, sat down near the adjoining wall, and got an earful. Did I feel guilty? Absolutely. And pulled my chair closer.

It became a game to figure out who said what. Half the time I didn't know because I'd hear chatter from the foreground and the background, mixed in together. I ran upstairs, grabbed my journal, came back down, and sat down at the table, pen at the ready, all the while chomping on my delicious appetizer. They chatted about the latest world news, political events, films, even fashionista news, the usual conversations. Until it got real.

I heard Dana's distinctive, throaty voice: "Stay away from her, she's straight."

Someone, possibly Jamie, disagreed: "So? Straight women need a good orgasm, too."

Unable to move, I held my *crostini* in midair until olive oil dripped down onto my palm and a ribbon of wetness ran down my wrist. I'd swear they had pulled Kate over to stand next to our common wall.

"You're recovering from a nasty breakup. You're vulnerable," Dana said. "I'm tellin' ya, Kate, don't go any further. Ninety-five percent of rebounds never work."

"A wise recommendation," I whispered to the dogs, who sat wagging their tails and eyeing my dinner. I tossed them each half a toasted *crostini*.

"On the other hand," Brittany the psychic said, "Listen up and pry your heart open. You'll know when you know. Until then, explore your psychic abilities." A thump on the wall made me jump.

"Brittany, you're weird," Dana said.

Stunned, I felt olive oil dribble from the corner of my wide-open mouth. Did Brittany intuit that I was listening? I felt her eyes looking at me through the wall. Brittany's website described her as a naturopathic physician, medical intuitive, astrologer and psychic. Was she telling me through the wall that she knew I had psychic abilities, just like mama said? I had been unusually perceptive as a child, knowing the moment when my father would walk through the front door, or remembering going to places my mother knew I'd never visited, or having vivid dreams, but I also saw auras or spirits around people and had an imaginary friend who was very real to me. I'd let it all fade away as I grew older, until Brittany "spoke" to me through the wall to remind me.

The "wall talk" continued. I heard Kate say, "*Foo*, I don't need to be psychic to know nothing will happen."

Nothing will happen?—How did I feel about that? And what did "foo" mean, if anything? I decided, jotting it into my journal, it must be an affectionate California slang word. Too much going on to continue journaling, besides I felt guilty breaking their privacy. Instead, I leaned closer to the wall, listening, hooked on their personal version of *The L Word*.

"To heck with them, Kate, I'd go for it," Erin butted in, walking past them. It had to be Erin, it sounded like her cheerful, direct tone.

"But take it real slow," someone said. It sounded like Jamie.

"Not! Real women don't go slow," Erin said. "You can't afford to waste time. Find out now if she eats from both sides of the buffet. Do a drive by."

"A drive by?"

"Yeah. Cruise the cherry. You know, accidently, like. Send your hand on a fact-finding mission. See how she responds. Well, have you?"

"Shut it! As if I'd tell you lot," Kate declared.

I felt a heat at the base of my spine and lower areas. "Wooo."

"Good call, Kate. Must be depressing, though, not knowing either way," Jamie noted.

Luciana's Spanish accent interrupted, "Whenever I feel depressed, I just put my hands on my vagina for a minute. Holding that much power always cheers me up. *Es cierto!*"

"You are so bad ass, babe," Bibi said with a noisy smooch.

"That reminds me, remember the pink Viagra pill for women? Tried to convince us we needed it. Typical bullshit," Renee said.

"I've already got Viagra. It comes with batteries." Laughter all around. I didn't get it until I heard the next person.

"Yup, vibrators can do the trick, not that I'd ever keep one in my house," Dana said.

"Oh sure, come on."

"I'm serious. My brother is the executor of my estate. When I die, he'll have to go through my stuff. I can see him now, waving my vibrator around like Obi-Wan Kenobi's lightsaber."

More laughter.

"Try verbal vibrators," said someone who accentuated the words with a dramatic flair, "Like stimulate, smolder, succulent, stroke, you know."

My mouth dropped open again.

Tracy, Renee's girlfriend, joined the conversation, "Once, I gave one of my girlfriends a flat panty vibrator. I controlled the vibrator from a mobile app. She'd be at work and all of a sudden, it would vibrate in her underpants. Her grumpy boss never guessed why she was so happy most days."

The clatter of plates stopped dead. Silence in the kitchen. I covered my mouth, muffling my laughter, afraid they'd hear me snorting through the wall.

"It's true, I swear!" Tracy insisted.

I wrote down "panty vibrator."

I heard Vera in her distinguished British accent along with the rattle of dishes: "One of my straight friends told me that it wasn't until after her divorce that she read a book about orgasms and vibrators. Having never had either and being the resourceful gal that she was, she used the only vibrating device on hand: her electric toothbrush."

Clang went a pot dropped on the stove. "Oh, great! That image will haunt me tonight when I brush my teeth," Bibi said. "Or tempt me."

"Ridiculous," CJ admonished. "Shifting subjects, what are we doin' tomorrow? How about Lugano and the casino?" A few agreements.

"How about we rent another boat?" A few more agreements.

Meanwhile, Erin segued: "Anyway, Kate, I think an affair is just what the doctor ordered, or in this case, the chef. A few tasty appetizers *á la carte* wouldn't hurt."

I gulped hard.

Feisty Bibi piped in, "Nah, Kate's a picky eater. Likes hot 'n spicy Latinas. Otherwise, it's dine and dash, lick and split."

"Whoo-hoo!" A smash of glasses for quick toasts all around.

"Okay, that's enough," Kate said, serious. "I appreciate everyone's concern but, like—F-off!" Kate poured herself some wine.

Dana's heels clicked back closer to the wall between us. "Kate, I've been meaning to ask you, let me book us a trip to Palm Springs, just the two of us, to the Dinah Shore Open. You'll have your pick of balls and women, now that you're single again."

Noooo! I felt like yelling, don't go, Kate! I heard a weird, frantic hissing and looked over to see my pasta boiling over! "OH SHIT!" I shouted, dashing to the stove. Did they hear me? I froze. Waited. No noticeable change in the dinner prep sounds, so I deduced that with so much going on they hadn't heard me. I hoped Brittany didn't pick up on it.

Feeling guilty, I threw together my pasta with the homemade pesto sauce and tiptoed outside to eat on my side of the property. The dogs stayed close, eyeing my pasta. I sneaked over to the private spot where Kate had drawn me, under the flowering arbor with table and chairs. It overlooked the town below; the night air cool, refreshing; and the lake sparkled magically. I sat at the small table, enjoying my meal.

Their music played on until late, but I didn't mind, they enjoyed themselves. As their concierge, I now knew my place. Later, I sat in bed writing in my journal all the day's activity, even writing a few things in code in case my daughter read it later. "K" for Kate; "Ks" for Kiss. I also taped in a few souvenirs: a leaf from the Holm oak tree at the Villa del Balbianello; my grocery, bra, and silk scarf receipts; a ferry ticket stub, the day's reminders. Rich, beautiful memories already.

A water creature swims like a dolphin. Its black slithering body and long tail skims below the surface. From land, Artù the owl takes flight, skimming inches above the water, his strong wide wings the same length as the serpent. I am the serpent. I am the owl. I see out of both eyes. They lean against the gravitational pull of the Earth, gliding inches apart, together. Then Artù does something daring. He dives into the water on top of the serpent. They float together in the water side-by-side, the current pulling them along. Then they morph into two human figures. They make love, caressing one another. Two opposing creatures become united. I see their faces: the liquid solidifies, and the figures change into Kate and me, embracing and kissing; caressing each other underwater in a slow-motion dance. We morph back into Artù and the serpent once again. Artù, the beautiful owl, surfaces and lifts off into flight.

I felt a light touch on the top of my head and sat upright in bed with a short gasp for air. I had fallen asleep, my journal on my lap. As my consciousness slowly returned, the strange vision of Kate and me making love made me feel warm all over. I heard something outside, perhaps the clinking of shattering glass.

"What the heck?"

I stumbled out of bed, wrapped my dressing gown around me, slipped into my thongs, as I glanced at the bedside clock: three in the morning. "Where's it coming from?"

I opened the door to our upstairs adjoining hallway and listened. The entire house full of women purred and snored as they slept. I'd never heard women snore together. It comforted me. The other mysterious noises came from somewhere outside.

I found the courage to investigate, rushing downstairs to my lower suite. The dogs whined at my feet but didn't bark. I held them back as I opened the front door, slipping past them outside into the chilled night air. I edged closer to the corner of the villa, the dark side nearest the olive grove forest and front driveway. More noises came from the woods:

Dark figures, strange movements, unreal, dark see-through images. Shadowy human forms ran between trees in the darkness.

As I approached the corner, the vision disappeared, like the closing of a camera lens. I blinked a few times, unsure of my eyes since I now saw no one. At the end of the driveway, hidden behind the garage, and close to the entrance path that led into the olive grove, I saw a double-seated scooter. Someone walked up to it and sat sidesaddle. A broken beer bottle lay on the ground, leaking a river of wasted beer. A curl of white smoke drifted into the cool air. I crept closer and peeked.

A blond, long-haired person, either male or female, smoked a cigarette. By then the cloud of smoke reached me, unmistakably marijuana. The blond head turned, and I recognized Shaun, the American surfer-hippie dude. Moments later, I heard a shrieking giggle as a young girl ran from the olive grove path into Shaun's arms. She looked young, maybe seventeen. They kissed; sweet, tender, as you would after sex. He ditched the joint and jumped on the scooter. She kissed him once more and then hopped on the scooter to sit behind him. He quietly wheeled the scooter onto the roadway and glided down the hill. I heard the tiny engine cough to life as they rode away.

It didn't take much to guess what Shaun was doing: having a secret rendezvous with a young village girl in the olive grove. Clandestine, but not sinister. I wondered if they used a certain white chalk mark on a village bench as their signal to meet-up; but, no, they wouldn't use Carlo's mason mark.

I tiptoed back toward my guest house, taking a different route. On my way past the villa, a light shone across the pathway from a ground floor window, with a shadow moving inside it. I peeked into the living room window and was surprised to see, at this late hour, Kate. She stood in front of a large canvas set on an easel. Her hand moved swiftly, expertly, as she painted over a charcoal drawing with large brush strokes, blocking in the background. The portrait of Angelina over the fireplace seemed to watch Kate with an encouraging, intimate gaze. I wanted to stay and watch her, too, but I didn't wish to intrude on the rapture between an artist and her muse.

CHAPTER 12
Wildflowers and Headstones

If life is the dancer and we are the dance,
Then our rich memories are its music.
So kick up your heels under the moon,
Dancing to the rhythm of life,
And live to live!

—G. A. McKenna, journal entry

E arly the next morning I heard Isabella singing downstairs in the villa's main kitchen. I opened the drapes. I couldn't see any parked rental cars, which meant the guests were away on day trips. I jumped into a bright blue pullover, white short shorts, and the new blue floral scarf—nothing black. I heard Isabella singing what sounded like a Renaissance madrigal and opened the bedroom closet to listen.

"...voi cantata, spargend' e rose e fiori, Viva la bella Dori!"—You sing, scattering roses and flowers, Long live fair Dori! That's all I could translate.

No one was around, so I chose to go down the secret staircase into the villa's kitchen. Isabella was gathering dusting supplies.

"Buongiorno—Good morning, Isabella," I greeted her.

"Ay-ay!" The poor woman jumped a foot. "No use secret stairs, Miss Gerri." Her hand clutched her chest. *"Sì, buona giornata.* You wake early."

"Yes. I need to ask you something. Someone was here last

night, well, not here, but using the olive grove."

Isabella said, "It wasn't Alex. Last night he—"

"Hey, why did you think of Alex?"

She raised both eyebrows, "Couldn't have been him. He sleeps my home, most nights. He likes my cooking," she smiled. "Besides, in the evening he help Signor Lazzaro at his hotel."

"Vincenzo Lazzaro? Where is his hotel?"

"In Menaggio. The Hotel Carmela."

I snickered, "Of course it's named after his wife."

"Is okey-doke hotel, nightclub, casino, small but fun. Vincenzo is rich man, owns real estate. Alex, he's in pressure."

"*Under* pressure. Why?"

"He, I would like to ask question, for him. The lawyer, the tall one, she can do papers?"

"You mean Vera?"

"*Sì*, immigration papers. She can do?"

I squinted at Isabella, "Let me understand. Alex needs immigration papers. To what? To stay in Italy? And you want Vera to do them?"

"Yes. Easy as pie."

"Not so easy as pie. She might not be an immigration lawyer. Where's Alex from?"

She hesitated, looking sheepish.

"Isabella, how can I help if you don't tell me the truth?"

"Syria. He is refugee, came by boat, sneaks into Italy from Albania. There, is good?"

"Are you sure? I mean, do you even know the truth?"

"Believe me, he is desperate. If he does not get papers, bad things will happen."

"What bad things?"

Isabella made a zipper gesture across her lips, and her voice became low and conspiratorial, "Vincenzo, he wants Alex to do not nice things. Gambling tables, you know, like cheat the tables. And other things. No-no-no. Please, I can say no more. Can you ask for Alex?" She placed her hands in a prayer position.

"He's being blackmailed by Vincenzo to do illegal things?"

"Shish, Miss Gerri, quiet!"

"Or else Vincenzo will have him deported?"

I watched her expression turn from hope to fear.

"You're so young and so in love with Alex. Be careful, Isabella. A young heart is a fragile thing."

She smiled at me, whispering, "*Vero amore*—True love, Miss Gerri."

I worried for her. Alex could be from Syria or Turkey, or anywhere; I feared for him, too. If he escaped Syria in the fleeing refugee tidal wave, why did he not register legally? I speculated he was actually Macedonian who had hopped a ride on one of the many illegal ships via Albania that, according to the media, had arrived at the port of Bari, Italy. He might have lied to Isabella.

"By the way, I had a dream last night, about the water serpent from the castle in Varenna, do you know about it?"

"Aye-ya-ya! Bad luck to talk about serpent." Isabella's eyes widened; her hands shook at me, "No-no-no, it will come from Milano. The serpent of Milano on the statues, they come alive. Last time I cursed it I got breast cancer. Lost my hair."

She pushed back her reddish-orange hair to expose her nearly-bald head underneath the wig. Her hair was growing back, about half an inch. I had no idea—how stupid of me—preoccupied with my own life. She straightened her wig, fussing a bit, then kissed a gold horn pendant hanging around her neck.

"Protect against Evil Eye. Shish, now. I finish and go."

I wanted to hug her. "Sounds good. I'm taking the dogs for a walk." I heard stirrings upstairs. "Someone's waking up?"

Isabella grimaced, "*Sì*, people wake up. Those who did not go out, wake up."

"Do they know you're here today, cleaning?"

She nodded, "*Sì*, they're requesting. They no like spiders. It's in the guest book." Isabella swatted at a black spider.

"Wait! Don't kill it."

"It's a spider, I kill."

"No, please."

Grabbing a paper towel, I helped the spider crawl onto it and gently set it outside the doorway. We watched it crawl away to freedom.

"Do you save birds with broken wings, too? And people? So you will help Alex?" Isabella insisted.

"I guess you got me. Yes, of course I will—I'll try."

Isabella gave a little sob of joy and hugged me tight. Pulling back again she waved the duster, "Then you can save the spiders, too, every few days," she said gleefully, and with a slight curtsy she went about dusting, singing again.

She had said "every few days." How long had I been here? I counted on my fingers: Tuesday, my fifth day in Italy. It felt like a month. The days had been jam-packed: Bellagio, Balbianello and Lenno, and Varenna. I should be exhausted, but instead felt invigorated.

"I'm off," I said, skipping out the door with the dogs.

Heading past the pool and down the garden pathway, I decided to visit the church and cemetery. Pucci and Goldie romped through the tall grass, barking. I worried they'd wake the rest of the household. I called the dogs and put them on leash as we approached the graveyard near the church.

I thought of the young lovers: Alex an illegal refugee, hiding in a small town and falling in love with Isabella, a local girl. Do young people nowadays have a plan for the future, or are they fearful, too, like me and my friends? We used to be brave. We used to be courageous. Now all my friends talk about is retirement: Do you have enough money to live on? Can you remain healthy? Do you have a medical plan? When will old age set in, and what about old-old age? I want to leap out of my skin, to get past the fears and imagined insecurities.

What precipitated these thoughts? Oh, yeah, I kissed Kate yesterday. So what was the big worry? Fear I wasn't worthy to be loved again? Fear I might be falling in love with her? Fear of a relationship? Do I dare?

Isabella had said, "*Sì*, people wake up." I want to wake up, but what do I really, really, really want to wake up *to*? Am I getting what I want from this lifetime? I wondered.

I stopped on the hill overlooking the town of Argegno, modest and unpretentious with its orange rooftops. On the opposite side of the narrows, the slopes of the mountains resembled green fjords rising out of the water. Right in front of me stood the church steeple and its cemetery.

A screen door slammed up the hill behind me at the villa, and I turned. Out popped Tracy still in sleepwear and Renee in a swimsuit. Obviously, not everyone had left on a day trip. The loud splash ricocheted down the hill as she jumped into the pool. I knew that Kate usually hung out with them. Was she still here? Once I entered the church grounds, I pushed aside thoughts of them as I focused on my mission.

Isabella had told me that Winston Churchill, vacationing in 1945 just after the war ended, had painted a watercolor of the 17th century *Chiesa di San Sisinnio*. Most striking was its tall Romanesque bell tower, but I had never heard any bells ringing. A plaque told me that in 1848, during the invasion by Austrian soldiers, local patriots used the Saint Sisinnio Church as their secret headquarters. Here, the partisans planned their resistance operation. The open wooden door invited me to enter, but I was here for a different reason.

Through the overgrown grass, I prowled the churchyard cemetery inspecting the gravestones and mausoleums for one in particular. I was drawn to an elaborate marble tomb, the largest one in the cemetery, and around it grew a patch of blue wildflowers. And there she lay. The inscription carved into the marble read:

Angelina Lucia Beatrice Merosi-Ferrario
La bella cantante di Argegno
[September 3, 1908 - April 6, 1945]

"The beautiful singer of Argegno," I translated out loud. Above the inscription was a large porcelain cameo portrait of Angelina, identical to the image used on the Villa della Cantante's olive oil bottles.

"There be none of Beauty's daughters, with a magic like Thee," I recited the first lines from Lord Byron's poem, the one Carlo had mentioned. "She died so young."

Her husband Max's grave marker, located on the outside of the tomb's building, read Marco Silvio Ferrario with a picture next to his name. Angelina's parents were also listed, and space had been cordoned off for burials on either side of hers, presumably for her daughter Marcella and family. Marcella's first husband Giorgio Romano's grave was nearby. Missing was another grave marker, the one I'd wanted to confirm more than anything.

"*Buongiorno, signora.*" The voice startled me, and I stumbled to turn around. Kate Bradshaw stood a few headstones away, wet and wearing a swimsuit, a towel on her shoulders; the luminous droplets glistened on her bare skin and wet hair.

"Hunting for graveyard treasures?" Kate asked, drifting toward me. "I saw you from the pool, came down to investigate." Her one-piece swimsuit exposed her lovely cleavage and accentuated her fit figure. I started to sweat, feeling wet underarms; must be the hot sunshine.

"La Cantante's grave is there," I pointed. "And I'm looking for the grave of Marcella's illegitimate baby."

"That's right, the baker said it was here. Did you check the local registrar for a death certificate?"

"Good idea. He said the baby died at birth or thereafter. Carlo also said Marcella got pregnant by a transient olive picker. It's a mystery who the father is, and I assume she's never confessed. All hush-hush at the time."

"I remember he never said whether it was male or female. I love solving a good mystery, and this one is *très-très* interesting."

"You've got paint all over your fingers," I noticed, touching her hand. It felt warm; I smelled fruity peach and blushed.

"I set up a canvas, been painting all night. When the Muse strikes, you know." She bent down over a headstone, "I wonder what year the baby died?"

"Hmm, good question. Let me see, if Marcella was born sometime in 1944, and she had the baby in her late teens, but let's say at twenty-years-old, that makes it 1964. Right? Or, plus nine months, which means Marcella's baby might have been born in 1965, or even 1966." Something felt odd, but I couldn't think what.

"Illegitimate. Catholic churches disallow cemetery burials for illegitimate births, don't they? Might be in a separate area?" Kate wondered.

While we walked around reading the headstones, Kate said, "Some of us might drive to Lugano tomorrow. Or else rent a boat. Can we do the cooking class on Thursday?"

"All good, yes. Let's meet in the kitchen at nine, no, make it ten o'clock sharp, ready to go to market," I suggested. "I figure including the cost of food and wine, a light lunch, and a full course dinner, should be around forty-euros per person. Is that all right?"

"Sounds more than fair. I'll tell the others," Kate said. We both continued searching but couldn't find the baby's headstone.

"Are we sure Carlo never mentioned the baby's name?"

"No, he didn't." Kate said, "Well, we've done a sweep of the graveyard. There are no baby headstones here. It's not here. Or, he could be lying. Years ago, an illegitimate birth was scandalous. I suspect they did a cover-up. NFA: No further action."

"My, aren't we suspicious. Why would he have reason to lie?"

I stepped on a flat grave marker, unkempt and neglected, surrounded by tufts of long grass. I froze.

"Dunno." Kate leaned in toward me to touch my shoulder, "You look like you've seen a ghost."

"Look down at my feet, read the gravestone."

"It says Otto Weber.... Oh my god, he's the one who murdered her. He's Angelina's murderer, the young general. What the hell? And so close to her grave."

A voice from behind us: "Gerri, telephone!"

We turned to see Isabella running through the grass field to the rock wall. "It's Signor Vacchini for you." Excited, Isabella held up my mobile.

"He called *my* phone?"

Isabella got stuck with one leg over the rock wall. "I was upstairs cleaning, heard your phone. I answered. I thought maybe Rosie from England again, but it's Davide Vacchini."

I nodded, taking the phone from her, while Kate reached over to help Isabella get off the rocks, but she kept glancing over at me.

"Thanks. By the way, Isabella, can you work for me at the villa on Thursday, about noon? I'll pay you." Isabella, still caught on the wall, agreed with frantic nods.

"Hello, Davide? How did you get my phone number?"

A faint voice on the other end of the line said, "Ah, Signora McKenna. This is Davide Vacchini. You would like a boat ride tomorrow? I can be there at eleven. Please say yes. I feel terrible about yesterday. Please, you will come?" he implored.

I hesitated. He didn't answer my question. Did it matter? Yes, it mattered. "How the hell did you get my phone number?"

He was taken aback because he answered with a sheepish voice. "Your friend Rosie, is that all right?"

"Yes, sorry, that's fine."

"So, you will come to the village dock?"

I didn't want to, but he is Rosie's friend. "Um, well, why not? Sure," I answered, wondering why the hell I'd want to go for another boat ride. I hung up.

"Looks like I'm going for a boat ride tomorrow," I said to Kate.

"Cool, so are we. Erin rented a motorboat for us. I was going to ask you but—too late now."

As Kate and I walked through the grassy field toward the villa, we talked about what Carlo had told us.

Kate reminded me, "You think Carlo is Marcella's father, right? Isn't that what you asked him at the hotel? You've got nerve, girl. Except he didn't answer. We can't assume he and Angelina had an affair."

"Then I'll ask his son Davide, tomorrow."

"You're brazen. Or naughty," Kate said, chortling.

On the main roadway, a few cyclists whizzed by on their way down the hill.

"Hey, I saw some bicycles in the shed. Wanna go for a bike ride?" Kate asked.

"Huh, ah, I've forgotten how to ride a bike."

"Then I dare you!" she grinned, leading me toward the villa's garage.

We peeked inside at the bicycles and the two convertibles. The two Alfa Romeos glinted behind the garage door windows.

"Forget the bikes. Let's take a convertible. The newer one." She tried the garage door. Locked.

"No way," I said, remembering Isabella's instructions, "No one uses the Alfa Romeos."

"A late-1960s Alfa Romeo. It's a beauty. A Spider or Giulia? Who cares, let's go."

"Are you kidding me? No way!"

"Keys please," Kate said, her hand waiting. I didn't budge. "Professor McKenna, life is like a game, it's a daring challenge, and at the end of the day, you're the prize. So, win it."

"Win at my own game of life with no other contestants? Hmm." I took the key ring from my back pocket and held it up, just out of her reach. "All right, but on one condition: I drive. If anything happens, it's my fault."

"Ooooh, you really are naughty," she laughed.

While Kate went to change out of her wet bathing suit, I put the dogs inside my suite and checked the car's logistics. I remembered Isabella told me Marcella drove the 1960s one, but I still checked its valid license and insurance, and how to take the convertible top down, and if it had any gas.

When she returned, Kate reminded me how to drive a manual shift without grinding the gears. Surprisingly, she appeared a little shy with me now, but sweet; keeping her distance, yet she held my hand on the stick shift, tightening my grip. Then her hand on my knee, pushing it down into a shift motion, sidetracked me. We drove off with a roar.

The winding double lane roadway with hairpin curves followed the lake, a fun road for a fast roadster. I felt exhilarated, driving Signora Marcella's Alfa Romeo. Even more exhilarating was driving the red convertible while seated beside a gorgeous brunette, still not touching, keeping a beautiful distance.

Kate turned the radio on and punched in a few buttons to find a radio station. Her flimsy blouse beckoned me as it rippled in the wind. As the music blared, she touched my leg, cueing me to shift with her firm hand. Sitting closer, when she touched my knee, I wanted to break out of myself, ecstatic. Recent memories energized me: kissing her at the Villa del Balbianello, the kinetic attraction between us while she sketched me, our touching in the steam room. We drove in easy silence, feeling the wind in our hair and reveling in the saucy growl of the Alfa's engine.

I felt Kate watching me. Finally, she giggled and said, "I like it when you're being butch."

"Butch? Are you putting me into a mould? I don't want to fit into anybody's mould. And I won't. I'm tired of it."

Flabbergasted, Kate said, "Okay. Where did that come from?"

"I don't know. Sorry, ignore me."

"No, I want *you* to know where that came from."

I drove along for another moment before answering, "My husband. He was caring, thoughtful, lovely, as long as I fit into his mould. When I stepped out of it and became myself, the woman I am, he went off to some young chick to mould her. That's where that came from. Sorry. It has nothing to do with you."

Kate listened, smiling. I pumped the brakes, cranked the wheel and pulled over, sliding on the gravel at the side of the narrow road. Kate hung on for dear life.

"What are you doing?"

"Being butch."

I leaned toward her and pulled her to me. I kissed her long and hard.

"Hmm, I could get used to being butch," I said, laughing.

Kate laughed as I checked the rear-view mirror for oncoming traffic and pulled back onto the road. Feeling braver but still keeping to the speed limit, I followed the switchback road to Laglio, past the villas owned by celebrities, down to Cernobbio and back again.

After an hour of joyriding, we parked at a roadside pullout to stretch our legs and enjoy the vista. Kate grabbed my hand and pulled me, running down a hillside laden with wildflowers. The vision of purple, red, yellow petals and the long grasses bending in a breeze reminded me of a Monet painting. She pulled me down into the long grass.

"Can I take a selfie of us?"

"With my wild hair?" I said, crunching it with my fingers.

"I like your wild messy hair." She took out her phone and a small telescopic selfie stick from her vest pocket, attaching the phone to the universal mount and cable, and then positioned the selfie stick. "Turn around and come close."

We both turned around and, with the lake now behind us, I leaned into her, close, wanting the closeness, I placed my hand onto her leg and my face close to her cheek. She pressed the button on the handle to take a video of us with the lake's landscape behind us. I kissed her cheek. She pulled me down into the long grass, laughing, rolling me over in the flowers, still filming.

"Stop it!" I yelled at her, laughing, trying to grab the selfie stick.

"Go on, fight me off."

She dropped her phone into the long grass and tickled me. Pretending to hate it, I slapped her arm. She kissed me then, taking me by surprise and pinning me down, my hands above my head. I stopped struggling. She bit my lip gently and slipped her hot tongue inside my mouth, searching, probing, as one of her hands glided down my arm, slowly, until she went underneath my top. She cupped my breast, softly rubbing my nipple with her thumb, then pinched it between her fingers. I let out a soft wordless cry.

Kate buried her head onto the side of my neck, kissing it, nuzzling me while my nipples grew harder from her touch.

She laid next to me, up on one elbow, her other hand exploring my body, and we smiled at one another. Her face glowed in the sunshine, the long grasses creating a private world for us. As she looked at me with those hazel eyes and long lashes, I felt her hand edge south toward my groin, which ached, wanting her touch.

She rubbed the inside of my leg, teasing me over the top of my clothes, edging closer to my genitals. But then, she stopped to see my reaction, waiting.

I whispered, "I'm so wet right now."

Her hand slipped down a little further, pressing lightly. She touched me with the heel of her hand, pressing on my swollen mound in the direction of my clitoris. Still looking into each other's eyes, I waited for her to cradle my sex in her warm hand. Intensely aroused, I gasped when she undid my pants button and zipper.

We heard car doors slam at the roadside and then children's playful voices coming nearer. I sat up quickly, brushing away Kate's hand and zipping up my pants. The children and their parents came closer, playing in the wildflower field, but then they went in the opposite direction.

Kate touched my back and moved to sit beside me. We heard a phone "ping!" She searched in the long grasses for her hidden phone and found it. She leaned over and kissed the back of my neck with her open wet mouth, nibbling.

She whispered, "I want you so much. Maybe too much too soon. Slower next time." Another text pinged on her phone. Reading it she said, "I have to head back."

I leaned into her, turning to gaze into her glorious eyes. Kate's entire face was alight with her sweetness. Suddenly I felt willing to trust her. Her hand wandered teasingly across my belly. Just as I was wondering where her hand would go, I heard the children again in the distance. I felt her hand gently withdraw. We both knew our brief moment of passion had to end.

On the drive back, Kate's hand lay easily on my leg. We didn't talk for the longest time. The views were spectacular and words felt irrelevant. I spoke first.

"I'm curious. You've been a lesbian since age fourteen, that you knew of, right?"

Kate smiled. "Yes, before age fourteen I was asleep, don't remember much, except hanging out with my girl buds. My first time was with a much older woman. My gym teacher."

"A teacher! That's inexcusable."

"Guess that's why I like teachers, huh, Professor?" She squeezed my leg, nearly making me swerve the car. "My fault, not hers. I suffered for two years in her class, wanting to be near her but not knowing why. I even became teacher's pet, hanging out after school to help her with gym supplies. On my sixteenth birthday, she kissed me on the cheek, and that was it: head over heels in love. I stalked her for another year until she finally gave in. She took me in the back room, on the gym mattresses. They were all smelly and sweaty, and it stunk. Not at all romantic."

Kate's hair blew in the wind, the convertible roof down; the wind and the warmth of the sun embraced us. She continued, "The next day, she moved away, having already transferred to another school. Guess she didn't want to leave without helping me come out. I saw her drive away in a moving van. Her girlfriend drove the truck, a real dyke, strong arms and slicked-back hair. I even tried that haircut, but it looked ridiculous on me," Kate said, chuckling.

"God, I was heartbroken when she left. After that, it took me a few years to find the courage to walk into a lesbian bar. Immediately, when I set foot inside, four women came on to me. I'd found my tribe. Meaning, I hung out at Gay bars and got wasted, had a lot of sex, but it's a blur. Thankfully, I fell for someone who pulled me away from all that."

Kate waited for my reaction. "Does that answer your question, Miss McKenna?"

"Oh, yes, yours was a sexy first time. I had a totally different experience for my first time. It happened in a 1978 MG. Tight quarters. He bungled it. A disaster."

Kate laughed along with me.

"How about now, in an Alfa Romeo?" she said.

"Tempting. But too late."

When we pulled into the villa's driveway, Kate's friends were waiting for her so they could all go on a tour. She waved goodbye to me, looking sad for a moment, then secretly threw me a kiss.

For the rest of the afternoon, I relaxed in my suite, not wanting to see, talk, or connect with anyone else. I needed to process what happened with Kate. Her closeness had penetrated me, similar to the essence of a succulent peach. I wrote in my journal and pasted a few wildflowers alongside my notes, then emailed fun but vague updates to my children, read my guidebook, ate everything in the fridge, totally unable to think of anything but Kate.

Later I learned that most of them had taken the ferry to Como town to shop, while a few others hiked the trails. In the evening, all of them drove up the lake to Vincenzo Lazzaro's Hotel Carmela and casino complex in Menaggio. They didn't return until 3:00 a.m.

That evening, Angelina and Marcella's villa stood in quiet repose, all the ghosts lulled to sleep by the soft lapping waves of the lake and the cries of distant geese. Before going to bed, I took the dogs for a walk down the main road. Our stroll gave me a chance to snoop at the other extravagant villas in the area. Lots of rich people on Lake Como. If anyone ever wanted to, they could house-sit forever in these parts.

Returning to the Villa Cantante, I sat under the farthest arbor of vines and latticework, overlooking the church and graveyard. In the near-darkness, I saw that someone stood over a grave—a shadowy, hunched figure dressed in a black jacket and hood. Was it an imaginary vision? Walking to the rock fence, I realized he or she stood at Angelina's gravesite. When the dogs barked, the person hobbled away.

CHAPTER 13
Oh, Madonna Mia!

Willing to trust again, the past held me back.
I had to shut that book before I created a new story,
hoping history wouldn't repeat itself.

—G. A. McKenna, journal entry

Wednesday morning I slept in, dreaming of Kate—a sweet, hot dream—and regretted agreeing to meet up with Davide Vacchini. The villa was completely quiet. I assumed the guests had either left early for their road trip to Lugano, or else to rent a boat.

When I opened my front door for the dogs, a small gift sat on the doorstep. I undid the purple bow and took the lid off. Inside were chocolates molded to resemble wildflowers, with no card necessary for the sweet memory.

I took Pucci and Goldie for a quick jog. They ran toward the trail leading into the coniferous forest, but we steered clear of the olive grove. I had begun to feel at ease on the tree-canopied pathways. Trees are magical beings, at least to me, perhaps because I believe that all trees have roots intermingled with the roots of other trees and who's to say that those roots don't travel around the globe, one tree to the next and, thus, send messages energetically? Whatever the reason, I felt "at home" in this forest and less frightened to go walking on my own in these unfamiliar woods.

At eleven o'clock I had just finished dressing when I received a text and heard a long-sustained honk echoing off the lake. I hurried down the cobblestone pathway, past the church, and minutes later, across the main road to the villa's small boat dock.

Davide had moored his boat alongside the villa's sixteen-foot runabout. His yacht dwarfed the entire dock. I didn't see him and figured he must be below deck.

I stepped onto the wobbly dock but soon stopped; my hands trembled, my breath grew shallow. Then I reversed course, knowing, "I'm a brave, adventurous woman, so win it!" I edged my foot along the wooden slats, one baby step at a time.

Davide popped up from the boat's cabin, "*Signora*, let me help you." He came to my rescue and helped me into the boat. Without any small talk, we took off into the narrows of the lake. Both of us stood inside the enclosed wheelhouse where Davide steered the boat. The cruiser smelled brand new, with new luxury leather seats along its nine-foot width.

He noticed my inquisitiveness and said with a proud smile, "I pick up special guests in Como town for the hotel. It has a toilet and shower, a full kitchen, and even a television. It sleeps four. For special guests."

"You mean, women guests?"

"Sometimes." He winked at me. I rolled my eyes.

Davide was, as I had previously noticed, a very handsome man. He wore his wavy dark chestnut hair a bit long, giving him a slightly untamed air; today he wore tight khaki shorts, a crisp white shirt that showed off his tan, and sturdy-heeled, slip-on leather deck shoes, no socks, and, of course, sunglasses. Clooney on steroids.

I had reservations, worrying about encouraging his ardor, and had dressed accordingly. Due to the limitations of my suitcase, I once again wore my capri pants and non-slip sandals, this time with a bright blue linen blouse and my new lacy orange bra underneath. I have no idea whether I impressed him, nor did I care, but I found myself warming toward his exuberant yet courtly Italian demeanor.

He gestured grandly with his hands as he talked, which meant the boat veered whenever his hands did, causing me to feel a little seasick. I wanted to offer to steer, but thought better of it, unsure how an Italian man would react to a woman driving his new boat.

"Be right back," he said, leaving the boat in low gear, and hurrying into the cabin below.

Seeing the steering wheel unattended, I yearned to take hold of it. So many times I had steered a boat out of Vancouver's harbor, and now here I was in Italy. Our family boat had been older and nothing like Davide's fancy yacht. Excited, I gripped the wheel. As I gently edged the throttle handle forward, I felt goose bumps all over my body.

I heard Davide rummaging in the cabin, but soon he returned, "Nope, can't find it." He looked flushed and agitated until he saw me driving the boat.

"*Brava!*" he said, raising one hand and swirling it in the air.

His mobile on the dash rang. Without looking to see who called, he clicked it off.

"Go ahead, take the call, I've got this," I said, feeling confident.

"Nothing is as important as now, *cara mia.*" He winked at me again.

For the next hour we tootled about the exquisite lake, delighting in the clear blue summer sky, the green cascading slopes, and the soft-purring boat motor. Davide let me drive while he pointed out the waterfront villas owned by celebrities, including the one that belonged to fashion designer Gianni Versace until his murder in 1997 and, of course, the villa that will always be known as George Clooney's. Then Davide drove us back toward an island.

"And now, here, we will picnic on Comacina Island. The only island in Lake Como," Davide announced as he drove us toward a small, wooded island. He slowed the boat into a public dock near a stand of willow trees and tied up. As we grabbed the wine and picnic basket and hiked into the woods, Davide told me about the island.

"Comacina is the island of the *Magistri Comacini*—Como's Master Workmen, an important Masonic guild in Europe for master builders. My father, his father, and his grandfather were Master Masons in Europe."

"Yes, I saw the Masonic emblem in your father's bakery."

"Unfortunate, but I stop the tradition at my feet, to own a hotel instead."

I couldn't help it and took the opportunity to ask, "I'm wondering if Signora Marcella was named with an 'M' for Mason in honor of your grandfather, or because of your father Carlo's relationship to her?"

Davide's eyes widened in surprise, hesitating. "And, Marcella was my grandmother's name." I raised my eyebrows at him. Then he changed topics saying, "And this is their headquarters for secret meetings."

Did he just admit that his father, Carlo, was Marcella's real father? He nattered away as he led me along a worn pathway toward a roofless stone ruin hidden by a circle of trees, a very secluded place.

"The Masons used the island as their hideout during the Second World War, including my grandfather." Through the brush, we climbed the rockery to an ancient stone ruin. "Here we are in Basilica of Saint Euphemius, an ancient crypt, as you see."

Three arched windows in the stone ruin opened to a private view of the lake. The site also contained a plethora of empty wine bottles, campfire ash, and other party remnants, plus several hungry cats.

The most striking feature for me was the Rune and Masonic symbols carved into the ancient stones like hieroglyphic graffiti. He watched me run my fingers over the carvings.

"Mason's marks are the sign of the *Comacini* masters who liked to *immoralize* their secret meetings."

"*Immor-ta-lize*," I corrected, smiling.

My eyes caught the sunlight, and I experienced a momentary, imaginative vision:

Souls rose out of the ruins wearing dark clothing, their faces hidden behind hoods. Under cover of darkness, they followed one another into the forest. Before leaving, they each carved their mark into the stone.

Davide shooed the wild cats away and tossed the debris into the bushes, making a cleaner spot for us to sit. He spread out the picnic contents on the stone bench: cheese, bread, grapes, and olives; and then unwrapped two wine glasses from a tea towel and a bottle of rosé wine. He grumbled to himself, shaking his head, annoyed while searching in the basket.

"Ah, *merda!* The wine opener. It's always in the basket, but today there is not."

"One of your girlfriends must have taken it, a souvenir, eh? Give me your shoe," I demanded, tongue-in-cheek. He didn't understand. "Your shoe. Either one. I'll show you a Canadian trick."

He still didn't understand but took off one shoe and handed it to me. I snatched the wine bottle and read the label: "Hmm, from the Dolomites. Perfect for this trick." I placed the bottom of the wine bottle into the empty heel of his clearly expensive Italian-leather deck shoe. Carefully holding onto the bottle's top with one hand and the shoe's heel in the other, I rested it against the wall of the stone monument, "Ready?" and slammed it down hard against the stone.

"No! The bottle, she'll break!"

"Then you'll have to drink fast," I grinned at him, taking aim again and slamming the heel hard onto the stone ruin. After a few more bangs on the stone, the pressure pushed the cork up. I pulled it out, allowing the air to escape first. Now, he was impressed.

"*Favoloso!* All my years, I never saw this." And he proceeded to kiss me on both cheeks as I poured the wine. "You are fabulous, *gentile vedova.*"

"Enough with the widow thing, okay?"

He nodded his head like a good little boy.

Having wine with our lunch on a warm day, I got a little tipsy. Davide did, too. I listened as he talked about his life on the lake. His delightful and charming repartee made me smile. And because I was a cook, he charmed me even more by talking about his attempt to get a Michelin Star for his restaurant, how his chef was lazy, and he made me feel special by his subtle job offer of perhaps one day being his head chef. He also talked about all the people he met from all over the world, especially the women, the lonely divorcees, and then, about his family.

At a lull in the conversation about his family, I said point-blank: "I know your father Carlo is Marcella's real father, right?" Davide froze. I waited a moment, and when he continued looking flabbergasted, I pushed on, "I mean, Angelina and her husband, Max, had tried for years to have a child, and then suddenly, when Carlo comes on the scene and develops a close friendship with Angelina, she gets pregnant. It's obvious, and Max might have even given his blessing, wanting an heir. Are you close to Marcella, your half-sister?"

Davide's worried frown and hesitation told me all I needed to know, that, yes, Carlo is Marcella's real father. Perspiration droplets sprouted on his forehead. He finally said, "My father told you this? Then I am happy."

"Um, not exactly…"

"No more secrets between us. Except *the one*."

"What? What secret?"

"No-no, *bella mia*," Davide looked flustered, he scratched his chin, turned red-faced, and surprised me by saying, "For later. For now, together, we love the day."

"Yes, I love it here. Is it for your special women clients, your secret necking spot?"

I think something got lost in the translation because he leaned over to kiss *my* neck, moving his hands closer to my breasts.

"No more talk," he demanded. He gathered me up in his arms and drew me close for a kiss. I held him at bay, away from me.

Between his charm, good looks and admiring attention, I felt flattered and a little aroused, no doubt the buzz from the wine. But I thought about Kate's lips, her shapely curves and firm figure. My mind raced; my heart pulsed. Whoa! I can't do this.

I pushed him away, "We need to stop. Sorry. Time to go," I announced and stood up.

He stood alongside me, "You not want my kisses?"

I tossed things back into the basket, "Davide, you're very handsome and charming, what girls call 'dreamy.' If I were straighter, everything about you would totally do it for me. But it just doesn't. Sorry. We gotta go."

"What mean 'straighter'?" He sputtered but took it like a gentleman. We walked through the trees, back toward the boat. As we reached the boat, Davide helped me aboard.

He said, "You are a sweet woman, I want to take you in my arms, to take you to bed, make you very happy." He then reached for me and held me in his arms, not letting me go.

At that moment, a speedboat drove by. Loud laughter echoed off the water. Inside the boat, five Villa Galz were enjoying their outing, including Kate driving the boat. They spotted us. Davide's arms were around me and, against my will, he pulled me in to kiss me. I saw Kate stand up in the boat as it whizzed past us.

Erin yelled, "Whoo-hoo, Professor!" along with catcalls and taunting hoots.

Red in the face, I pushed Davide away. Shit! Kate had seen us kissing. I felt embarrassed and wanted to kick myself. It happened so fast, and they were gone.

Davide leaned in and I stepped back. His eyes had hardly left my breasts all day and now he just *had* to touch the voluptuous 'girls.' He reached for me, and as I swatted his paws away some buttons on my blouse came undone.

"Stop it!" I yelled.

I heard a loud roar and honking. Their speedboat roared past again, violently rocking our boat with its wake. I knew Kate and the Villa Galz had done it on purpose, which pissed me off. As they whizzed past, they gave us an all-tits-up Boob Flyby, flashing their breasts at me, their shirts over their faces so I couldn't tell who's who—all four of them had bras on. Kate drove the boat. She laughed, but then her mood went sour, frowning. She looked pissed off.

I turned around to Davide. When he stared at my cleavage in the sexy orange bra, I realized my buttons were half undone— "Fuck!"

"You want to fuck now, yes?" Davide said, excited.

"Nooo! Take me back home."

"*Oh, Madonna mia!*" he moaned in frustration.

CHAPTER 14
Breaking Rules

I wanted to walk on water to be with you.
Instead, I drowned in a puddle of absurdity.

—G. A. McKenna, journal entry

"Let me drive, okay?" I took hold of the boat's steering wheel like *el capitano*. Davide was lucky he had untied the boat because I gunned it backwards, cranked the wheel, and the boat spun effortlessly out from the island's dock, like a wheelie on water.

"Another Canadian trick?" David said, amazed. He excused himself and went below to the cabin.

Discreetly searching for Kate's speedboat, I piloted up the lake. With the wind in my hair, I felt free, unencumbered, and sexy, feeling as if I could do anything, and go anywhere. I had become me again, but more. I had become undone, experiencing a definite shift, because now I knew I wanted Kate. Just the thought made me wet. My already stimulated body ached for orgasmic release. I wanted Kate to touch me, not this suave gigolo.

Davide came back topside with two shot glasses and a bottle of bourbon. He stood beside me, gawking. Was he wondering where my newfound power had come from? Doubtful.

I grabbed a shot glass of bourbon. "Down the hatch!" I rejoiced, quaffing the shot.

He purred into my ear, "You are most amazing woman, Gerri McKenna. I still want you."

"Seriously? Sorry, Davide. It'll never happen, not now." I wanted Kate, period. "Let's skedaddle."

"What is skedaddle?" Davide asked, boyishly.

We tied up at the villa's dock in Argegno and consumed more bourbon while we talked about how he knew Rosie. I was surprised to discover Rosie's Devon neighbors, Marcella and her husband "Mister Eaton," had invited Rosie and her husband, Bill, to visit the villa, and that's where Davide had met her. Apparently, they'd hit it off immediately.

By the time I was ready to leave the boat, half a bottle of American bourbon whiskey was drunk and so was I.

Davide had to help me step off the boat. "You feel good?"

"Never better," I said, staggering on the wobbly dock. "*Ciao!* Thanks for the ride. You're a sweet man."

Davide chaperoned me towards the villa, insisting on making sure I was all right. I shivered in the cool breeze, and he wrapped his jacket around my shoulders. Feeling woozy from the bourbon, which I never drink, I barely managed to traverse the cobblestone path leading uphill toward the church and the villa.

"Please, you'll see me again?"

"Of course I'll see you, but no more funny business. I'm interested in someone else."

"Impossible! Who interests you?"

"Good night, Davide. Time to go home. Thanks again."

I waved and hurried uphill, zigzagging, exhausted, and trying to digest the day's information, especially the confirmation that Carlo is Marcella's "secret" father. As I forged the hill, the sun went behind the mountains and the long day was coming to an end. The purple light made the pathway glow. My legs felt deadweight, I barely made it to the villa. I needed to see Kate, but I needed a ruse so the others wouldn't guess why.

I broke my own rule and knocked on the guests' kitchen door. Jamie, the birthday girl, opened the door. In the background, several guests made dinner while laughing and enjoying themselves. I heard Erin yell, "Where's your boyfriend, Professor?" Jamie shut the door halfway.

"Sorry to bother. I'm a bit embarrassed, but…Can I buy a

bottle of wine?"

"What happened to you?" Jamie raised her eyebrows, alarmed.

Her wide eyes scanned me up and down. I shrugged, but realized my hair was disheveled, my white capri pants were stained, my neck had red stress blotches, and my nose felt burnt.

"Uh...come in."

"No, no, I don't want to disturb. Need wine. Maybe Kate can bring it for me."

Jamie went into the kitchen while I waited outside leaning against the door jamb. I heard Jamie elate, "It's for you." After a few whispers, Kate appeared and came outside bringing a bottle of Chianti.

Kate's eyes widened at my appearance, "Are you all right?" and she touched my cheek.

"Yup, fine. Just want a bottle of wine, pay you later."

"Haven't you had enough to drink?" Kate smiled, likely smelling the bourbon.

"Would you believe I hardly ever drink? Honest. Can we talk please?"

Kate came outside, "You're mad at me, for the boat thing. Just a bit of fun." She followed me as I stumbled on the rocky path. "You haven't forgotten about tomorrow?" Kate said in a soft voice. "The Cooking Class. Tomorrow. You said ten o'clock sharp."

"Oh, shit! Thanks for the reminder."

I bumped into Kate, losing my balance. She caught me.

"Are you upset that I went boating with Davide Vacchini?"

"You're free to do what you want."

"Smart answer. Without answering." I stared at her lips, her soft, sweet lips, wanting to kiss them. But I quickly pulled back, saying, "Hey, you're not even a little jealous? You can go now."

I turned and bumped into a wall trellis.

Kate knew I was in trouble. She followed behind me, and when I stumbled, she caught me. She put her arm around my waist, holding me close.

"I like you," I said, then hiccupped.

Her closeness felt good, with her strong arms around me. We reached my entrance. I couldn't find the keys in my pockets. Kate leaned me against the door and had to reach into my pockets and fiddle about to search for keys.

"Thanks for worrying about me. I'm fine. Honest."

"Yeah, right. You can barely stand." Her one hand held me against the door.

"Where's my wine?"

"On the doorstep. Better not open it. Cooking class tomorrow, remember?"

"Right. Don't give it to me. I didn't really want it. I just wanted to see you."

I leaned into her as she searched my body for the keys. I kissed her cheek close to the crease of her lips.

"No, no, stop that," Kate said, "I don't take advantage of intoxicated women, as much as I'd like to oblige you, because you are very intoxicating."

"Good for you." I tried to keep standing. "You like me."

Kate chuckled. Luckily, before I made an utter fool of myself, she found the keys in my small purse that had shifted around to my back. Kate opened the door, and I fell into my kitchen, literally. Goldie and Pucci rushed past me, jumping over me, heading out for a pee.

"Poor dears, they've been inside for hours." Hiccup. "Since Isabella left."

Kate helped me off the floor, and I leaned up against her, my arm around her shoulders.

"Sweet of you to care. But I'm okay. Nope, maybe not. Gotta throw up." My head spinning, I kicked my shoes off, threw my purse on the floor, and staggered around in a circle. "Where's the toilet?"

Kate steered me in the right direction, "I'll make coffee."

"No, go. Please," I said, kicking the washroom door shut, before puking.

Kate was gone by the time I came out of the bathroom. I felt better, but also pretty embarrassed at having her see me so inebriated. Slowly coming back to sanity, I fed the dogs and left the door open. After pouring a big glass of water, I grabbed my tablet and mobile, and toddled outside to what had become my favorite spot. The dogs followed me, not letting me out of their sight. We sat near the overhanging bougainvillea and wisteria, watching the sunset's afterglow. I had privately named it the winter garden because I could see the lake and the tips of the snowy Alps.

I turned my tablet on, intending to continue my cooking class supply list, but couldn't concentrate. Then I heard a ringing sound on my tablet. Amazed at the strength of the villa's Wi-Fi, I clicked the video call button and saw Rosie's face on screen. She sat at her home desk in Devon, England.

"I'm glad to see you, actually, really glad," I cried, my words slurred.

Rosie's face came closer to fill my monitor, "You're upset. What's happened? Why is your face dirty?"

"Upset? Me? Nah. Except…I almost had sex with an Italian walking groin, your dishy friend Davide tried his best to 'look after me' like you said. And I've been kissing a lesbian. On the mouth. My nose is burnt to a crisp. And I want outta here!"

"Sounds like you're fitting in perfectly."

Someone turned up the music in the villa's kitchen; the guests must be getting an earful. They closed their kitchen window with a bang. I felt sorry for Kate if she overheard me.

"The thing is—" Rosie started to say.

"No, stop it. I want to go home."

"Not yet, Gerri. You can handle it. You're a big strong woman, my brave friend. Hang in there a little longer."

Incredulous, I pushed my face toward the screen, "You're kidding, right? What are you not telling me?"

Rosie's face turned sad, her teary eyes and raised eyebrows told me something else was going on. She said, "I'd never put you in harm's way, at least, not on purpose. I love you dearly. Now, stop whining and get some balls! Better still, grow a pair of tough labia!" Her call ended abruptly.

I felt dumbfounded. I wanted to fly to her in England, to wrap my arms around my very best friend. I dialed Rosie on Paul's phone, but no answer. Three messages flashed in: two from my daughter and one from the Freighter Girl. I texted my daughter and then gulped down the entire glass of water. Tomorrow was another day. What else could happen?

CHAPTER 15
To Market We Go

My eyes are too wide open to see clearly.
Let me see myself through the eyes of others.
Especially her eyes.

—G. A. McKenna, journal entry

The alarm clock blasted me awake at 8:00 a.m. I found myself all scrunched up on the small couch, a whirring helicopter inside my head, my mouth as dry as the desert, I lurched over to the kitchen counter to shut off the clock.

"Geez. Why did I set the alarm? Oh, yes! The class. At ten o'clock. I gotta hussle."

After letting the dogs out for a pee, I stood at the kitchen counter and noticed the Bodum coffee maker was all ready to go. Kate must have done it while I was in the bathroom. "Bless you, Kate. So kind of you." I added another scoop of ground coffee to make it extra strong and turned it on. "Oh, my aching head."

As I popped a headache pill, Goldie and Pucci ran back in and nuzzled up to me. Hungry, no doubt. I fixed their favorite breakfast and headed for the shower.

Mindlessly putting on a bit of makeup and getting dressed, I tried to drink my brewed coffee but my hand shook the cup.

"There's nothing to be nervous about, Gerri," I told myself. "You've taught a thousand cooking classes. Just ignore her being there." Taking a few deep breaths, I drank the coffee with a steady hand, then looked down and realized I had changed into all black clothes again.

Running up to the loft, I threw off my clothes and dove into a lightweight knee-length flared skirt, a loose silk-blend shirt, and my comfy sandals. Minutes later, I was back downstairs, pacing around the room, waiting.

Ten o'clock sharp the villa guests arrived, milling around outside my front door. I did up my top two buttons, bit down on the bullet, and strode outside in full Professor McKenna persona, pretending that last night never happened.

"Ciao, ladies!" I exclaimed, noticing Kate's face lit up when she saw me. "Are we ready for market day? Hope you don't mind the term 'ladies,' I say it with utmost respect." I counted them. One was missing. "Where's Bibi?"

Wearing a summer dress, her big cleavage and tummy bouncing, Bibi ran up to us. "I'm late but I'm worth it," she proclaimed. Luciana kissed her lovingly on the cheek.

"And so, it begins, the nine-course meal. The *Aperitivo*, *Antipasto*, *Primo*, *Secondo*, *Contorno*, *Dolce*, *Frutta*, then on to the *Digestivo* and *Caffé*. I hope you have good appetites like the Italians."

The van fit four Galz comfortably, plus me, the driver. The rest of them, including Kate, either walked down the cobblestone Roman pathway or drove rented electric Vespa scooters to the village. As everyone sorted out their transportation choices, I slipped over to Kate. She wore a pair of light stretchy blue jeans and a summer top, the wide scoop neck lingered off one shoulder.

"Kate, ah, thanks for last night. And for the coffee this morning. Kind of you."

"No worries." Kate winked with a smile—I drowned in her eyes—and she sauntered over to the other walkers, pausing to help Bibi get on the back of her girlfriend's scooter.

"Okay, everyone! Let's meet in the *piazza* near the fountain," I yelled.

"I'm a lousy cook," I overheard Erin grumble.

"Not to worry. I believe Julia Child once said, I was thirty-two when I started cooking; up until then, I just ate." Everyone laughed.

Giving the walkers a head start, I made sure Goldie and Pucci had one more run-around before we left. After the five-minute drive into town, I parked the van a block away and we walked to the *mercato*, the outdoor market, where we met the others. My research had revealed that once every two weeks both the *piazza* and promenade were lined with market stalls. Bright canopies and large patio umbrellas kept the seller's wares in the shade: locally grown fruits and vegetables, locally-caught lake fish kept in crushed ice, local honey, plus spices, herbs, truffles, and lots of La Cantante's bottled olive oil.

We waited by the fountain for the others to arrive. Carlo Vacchini had a bread cart outside his shop, and there were other carts around the fountain and down the street. Even the Limoncello boy sold his golden happy juice from his cart. I noticed the bench beside him had no white chalk mark, I assumed it had been someone's secret signal for something, no doubt a secret meet-up. On the other side, along the lakeside promenade, there were antiques, used furniture, and everything from kitchenware to nuts 'n' bolts. A smattering of tourists arrived by ferry and swarmed around the stalls of clothing and leather goods, snapping up the T-shirts and handmade purses.

The other Galz joined us, and we came together to form a rather large, conspicuous group of women. After all, large tour groups never came to Argegno. Lia's friend had declared the town kaput; nothing to do in Argegno, why would people want to visit? No museums, no historical architecture, no hot spots to dine or dance, not even a supermarket. No celebrities came, either. All they needed was one George Clooney and voila!

Well, Argegno did have a celebrity of sorts—a murdered opera singer—and tourists love a good scandal. Why haven't the villagers ever capitalized on the story of La Cantante? Angelina Ferrario doesn't even have a commemorative plaque like Mussolini and his mistress, murdered a few towns away in Mezzagra. Thousands of tourists flock there annually to see the spot, and the town benefits financially. However, even if it would save their town, the villagers of Argegno devotedly downplayed La Cantante's murder story.

Shop owners and locals came out to watch my group of stylishly dressed women. Curious, excited villagers followed our every move as we headed for the vegetable carts first.

As I passed each stall I pointed at an item and asked how much,

"*Quanto costa, per favore*?" I also explained to my group, "Never touch the vegetables or squeeze them like we do in North America, unless you want an irate Italian yelling at you."

Bibi carefully placed a ripe tomato back onto the cart and smiled at the frowning vendor, as did Jamie and Hannah who abruptly finished playing crossed swords with a large scallion and a long white asparagus, respectively.

"Tracy, why don't you count out the Euros and pay for us?" Then I spoke to the whole group, "Most Italians are very polite. Remember to say please in Italian, *Per favore*—Pear-fa-VO-ray," I repeated the pronunciation so they could hear this important word. Then I did the same with thank you—*grazie*, and hello—*Ciao,* and goodbye—*Ciao* or *Arrivaderci.* All of this was straight out of the guidebook; the chapter on the rules of buying food at a market.

Off to a great start, we filled our shopping bags with seasonal fresh vegetables and herbs. A middle-aged woman, possibly a widow because she wore a black dress, black stockings, and black shoes, sold us homemade flat tortellini squares from her daughter's stall, and also buckwheat flour squares for Dana, who was gluten-intolerant.

A row of widows sat on a bench, black ravens alongside a row of elderly men. I looked for my toothless *vedova*, but of course her regular bench is in Varenna. Why don't widowed men wear all black?

As we approached the *Macelleria* or butcher shop, the fat-bellied butcher in his bloodied white apron, lounging out front, noticed us and scrambled to his feet.

"Quick! They shop here."

When we entered the shop the butcher barked, "Tommaso, clean the cutter!" and a bored-looking teenager with purple streaks in his hair slouched into action. I wondered if he used the same hair dye as Lia, the Gelato Girl.

"*Buongiorno, come stai*?" I asked.

"*Bene, grazie.* My name Diego, famous butcher of *Lago di Como.* How can I help today?" he replied with a wide moustached grin, ready to help me spend my money.

An old man with a white beard shuffled out of the back room, frantically waving a bloody cut on his finger. "*Cheh-sh-ch!*" he yelled in a Polish dialect. Diego was torn about what to do, but followed the old man, saying, "So sorry. My daughter will help you."

I looked around for his daughter, but Tommaso the butcher's "son" stepped forward.

"Hey hi."

The young boy—or on closer inspection he was a *she*, or rather, in our modern vernacular, *they* were nonbinary, androgynous, and cute—was late teens, with a short, swooped-over haircut. Tommaso kept watching the Villa Galz while running around filling my order and kept staring at Erin and Luciana. With downcast eyes, Tommaso managed a few quick nods at them.

I ordered enough free-range chicken breasts for all but the vegetarians and taught my attentive Galz how to order by weight using kilograms, not American pounds. I wanted to impress them with my Italian but, feeling nervous, I spoke very simple English, except for the polite greetings and food names.

"I need volunteers to go to the deli, the *Salumeria*, for cured deli meats, some prosciutto, salami, and mortadella. Anyone?" Wanda and Brittany volunteered. "Ask for two hundred grams each for the *antipasto* course. Should be enough," I specified. "Keep the receipts." Three curious locals followed them across the street to the delicatessen. By then I also had an entourage of locals clustered behind me.

We passed Rocco's cafe and I waved to Lia, the Gelato Girl, who waved back. Next door at Carlo's bakery, I peeked inside, wanting to introduce my guests. I heard an angry male voice coming from a stairwell past the bread counter; I assumed Carlo's apartment was upstairs. I heard Carlo's voice arguing with another man in loud, fast Italian and decided not to bother him. Grabbing four *pagnotte*—longer loaves of bread, and some *focaccia*—flat bread from the basket, we left the Euros on the cart.

Outside, while we shopped at the truffle and spice stalls, Vincenzo Lazzaro exited Carlo's bakery, his face flushed red from the argument. He yelled back to Carlo, "And keep him away!" Vincenzo and his bodyguard jumped into his limo, parked at the edge of the square, and drove away.

A moment later, Carlo appeared in the doorway. He found the

money on his cart and scanned the crowd, perhaps looking for who left it. I hid behind Erin, the tallest lesbian in the group.

Across from Carlo's shop, his estranged wife, the white-haired flower-cart lady, yelled over at Carlo, "What are you up to, old man?" My thought exactly. What was going on?

"If you never see me again, know that I love you," Carlo said to her in dramatic Italian fashion. He blew her a kiss, which she rejected with a wave of her hand.

Alex and Isabella exited the stairway that led upstairs above the bakery. She kissed him and skipped away into the crowd like a schoolgirl. Alex noticed me and watched us, particularly me.

Feeling somewhat extravagant, I splurged and bought an expensive truffle, then herded all my Villa Galz toward *La Formaggeria*—the cheese shop. Alex followed us.

I kept wondering, why would Vincenzo Lazzaro and Carlo be arguing? I got the feeling they argued about Carlo's son Davide, but why? "None of my business," I muttered, knowing that I keep being slowly drawn into their lives.

At the cheese shop, we watched as the owner, an old burly man, shouted: "Quick, back to work!" clapping his arthritic hands at his two young staff who lounged outside.

"*Grüß gott!*" he said to us, which I believe to be Austrian for good morning; not unusual as Austria lay on the northern border with Italy. It didn't sound like an Italian dialect, nor the traditional German *guten morgen*. His bleached-clean white apron matched his thinning white hair. I asked for a big square of parmigiano reggiano, ricotta, burrata, and fresh bocconcini balls, all with a hint of grassy or earthy aromas.

After my request, he struggled with a grand round of parmigiano, bringing it out from the back. His young employee hurried to help him. It seemed to be a familiar story in Argegno: elderly shop owners mentoring younger relatives or staff who worked in their shop. I admired this cultural tradition. I also mused that some of the shop owners were not originally Italian.

Kate and I kept touching at odd moments. In the crowded market street, we walked alongside one another, unintentionally touching or knocking into one another. Handing over the wrapped parmesan cheese, my hand touched Kate's as she stuffed it into a cloth shopping bag. Reaching for the ricotta cheese, our bare arms touched; when she reached for the tomatoes, her breasts brushed past me; walking through the throngs of villagers in the crowded street market, our hips bumped together. At one point, Kate put her hand on my shoulder and leaned in. Of course, the sexual tension excited me, and Kate must have felt it, too.

Finally, she placed her hand on the small of my back, and said, "Good to see you smiling."

"Ha! Yeah, um, good." Blushing, I dropped the bag of cheese and bent down to retrieve it.

Taking a few minutes for myself, I stepped back to admire Kate as she roamed the stalls. A thought dawned on me. Had I entered the phase of life that Margaret Mead called "post-menopausal zest"? Apparently, after years of hormonal changes through perimenopause, or men-on-pause as I like to say, a woman's sexual passion can explode wide awake! I remembered reading about a middle-aged nun who, after ten years of being in a nunnery, went for a therapeutic massage and was so aroused she left the nunnery to explore her libido.

I felt like that nun. For years, my libido went out the window, my marriage being a sporadic no-sex-zone. I'd given up any hope of awakening my sexual passions. And just like that nun's masseuse, Kate had ignited my paused erotic libido. I found myself wanting her now, right in the middle of the market. A part of me was delighted and whispered, "Oh, let go, Gerri. Enjoy these lustful feelings. Why suppress them?"

"What?" Dana asked me. "Did you say something?"

"Uh, nothing."

I regained my focus and said to everyone, "Now, you will see, the first course in an Italian dinner is the *Aperitivo*. A pre-meal drink meant to stimulate the appetite and open the palate. My preference is Prosecco, a sparkling white wine, with a dash of Aperol."

I pointed at Dana and Kate, who happened to be standing next to me. "Can you two go to the wine store? Wait!" I had noticed Vera's head bob down and kicked myself for not sending her with Dana. Vera obviously had a crush on her. "And Vera, help them out, please." She lit up, smiling.

"Kate, please buy enough white wine for all of us. A few reds, plus four bottles of Prosecco. Thanks. Uh, Jamie, can you and

Hannah help them carry? Bibi and Luciana, please take all the shopping bags to the van—Do you mind?"

Kate stopped to hold the door open for Vera and Dana, Jamie and Hannah, Bibi and Luciana as they all filed out. Then Kate stopped and leaned toward me to whisper, "You're doing a superlative job, Professor."

I felt butterflies in my stomach but disguised them with a curt Miss McKenna smile. "Am I forgetting anything?" I looked down at my list.

Kate leaned over my shoulder as if to look at it, too, but whispered, "You look cute in your teacher's eyeglasses." And then she followed the others out and I continued scanning my list.

"Mozzarella!" I yelled to the shopkeeper who jumped. "Oh dear, what would an Italian meal be without mozzarella? For the *Antipasto* course, of course."

To the remaining Galz—Renee and Tracy, CJ and Erin—I said, "The *Antipasto* is after the *Apertivo*. It's usually cold meats, hams or even salmon, a variety of cheeses placed open-faced on panini or *bruschetta*."

While getting the mozzarella, the cheese shop owner and staff listened in, as did a few curious local women who had followed us inside the shop to gawk. Their interest had to be motivated by my large group of Galz, or by my being the villa's *vedova*. Odd, but I hoped they enjoyed my lesson.

I pointed at Renee and Tracy, "I forgot to ask Wanda and Brittany to get some Sicilian olives, some small crisps, nuts, and perhaps sauce dips at the deli. All good for the *Apertivo*, nibbles with the wine. Off you go. Keep all the receipts for later. Thanks. I'll meet you at the van. Have fun and practice your Italian, say *per favore* and *grazie*."

"I'm useless with languages," Renee admitted. Tracy kept repeating the deli list as they left.

Once outside, my cooking class got separated. Erin and CJ went to the tourist stands along the promenade to peruse the leather goods, and Bibi skipped over to the *gelateria* for an ice cream. I had lost them.

Realizing this is going to be harder than I thought, I yelled to anyone who might still be able to hear me, "Be back at the van in ten minutes!" Worried the hot sun might ruin the food, I headed for the van parked up the street and put my shopping bags inside. Wanting to get out of the sun, I stood along the street's storefronts, waiting under a trattoria umbrella in front of the hotel *Albergo Argegno*. Along the street off the main piazza was a row of business fronts near the hotel. I spotted Alex standing in a shaded doorway.

A few locals stood in the sunshine outside their respective office storefronts, partaking of their morning espresso together. The conversation seemed serious. As I drew nearer, I overheard them mention *the Americano*.

An exceedingly fit, platinum blonde beautician, with thin tattooed eyebrows, slouched in front of the hair salon and stated, "I heard the Americano's badly beaten."

"He deserved it. That girl is too young to have sex. Her father probably beat him," said Dr. Sergio Valente, the late-thirties dentist in a white smock and denim jeans who stood in front of his dental office.

A young girl? It might have been the same young girl I'd seen Shaun with at the entrance to the olive grove.

"A client told me the girl didn't have sex with him," the beautician corrected what everyone might be thinking.

I recognized Johan the pharmacist in his white smock who cupped his ear and asked her, "Eh? Do you mean the boy Shaun who works for Vincenzo?"

My ears perked up, too.

In the law office doorway, stood a lawyer in a tailored suit with his tie undone. "Yes, he does odd jobs for Lazzaro, so what?" the lawyer asked.

"I'll bet his beating had nothing to do with the girl. It's that Vincenzo," Johan said.

I felt badly for Shaun and the young girl because I know the ways of young people, and because I also knew there had to be more to the story. But why would Vincenzo be involved? Rumors and gossip can quickly get out of control in a small town. And yet, in every rumor there is always a kernel of truth.

An elegantly dressed woman exited the hotel connected to the *Ristorante Barchetta* and listened in. She also watched me. Her auburn streaks in an otherwise brunette short-cropped hairstyle looked striking.

She announced to the others, "It's not about the girl. Shaun crossed Vincenzo by tempting his wife. That's why Vinnie had him beaten. I'll bet you a season's paycheck."

And so cometh the truth behind the rumor.

This hotel woman strode over in her exquisite high heels to the dentist next door. They exchanged a few whispered words and eyed me. She gave him a quick smooch and within thirty seconds of turning on her high heel she was in my face.

"*Buongiorno, signora. Quanto costa?*"

"*Pardoni?* How much for what?" At first, I thought she wanted me to buy something at her restaurant because I stood underneath one of her hotel's umbrellas. She sputtered Italian off her tongue, too fast for me. "Ah-ah…?" I stuttered, glancing around for help. I spotted Alex lurking around. He knew I saw him.

"Alex Pandev," I yelled at him.

Two teenage boys roared past on loud Piaggio scooters, weaving in and out of the crowd, so he pretended not to hear me.

"Alex, come here, please."

Alex sauntered over with a Fonzie swagger which hid his embarrassment, his large cowboy boots clomping along. "*Buongiorno*, sweet Miss Gerri," he cooed.

"Yes, *buongiorno*, now please listen-up. What does this woman want? Can you translate for me?" I asked him, grabbing his arm to pull him closer, my hangover making me too fuzzy to translate. He nodded like a frightened student and the Italian flew around, their hands waving in the air at one another.

After a few moments, Alex explained to me, "Signora Sofia Valente, the hotel owner you see here," he pointed, "asks if you are a famous Canadian chef?" He pulled out his mobile phone and showed me his Google search: a photo of me receiving the Order of Canada for my Culinary Arts curriculum. "You do cooking class? To teach, here in her hotel, Signora Valente wishes to know how much. She say, your cooking class will bring tourists, will help the town. How much you charge?" Alex looked proud of himself, grinning from ear to ear showing those two rotten front teeth.

"Is she serious?"

Alex nodded several times in succession, and Sofia the hotel lady followed suit.

Sophia said, "Need to know before the Strawberry Moon Festival, to set up. *Tutto a posto?*—Is all in order?"

"What's she talking about?"

Alex said, "The festival celebrates the June-bearing strawberry harvest. We celebrate on the full moon. Hundreds of people will visit Argegno for this festival."

"Ah, yes, the festival. Um. Is the dentist her husband?" I asked Alex, who stared back at me, surprised.

"What's a-what she say?" Sofia Valente asked Alex.

He nodded at me, "Here, her husband Dr. Sergio Valente, the dentist." Both of them scrutinized me. The lady's eyebrows rose as high as her short bangs. "Her parents, you not know, were famous journalists in Austria."

"Fascinating. So, Alex, here's the deal," I said. "Alex, pay attention, please. Translate to her. Signora Valente, I have three requests." He translated correctly, I hoped. "First, she'll need to take care of advertising the cooking class. And, if she wants, she can charge for the class. But she must advertise it. Second, she provides all kitchen and cooking supplies." Alex translated to her, and Sofia Valente nodded consent.

"And three?" they both asked, in English and Italian.

"Third, I will do the cooking class and keep any tip money, but for my fee, her husband fixes your teeth for free. Got it?"

"*Che?* No! I too afraid of dentist."

"Tell her," I insisted.

Alex balked for another moment but then relayed my terms in Italian. The lady cocked her head, but then smiled. "Is deal!" Sofia took hold of my hand and shook it. She proceeded to grab Alex by the ear and pull him into her husband's dental office. After a loud Italian exchange between them, I saw through the front window that Sofia pushed Alex into the dentist chair, ordering her husband to fix his teeth or else. I was pleased as punch, except now I had to do another cooking class. Actually, I felt pleased to be able to offer something that would help bring tourists to the town.

I turned to head toward the van and ran into Carmela Lazzaro. Up close or afar, Mrs. Lazzaro was a striking beauty. She had her unibrow daughters in tow; all three dressed identically, even the older one who probably hated dressing like her younger sisters.

They waited at the curb. The youngest one was unruly, tired, and whining for ice cream from a vendor's cart.

To get to the van, I had to walk past her, even though I looked for an alternate route. As I passed by the youngest girl yanked and broke loose from her mother's grip and fell off the curb into the road. Two Piaggio scooters roared toward her, their teenaged riders laughing, inattentive. It happened so fast. I jumped to grab the girl out of the way, yanking her arm and pulling her towards me. The motorbikes swerved and skidded around us without caring to stop.

"*Mia bambina!*" Carmela wrapped her arms around her frightened little girl and deposited her on the sidewalk. Then Carmela threw her arms around me in a big-breasted bear hug, spouting off so much Italian I got dizzy, or was it from the tightness of her grip? A crowd gathered to watch.

"*Dio mio*, I owe you my life!" she cried, pulling back to see me. "It's you! The one with the—"

"The dead bra. Yep, it's me."

"I remember, at the train station. I am in gratitude, thank you, thank you," she kept repeating in a thick Italian accent, grabbing my hands. "What is your name please? I must know."

"Okay-yup," I wiggled away. "It's Gerri McKenna."

Carmela gasped for air, her eyes as wide as two brown truffles. "No-no, please, you are not the old widow McKenna from Canada with a dead bra? You are not old. You are young and beautiful." She shook her head and blinked rapidly, then seemed to recover. "I am forever in your debt," she proclaimed, kissing both my cheeks. She spun around and announced publicly to anyone listening, "Forever, I am in her debt." A few locals nodded.

Carmela Lazzaro backed away, taking a good look. Her little girl tugged her sleeve, still wanting ice cream, but Carmela continued to stare at me, mouth agape.

I spotted my group heading toward the villa's van. "Take care," I called to Carmela, waving as I hurried away and met my group at the van. With all the food supplies, only three passengers could ride in the van; the rest of them either walked or rode double on the scooters. I drove past Carmela, her hands waving every which way as she ranted into her cell phone. Her words "the *old* widow McKenna" rang in my ears.

CHAPTER 16
Lust on the Menu

Find something you're passionate about.
If not, life is lost on endless distractions.
And learn to cook. Not only is it good for your soul,
it teaches you to be fearless of mistakes.

—G. A. McKenna, journal entry

I drove to the Villa della Cantante and we unloaded the market food from the van into the kitchen. Finally, I turned to face the incredible stove which became mine for the entire day.

The ILVE gas stove gleamed with sixty inches of pure perfection: five burners, a griddle, a rotisserie, and digital controls for European convection cooking at its finest. You could grill, bake, broil, wok, rotisserie, steam, defrost, you name it. Along with loving the shiny knobs and electronic components that resembled a Mercedes-Benz's dashboard, I had to stop myself from hugging it.

Shortly after preparing the kitchen's long table with my teaching tools, the rest of the Villa Galz arrived heated from the uphill walk, excited, and proclaiming their thirst as they gathered around me in the kitchen.

"First on the list, a quick lunch and the wine." They watched me as I prepared the First and Second Courses. "The *Apertivo*, in our case Prosecco, is served with the light nibbles Tracy and Renee bought from the deli: marinated olives, cracker crisps, with an artichoke and gorgonzola dip, no onions, along with a variety of nuts and, of course, Prosecco wine—to get you in a fun mood for the class, eh?"

"Eh? Eh?" a few of them made fun of my Canadian speech. We all laughed.

"Next, a little later, we'll have the *Antipasto* with the ingredients Wanda and Brittany bought: cold meat slices of prosciutto, salami, and mortadella, and the buffalo mozzarella and burrata cheeses on crostini and focaccia, topped with a sprinkle of olive oil and fresh basil." They all helped arrange it onto platters and watched me as I prepared the crostini using burrata cheese and marinated sun-dried tomato antipasto on the local *pagnotta* bread.

"Burrata is a special cheese from Puglia made from buffalo milk and means 'buttered' in Italian. When fresh, it is soft, creamy, and buttery."

With everyone happily chatting, we carried the prepared platters and the wine outdoors onto the terrace. A long table was already setup under the larger arbor over by the pool and gardens, as opposed to the smaller one over by my guesthouse where I'd found Kate drawing. The trelliswork flowed with wisteria and hanging grape vines, surrounded by potted magnolia trees. Everyone sat around the table, eating and enjoying themselves while I returned to the villa's kitchen to prepare for the class.

A few minutes later, on time to help me, Isabella arrived like a windstorm. "Did you hear? It's all over the lake! Shaun the *Americano* was beaten. He's in Como's hospital," she grimaced, washed her hands, shook them dry and stood with arms akimbo to face me.

"Later. There's lots of work to do. By the way, I saw you and Alex together at the bakery."

"*Sì*, I live above the bakery."

"Oh. Um. Where are the aprons?" I scrambled around looking everywhere, thankful to find the villa's dream kitchen fully stocked.

"*Dio mio!*" she yelled, "Gerri, the police, they think your Davide beat up Shaun."

That got my attention. Isabella crossed herself, then opened a drawer in the buffet and tossed me an apron.

"Isabella, he is not *my* Davide. He couldn't have done it. Yesterday he was with me on his boat. I heard Vincenzo was involved. Please hand me the chopping block."

I chose an exquisite knife from the rack—sharp, balanced, an excellent brand—and chopped the rosemary, thyme, parsley, and garlic cloves in a flash.

"Can you get the thirteen chicken breasts, in the fridge?" I asked, while Isabella continued in panic mode.

She opened the fridge door. "Thirteen? It's bad luck to seat thirteen at a table. Twelve is good, like *il Cenacolo,* what you call Da Vinci's *The Last Supper*. Thirteen is no good."

"All right, so kill someone off."

I halved the lemon and squeezed the juice into the bowl with the herbs, then added one cup of olive oil, "Now, some garlic and lemon juice to make the chicken marinade."

"Ah-no, Shaun and Davide, they argue. Terrible scene," Isabella proceeded to crush a red pepper. "Alex, he knows. Oh that Carmela, she is *stupida*," Isabella blurted out, then added the crushed red pepper to my pesto sauce.

"Hey, stop that!"

"My mother, she adds pepper to pesto. But how can you eat pesto anywhere but Genoa where pesto comes from? Genoa basil is the best in the world."

"Lovely, but I'm still making *pesto alla Genovese*. Hey, wait a minute, Shaun argued with Davide about Carmela? Why? Are Davide and Carmela, I mean, was Shaun stealing his thunder?— Hand me two baking dishes, please."

"What is 'stealing thunder'?"

"In other words, Shaun became too friendly with Carmela, Davide got jealous, they argued, and that's why the police think Davide beat Shaun."

"I know nothing. *Piccoli segreti*—The little secrets. I shut up now." She fixed her eyes on me, a panicked gaze. Then she rummaged around the kitchen and handed me two 9-by-13-inch nonreactive baking dishes.

"Okay, here's another guess. Vincenzo beat Shaun up because Carmela said he's the one she's having an affair with, and not Davide."

Unsure, Isabella nodded but also shrugged while I arranged the chicken in the dishes and poured on the marinade. "Maybe, but no-no." Glancing out the window, she ran to open the kitchen door.

"Okay, I've got it. It's a threesome!" I barked, just as Kate walked in.

"Yo! Sounds like fun. Is that on the menu?" Kate laughed. "The wine's all gone, so we're primed and ready."

The others followed Kate into the kitchen, ready to begin.

"We have a gift for you." Kate handed me a brown paper bag. "Sorry, no wrapping paper." I opened the bag and pulled out a tall white chef's hat. On the hat was an Italian flag stitched with the words, "Made in Italy." A hopeful sign, I chuckled. They all cheered for me to wear it.

"How sweet of everyone. *Meraviglioso!*—Wonderful. Thanks, all of you."

I tried to position the chef's hat on my head, but it flopped onto my face. Kate helped me, standing in close, putting the floppy bit to one side. I felt her heat, or perhaps my own heat radiated from inside. My knees felt weak. I was falling for her eyes, her smile, and the sound of her voice. I didn't dare look at her for long. I felt the others watching us. My cheeks and neck blushed.

Kate said, "There, all fixed," and she moved away. I wanted her closer. I showed off the hat, and they all applauded. It fit perfectly.

In preparing for the cooking class, I had all the supplies we needed laid out on the enormous kitchen table in order to create the four remaining courses of our Italian meal, having already done two courses. The villa's huge kitchen had plenty of room for everyone to participate in an interactive hands-on lesson. Pucci and Goldie stayed underfoot, happily running about, enjoying the excitement and company.

"Tortellini Lesson. We'll make tortellini from the pasta squares we bought at the widow's market stall and the ricotta cheese from the cheese shop."

Each woman stood at a station around the table. I advised Dana to keep her gluten-free buckwheat tortellini squares separate. At first, Kate stood next to me, but I couldn't concentrate. Whenever we brushed up against one another I felt a fiery flush from the top of my head down onto my chest. I had to move away from her. I walked around the table in my Miss McKenna persona and stationed myself at the head of the table.

Every so often I got caught in Kate's eyes, seduced by a clandestine gaze in that beautiful distance between us. I was falling for this woman. After years of feeling sexually dead in an expired marriage, something was being unleashed, or released; a private part of me long buried, that I had forgotten. Varenna's toothless *vedova* came to mind, and my heart surfaced. I was feeling reborn, joyous, and innocently wicked—Okay, Gerri, never mind, concentrate. Back to the business at hand.

Jokes flew around the table, and everyone laughed, except me. I had to remind myself to smile, to make it enjoyable and amusing, and fun.

"We're using one-and-a-half-inch pasta squares. In Italian homes they make the pasta from scratch."

"Not all homes," Isabella muttered. "We get lazy, too."

I placed a few squares next to Bibi's station. "What you do is put a small dollop of the ricotta cheese mixed with the chopped basil pesto filling in the middle of each pasta square. It's an easy recipe for you." I paused, waiting for them to catch up. "Fold the square in half, diagonally, with the edges not quite meeting." They watched me fold a few squares. Isabella tried to correct my fold, and I swatted her hand away. "Then, press down to seal the edges and pinch it shut, like this."

I glanced at Isabella who nodded with a smile.

"Bend it around a finger and press one corner over the other. It should resemble little peaked hats, like so." I held it up, perching it on the top of my finger.

"Uh, Gerri," Bibi said, "it looks like a little peaked clitoris," she noted with raised eyebrows. Each of them had to take a closer look, even Isabella.

They stared at me, waiting for my reaction.

I held up my tortellini, "Hmmm, you're right. No wonder Italians love to eat tortellini."

That deserved a toast of raised wine glasses. Isabella laughed her head off. I relaxed. I heard Kate snicker but didn't dare look at her. Of course, when you're forcing yourself not to look, what happens? You look. One brief glance and our eyes met. I felt my legs wobble from under me and a hot rush between my legs.

"Lust is definitely on the menu," Bibi murmured to her girlfriend Luciana.

I smiled, then said, "Carry on making the tortellini. It will be our *Primo* or First Course. This course is served cold or hot."

Tracy kissed Renee and said, "You're my hot Primo," her arm slipping around her girlfriend's waist. Sweet to see these two classy women adore each other.

"Ah..., okay. Where was I? The *Primo*. It's heavier than the *Antipasto,* usually pasta, lasagne, or soup. The French would have *crepes.*"

I made the mistake of peeking at Kate and a red flush emerged full-blown from my body, down my chest onto my breasts. My nipples felt so hard they could cut glass. Oh, please don't notice my erect nipples through the thin blue blouse. I unbuttoned my shirt a little, the heated flush unbearable, and pulled the apron up to cover my breasts.

On one side of Kate, Dana flirted with her, touching Kate's hands, squeezing the tortellini, brushing up against the side of her body, and whispering sexy remarks in her ear. Meanwhile, Vera glared at them, as did I.

My breathing became rapid. Sweat beaded on my upper chest and ran down my cleavage. I hoped no one noticed, though Tracy and Renee raised eyebrows at one another. Isabella brought me a glass of water, which I easily drank down in a few gulps.

"As Chef Anthony Bourdain said, good food is often simple food. Basic cooking skills ought to be a required skill as you grow up. Learning to feed yourself and your friends can be taught to everyone as a fundamental skill."

"Like your culinary arts course in school," Erin added.

"Yes, by the end of session all my students know how to prepare meals."

Erin handed her freshly-made tortellini to Isabella who walked around the table with a large bowl. Watching, I wondered what Isabella thought of all this? Does she even know about lesbians?

"Your students go on to become famous chefs," Erin said. "We googled you."

"You're a famous cook, McKenna," the athletic CJ shouted, pinching her tortellini shut and tossing it the length of the table into Isabella's large bowl. "A hole in one!"

"My students go on to train with famous chefs in restaurants. I'm just the teacher."

"Disgustingly self-effacing," Dana, the feminine beauty hissed. She touched Kate's arm, asking, "Are you finished with your little clits, dear?"

Kate snickered. I reminded myself, both women were single. With Dana's fit figure and long amber-blonde hair, Kate might be attracted to her. I needed to step away.

"I'll create two types of sauces for the tortellini. A tomato and cream sauce for those who are allergic to onions and garlic; and the fresh basil pesto with garlic, pine nuts, olive oil, and cheese. Now for the chicken. Isabella, please, if you don't mind."

Isabella acted fast; a good helper, she knew what I wanted. Erin went to the fridge with her to lend a hand, touching Isabella's shoulder. Did I imagine sexual overtones instead of legitimate kindness? I had to be careful not to make up a story.

"The next two courses are the *Secondo* and *Contorno*. The *Secondo* is the main dish with meat or seafood. Today we have chicken breasts to make a northern Italian-style chicken recipe. Don't worry, I've already deboned the chicken. I can explain how to do it using a boning knife and poultry scissors, cutting along the backbone, if anyone—"

"Nope!" Bibi went white as a ghost, "Too much Julia Child for me."

Isabella brought out the marinating chicken from the fridge.

"Who'd like to flip the chicken breasts in the baking dish?"

Luciana the cop, and Tracy the realtor, each grabbed tongs to turn the chicken in the dishes while I poured on more of the marinade I'd made yesterday, explaining all the ingredients. The aroma of this marinade even impressed me. I managed to splash some onto my loose silk-blend blouse, above my apron.

"*Fantastico!* Our chicken normally marinates for two to six hours in the refrigerator."

Isabella took the baking dishes and shoved them back into the fridge.

"As you can see, *Issy* my assistant is a great help," I said, realizing I had given her a nickname. Everyone cheered for her. Isabella, overcome, teared up and gave a little curtsy.

"Hang in there, girl, you're the bomb," Bibi said, giving her a quick hug.

"I'm a *bomb*? Big bomb boom!" She straightened her wig and waited for the next chore.

"Ha! You effin kill me, Issy," Erin laughed and high-fived her. Everyone, myself included, had grown quite fond of her.

"Issy, do you know how to start the barbeque?" I asked.

"No, too much danger, so sorry, not me," she said, backing away.

"I've got this. Come along, Issy," Erin said, tugging at Isabella's arm, but she wouldn't budge and shook her head. "It won't explode, I promise." Erin went out the door toward the pool area.

"Time for a wine break?" Jamie suggested.

"Right. Good idea. You had the *Aperitivo* and *Antipasto*, now we prepared the *Primo*, next the *Secondo*, and *Contorno*. Be back in, let's say, fifteen minutes?" I wiped perspiration from my forehead, removing my chef's hat.

The women ran outside into the heat of the day with full glasses of wine or a Peroni Nastro Azzurro beer. Kate seemed to hold back, edging toward the kitchen door behind Dana. Did she want Dana to leave, or was I making it up?

"Kate, do you have a moment?" I said, surprising myself.

"I'll meet you at the pool," Kate said to Dana.

"I won't keep you. Is today actually Jamie's birthday?"

Kate glided up to me. She lowered her eyes to my half-undone blouse, then raised her eyes to meet mine and said softly, "Yes" as if it meant more, much more.

"Good. Um. Is there a birthday cake?"

"Unfortunately, no cake." She grabbed a pre-moistened towelette and proceeded to wipe the marinade spill on my blouse. "You, ah, spilled some. Let me…"

The spill was above my left breast. One edge of Kate's mouth curled into a smile as her eyes lowered to the top of my lacy orange bra. I held still like a good girl. My breathing became heavy, the heat rising between us. She took charge, and I liked it. And that's when I slowly started going crazy.

"There, all done. Might leave a stain though."

"Thanks." I cleared my throat as a subterfuge, noticing Isabella trying to be invisible at the counter.

Then Kate left for outside. I felt faint, wondering, does she know I want her? I knew she felt the heat between us. Shit. I slumped into the nearest chair.

Isabella poured some wine and held it out to me. "You need this?" she smiled.

I shook my head, "I'd better not. Um, everything all right?"

"A-okay. It's fun. I like," she snorted, gulping the wine then pulling out her cigarettes, ready to go outside for a smoke.

"You still smoke?"

Isabella frowned, "I know I must quit. Okey-doke, I will quit. Tomorrow." She smiled and went outside to light her cigarette.

I shut my eyes for what seemed a lifetime, but then my eyes had already been shut for a lifetime. The sounds of distant laughter and splashes in the pool brought me back. The air shifted. I felt my chest pumping air, heard the sound. Felt the kundalini serpent energy rise up my spine, wanting an outlet. I opened my eyes. "Okay, enough!" I declared and scooted outside with the dogs. I needed fresh air.

I hurried to my special spot overlooking the lake. Goldie brought me a ball, all wet and gooey, I threw it as far as I could and off he went to retrieve it, Pucci barking along after him. Feeling the sunshine on my face, I was beginning to feel better. About ten minutes later, I joined everyone as they strolled back into the villa's kitchen, mostly to open more wine and beer, and then we all stood around the table.

"Next comes the *Contorno* served with the *Secondo* as a side plate. It's vegetables, whatever's in season, either raw or cooked. The farmers had an early eggplant crop, plus hothouse carrots, and a special treat, truffles, but they might be from last harvest time. There you have it. Oh, does anyone want a side salad?" A few raised hands. "Issy, can you check to see how Erin is doing at the barbeque? Who wants to help prepare the veggies?"

"Yes please. I'm a takeout queen, need to learn," Vera said.

"We'll help," Jamie and Hannah also volunteered.

"The rest of you can either watch me create two tortellini sauces or go play. Up to you." Then I asked with trepidation, "Is everything all right so far?"

"Totally Gucci!" Bibi said.

"Are you kidding? You're great," CJ said.

"Lovin' it!" Renee concurred, and they all agreed, some of them giving me quick hugs. I was surprised and touched. I'd been worried and kept forgetting to have fun. After all, they were paying for this themselves, unlike my school students.

Jamie said, "Gerri, we're going to Milan tomorrow to see Leonardo's *The Last Supper*. We have an extra ticket. We'd love it if you came with us!"

"Really?" I glanced at Kate, realizing it must be her ex-girlfriend's ticket. "I might, yes, thank you."

About fifteen minutes later, all the veggies and a fresh *Insalata* had been prepared. Isabella had prepared the fresh pesto while I made the other tortellini sauce: Italian tomatoes, finely chopped carrot and celery, pureed and simmered in a pan with herbs and butter. I would have added yellow onions, but Jamie was allergic to onions, so I used a pinch of garlic instead, then added a half cup of heavy cream as no one was lactose intolerant, thank goodness, and salt to taste. Delicious, even without onions.

We carried the trays of marinated chicken out to the barbeque. The "Alpes Inox" barbeque had a freestanding stainless steel, multifunctional five-burner gas cooktop on wheels, complete with sink and drawers. Amazing design.

I had asked Erin to preheat three bricks for about twenty minutes. Everyone watched as we placed the chicken, skin side down, on the grill and placed the three bricks on top of the chicken to cover and flatten the breasts.

"This northern Italian-style chicken dish is popular throughout Lombardy. Erin will cook them, I hope." She nodded, listening intently. "Cook until the skin is grilled, about twenty minutes. Then remove the bricks and turn the chicken over and cook for another fifteen minutes. Thanks. You deserve the chef's hat."

"Honey, you're the chef; I'm just an old barbie," Erin grinned, tongs in hand.

"All right, thirty-minutes until dinner," I announced. I turned around only to see Bibi whipping off her clothes, "Oh, my!" and jumping into the pool.

I hid my gaze but then heard two honks from a car pulling into the driveway and went to investigate. To my surprise, Davide Vacchini arrived and leapt out of a baby-blue Maserati convertible.

"*Buonasera, signora!*" A bouquet of pink roses came forth with a flourish.

"No, you can't be here!" I tried to keep him hidden behind a bush, not wanting Kate to see him.

"I want to apologize for yesterday, to see if you are all right, *cara mia*. Are you all right?" he moved closer to me, kissed my cheeks three times. I felt his beard stubble on my skin. I moved away from him to dodge the unwanted attention.

"I'm fine. Thanks for the flowers."

Speechless, he paced back and forth.

"What's wrong?" I asked.

He sputtered, "The police think I beat up Shaun, the American."

"You were with me. It's not your fault what happened to Shaun, unless.... Are you hiding something?" I nudged him toward his car, not wanting the guests to hear.

"This morning Vincenzo threatened my father. He thinks I have an affair with Carmela."

"What a surprise," I smirked. "Are you?"

He took hold of my hand, "Come with me to the village, everyone will see I am with *you*, not her." I stepped back. "Gerri, if we pretend to make-out in public, everyone will see I want you, not Carmela."

"You're kidding, right? You'd use me so Vincenzo won't send his bodyguard to beat you up, huh?"

I saw Kate and Dana, and then the two doctors saunter around the corner from the pool. They carried empty wine bottles, tidying up by taking them to the kitchen. Shit!

"Love is what I need, everything else is a want," Davide cooed. I hoped no one overheard him.

"Where do you get this crap, old Marcello Mastroianni movies?" I pulled Davide to his blue Maserati and gave him a quick peck on the cheek. "Now, go."

"I need you for a quick ride?"

"Sorry, no quickies."

"To talk."

I glanced back at Kate with her hands full as she slowed her gait to watch us. Then I heard cat-whistles from the others. Dammit! I stepped away from Davide and opened his car door, telling him, "I'm busy teaching a cooking class. Go."

"I heard you are a great chef. Tomorrow, come to me. We need to talk."

"About what? Can't. I'm ah, what am I doing? I'm going to Milan, to *The Last Supper*."

"*Oh, Madonna mia*! I must see you."

"Off with you." Wouldn't you know it, the meaner I treated him the more he wanted me. Or did he just want to talk to me? He tried to kiss me goodbye on my cheeks. I knew the girls watched us. He finally drove off in his Maserati GranTurismo convertible, honking and waving to everyone who came to watch. Shit!

"Whoo-hoo, Miss McKenna, a Maserati Man!" More cat-whistles and innuendos, except from Kate. She looked unimpressed and a little sad.

"I'm not interested!" I yelled loud enough for Kate to hear me.

I hid in my guest suite to cool down. A few moments alone before a loud knock at my door. "Now what?" Hot under the collar, with my erect nipples sore from rubbing against my stained blouse, I threw off the apron and answered the door rather like a mad bull: "YES!"

Isabella stepped back, "Ah, my heart she jumped."

"Issy, I'm sorry. What's up?"

"The chicken, she's ready."

"Good, good." She handed me an envelope. "What's this?"

"From the girls in the cooking class, for you. And a big tip."

I opened it and saw several large bills, way more than forty euros per person. "Way too generous of them. We'll divvy up later. Keep it safe." I shoved the envelope deep into her apron pocket for safekeeping.

As we hurried around the villa's corner toward the pool and barbeque area, Isabella spoke to me in a hushed tone, "She said, 'she'll break you.' She say that."

"What? Who said?"

"Signorina Dana says you will break Signorina Kate's heart. And Kate, she say, 'it's not going to happen between you and me,' meaning Dana and her. Is good, no?"

I stopped us in our tracks, sliding on the white stone gravel. "Is good, yes. Your English improves by leaps and bounds." I paced, turning around twice, asking, "Are you all right with, you know…. Not that I am, you know…"

"Gay? Gay is Gay, is no big deal. When you're in it, you don't see it," she smiled.

"What d'ya mean?" I gulped as we carried on, slipping on the gravel toward the pool.

"The French, they have an expression. They say *coup de foudre*—love like a bolt of lightning, comes."

"You mean, love at first sight? The first attraction?"

"*Sì*. When was your *coup de foudre*, the first moment with Kate?"

I stopped, again skidding on the gravel. "No. No-no."

"Me with Alex, I saw him on his motorcycle and bam!" she clapped, "That's it! And you, Miss Gerri?"

"Huh? No bam-bam. Well, all right, the steps, the front steps of the villa, that first cheeky meeting. Enough. No more *coup de foudre*, we have work to do." I grabbed her arm, and we went to the barbeque.

Dinnertime held a magical aura, the air filled with a veil of mystery as if anything could happen. My Villa Galz wined and dined on the outdoor garden terrace at a beautifully set table. They loved the scrumptious cooking; every bit of it as close to an Italian mama's meal as I could manage without cooking for days. For the dinner wine, I surprised them with unlabelled local wines bought at a market stall, a white wine and a red. I'd sampled them from the vendor, so knew they would taste perfect with the meal. Vera had also purchased an expensive wine bottled northwest of Lake Como, two bottles of *Valtellina Superiore Riserva*.

They asked Kate to do the wine tasting. I poured her a taster's amount of the aired bottle of red wine. She took her time, swirling the wine, smelling it twice, sipping and gargling enough to release the aroma, and announced, "Dry, slightly tannic, but velvety, characteristic and harmonious."

CJ whispered an aside to me, "Try not to look impressed. She grew up on the family vineyard." But Kate did impress me, in more ways than one.

Isabella also impressed me by helping serve and clear the dishes like a pro. As sunset approached, strings of little white lights turned on, all over the terrace and pool area, and under the terrace's canopied vines, infusing everything with a romantic glow. I stayed in the kitchen as much as possible, watching them through the open door and the windows to see when they needed something. They invited me to join them for dinner more than once, but each time I declined. It's their night and Jamie's birthday. Besides, I had to prepare the *Dolce, Frutta, Digestivo*, and *Caffè* courses. Isabella stayed in the kitchen doorway as my go-between and carried out her duties with diligence.

Kate came into the kitchen, "You sent for me?"

"Would you please help me with the birthday cake?"

"You made her a cake? Thanks, Professor."

Together, we placed the candles one by one, preparing to light them. Isabella and I had whipped up the *Dolce,* or dessert, off to the side on our own. For the *Frutta*, we decorated the cake with fresh strawberries.

"You're an excellent chef. These gals, I know they'll appreciate it. It's pretty special." She looked at me, "You're pretty special." She leaned in to kiss my cheek, close to my ear where I heard her moist lips.

My energy had been waning, but she filled me up. Together, Kate and I carried the dessert and plates outside as all the Galz sang Happy Birthday to Jamie. The simple-to-make but fancy-looking *Torta Meringata* made a glamorous Italian birthday cake, with four fancy birthday candles for Jamie's fortieth. Kate and I gazed at each other across the table. Making a wish, Jamie blew out all the candles, and everyone cheered and clapped.

As I left for the kitchen, I noticed they did a special circle toast around the table, one person to the next person beside them, and so forth. And then Renee tapped an App on her phone and the terrace exploded in dance music from small speakers.

Isabella and I discreetly cleared the larger dishes and let them have their space. I decided to start collecting the glasses and dishes scattered all over the villa. Isabella began rinsing and filling the large dishwasher.

"You know, now's a good time to ask Vera about Alex's legal papers," I suggested to her. "It would be better coming from you, and Vera's in a good mood, eh?" Isabella wiped her wet hands on her apron and straightened her wig. "I'll check the living room for glasses," I advised, taking a tray. Truth was, I needed time away from Kate, but I also had another objective.

CHAPTER 17
Daring To Be Bold

Where I came from is important, yes, but
only because it launched me to where I'm going.

—G. A. McKenna, journal entry

Wine glasses were scattered about in the villa's living room where the Galz had lounged before dinner. I had not been in this part of the villa since Isabella first showed me around last week and when Kate showed me her drawing under Angelina's portrait. Kate's easel stood in the corner, her painting covered by an old cloth. Tempted to take a peek, I started to lift the cloth but a noise in the hallway startled me, and I hurried over to where an iPad had been set up on an end table.

It must have been Renee who had set up her iPad for a revolving slideshow of everyone's photographs. I stopped to watch when I saw photos of me. Kate had taken quite a few of me at Balbianello near the Artemis statue, almost all of them close-ups. I was taken aback, yet mesmerized at the same time, feeling suddenly vulnerable. But I needed to stay focused on my objective: to get to the library.

I collected the wine glasses onto a tray and hurried into the library. The photos in the alcove were crooked, so I paused briefly to straighten them. I found the cement brick with the Mason's mark, the one I'd first seen when Isabella showed me the library.

The carved marking had faded over the years, but I made out a triangle.

I wanted to see it better. Choosing a pencil and a piece of paper from the desk, I rubbed over the carved mark. To my amazement the rubbing showed a large triangle with an eye carved inside a smaller triangle. I instantly recognized that the two triangles meant rebirth and the eye meant protection. I knew this because the same symbol was on the Third Eye pendant I always wore. Putting the rubbing and my gold pendant side by side, the symbols were identical.

"Fascinating."

More than ever, I needed to see what was inside the secret brick drawer, remembering how it had opened by accident. I put the rubbing into my pocket, and then pushed on the brick. It popped open like a small drawer. Inside lay an antique brass skeleton key and two smaller keys.

"Keys to what?" I turned and glanced over at the walnut-veneered writing cabinet and figured the brass skeleton key must fit the brass keyhole or, if not, something else in the library.

"Do I dare?" I murmured, holding the key and staring at the cabinet's keyhole. Isabella had said it's private.

A second later, I heard a loud click from the bookcase. And a creaking sound. I turned around to witness one section of the bookcase moving. I jumped back.

"What did I do?"

The section of the recessed photo shelf opened like a door on hinges. The door's side view showed that the brick façade was actually composed of fake half bricks. The secret door opened onto a small, dark room with another smaller door inside. "Curiouser and curiouser," I whispered. Words came back to haunt me: *"Be bold where you stand, I dare you. Why risk standing still?"*

Nervously, I went inside to open it. Suddenly the bookshelf started to close. Afraid I might get locked inside, I pushed my way out.

The masonry brick had slid back into place as the door closed. My curiosity battled with my trepidation until I pressed the brick again; after a slight pause it slid open again, as did the secret door in the bookshelf. I lodged one of the many books at the opening, took one of the smaller keys, and hurried inside. I unlocked the small inside door as the bookshelf moved to close automatically, but the book stopped it. Behind the door was a low tunnel and narrow steps going down into pitch blackness.

"Okay, that's enough," and I ran out, feeling afraid. I removed the book and the fake door shut tight.

I heard noises from the living room. The sound of footsteps on the marble floor came closer to the library. Damnit! There wasn't time to investigate the writing cabinet. I ran to the brick, returned the key, and clicked it shut.

Needing a subterfuge, I quickly turned on the vinyl turntable. A guest had been playing the impressive album collection. A 78-record spun and a 1930s recording of Ethel Waters singing "Moonglow" crooned and echoed out the living room and hallways.

While pretending to sing along with the recording, I canvassed the massive floor to ceiling bookcases and found the poetry section. After all, it was the real reason I'd come to the library.

Even having to stand on my tiptoes, the book wasn't difficult to find: a red leather-bound book with faded gold lettering on the spine. I took it off the shelf and opened the book at the title page: *The Poetical Works of Lord Byron*. The same book Carlo Vacchini recommended I investigate. I flipped the page and noticed the First Edition info: Publisher P.F. Collier (1884).

I felt a presence behind me. I turned to see Kate enter the library. The hardcover book slipped from my hands and landed flat on the hardwood floor with a thud.

"Lovely singing voice, don't let me stop you," she smiled, and I blushed. "I've been sent to fetch you. We have a surprise."

Kate reached down to retrieve the book. "Lord Byron's book. Isn't this the book Carlo, the baker, told you about?"

"Yes, that's right. I'll be there in a minute, I'm tidying up," I said, stalling, and while collecting a few more glasses, I watched Kate nonchalantly flip through the book.

"Hey, this is interesting. An old photograph." Kate held a small photo.

"What?"

"An old hospital photo, baby and mother. They used to take black and white photos after a birth, with a number. They didn't want to mix up the babies. It happened back then."

She handed me the small 3x4-inch photograph. I stared at it for mere seconds—a lifetime of images flashing by—and then dropped it as though my fingers got burned. In slow motion, the photograph fell to the floor.

"What's wrong?" Kate bent to get the photo.

"Don't touch it! Where'd you find it, what page?"

"I dunno." Kate flipped through the book, "Here, it's tagged on the corner."

Sure enough the corner was folded down halfway.

"Please read where the bent corner touches."

"*There be none of Beauty's daughters, With a magic like Thee.*"

"No, it can't be. What's happening? Oh, my god."

"I guess this is the missing baby, right?" Kate said. I stared at her but couldn't answer. "*Beauty's daughter*, Marcella is beauty's daughter, meaning daughter of the beautiful Angelina. Right? Why tell you that? Feels like there's more to the story," Kate said. "Like, who is *Thee*?"

My hands trembled. "Carlo said there are no secrets on the lake, unless you swim below the surface. I have a feeling we're about to take a dive, as in…" I paused, then, "Beauty's *daughter*, he's telling us her baby was a girl."

Kate's back straightened, at attention. "Good one, Professor." Kate carefully retrieved the baby photo off the floor and walked over to the special alcove reserved for framed photographs. She held the black and white photo next to a framed photograph on the wall of a young Marcella with her father.

"Yep, confirmed, it's Marcella in both photos." She handed me the photograph that had been hidden in the book.

I ventured a closer inspection. The young girl's photograph resembled Marcella. She held a swaddled newborn baby. Behind her a white hospital crib had one side down and in the crib were two items, a toy rabbit with long floppy ears and a hospital card with the numbers AL10-660513.

"No. This is crazy." I felt my heart palpitate, beating hard against my ribs.

"Gerri, what is it? You're freakin' out."

"Like you said, there are millions of these photos, right? It doesn't mean anything."

"Yeah, but we can assume it is Marcella and her baby, unconfirmed but it warrants inquiry. Would you like me to investigate?" Kate asked, expressionless.

"Meaning how?"

"Birth records, locally or else in Milan. We're in Milan tomorrow, right?"

"No-no, please, ah, don't trouble yourself."

Interrupted, Luciana's voice yelled from the corridor, "Kate, Code-99, bring the chef!"

"Sorry, it's a Code-99. Police slang, it means tea break, or in our case, wine break. Come on, it'll be fun."

Putting the photo safely into my pocket, I said, "I hope it involves copious amounts of wine."

Kate held my hand as we walked back to the villa's kitchen. Her touch felt safe and loving. I slipped the priceless photograph into my purse on the counter.

Kate had made a ring of flowers from five-petal, blue Forget-Me-Nots, which she brought forward and placed on my head.

"How lovely. Forget-Me-Nots, a symbol of remembrance. Are you saying don't forget me?"

"Who could forget you? And they match your Forget-Me-Not pin, the one Carlo gave you."

"Sweet of you, for making me feel special."

Standing at the kitchen doorway, Erin held up a scarf, "It's a blindfold, for you."

"Is that necessary? I've got to bring in the tray with the *Digestivo* and the *Caffè*. *Digestivo* meaning digestion and—"

"Nope, stop! That's an order, Chef. Leave it with me and Issy," Erin insisted.

Erin helped Isabella bring out the tray of *Digestivo* and shot glasses: bottles of grappa, the bittersweet Amaro liqueur, and Limoncello, along with a coffee tray. The sun had set and fireflies began appearing and several of the women lit two of the Villa's elaborate candelabras. The dogs barked and ran around them in circles, a little crazy.

Erin passed me a small brass cup, saying, "Bottom's up." I drank it down and felt the strong grappa titillate my tongue.

"God, I needed that."

CHAPTER 18
Initiation into the Mysteries

Keep your head up; don't look at your feet.
Feel the music. Just dance!
There are no wrongs.

—G. A. McKenna, journal entry

K
ate and Erin walked me to the edge of the purple wisteria-
filled arch. I saw twelve Goddesses, each unique and
beautiful, with blue Forget-Me-Not flowers in their hair.
They stood six to a row, holding the lit candelabras. Several
fireflies flew about them. Brittany and Hannah had taken the
wooden flute and conga drum from the foyer and played them
carefully with a processional beat, along with Renee's choice of
music.

Kate stood behind me, tying the scarf blindfold over my eyes
and around my head. With her arms stretched out around me, I felt
her breasts brush against my back. My covered eyes went off, but
my heart turned on.

Kate whispered in my ear, "It's a procession of light. I won't
let them do anything weird."

"I trust you. Did I say that out loud? Why do I trust you, I
hardly know you? But I do."

"Trust your own instinct," she whispered, and I felt her warmth
beside me. "I'm going to lead you to the swimming pool and
statues. It's all in fun." She held onto my arm to reassure me.

Through the chiffon scarf over my eyes, I could make out shapes, light and dark, and discern people. Kate led me among the twelve Goddesses and the lit candelabras. I heard the wooden flute and conga drum following behind me. We made a Goddess procession similar to the ancient Greek Eleusinian Mysteries, which had an initiation ceremony with secret rites. Sensing among us the Goddess Demeter and her daughter Persephone gave rise to my acceptance of a spiritual awakening, as in the archetypal energies within the ancient ceremonies of death and rebirth, rebirth into a new life. Like coming "home" to one's Self. What kind of life was being revealed to me? I've had other similar physical sensations of entering a new life: like walking down the aisle to accept my university diploma, or walking down the aisle to get married, or entering the hospital corridor to give birth. This felt similar in that something new is coming; yet, it felt cryptic.

My inner voice spoke to me:

In the library lay another secret initiation—a discovery.

In a flash I connected the secret brass key to the Mysteries. I had a vision of the statue of Artemis at the Villa del Balbianello; she, the Goddess of the Hunt, Lady of the Beasts, the moon, chastity and childbirth, and a Lesbian icon. The ceremonies and beliefs had been kept secret through the centuries. Like the secrets I'm slowly uncovering.

In my inner vision the marble statue of Artemis came to life, moving her limbs to put an arrow in her bow, her wild braided hair and tunic flowing in the wind. She let go her arrow and it shot straight toward my heart.

When someone removed the blindfold, I felt dizzy. Kate steadied me, a touch that echoed through centuries. We stood at my special spot overlooking the lake. The thirteen Goddesses toasted me with raised shot glasses of grappa brandy, the golden nectar.

Do they know I found the secret treasure?

Jamie the Birthday Goddess said, "We honour you and welcome you into our circle."

Erin held her glass up and said, "Here's to you, and here's to me, friends for life we'll always be, but if by chance we disagree, fuck you and here's to me!" Everyone laughed.

Jamie continued, "To the best chef on Lake Como. *Saluté!*"

Everyone downed their brandy, only Dana refused to toast. My Judas glanced at me, no doubt pissed off because I held Kate's attention.

I sipped mine, making a face, and said, "Issy and I thank you for your generous tip. *Brava* to the Goddess!" Then I downed the last bit in one gulp.

Erin stuffed a cigar in my mouth and poured me another grappa, "You're off duty, Chef. Drink up." She passed around Brissago cigars. "Light up, everyone!"

"Now this is definitely a *Digestivo* tradition."

Using the lighter, Kate helped me light it. As I sucked on the cigar she said, "Gotta suck hard to get the luxuriant gratification." She made me laugh and I choked at the same time. I washed it down with a bit of brandy.

"Enough for me, no more. For someone who doesn't drink, I've been drinking way too much." I passed Kate both the cigar and the grappa.

Isabella stood shyly beside Vera, who lit a cigar for her and passed her a brandy. They were bonding. She also choked on the cigar smoke but tried her best.

Down the hill from us the San Sisinnio church bells rang. First time I'd ever heard them. Light from inside the church spilled out the open doorway.

The villa's outdoor terrace exploded with loud Greek music. Renee had changed the music, and we all ran back to the terrace and moved the long table out of the way. Why Greek music I had no idea; perhaps to represent the Eleusinian Mysteries?

Under the twinkling lights, the women formed a ring around Jamie and danced for two songs, ending each song yelling, "Opa!" They pulled Isabella and me into the circle. I tried to follow the Greek dance steps. "Opa!" In a swirl of dancers and music and lights, I allowed the frenzied revelry to take me, loving that moment when your self-consciousness is taken over by opening to the music, suddenly entering your soul, swirling you into the dance of life.

Take me below surface into the Mystery.

The impassioned Greek music segued when Renee changed tracks to a slow Latin-type song, and partners met to dance under the starlit sky. Renee and Tracy danced a romantic waltz, as did

Hannah and Jamie, CJ and Erin, and the others. Light on her feet, Bibi with Luciana did a gentle Swing Dance to the music. Isabella and I were heading back toward the kitchen when Kate approached me.

A little tipsy and a lot perturbed, Dana watched Kate ask me to dance. Dana scowled and in retribution, grabbed Vera for a dance. Vera seized the opportunity to hold Dana close, gazing lovingly into her eyes. Dana reacted with surprise.

Kate and I stared at one another, not knowing who would make the first move. Kate stepped forward, toward me. I felt impelled to take a step closer to her. She took me by the hand, and we danced together in front of the others. I found Kate delightful in her nervousness, and her shyness gave me a feeling of dominant advantage. I liked it.

Dana continued scowling at us. Vera got her attention by pulling Dana closer and surprising her with a kiss. At first Dana resisted, pulling away, but Vera held fast, bravely showing her heart in her eyes. Stunned, Dana stopped dancing to plant a forceful yet tender kiss on Vera, not letting go.

Sweetly and shyly, Kate waltzed with me at arm's length. Her shyness was a side of her I hadn't seen.

"Hold me," I whispered without filtering. "I need to be held."

It had been a long time since I danced with someone. I took the lead and held her close, our bodies touching openly at last. Feeling the curve of her waist made my heart race. Our breasts touched lightly, and I felt her swollen mound press against mine; our bellies grew warm together. I wanted to kiss her. My mouth opened so close to the side of her neck that she must have felt my hot breath on her soft skin.

Against all reason, I whispered a quote from Shakespeare's *Romeo and Juliet*: "My lips, two blushing pilgrims, ready stand, to smooth that rough touch with a tender kiss."

In response to Shakespeare's words, I felt a slight body quiver from Kate. At one point I felt overwhelmed and moved a few inches away from her. Remembering my Latin dance class, I placed my hands on her hips and moved them side to side in a half circle. With a few lambada moves, I took her hand and slowly spun her, pulling her into me. I felt shy in front of the others.

Dancing close to us, I heard Dr Wanda say to Brittany, "Oh, I like that move."

Moments passed, my head in a cloud, nothing else existed.

Suddenly ABBA's "Dancing Queen" assaulted us, and the Villa Girls formed a long line following Bibi who took the lead, dancing past the pool, onto the terraced lawn, and down the slope toward the church.

I pulled out of line when I spotted people coming out of the church. The darkness kept me from seeing the faces of a large group who got into several cars and drove away, but then the car headlights blocked my vision to see inside the cars. Must be a town meeting, I figured. Isabella also watched them.

"It's about the casino. Most villagers are against it," she whispered to me.

CJ caught my shirttails and pulled me back into line. We danced back to the pool area and around the statues. All of us touched Aphrodite's right breast for good luck, except for Isabella who preferred to rub the penis of Michelangelo's David, of course. Isabella broke rank and headed into the villa's kitchen. That's when I also escaped.

Having felt my Wild Woman come out tonight for the first time in twenty-years, I hurried away from them, dancing across the grass into the other smaller arbor, the one away from the villa's terrace. To catch my breath, I hid under the climbing vines and little white lights in the latticework. The lights attracted magical fireflies that darted about.

I watched Kate looking for me, and then I made my whereabouts known by stepping out into the moonlight so she could see me. We gazed at one another for what seemed an eternity. As if propelled by my bewitching pull, she made a movement to come to me. My eyes transfixed upon her, steadily, eagerly, watching her sleepwalk toward me. The music and laughter faded away. There was only the gaze.

When she reached me, she stood motionless, speechless. The fireflies illuminated her, their light shining on her enchanted face. Her mouth opened as if to say something, but she didn't.

Finally, I said, "Come closer."

Kate took a step closer as though beyond her volition, spellbound. I took her hand and pulled her under the arbor, hiding among the climbing vines and latticework. The beautiful distance between us closed and we melded together.

I kissed her then, clutching her, clumsy, falling into her against the trellis. Her hands curled around my waist to steady me. Watching me while slowly lifting my skirt, exposing my underpants, she gently placed her knee between my legs and with her strong hands pulled me into her, closer; waking a part of me I never knew existed.

I heard the others close by, laughing and dancing, but I held Kate's gaze so I could look into her eyes, saying, "Don't stop."

We kissed, unable to stop even if they discovered us, which titillated me even more. Her hand went under the front of my shirt; she touched my breast, fondling it with a luxurious touch, gentle, loving, firm. She kissed me harder, unbridled, as if finally released from the enchantment.

"Do anything you want," I whispered while imagining the thrill of what she'd do next, until...

Rounding the corner the Villa Galz line-danced on the lawn in front of the arbor, coming close to us. "Oh, fuck a duck!" I swore.

Kate chuckled at me. I hid my flushed face into Kate's shoulder, feeling suddenly shy. I kissed her and ran off, taking the dogs back into the villa's kitchen.

Inside, Isabella cleaned the kitchen while the dancing and revelry continued outside. I caught my breath, drinking a few sips of cold water.

Looking at her watch, Isabella said, "I go soon." She kept glancing at the kitchen table.

Still breathless, I couldn't stop smiling. "Yes, of course, it's late."

All the Euro bills from the guests lay on the table. I added all receipts, took out my expenses and left cash to repay those who bought food, leaving a stack of Euro bills and some coins for Issy and me to split.

"Take what you think you're worth. I'm good with it," I suggested. Isabella looked shocked, then frowned. She took one bill and the coins.

"Fifteen euros? My dear Issy, you're worth way more. Please take fifty percent. You deserve it as much as I do."

"Hooptedoopte! No, you're chef," she insisted. "Half is more than I make all week."

I grabbed the bills and stuffed half into her pocket. "I insist. It was a joy working with you. And, well, I have another cooking class, if you're interested?"

Her face beamed. "*Sì*, I would honor to be of help. Next time I take one quarter. Okey-doke?"

"One third, I insist. A deal?" I made her shake on it, "Hey wait, I'll give you a ride home."

"No, is all good to go. And I want to find out about the meeting at the church. Maybe about the casino. Thank you, Miss Gerri." She gave me a big bear hug and bounded out the door before I could protest.

Since the guests were clearly occupied, I indulged myself in using the secret spiral staircase up through the closet into my bedroom, the two dogs at my heels, and thinking of Kate. Will she ever make her way up these stairs to me?

I loved the weight of place—the structure, the furnishings, the ambience—of my bedroom at the top of the stairs, so quiet, away from the world. I opened the draperies on both windows, allowing the moon to paint its light in lucid strokes inside my bedroom. Not quite full, the thirteen-day moon lit up the garden and lake, creating crisp shadows.

"What just happened?" I asked myself, cherishing the close encounter in the arbor, but also thinking about what had happened in the library.

Before flopping onto the bed, exhausted, I desperately needed to face something: an elusive Pandora's Box of haunting memories long forgotten.

I sat at the small desk and opened my tablet. While waiting for it to boot up, I scribbled in my journal the words that had infiltrated my mind during the procession of light ceremony:

In the library lay another secret initiation—a discovery. Do they know I found the secret treasure? Take me below surface into the Mystery.

The Wi-Fi connection seemed faster than usual. I logged into the cloud and went to "My Photo Gallery." As I searched for one image in particular, a lifetime of scanned pictures flew by: school graduations, my marriage, photos of Julie and Thomas as youngsters and older, all grownup, of me accepting the Culinary Arts award. Oh, why hadn't I put them in separate folders? Christmases, birthdays, Thanksgivings around the table. Photographs of myself as a child in Vancouver, of my wonderful parents as they aged, and as I aged, going backward from my first day at school, my parents holding me as a child, and then I clicked "pause."

Here was the first known photo of me as a newborn, alone in a hospital crib.

I held up the old black and white photo that had been hidden in Lord Byron's book, of young Marcella holding her newborn baby. It was the same type of crib, the same toy rabbit with long floppy ears, the same baby with a full head of hair, and the card with the identical number AL10-660513, the digits being the date of my birth: 1966-05-13.

On the back of the photo, someone had handwritten the now faded word "Allegra." My memory was unclear, but I had a feeling the same word was written on the back of the photo I had at home, the photo I now stared at on my tablet. Allegra is my middle name.

"This doesn't make any sense. How can I be Marcella's *dead* baby?" I said before falling into a deep sleep.

CHAPTER 19
The Olive Grove Lovers

I overthink everything.
It's like when you stand at the top of a slide,
you can't hesitate, you have to take your turn.

—G. A. McKenna, journal entry

I awoke, panicked, in the middle of the night to the barking of dogs downstairs. The bedside clock read 1:11 a.m. I jumped up, still dressed, and ran downstairs. I tried to quiet the dogs, but then heard voices outside and opened the top section of the Dutch door. I saw two figures at the corner of the villa, one was hunched over. Kate's face turned into the moonlight and I opened the door. The dogs took off and tore uphill, away from Kate in the opposite direction. Kate hung on to Dana, who was kneeling, apparently too drunk to stand.

"Is she all right?"

"Ah, no," Kate said, startled. "She's not a happy camper. Too much grappa."

"Yeah, it sneaks up on you." The dogs barked uphill, already near the olive grove. "Damnit! See you later." And I started off uphill into the dark.

"Hang on! You can't go there alone. I'm coming," Kate offered.

Dana groaned, "No, stay with me," and heaved again.

Just then Vera arrived to help her. "What's wrong? You okay?"

I ducked inside for a flashlight and sweater, then started up the hill. Kate caught up to me.

"They've never run away before," I said.

"We can follow the barking. They'll be fine. No wild boars, are there?"

"No, only goats. Hopefully."

We hiked along a well-defined path into the olive grove, the one place Isabella had warned us never to go. My small flashlight helped a bit, but the gibbous moon lit our way. The deeper we went, the darker it got, the moon now mostly hidden. The ancient grove came alive with iridescent dark magic. Owls echoed in circles around us, caterwauling a warning. The shadows shifted as we walked, creating moving figures out of the twisted outstretched branches of the ancient olive trees.

I collected some fallen olive twigs that still had their leaves. "I love olive leaf tea. I'll make it for you." I heard the dogs bark. "They're over this way," I said, following a worn earth trail uphill. How did I know this trail? Then I saw them as if from the past:

Visitors in the grove, clutching their belongings, clutching one another, scarves on the women's heads, work caps or berets on the men. They held children and carried leather suitcases and hurried through the woods, afraid, afraid of me, running from me, the watcher in the woods. Who am I? I looked down. I wore men's high black leather boots. One of the visitors turned and saw me, his eyes fearful. My hand took a boy's cap from my head—the cap's insignia was an eagle and a swastika, belonging to the Hitler Youth. The man hurried the others onward. I said nothing, did nothing. I let the refugees escape.

I stumbled. Kate's voice cut through my waking dream vision. "You okay? Where'd you go just then?" I felt Kate beside me, felt her near, walking close and touching my arm.

"I'm not sure...ah, I had a weird vision. It feels like I've walked this trail before, in a different time."

"A déjà vu?"

"Yes, similar. Or from a past lifetime."

"Shhh." Kate grabbed my hand. "Do you hear that?" Kate

whispered.

We heard voices in the distance. We listened. The dogs barked, but this time, an excited happy barking.

"They must have found someone they know." I heard them whining as though someone familiar patted them. Then they stopped barking all together.

"It might be lovers making out," Kate said.

"One night I saw Shaun, the American boy, with a young girl coming out of the olive grove. Perhaps he's out of the hospital and they're together?"

Presently the dogs ran toward us, tongues hanging and tails wagging, excited to see us.

"Good puppies." I patted them, overjoyed with relief, but wishing I'd brought their leashes.

"Thank God, they're safe," Kate said and then moved closer to me. "Do you mind if…?"

She led me behind a huge hollow olive tree trunk; the tired dogs following us, not leaving our side. Kate touched the side of my face.

"Hope it's all right, here, in the olive grove where lovers go."

Kate leaned in, kissing me on the small indentation where the cheek meets the far corner of the lips, a gentle kiss, lingering, her lips touching mine lightly, and a slow movement of her breasts brushing past mine to the other side. And another kiss, this time with her sweet lips on my blushing cheek. A pause. We looked at one another. The stars sparkled in her eyes.

"You want more?"

My stomach flipped. She waited for a sign from me whether to continue. I was deciding. Then I gently bit her lower lip and whispered, "I want to go inside you."

She drew me to her. I didn't resist. She kissed me hard, her full-blossomed lips warm. Our groins touched. I felt a fire rage inside and watched her quiver as I glided my hand underneath her shirt, gathering her breast into my cold palm. Braless, her breast felt warm and inviting. She leaned into the hollow of the tree, hidden in the forest, as we opened ourselves to each other. Face to face, I watched her quivering lips, a strand of hair that fell across her cheeks, the shadow play of branches on her lovely face.

I slowly unzipped her pants. My hand greedily reached inside her mauve panties, past her soft pubic hair to seek her wetness. Gently, I pushed a finger inside her, and then another. It took my breath away as her ravenous vagina throbbed around my fingers and, then, the heel of my palm pushed against her clitoris. She moaned. The dark woods called back with night sounds, waking the birds and the animals. I witnessed her complete arousal as she lost control, as she let go and arched her back, her luscious mouth wide open. Her body rocked to my rhythmic thrusts, rubbing her in the perfect spot. I didn't stop until she bore down, yielding to my touch, and her contractions erupted. She made a low, steady continuous sound as her entire body moaned and *orgasmed*—is it a verb? An orgasm, free of ulterior motive, uncomplicated, and passionate; thank you, author Erica Jong. The tree held her from behind as I embraced her from the front. Neither of us moved, simply breathing together for several beautiful minutes.

I felt euphoric, almost delirious with pleasure from giving her an orgasm. Being a woman, I knew what she needed me to do, initially, now I wanted to learn how to please her even more. I kissed her gently before slowly, gently removing my fingers. We both smiled, having shared a silent communion.

"I wasn't expecting these feelings," I whispered. A few tears emerged. They must have run onto her cheek as well. She pulled back to wipe the wetness off both our cheeks.

"That makes two of us. This complicates matters."

SNAP! Suddenly we heard the loud snap of a twig not far away. The dogs whined at our heels but did not bark. I hung onto Kate's arm. The sound of another twig snapped metres away.

We heard the voices. One of the voices was familiar but whose? We could barely make out the dark shadow moving toward us.

Kate pulled me deeper into the hollow of the tree. I held onto the little dog, but Goldie got away, running up to the shadowy figure whom I recognized as he came into the moonlight.

Davide yelled, "Goldie, go home, boy. Go on!" and the golden retriever ran down the hillside toward the villa. Pucci bolted from my grip and ran after him.

I whispered to Kate, "What's Davide doing here?"

"There's someone else."

"Where?" And then she came into the moonlight, too.

It took me a moment to recognize her, with her long hair hidden under a cap, her denim jacket and skirt covered in leaves and twigs as though she'd been lying on the ground. Carmela Lazzaro ran up to Davide and caught him in a whirl of kisses.

"Tuck in your shirt, you bad boy," she said, laughing while helping him.

"You know I'm in love with you. Run away with me, tonight," Davide pleaded.

"I've got to go, the casino is closing, he'll be home soon," she said, her voice breaking. "Oh, Davide, I don't want to leave you."

Had I translated it correctly? "What are they saying?" Kate wanted to know.

Davide kissed Carmela and they hugged, reluctant to part. Finally, they hurried along a different path leading away from us, back towards Argegno.

I whispered to Kate, "Well, whad'ya know, both Carmela and Vincenzo are having affairs."

Kate and I waited several minutes before we crawled out from behind the tree. My leg was asleep. I lost my footing and fell backward, falling through some brambles onto wooden planks, which creaked under my weight. Kate grabbed me as the old wood broke, falling away to expose a dark hole as tall as a hunched-over man. A wave of musty air escaped, almost choking us.

"Must be an old mine tunnel, or something?"

"Unless, depends on where it goes." I stopped, and then leaned in to inspect it further.

"Oh, no you don't. Let's get out of here."

The dogs ran back to us as Kate and I leaned into one another, heading toward the villa through the olive grove. As we exited the grove path, I spotted a swirl of white cigar smoke caught in the light of a street lamp. Someone sat at the old rickety picnic table at the end of the driveway, his white hair and hunched shoulders unmistakeable. He wore a black jacket with a hood.

"Kate, do you mind taking the dogs to my suite? I've got to speak with Carlo Vacchini."

"I'm not leaving you."

"Please, Kate, I need to speak with him in private. It's important."

Kate relented and called the dogs, taking them to the villa.

Carlo had his back to me as I approached. With a walking stick at his side, sitting on the picnic table, he faced the dim lights of the village and lake.

"Good evening, *signora*," he said without turning.

"What are you doing here at this time of night?"

"I might ask you the same. We both take a midnight stroll, I see. But I am looking for my son. I've checked all his usual haunts. Except the olive grove. There's been a threat."

"Whad'ya mean?"

"My son has been, how you say, fooling with Vincenzo's wife and he found out. Do you know where my son is?"

"Who, me?" I tried not to lie. "You could have phoned me."

"I had no energy to check inside the olive grove. It's where they go, you know. Lovers. Secret trysts. Always been that way."

"Is that where you met with Angelina in your younger years?"

He chuckled a little. "Walk with me." He snuffed his cigar and pushed himself up with his walking staff. Carlo walked me arm-in-arm along the roadway toward the lights of the village. For an old man, his footing was steady. The air felt chilled and weighted with moisture from a thin veil of moonlight as the moon dropped lower.

"You have questions for me?" He knew I did.

Desperate to ask only one question, I found I couldn't speak it. When I first compared the two baby photographs, my brain wouldn't compute what it meant. My rational mind tried to explain it all away, but I couldn't explain away the birth number.

As we wended our way along the moonlit road, I finally stopped alongside Carlo to ask him, "Who am I?"

"You found Byron's poetry book."

"You knew I would. You meant for me to find the photo of young Marcella with her newborn. It's identical to my baby photo at home, except in mine Marcella is missing. I've always known I was adopted."

I watched Carlo for clues, but his expression told me nothing.

"My parents never hid my adoption from me. But there's no record, you see, none. No government paper of my adoption, no registration of the birth mother's name, no nothing. I assume my birth certificate was faked." I became angry, wondering whether I could handle it, hoping I could accept whatever came next, could swim along with the fluidity of change.

Another nagging question, "How did you know I was coming to the Villa? Why all the subterfuge? Why not tell me everything right away?"

I stared at Carlo, waiting. True to his inherent chivalry, he hesitated long enough to choose his words carefully.

"I not understand that part, not up to me," he smiled. "Until recently, we didn't know where you were. We never stopped looking for Marcella's baby—for you." He stumbled a little, but his staff steadied him. "*Tesora mia*, my dear treasure, Stephanie and Felix Bianchi, the young Italian couple from Milan who adopted you, emigrated to Canada without telling the nunnery, and neither Marcella nor her father Max knew. Eventually we learned they had emigrated to Canada."

My entire being gave way to utter relief. Let me hold on to that feeling for a moment, before the world starts to spin again, and more change arrives.

I turned at the distant screeching of an owl that echoed in the darkness. Something had startled it. My eyes played tricks. Did a dark figure move behind us, further uphill along the road? Why would someone follow us? I listened to my psychic Gift and thought of Kate; she might have wanted to keep me safe.

Carlo hung on to my arm as we continued to walk slowly downhill toward the village.

"Where was I born?"

"*Milano.* When he discovered his daughter's pregnancy, Max was furious. 'My daughter will not have an illegitimate baby,' he vowed. Being a stout Catholic, an abortion was out of the question. She refused to marry just anyone. No one has an illegitimate child in a small town." Carlo wiped his sweaty brow with his handkerchief. "In Marcella's fifth month of pregnancy, the village rumours started. Max set her up in Milan to have the baby at a nunnery. Alyssa Leoni was the midwife," Carlo said.

"Leoni? The midwife is related to Emilio Leoni, the village doctor?"

"His mother."

"Is she still alive? Would she remember my birth?"

"Absolutely she would remember you—if she were alive. I believe you were her tenth delivery that year. 'AL10' is in your birth number. 'AL' stands for her name, Alyssa Leoni, and birth number 10. She kept the secret of your birth, never talked about it to the villagers, until her deathbed. Max Ferrario paid her well."

"Hush money?"

"Sort of, but no. With your birth money she became a registered nurse. And because of that, her son could afford to become a doctor. Dr. Leoni is also beholden to Marcella's family, as are many others."

"Others? I don't understand." As he spoke, his words became a river in my mind, and flooded me with long-ago memories, before my time. I watched the pictures swirl and move like a film in front of me. I had to be careful not to carve the images out of thin air and make them my reality, my story.

"Yes, many others are beholden."

Walking beside Carlo, something else dawned on me, but instead of facing it, I asked another question. "Did my parents name me, or did Marcella?"

"Geraldine is an anagram, chosen by your adoptive parents. It means 'realigned.' It's an old Masonic trick, hiding secrets in anagrams," he smiled. "Marcella chose your middle names. One of your middle names is Allegra, is it not?"

"Yes, but I never use it. I believe the word is written on the back of my baby photo at home."

"Marcella chose it because Allegra was Lord Byron's daughter's name. As I said, the young Marcella loved Byron's romantic poetry. But Allegra Byron died five years after her birth in Ravenna, Italy. Her name seemed fitting somehow, because we told everyone you had died."

"No doubt because Marcella's father feared a backlash and village gossip. But why tell me the baby was buried in the cemetery? You lied to me."

"Sometimes I am a foolish man. And you seemed so fragile. Forgive me." Carlo looked tired. His eyes no longer held a childlike curiosity but more a determined grit. He placed a comforting hand on my shoulder and said, "Now, I look forward to watching what you will do. *Luce dei miei occhi*—Light of my eyes."

"I would be honored to call you *Nonno*—grandfather. If I may."

"There will be time for that. Now go. I can manage from here. Rest. It is much to digest," he said.

"Yes, thank you, *signor*, you are most kind. I'm in overwhelm. *M'illumino d'immenso*—I illuminate myself with immensity."

"Ah, the poem by Giuseppe Ungaretti, his search for harmony. Yours will come, *cara mia*."

Carlo kissed me on both my cheeks, and a third kiss for good luck. I watched him go, slow but sure-footed, back toward town. He knew the hills and valleys, each trail, each vineyard and olive grove, as only a local could.

In that moment, I chose to whisper another truth, forming the words and putting their vibration out into the world: "Carlo slept with Angelina and is Marcella's biological father. Marcella is my biological mother, and she's Davide's half-sister. That makes Davide my distant blood relative. Thank goodness, I didn't want to sleep with him." I chuckled nervously, but it suddenly disappeared when I whispered into the wind....

"But, who is my biological father?"

CHAPTER 20
Bellezza, Bella Mia

*While sleeping, love sneaked up on me and
unlocked the gateway. Dear woman, how you
have stirred my soul and awoken my heart.*

—G. A. McKenna, journal entry

Hoping Kate waited for me, I tiptoed around the corner of the villa to check the pool. No one there. Close to three in the morning; I assumed everyone was sleeping. The cool water beckoned me to enter. I stood at the edge and took off my clothes, then tiptoed into the pool onto the blue turquoise steps and felt the cool sensation of water rush onto my skin, awakening cellular memories of youthful dalliances.

"Oh my god, I'm naked in a pool," I whispered.

I floated on my back, my breasts above waterline; moonlight filtered through the surface, lighting the pool's blue bottom, my head swirling with thoughts.

I felt uplifted by the discovery of my birth mother and finding out she had searched for me all these years. Still, I had so many unanswered questions. And who was my biological father? Some transient olive picker? Someone passing through from one orchard to another and partying with village girls in the olive grove? I'd been created out of passion, not hate. That's as far as I would let myself envision a story; the rest might never be uncovered.

I heard footsteps crunch on the white gravel rocks.

"I was worried about you," the soft voice said. Kate stepped out of the shadows and sat with legs crossed at the pool's edge, dipping her hand into the water, sending tiny ripples toward me.

"How much did you hear? That was you following us, right?" I asked, floating vertically, my head and shoulders above the surface.

"Too far away to hear," she shrugged, then said, "I wanted to protect you."

"You are a kind, sweet woman."

I swam to the pool's edge and gazed up into her sleepy eyes. I melted, a sudden release and sense of freedom, which made me want her even more. Enjoying my own sexy amble for the first time in years, I strode up the steps out of the pool—naked, bare to the world, finally brave—braving love at all costs.

Kate grabbed a pool robe and wrapped it around me, pulling me in close. "Remember at Balbianello? You kissed me, stoned. Would you have kissed me sober?" Kate asked.

"You had me at *hiya!* The first time I met you." I held Kate's hand.

I was wet, half-naked, getting cold. Her lips were wet, smooth, warm. I went to kiss her, until I caught a glimpse of two brats in the Villa's window: Erin and CJ peeked out of the master bedroom window, nodding to one another. But I no longer cared.

I snapped up my strewn clothes and pulled Kate toward my suite's entrance. We climbed the stairs to my bedroom loft, and I took her to bed. I undressed her, all except for her sexy mauve panties because they excited me. Kisses and caresses in the dim light before sunrise, as the curtains fluttered in a cool lake breeze. She kissed my waiting lips, no hesitation, no need to second guess my desire. I was ready. My mind started to swirl a mile a minute: Marcella is my biological mother, what will it be like to meet her?

Let go! Enjoy the smooth, naked body on top of me, caressing me with kisses, slowly unpeeling my robe, touching my skin with her soft firm hands, smoothing over my skin; her hot tongue against my earlobe; more kisses on my neck, my shoulders, then my breasts, where she took a nipple into her mouth, her fingers walking down my body, searching for the mystery and the wetness between my legs.

"Gerri, are you sure about this?" Kate whispered.

"Why? What's wrong? Yes, I'm sure. I've had babies. I have stretch marks."

I envisioned Artemis, the statue at Villa del Balbianello, her strong fit body now living and lying next to me. I felt unworthy that such a breathtaking woman wanted to make love to me, this time real lovemaking, not secret quickies under the arbor or in the wildflower field or in the olive grove. It petrified me. Then she set my mind at ease.

"I love your body. There's no goal, simply enjoy."

"Simply, simply, Artemis, bend me, restring my bow." She smiled at my schmaltz. "I'm a little nervous. But I'm loving this. Honest."

"Is it all right to taste you?" she asked.

My nervousness made me laugh. Then I realized: oral sex isn't necessarily safe sex. She's been a lesbian for years; she knows what she's doing. I had no signs of a sexually transmitted disease from my husband's extramarital affair, or affairs; after all, we hadn't had sex for years.

"Absolutely. I mean, yes, it's all right."

"You're flushed, are you okay?"

"Yup. Ah-huh."

"Try to relax."

"Easy for you to say. It's as if I've never done this before. I mean, yes, I'm new at *this*. But I trust you, yup, and want to share this experience with you." My rapid nattering sounded funny. I had an adrenaline rush, my nerves felt rattled but titillated, and on fire.

Kate didn't laugh at me. She moved back up and kissed me; a long, lingering kiss. The sensation tingled on my skin and relaxed me. I felt safe with her.

"I love it when you kiss me."

"I love kissing you."

Kate moved down a bit, her soft hair brushing over my chest as she licked my sensitive nipples, gently squeezing them with her lips, kissing them. She slid further down, rimming my belly button with her tongue, covering my pubic area with her hand between my legs, soft, smooth, teasing and touching me with her fingers way down into the mystery of a woman's ecstasy. Her hands went around my waist, pulling me to her and parting my legs.

I swear, I could have come right then. My body burned with passion for her.

She took her time, slowly kissing my inner thighs. Closer, I felt her wet lips, felt her soft hair sweep my belly; every caress a prelude to her hot mouth tasting me.

"You all right?"

"Nope, thinking too much. Amazing, isn't it, the sole purpose of the clitoris is for pleasure; it has eight-thousand nerve endings," I said, not knowing what part of my brain that came from.

"Let me take care of you."

And then I felt Kate's warm tongue inside me—instantly, the world of erotic sensation opened. Swept away, I became an ocean wave rolling in over and over onto the soft golden sand, conscious of Kate's tongue and nothing else.

"Don't move," she said softly.

She kept moving her tongue, gently, lightly, and then teasing in steady waves. She avoided direct contact with the clitoris— Shut up, Gerri, stop analyzing!

I watched the moonlight coming through the window and creating shadows on the ceiling, the candlelight flickering on the walls, heard the gentle lapping sounds of the lake. Then I came back when she concentrated on the clitoris, increasing the pressure with gentle, steady movements of her tongue.

If this is ecstasy, give me more. "*Bellezza, bella mia*—Beauty, my beauty," I whispered. "Oh my god, keep doing that. Yes!"

I undulated to the rhythm of my aroused pulsating body. I tried not to move. She gripped my hips to hold me in place. I almost couldn't take any more, the sweet trembling between my legs expanded, vibrating to all body parts, a rocking motion, was I on a boat again? I opened my eyes. No, not on a boat. In bed, in ecstasy, with *La grande bellezza*—The great beauty. A long heave, like giving birth, and the world expanded into infinity; in rapture I felt my body push and ignite, push and burst out, until one last erotic heave and a long, sensuous moan.... Or did I scream? Then relax, give way, allowing myself to open up and accept. The waves faded and the world flooded in.

"You 'flow from my belly like honey,'" I whispered to her.

I hugged Kate tight, feeling her nakedness on mine, realizing that our intimate melding didn't resemble sex, but rather, creating love. I had experienced breathless orgasm in a back-arching, please-don't-stop way, the feeling of pulsating waves washing through my body again and again. With our limbs entwined, the sun rising, my heart dawning, she fell asleep, but I awoke, my entire being awoke.

"That was amazing. Dear woman, how you have stirred my soul and awoken my heart." I whispered to Kate's sleeping face, the quote attributed to Anaïs Nin: "I want to love you wildly. I don't want words, but inarticulate cries, meaningless, from the bottom of my most primitive being, that flow from my belly like honey."

I must have eventually fallen asleep and moaned because Kate's hand caressed my cheek, "Shhhh, it's all right." She lay beside me, her head on my shoulder.

I opened my eyes. "I'm regenerating my passion for life, aren't I?"

"Uh-huh." Rolling onto her back, Kate chuckled, and stretched an arm into the air.

As I rattled on, she sat up and, naked, ran over to the desk to grab some paper and a pencil. Then she jumped back into bed and sat there drawing me, again. This time, she concentrated on the eyes.

"It's *regenopause*. When a woman remakes herself to become her most authentic self."

"Whatever you say, Professor McKenna."

"Turns you on, doesn't it, that I'm a teacher?" I grinned.

"In a sexy-prurient kind of way." Her sketch hand moved quickly on the paper. "I love your mouth, and the way you kiss me. I love your smile. Your eyes, especially your eyes. And I love the way my arms love you." She kissed me, playing with my hair. "That was amazing."

"*You're* amazing, my sweet American woman."

I grabbed the sketch, threw the paper into the air, and kissed her. Rolling her over, I massaged her back with one hand. Eventually, we both snoozed.

When I awoke, the room looked different. The pomegranate-colored sunrise splashed the walls and gave a golden sheen to Kate's hair. I caressed her hair and brought her head onto my shoulder, hugging her skin to skin. When my eyes focused, the colors and edges looked crisp and vibrant. Had the world shifted, or my worldview? Was I being ridiculous? Gawd, I hope so. For once in my life, I welcomed having no sense whatsoever.

I caressed her as she snoozed, kissing her forehead.

Kate snuggled closer, half asleep, opening her eyes. The sound of Kate's sweet whisper enchanted me. "I forgot to ask, are you coming to Milan, later today, this morning—what time is it? I'd like it if you did, so would the others."

"It's going way too fast." I paused, then, not wanting to think about her eventual leaving, I jumped ship, "I almost slept with my sort-of half-brother."

"Say what?"

"Carlo and Davide Vacchini, we're related. I'm Marcella's illegitimate daughter. I'm the dead baby, except I'm obviously not dead."

"What the heck?" Kate said, now fully awake, up on one elbow. "I'm missing something, like the whole story. Unless… are you adopted?"

"Yes."

Kate did a double take. "You forgot to tell me that part. You're Marcella's baby?"

"Uh-huh."

"Is that what Carlo and you talked about?"

"Yes. But, I first suspected it when I saw the black and white photo hidden in Lord Byron's book. The one you found." Kate nodded with a catatonic stare. "I'm convinced Carlo got Marcella's mother Angelina pregnant during one of their olive grove trysts. Or it might have been planned. I mean, let's say Max was sterile and he wanted an heir. They might have arranged it with Carlo, or not. Carlo as the biological father of Marcella makes him my relative. My grandfather, actually," I acknowledged, saying it out loud in the wash of dawn's light, hearing the birds twittering in the silence between thoughts.

Kate raised her eyebrows in a quizzical look, "Yes, and…?"

"Carlo slept with Angelina, La Cantante. And, of course, you know that Carlo is Davide's father by Liliana, the flower-cart lady. So, we're related but, I can't make sense of it. He's my half-cousin, or half-brother, or…?" I trailed off into a void.

"Hella, okay, this is a bit of a shocker," Kate said. "No way, Davide's not your half-brother, but he is Marcella's half-brother. They had the same father, your grandfather. That means Davide's more like your uncle."

"My uncle? If Davide already knew we're related, why would he try to have sex with me?"

"He's a man," Kate chuckled, but then frowning, she got up onto one elbow and asked, "It only matters if you're considering having sex with him."

"No, absolutely not," I sputtered. "It's all so strange. Here I've been living in my real mother's home without knowing it." A strange sensation swept over my entire body as I hyperventilated. "How the hell did Carlo Vacchini know I'd be at the Villa? Or get my mobile number? There's got to be a connection. I need to call Rosie to find out about—Ohhhhh, wait. Of course, Rosie's the connection. What a knucklehead I am."

"Who's Rosie again? Sorry, I'm still back at *you're the dead baby.*"

"Rosie's my best friend. If she knew, then this, all this, she planned it."

"A reasonable assumption. But why wouldn't she tell you? It's a real shocker for you."

"Good question. Issy told me that Rosie and Marcella both live in Devon, England. Carlo told me that, until recently they didn't know where my adoptive parents had moved to. What if, Rosie met Marcella in Devon and they clicked, it all came together, and then they arranged all this?"

"Good detective work, foo. Or maybe your friend Rosie doesn't know, and it's a big coincidence?"

"You think? Nah, too much of a coincidence." I had to repeat it to myself for clarification: "I can't believe Rosie didn't tell me. She'd better have a damn good reason."

"Wow. Unbelievable. All right, let me ask you something. Did you ever want to meet your birth mother?"

"Of course. Back in my university days, I searched but couldn't find any birth records in Canada or Italy. And my adoptive parents never knew the birth mother's real name. I gave up after that. I love my adoptive parents, Stephanie and Felix Bianchi. Mom's in her eighties now, living in a retirement community in Vancouver."

Kate leaned in closer, her hand rubbing my stomach under the sheets, comforting me.

"Funny, you know, I'm not angry. I wonder, should I fly to England to visit Marcella, to see her, to talk to her?"

"It's a start." Kate touched my chin, "Can I change the subject for a minute? This might not be the right time, but I need to know."

I nodded, with a little trepidation.

"After I leave, will we see one another again? Like, women do come out later in life. Late bloomers."

"I know that. Over the years I've been attracted to women. In university, I had a girl-thing for a few semesters. More like sexual experimentation. You remind me of her."

"I see."

"Guess I wasn't ready. I married, to a guy. Had two children. I had to carry on."

"By ignoring your desires. Could be time to let your heart lead. Be a LYLA: Love Yourself, Live Authentically." Kate smiled. "After all, your training wheels are definitely off."

I smiled at her. "Yes, but, tons of women are attracted to other women, that doesn't make them a Lesbian. I don't need to label my sexuality, do I? For now, let's say I'm carrying on with an experiment."

"I get it. In other words, like me, you don't trust falling in love again because your last lover cheated on you."

"You need to slow down. Who said anything about 'falling in love'?"

Kate bit her lower lip. "Right, yeah…"

We both took a pause, both silent, not wanting to hurt one another.

Finally, Kate said, "Am I getting too close? What if I want to be more than your experiment?"

I felt my body melt, and then Kate said, "Gerri, I'm over-the-moon for you."

My mind went blank, dead air, as if it had shutdown. In all

innocence and unfamiliar with the rules, I said, "I don't know how to answer you. Does that mean, I mean, are we done here?"

Kate winced, "Double-ouch. In that case, I enjoyed being your test subject, Professor." Kate jumped out of bed to put on her clothes. "I guess I'm not the one for you. I'm not your person. And I won't be your experiment."

"Kate, I'm sorry, I don't know what I'm doing. You're lovely, the sex was amazing. It's not as if I sleep around."

"Hella no, just an Italian walking groin and then a lesbian."

"Not fair. And for the record, I did not have sex with *uncle* Davide."

"Good to know, thanks." Kate let out an upset sigh. She paused as if deciding whether to continue. She said, "You've got my heart, Professor. What d'you intend on doing with it? Let me know when you've made up your mind."

"Don't go. I'm sorry, sorry my life's a mess. Nothing I can't handle."

"Stop *handling* and start *feeling*—You're scared."

"Of what?"

"Of letting go of your dead husband. Of falling in love again."

I felt blood drain from my body. "He's long gone. It's the grief that needs to go. Grief doesn't have a time limit."

"Yes, I know." Kate grabbed her shoes and her drawings of me, about to leave. She became distant and sad. I knew I had hurt her. She opened my bedroom door that led into the villa's upper hallway, but then hesitated. "We're leaving at nine o'clock for Milan. Are you coming with us?"

Distracted, I said, "No, yeah."

"Is that a no or a yeah?"

"Yeah, no, for sure."

"Grrr, Canadian-English, I need a translator." She paused, taking her time to speak, then said, "We're both wounded. But time is slipping away. Don't deny your feelings, Gerri, either way. Love happens when you forget to hesitate."

Once again, she took my breath away.

Kate left past sunrise. I sensed her absence, and the emptiness left its mark. Wrapping the sheet around my body, I got up, momentarily losing my balance, as if I was learning how to walk again. My clothes lay in a pile on the floor, sweet remnants of passion's embrace. Artemis had drawn her bow and shot an arrow into my heart. Now, awakened by her arrow, sleeping no more, I surfaced.

Olive leaves still clung to my clothes from hiding in the grove while spying on Davide and Carmela with the woman whom I, what? Admired. Appreciated. Wanted. *Loved?*

I sat down at the desk and taped a few leaves into my journal. An idea began to formulate, something about olive leaves. I felt a wave of euphoria, post-ecstasy, flow over me, initiating an idea, and quoted Lewis Carroll's *Through the Looking-Glass*, "'The time has come,' the Walrus said, 'to talk of many things....'"

I turned on my tablet and placed a video-call. It rang loudly in the early morning air. The video came on as Rosie's sleepy face appeared on screen.

"I found the baby photo," I said, deadpan.

"Congratulations. About time, goofball."

"Don't you 'goofball' me! Carlo told you I saw the baby photo and made the connection, didn't he?" Silence on the other end as my best friend's wide eyes stared into the webcam.

"I know you're angry with me."

"You'd better believe I am!"

"Two more days. I love you, old friend. Keep going. The game is afoot, pet," Rosie whispered and clicked off.

"The game? Are you kidding me?"

I didn't know what to think. I didn't want to think, I'd had enough. And when you think you can't handle another curveball, wouldn't you know it, the Universe throws you yet another one.

My phone vibrated: another annoying text from Paul's Freighter Girl, who possibly had a "Paul" in every port. Enough. I'd had it. I grabbed the phone, my hands trembling, and texted:

"This is Paul's wife. He's dead. Get over it. I have."

Obviously, she didn't know yet. Feeling badly for her, I surprised myself by typing, "Sorry for your loss." That seemed like an idiotic thing to say to your husband's mistress, but I felt a weight lift off me, a punctuated finality. It's finally over. But, now what?

CHAPTER 21
Milan's Last Supper

Hesitation is not facing up to truth.
It's as if we run headfirst into a fully loaded logging
truck, or stuff our emotions, then get sick or fat.
Not wanting either, I forced myself to realize that,
love happens when we don't hesitate.

—G. A. McKenna, journal entry

After sleeping a few hours, I awoke feeling refreshed and somehow different. The weather report predicted hot and sunny. I chose the only dress I brought with me, the one rolled up at the bottom of my suitcase, the little black dress no woman should be without. I still sensed Kate's kisses on my lips and her warm hands on my skin. Last night our love-making had been sensual, and I needed to be near her, even though the chemistry between us was at times overwhelming. I tried to fight it, but I lost. The woman was settling in my bones. I did wonder where this was leading.

When I met all the Galz out front at 9:00 a.m., Kate was pouting visibly, still pissed off at me. I had hurt her. How do I make peace? I wanted to run to her and throw my arms around her. Not knowing how she'd react, I didn't. Instead, I tried making myself invisible within the cheery group. Tracy and Renee, Kate's closest friends, seemed unusually cool toward me. Or did I imagine it?

All of us took the ferry to Como town. While on the ferry deck,

I couldn't stop thinking about Marcella's "dead" baby. And just then, Shaun, the American, limped past me, carrying his packsack. His face had cuts and bruises, his hand was bandaged, and he hunched over, clearly to protect a few broken ribs. He wore a T-shirt, ripped jeans, and a sad expression.

"I see you survived Lake Como."

"I'm splittin' this scene. These people are nuts! But you, you're a kind lady." With his good hand, he shook mine; I couldn't think why, perhaps California politeness.

"Will you be all right? What happened to you?"

"I didn't do what they said I did."

"Like what?" I paused, but he didn't respond. Then I said, "You worked odd jobs for Vincenzo, so, was he the one who beat you?"

"Yeah, his stooge. His wife Carmela, she likes to flirt. She's a fickle lady. She's a real *man-ipulator.*"

I nodded; I could see that in her.

"Besides, I was interested in a girl. We were makin' out, fooling around, you know. Her father caught us. That was the end of that."

"In the olive grove, right?" I said to his surprise. "Sorry this happened to you. Pleasure meeting you, Shaun. Take care of yourself." I touched his arm with a gentle squeeze.

"At least I got in some hiking. Alex, he took me with him on the trails, y'know?"

He hobbled away to stand near the railing and smoke a joint, but then called to me, "Ma'am?" I went to him, and he whispered, "Someone needs to know. They beat me pretty hard, I had to tell them. They made me tell Vincenzo that it's Davide who's seeing his wife, not me." He looked away sadly. "Tell Davide I'm sorry."

After the ferry docked in Como town, I never saw Shaun again.

Off the ferry and onto the fast train with the Villa Galz, I felt welcomed in their midst, mostly, traveling to Milan, the city of high fashion, opera, and Leonardo's famous fresco. However, Tracy and Renee sat on either side of Kate, protective, keeping her separated from me. I'd been bumped across the aisle to another compartment. We only had today and tomorrow to be together, and then their luxury villa rental would end. Seeing Da Vinci's *The Last Supper* seemed sadly appropriate.

Vera sat in another train compartment with Alex and Isabella. A litigation paralegal, Vera worked for a criminal defence attorney, handling all types of documentation and forms. Spread out on the collapsible tray table were legal immigration papers. Thanks to Vera, Alex was meeting with a lawyer in Milan to apply for his landed immigrant status. Dressed in a new suit and tie, Alex resembled another commuting businessman.

"You clean up pretty good," I said to Alex as I passed their train compartment.

He grinned proudly, flashing his beautiful new teeth. Isabella had come along for support, still dreamily in love with him. While we waited for the train to Milan in Como town, she had said to me, "Alex has a real chance to get his papers, so then Signor Lazzaro can't blackmail him. Miss Gerri, we thank you from bottom of my heart," she crossed her heart. "If you ever need anything…" she pointed to me and then to herself, "You come to me."

I watched Kate across the train's aisle and smiled at her. She wore a white straw fedora hat, a silky low-cut top and a long skirt with a long slit to show her long legs, apropos for a Milanese *fashionista*. In fact, all the women looked dressier than usual. Tracy went for a walkabout, vacating her seat. I took a chance and plopped myself next to Kate.

"Hiya," I said. She nodded but didn't look at me. Her buddy Renee winked at me and dove into reading her magazine.

While sitting together, the sides of our bodies touched. I couldn't think of anything except the feeling of my bare leg against hers and how our bodies had melted together in bed. Kate drew in a sketchbook; I leaned in closer, pretending to watch her draw, but I loved looking at her strong hands.

Finally, Kate murmured, "I'm glad you came along," and the clouds parted.

Once we arrived in Milan, we had to run from the Cadorna train station to make our timed entrance at *Chiesa Di Santa Maria Della Grazie*—Church of Santa Maria Della Grazie. A museum guard shuffled us to the left of the church entrance to the refectory of *Cenacolo Vinciano*. Leonardo Da Vinci had painted *The Last Supper* on a wall of an otherwise nondescript building that had been bombed in 1943; as Fate would have it, and thanks to the wall of sandbags put up by the monks, the fresco survived. For a maximum of fifteen minutes at a time, twenty people were allowed to view the famous fresco.

I stood behind Kate at the back of the line. Wordlessly, over her shoulder, Kate handed me the ticket that had belonged to her now ex-girlfriend. Handing it over must have felt like an announcement to the world that her girlfriend would not be returning.

I placed my hand lightly on her back and whispered, "I'm sorry we argued. You're leaving in two days. Can we make it fun?"

"Absolutely. Will we ever see one another again?" She leaned back, closer into me.

"I hope so. Anything is possible," I whispered, my lips almost touching her ear.

"After my art show in Venice, I might stay with Vera for awhile, in London. I can do some business there, visit art galleries, y'know," she said, her shoulders lowering. "I might visit Stonehenge, a few hours south of London, to get the vibration into a series of paintings. Who knows, might even set up a studio."

"That sounds wonderful," I said, my eyes downcast, my spirits crestfallen.

"Life can be uncomplicated if we choose, like, you could visit me. Anytime, anywhere."

"I'd like that," I brightened, feeling a tiny spark of hope. "I'm not sure when I'll go back home. Except, well, to teach school in September."

Kate leaned back against me, drawing our bodies closer in a spoon position. I placed my arm around her waist, touching her abdomen, smoothing my hand across her belly. So close, I kissed the back of her neck. Tracy and Renee in front of Kate turned around and, seeing our affection, smiled at us, no longer feeling the need to be protective of their friend.

Our group was next in line. A security guard stopped the blonde, beautiful Dana and wouldn't allow her entrance. He pointed to her bare shoulders. She wore a skimpy sundress; definitely not appropriate attire for entering a church. I draped my new silk scarf over her bare shoulders, and he let us pass. Six other tourists accompanied us through the revolving doors into a glass-enclosed chamber to dehumidify and regulate the humidity in the room.

The guard then shuffled us into a barren, dimly lit room. It had been the monastery's dining hall; thus, the painting of people eating. Da Vinci's restored painting loomed before us. He had painted twelve disciples and Jesus the thirteenth, sitting at a long table eating a last supper.

"Thirteen people for supper, just like us!" Jamie said.

While everyone else took flashless digital photos, Kate pulled out her small sketchbook to make a quick drawing of the fresco.

Bibi read the museum sign aloud in an actor's voice: "'Truly I tell you. One of you will betray me. These were the words pronounced by Jesus.'—Etcetera, etcetera. Hey, checkout Judas *escargot*, holding a bag of silver coins," Bibi pointed at the painting. "And that sure isn't John. It's Saint Mary Magdalene. Pope Francis declared Mary of Magdala the Apostle of the Apostles. Right on, Mary, you go, girl!" she laughed and fist-pumped into the air.

I peeked over Kate's shoulder, "The figure at Jesus' right shoulder, the one you're sketching, do you think it's Mary Magdalene?" I leaned into her, touching.

"Well, it looks like a woman, or an effeminate guy. Historians believe Leonardo was Gay, but unverified," Kate said.

I watched her beautiful, strong, deft sketch hand. I brushed her hair out of her eyes so she could sketch better. I wanted to stand there, close to her, all day. After several minutes, Kate showed me her quick sketch of *The Last Supper*. The faces depicted all thirteen villa women. And there was a fourteenth guest at the table—me—sitting in the triangular space between Kate as Mary Magdalene and buxom Bibi as Jesus.

"You like it? It's meant as a compliment."

"Sweet, thanks."

Erin interjected, "What're you lovebirds talking about?"

"Lovebirds?" I felt an instant rush through my body. "You told her?"

Kate gave Erin an exasperated look, then said to me, "I didn't say anything."

"What, so, now suddenly I'm a lesbian?" My voice got louder. "I don't feel any different because I slept with a woman. You're sexual stereotyping. Jesus!"

Did I say that out loud? Like an echoing boombox, standing directly underneath Jesus, no less, not meaning to, but loud, yes. The barren gallery filled with the echo of my voice and a Security Guard SHHH-shushed me. "*Mi dispiace.*"

Erin took a step back, bumping into Dr. Wanda and Brittany, "Yup. She's in denial."

"No kidding."

"I'm sorry, everyone. This has nothing to do with you. I'm going through a lot right now," I said, mostly to Erin.

"Hey, if the lady says she's not queer then she's not queer," Erin said to our group. "Love who you love, period. No rules, no judgments, no labels. F-off everyone!"

"SHHHHH!" said the Security Guard.

Kate lost her inner light, as if a shadow moved across her face. "I can't do this," and she headed for the exit.

"Time to go shopping," Dana said, nodding at the guard, wide-eyed and embarrassed.

Outside, feeling unsettled, I followed the Galz quietly along in the street. I figured that my anger was caused by a sudden rush of feelings for what was happening to me. And, I'd spent the last thirty-odd years tamping down feelings of being attracted to women, and now, I needed to open the closet door and let them out.

I put my arm around Kate's shoulders and she leaned into me to whisper: "If it's too much, everything, I'll understand." And I hugged her, nodding, knowing what she meant: discovering my birth mother, opening ourselves up to love so quickly, being conscious of the pending time limit; all of it was too much.

Before long, we stood in Milan's huge *piazza*. We stared at the amazing *Duomo*, the largest cathedral in Italy and fifth largest in the world. The massive cathedral, made of pinkish white marble, resembled a half-emerged spaceship with vast engine spires pointing skyward ready for takeoff.

Bibi, holding a guidebook, said, "Can you believe it? Thirty-four-hundred marble statues and over a hundred gargoyles."

"Look way up there," Hannah said, pointing skyward.

We all craned our necks to view the highest spire and the glinting gilded statue.

"It's the famous *Madonnina* statue, the Madonna, Saint Mary of the Nativity. At least they put a woman at the top. Equal pay, I hope," Hannah chirped.

A lull in the crowds allowed us to enter the church's turnstile. Kate removed her straw fedora, CJ removed her tennis visor, and a few others removed sunhats out of respect. Again, Dana wrapped my silk scarf around her shoulders. I stayed close to Kate in order to sit beside her.

In the pews alongside everyone, I prayed the high vaulted ceiling wouldn't crumble and fall on our heads from an earthquake. Here I was, not particularly religious, yet spiritual and ethical nonetheless, wearing a little black dress and sitting on a pew with thirteen lesbians. A few days ago I was a born-again-virgin, now I'm in full-blown lust. Mother Mary of God, what would she think?

Kneeling in the pew, I prayed for my son and daughter and their children and families; I prayed for Argegno, the young people and the old widows; I prayed for the Villa Galz; and for myself, and for wanting Kate, and... "And lead us not into temptation, but deliver us from...from what? This can't be evil. Why do I care what anyone thinks?"

I looked up at the high marble columns and the grotesque statues and serpents, remembering what Isabella had said, how the serpent of Milan comes alive when you mention its name.

Here, sitting in a magnificent cathedral, I understood how the church wanted us to feel: small and humble, way down low under the eyes of God. Yet I refused to feel guilty for having lain with a woman; in fact, I felt excited. I felt God didn't care which gender I slept with as long as I loved and practiced kindness, like the Dalai Lama suggested. And then a spiritual message sifted into my mind in whispers:

Love is love, not gender.

Startled, I got off my knees and sat back onto the bench, feeling Kate's closeness next to me. For some reason, my thoughts went back to Louise in university, remembering how my sexual orientation had leaned toward either sex. I never called myself "bisexual"—that word never fit me. I felt *ambi*sexual: whoever I fell in love with, I fell in love with. It's true! Love transcends gender. I've always believed that we fall in love with a person's soul long before we love their skin.

Kate held her hands folded in front of her, until her one hand gently touched my bare leg, my dress now above my knees and her skirt's slit wide open. "Are you all right?" she whispered softly.

"I can't think when you touch me." I felt a rush up my spine and then down into places you don't talk about in church. Kate removed her hand from my knee. I leaned against her, "You know, I'm kinda Gay, right? I mean, queer, like in lesbian. After all, we called Pluto a planet for seventy-five years; now we don't know what to call it. The astronomers can't make up their minds. I called myself a heterosexual most of my life, now what am I?"

"I feel a dissertation coming on," she chuckled.

"Human knowledge is acataleptic," I complied, "There's no true certainty, only probability."

"I'm kinda Christian. Do you think I'm going to Hell?"

"Oh, for godssake, Hell only exists on Earth." I laughed because my words echoed.

"Shhhhhhhhhhh!" people shushed me from all over the church.

Kate's touch had ignited me sexually; I had to disperse the energy. I was a cat on a hot tin roof. My body felt on fire, my heart wide open, but my mind was angry. Finally it hit me, I'm angry at Marcella for abandoning me as a baby—that fell ka-plonk into my lap—but I felt unprepared to admit it.

"*Mi dispiace*. Excuse me, gotta go."

I struggled to get out of the pew, tugging my short dress over my knees, and stepping on a few people's toes to get past. Storming out of the church, I heard my heels hitting hard on the marble floor, the sound echoing up into the vaulted ceiling. The others lagged behind, but they followed me.

I did turnabouts, walking around in circles in the huge hot *piazza*, walking it off. Erin and CJ, Bibi and Luciana, and the two doctors Wanda and Brittany, waited for me beside Kate. The others, Vera, Jamie with Hannah, followed a shopping-obsessed Dana along with Renee and Tracy toward the exquisite *Galleria,* a covered shopping mall.

Kate was about to say something, but I had to beat her to it:

"Kate! Kate, I have to tell you something. I know this sounds crazy, but God spoke to me in there. He or She or It, gave me a message. It said, love isn't gender, it doesn't matter. Love has no gender, when you love you love, period. That's right, right?" Everyone just stood there nodding at me. "I mean, heterosexuality is not compulsory. Thank God. I mean, yes, thank you, God!"

They stared at me calmly and nodded, "Uh-huh" and "Yup" as if it's nothing new to them.

Moving toward Kate, I met her in an explosion of feelings, kissing her square on the lips in the middle of the piazza and didn't care who noticed.

"I've been such a knucklehead." I announced to the world, "Love is about love, not about gender."

"Absolutely." Kate smiled.

"I want to love you, but I get so blown away. It's a normal reaction. I'm normal."

"Normal is no longer listed on the gender spectrum," Dr Wanda suggested.

"Okay, so, in other words, your sexual history does not define your sexuality. *You* do. And at the moment, there's no one word to describe what I am. Does it matter?" I turned to everyone.

They shook their heads. "Nope."

"It's a life long journey learning self-love," Brittany noted.

Erin wrapped an arm around CJ, "Gee whiz, Chef, whoever you are is normal for you. Just love yourself!" Erin happily boomed in a loud voice. Erin rejoiced, "Come on, everybody! Group hug."

In the middle of the piazza, Erin's long arms wrapped us all together, the *piazza* pigeons cooing and fluttering around us.

Kate and CJ took their hats off and threw them into the air, "*Viva Italia!*"

Catching their hats, we quickly ran to catch the others and spotted Dana, Vera, Tracy and Renee, Hannah and Jamie. I wrapped my arm through Kate's, entering under a triumphal arch into the Galleria Vittorio Emanuele II, one of the world's oldest shopping malls. Not your ordinary mall, the *Galleria's* impressive, glass-vaulted octagon roof covered the entire street.

"I'm in heaven." Dana sighed, drooling at the covered *Galleria* of shops: Prada, Louis Vuitton, Gucci, and others. Handing me my scarf, Dana said, "By the way, I'm sorry I treated you badly. You're all right." She hugged me and then reached over to take Vera's hand, no longer just roommates.

I whispered to Vera, "I see you're braving it. Congrats."

A smile and a nod let me know she had chosen to be vulnerable enough to take a chance on love. "And you, too?" she asked.

I smiled in acknowledgement.

Bibi yelled, "I found it!" Her voice echoed off the stained-glass dome four storeys above us and down the four corridors of glass. Bibi watched a tourist spin on his right heel on the stone floor, on a mosaic of a dancing bull.

"You're supposed to rotate with the heel of your right foot on the bull's genitals," Bibi said. "It's tradition. Brings good luck."

"Not for the bull," Erin snickered. She stuck her heel into the marble floor's indentation, a divot worn by countless tourists over many years, and twirled.

"Gerri, you're next, take a spin, fall in love," Bibi proposed.

"Come on, take a chance," CJ said, nudging me.

Bibi and Luciana pulled me over and positioned my foot on the bull's testicles.

Away I went, spinning for all my worth, wondering, "Am I brave enough to allow myself to fall deeper in love?" Kate caught me when I felt dizzy. I kissed her, feeling free to do so in public. We laughed.

I asked Kate, "Remember when you said there's no goal, simply enjoy. Does that still stand?"

"*Assolutamente.*"

I loved her response and kissed her a second time.

"Now you're making *me* blush," Kate said, squeezing my hand and holding onto my arm.

We kissed in the middle of the *Galleria* with hundreds of people around us. I felt a sense of absolute freedom. Yet, could I withstand the vulnerability that comes with letting someone inside?

Three hours of shopping exhausted all of us. I bought a pocket-sized Tuscan orange Gucci change purse the color of my bra, the one item in the entire mall I wanted to afford. Dana, on the other hand, had several shopping bags, all carried by Vera. By then we were all hungry.

We would have stayed in the *duomo* area to eat, but Dana the travel agent had made a reservation at a fashionable dinner club. Out popped several mobiles with their GPS systems on, but Dana wagged her finger. Instead of walking, we took cabs to one of the trendiest clubs in town: Just Cruizin' Club, a high-tech celebrity wonderland, designed by a local fashion designer. Not my cup of tea, but when in Milan…

The Just Cruizin' Club turned out to be a glassy, classy disco supper club with booths designed to resemble classic cars. We chose a chill-out lounge area near a crazy canopy of lights, glass, and metal designs with a fiber-optic lighting system. The dance floor's overhead sea of disco lights twinkled, highlighting the sparse crowd. Seven o'clock at night was too early for the Milanese to party, but we could order food.

Seated all together around a long table, our expensive dinner orders resembled works of art, thanks to the *elegantissimo* chef.

Dinner conversation was sporadic until I asked, "I realize, as your concierge, I'm not meant to get involved—"

"Too late for that," Tracy interjected with a chuckle, winking at Kate.

"Very funny. But, I'm curious. How did you all meet one another? You all live in California, except Vera, who now lives in London. But your professions are so different."

Bibi jumped in, "I'll tell you. It all started with Kate. Kate used to be a police officer in Sonoma, then a private dick, there was a murder, see, and—"

"Say what?"

"Shut it, Bibi," Kate glared at her.

"You're an ex-cop?" I stared at Kate for confirmation.

"My dad was the Sonoma Police Chief, he expected me to follow in his footsteps, like my brother. So I did, for a while. Then I quit. It's a long story. I'd rather dance."

Kate got up and walked briskly across the dance floor to the DJ's elaborate booth.

Bibi continued, "Anyway, Kate came to L.A. with daddykins to investigate a missing person's case, actually a friend of hers.

Turned out to be a murder," Bibi's eyes widened, "where she met Luciana an L.A. cop and Hannah the assistant forensic pathologist, and then—"

"Bibi, let's not talk about it here. It was a delicate case," Vera said, glaring at Bibi who clammed up.

Bibi eyed me for a moment and then changed the subject: "You must have freaked out after the death of your husband." Luciana kicked her under the table. "Sorry, I didn't mean to…"

"It's okay. What can I say, you deal with it, or you don't." They all looked at me, waiting, like they wanted more. "When someone you love dies, or even when someone betrays you, it takes courage to not give up, to not be a victim, and to keep on living. Basically, to keep your heart open. Broken hearts can stay closed for years. Without an open heart, you are already dead."

The word "dead" ricocheted around the dinner table, slapping each shocked face into abeyance. Kate returned and leaned on the back of my chair to listen.

I continued, "Giving up is tempting when you go through a dark night of Soul. Like my recent meltdown in Varenna," I paused to witness their surprised reactions. "Ah, never mind that," I said. "No matter what it's about, you'll eventually walk out of the dark tunnel, but you have to hold on until then. Toss the drugs and razor blades and hold on. Life will change, but it will also get better. I promise."

"Holy truth bomb, Batman!" Bibi quipped. We chuckled together, glad to lighten things up.

I figured everyone had come close to the edge themselves, having had a personal experience with a dark night of Soul.

"Bloody good we made it out alive," Vera said fervently. She reached for Dana's hand, old friends in a new relationship, and everyone smiled at them.

"You find love when you least expect it," Dana said. "Right, Gerri?"

"Yes, um. Let me ask you a question, one I've been asking myself recently." Kate, now sitting across from me, leaned forward to listen. "Do you agree with Alfred Lord Tennyson, it's better to have loved and lost than never to have loved at all? Do you think that's true?"

Right away Luciana said, "Yah, *absolutamente!* We've all

made mistakes in love, been taken advantage of. Some of us shut down. But we gotta keep the door open, right?"

"Here, here," Renee said. "Love takes courage. We all want love to be perfect, hey, but it's not, love can be messy. What else can we do, except keep on loving?"

Jamie piped in, "Loving is good for you. Don't give up."

CJ agreed, "Damn right. Onward! Stay in the game."

Dr. Wanda noted, "Keeping your heart open keeps you healthy in body, mind, and spirit. It can heal you, and it keeps you playful and childlike."

"Agreed. An open heart is one way to age well and stay youthful."

I looked at Kate. She responded. "It's all bullshit!" Everyone gawked at her.

"Okay, kidding." They all scoffed, throwing a few olives which she batted away. "But hella hard, first you've gotta be brave enough to dive in or want to take that leap. Sometimes blindfolded." She looked at me. "It's scary for everyone."

"Yup," Dana said, gazing at Vera.

"Brittany?" I asked, noticing her eyes were downcast, lost in thought.

Brittany glanced around at her friends, then said, "Have the courage to survive. We're all just hoping to find someone we're comfortable enough to be ourselves with. Simple, really." She held Wanda's hand. "Plus, practicing sexual ecstasy never hurts." Everyone broke out into raucous laughter.

I nodded, loving them. From deep within, a solution came to me, and I repeated it to them.

"All right then. Solution: *Brave the fear and fall in love. Let's leave the wallflowers on the wall and step onto the dance floor to dance.*"

Then I gazed at the delightful women who sat around the large table. "I want to thank all of you. Here I'm supposed to do the welcoming and you welcomed me. You're an amazing group of women. It's an honor to know you." I felt a lump of emotion in my throat. "I'll miss all of you. Guess I make a lousy concierge, huh? I get too attached, just like with my students."

"You're okay, Chef. Remember, no U-Hauls for a year." I didn't understand. "Never mind, old Lesbian joke," Erin whispered to me. Then she raised her glass high and said with exuberance, "Here's to all of us making it out alive, warts an' all."

Everyone clinked glasses. Then they did the special circle toast I had watched them do at dinner last night. Erin turned to CJ who sat next to her and both of them looked into each other's eyes and clinked their glasses; then, CJ turned to Tracy next to her and they took the time to look into one another's eyes before clinking glasses, and so forth around the table one by one, toasting in the round and validating the person sitting beside them by looking into their eyes while toasting.

I took my turn. Kate sat across from me, so I clinked glasses with Dr. Brittany the Hollywood psychic. When our eyes connected, Brittany whispered to me, "*Cin cin*, Gerri. May you get your wish."

I wanted to ask her what wish, but she had already turned to Dr. Wanda. After they toasted, she turned back and whispered to me, "You're psychic, too, I think?"

"A little intuitive."

"More than a little," Brittany said, tilting her head.

I smiled, unsure what to say, then risked it: "Sometimes I see visions but not often. Do you? They could be past life visions."

We were interrupted by the final group toast of glasses: "*Salute!* Health!"

Brittany raised her glass half-heartedly. Watching me carefully, she said, "Sorry, not sure what you mean by visions."

"Me, too. One day I'd like to develop it, as in intuitive channelling."

"Wonderful. Come to L.A., I give classes," she said and handed me her card.

After dinner, we split up, some to the bar, some to the sofas, some tried to get the dancing started, and others relaxed in the chill-out coves. And then an all-woman tour group arrived and filled the dance floor, ready to party.

Bibi said, "It's a British bus tour. Girls just wanna have fun, hey! " she yelled, pulling Luciana onto the dance floor.

The music switched to a romantic waltz: singer k.d. lang sang Jane Siberry's "Love is Everything."

"That's my cue!" Kate jumped up. She caught my worried look, "I asked him to play a Canadian song for my Canadian friend. Hope you like it." She put her hand out, "Dance with me?" And I took the cue.

On the dance floor, Kate took me around the waist, we sorta danced, but more like standing in close, touching, feeling a sensory arousal. My gaze never left hers.

"I'll miss you," Kate whispered in my ear. "We're leaving soon. I might never see you again."

"Come back to the villa with me, now." That made her smile.

In her beautiful eyes I witnessed the reflection of firework sabers that spewed small fountains of assorted colored sparks into the air on the dance floor. We continued our dance to the end of the song, not wanting to separate our bodies.

Kate leaned over to Erin and said, "We're heading back to the villa," and suddenly we were surrounded by Kate's friends in a dancing group hug. They made fun of us, of course, our sultry dancing together, refusing to let us leave the dance floor. Finally, we said goodnight to everyone and pushed our way out of the crowd and out into the night air.

Outside the club, Kate said, "Um, waitaminnit! Which way to the train station? Or a taxi stand?"

The streets of Milan buzzed with activity but not a taxi in sight. She pulled out her mobile phone and switched on the GPS, and we followed the little red dot on the phone's map that showed us where to go. Holding hands, we hurried toward a piazza through the historic, pedestrian-only neighborhood along *Navigli Grande,* one of only a few remaining canals that had once transported all the marble for that crazy Duomo.

The crowded, noisy area had festive lights strung across the floodlit canal where lovers sat adoring one another. Romance embraced the air. People strolled and held hands or sat at tables under cafe patio umbrellas. Kate held my hand, stealing kisses, and bought us gelato cones. Along the cobblestone lanes, her arm hugging me, we searched half-heartedly for a taxi stand, wanting to continue our lover's stroll. The twinkling lights and mist from the canal filled us with feelings of forever, encased in a protective aura, as if the night would never end.

Finally, going into a side street, we were able to flag down a taxi to the train station. Enjoying our closeness, now I couldn't wait to get back to the villa...with Kate.

CHAPTER 22
Awakening Allegra

Life is a piazza! It's extraordinary, if you choose it to be.
Gerri, it's time to come out into the piazza of life.
Move into a place of enjoying life, enjoying each other.
What is going to happen will happen, regardless
of what we want to happen. Trust...

—G. A. McKenna, journal entry

Arriving at Milano Centrale a little before midnight, Kate and I jumped on board the Como train just before it pulled away. We hid inside our own train compartment. Kate rolled down the blinds and kissed me. At that moment, no one else in the world mattered.

After sitting quietly together for a while, I asked, "Are you really a police officer?"

"I used to be a detective. It was a family thing until my dad retired to start a vineyard. I quit to paint full time. Trouble is, you know what they say: once a cop, always a cop. Nowadays, I help run the family winery and do way too many art exhibits." She paused, then threw out a careless "Come visit me."

Words stopped on my lips.

Then she said in a slow, sexy whisper, "Remember at the club, when we all talked about falling in love being scary? I wanted to tell you something," she held my hand, "One day you'll be ready to fall in love. And when you're ready you won't think about getting hurt; you'll trust what you need."

I felt tears in my eyes. "You filled me up. You put me back in my skin."

Kate's hazel-brown eyes widened, "Oh, Gerri, what am I going to do with you?" She smiled and kissed away my tears.

The train chugged down the tracks. I felt revived. She had breathed life into me and taken away the sad part.

"I remember you said once, that love happens when we forget to hesitate." I whispered as she held me, "I don't want to hesitate any longer. So, why am I?" My body trembled, knowing the answer, but I kept it to myself.

We spent the entire one-hour train ride from Milan to Como in a loving embrace. How many forevers are in one lifetime? When I first arrived at Lake Como, I felt old, finished with falling in love. Now, I felt ageless. Age was a state of mind until your body told you otherwise, but your age had nothing to do with your ability to fall in love. It amazed me that I fell for Kate so quickly and so hard. After all these years, I am finally coming out, unfolding as a blossom opens in Springtime, opening to myself. It is an "effortless grace" or *shibumi* the Japanese word for the simplicity and clarity of being where you are supposed to be.

However, the nagging thought that we live in two different countries made me realize our relationship has an inevitable ending because long-distance relationships rarely work. My angst surrounding this had possessed me all day, unconsciously. Now I realize that, at some point, we'll have to talk about it, and soon.

Once off the train in Como town we looked for a taxi to Argegno. I recognized the cute Tommaso, the androgynous butcher's apprentice moonlighting as a cab driver. Tommaso leaned against the car, waiting for clients.

"Tommaso, can you take us to Argegno?"

After we jumped into the cab, Kate put her arm around me and pulled me into a passionate kiss, necking in the backseat. I noticed Tommaso in the rear-view mirror, grinning happily at us while driving, and I broke us apart.

"Tommaso is a cute name."

"Thanks. I chose it." Tommaso flipped their short, swooped-over hair. "Your name's Gerri, right? Can I meet your lesbians?"

"Of course. They'll be at the festival. Say hello to Kate."

"Hiya," Kate waved.

From Tommaso's expression it was as if I'd said yes to meeting a Gay celebrity. Tommaso was likely the only nonbinary who lived on Lake Como. Meeting others on the gender spectrum like Erin or Luciana would be a dream come true.

We reached Argegno and Tommaso pulled up near the bustling main piazza. Tommaso said, "We are stuck, the road is closed. The festival is tomorrow. Everyone prepares."

The roadways were blocked with trucks and carts, the villagers busy hanging up mini-lights and setting up tables, all in preparation for the festival. Sofia Valente, the hotel lady, had called it the Strawberry Moon Festival, held on the night of the full moon and named after the June-bearing strawberry plants.

"It's okay, we'll get out and walk. Thanks Tommaso."

I pulled out my wallet but Tommaso said, "Nah, forget it. See you later at the festival." But I put a tip in their hand.

As we crossed the road, Lia and her friend were tottering on a tall stepladder in the middle of the piazza, attempting to hang a long string of lights. The ladder was not cooperating, and Kate ran over to help just as Lia almost fell off.

"Kate, I'll be back. Gotta, you know, find a washroom," I whispered to her and headed for the nearest open business which happened to be Sofia's hotel.

"Get us a couple of beers, will ya?" Kate asked.

I hurried to the hotel. Only the bar was open at this time of night, and it looked packed with clientele. A scantily dressed server ran around with a tray of drinks, but I managed to scoot past her, heading for the washroom. After a quick pee, I headed to the long bar for a beer, but stopped on my toes when I saw *her*.

Carmela Lazzaro's diamonds sparkled under the lights. However, Carmela's downcast eyes and sullen face betrayed an unhappy woman. Her husband, Vincenzo, sat beside her in the plush leather booth. The Asian bodyguard stood in wait as Lazzaro ranted into a mobile.

Carmela raised her eyes and saw me. Her jaw dropped open. I hid behind a mirrored post and pretended to put on lipstick. I didn't want Vincenzo to see me.

"You better not mess with me, Franco! You'll regret it," her husband yelled into the phone, "He'd never run for mayor, not that asshole Davide." He must be talking to Mayor Franco Rossetti.

Vincenzo told his Asian bodyguard, "You know what to do. Go!" And he left, storming toward the exit.

"No!" Carmela yelled, bolting to her feet.

"Sit down!" an angry Vincenzo pulled her down into the seat. "You'll pay for this later. Your boyfriend is kaput!"

Carmela, clearly heartbroken, dabbed away a few tears.

That's when I remembered what Shaun had told me on the ferry. Carmela watched me without her husband noticing. I could see her reflection in the bar's mirror.

"Try the house specialty, *signora?*" asked the outrageously cute Middle Eastern bartender with a lilting accent that only magnified his exotic good looks.

"What? Yeah, if it's special, sure. Tonight's a special occasion," I said, distracted. "Oh, and a bottle of beer, any kind."

He reached for a super deep martini glass and a bottle of Canadian Club-30.

"Holy mackerel, that's expensive whisky. I used to buy it for my husband at Christmas." My eyes widened, knowing CC-30 is 40% alcohol.

"You look as if you can afford it, *la,*" he said.

"I'm a college teacher. We deserve better pay."

The bartender grunted and continued to combine gin, vermouth, Chambord raspberry liqueur, and Canadian whisky in a cocktail shaker. What the heck was he making?

Glancing in the mirror at Carmela, I slowly took Euro coins from my new orange Gucci change purse and counted them out on the counter. The bartender raised an eyebrow at me.

Carmela said something to her husband, took her gold Prada clutch purse, and rose from the table. Vincenzo stood to watch the vision of Carmela glide toward the lady's washroom. Looking as if she'd walked off a Milan fashion designer's runway, she sauntered toward me, passing by the bar.

The bartender added an ounce of peach schnapps and three ice cubes. His head jerked in Carmela's direction, "*Buona sera,* Signora Lazzaro." She nodded at him. Before entering the washroom, Carmela turned to me and with a subtle come-hither cock of her head, bade me to follow.

I glanced over at Vincenzo's table. As soon as his wife left the table, the narcissistic nit flirted with the vacuous server, holding her hand, and ogling her cleavage.

I asked the bartender, "Can you hurry, please?" He eyed me and shook the cocktail shaker, then poured it with flamboyant expertise into the deep crystal cocktail glass.

"Good, thanks, can I have it to go?" I chortled, having expected to down one shot of whiskey and be on my way. About to grab the glass, his long index finger wagged at me, meaning it's not ready yet. Next, he lit a match and dribbled some orange zest oil which burst into flame!

"Flame Grand Tini," he announced with a gesturing swish, pushing the cocktail toward me. "Twenty-euro."

"Get outta here. That's thirty Canadian dollars! I hope that includes the beer."

By now Carmela would be wondering if I were coming at all. He tossed a twist of fresh orange zest on top before I could stop him. I had to count more Euro coins. The bartender grew impatient.

"Forget it. On the house for teachers," he whispered with a wink, then hurried over to a bill-waving customer who would give a big tip.

I dropped the ten Euros I'd counted out into his tip jar. Overcome with gratitude, I took a sip and carried it, along with the bottle of beer into the elegant washroom. Carmela held a cell phone to her ear, listening to the constant ringing.

"I'm trying to get Davide. Something terrible has happened."

She pushed me hard into a toilet cubicle, almost spilling my drink. Carmela locked the stall and pushed me down onto the floral-rimmed toilet seat cover. I was now almost eye-level to her voluptuous cleavage.

"Signora McKenna, please help me. Davide must be warned!" Usually so elegant, Carmela grew frantic, sweat pouring from underneath her dark brown bangs and her bare cleavage glistening. "He won't answer my calls. I've left messages. Please, you must warn him. Vinnie's bodyguard has left to hurt him."

"Who's Vinnie? Oh, you mean Vincenzo."

"My husband, he wants to have Davide killed!"

I pulled out my mobile and dialed Davide's number.

"No matter, he no answer, it rings and rings. Shaun, the hippie boy, he told Vinnie that Davide and I are having an affair. They will kill him!"

"I was afraid of that."

A LOUD knock on the washroom's front entrance made us both jump; I stood up, she grabbed me, her cleavage compressing against mine; I tried not to look.

"Carmela, you all right?" boomed a male voice in Italian. It sounded more like a threat.

"*Un momento!*" We heard the door creak open, someone peeked inside but then left.

Davide answered my call. "Davide, it's Gerri. Carmela needs to talk to you."

"I got her messages. All five of them. Tell her I'll be all right." And he hung up.

"He's all right," I told Carmela who looked faint.

Carmela hugged me hard, leaning in closer to whisper, "Give Davide a message? Just to him. Not on the phone. See him as soon as you can. Tell him I will meet him. Tell him tomorrow is the night. *Comprende?*" I shook my head, not understanding. "He'll know." She moved off of me to go. "Tomorrow is the night, *sì?*"

"Wait," I whispered, grabbing some toilet paper. She watched me inquisitively. "The sweat, it's a dead giveaway." I dabbed the sweat on her brow and prodigious cleavage. Carmela took a deep, bosom-lifting breath and left to join her possessive husband.

I waited until I felt more composed, finishing my drink, figuring out what to do. Ready, I stormed out of the washroom, almost forgetting Kate's beer, and hurried through the now-crowded bar area. The place was packed, as though everyone had finished setting up for the festival at once. I got crushed.

Carmela stood waiting for Vincenzo as he argued with his bodyguard, who said he didn't find Davide. Vincenzo grabbed his wife by the arm and they left in a huff.

Squeezing out the doorway, I witnessed Vincenzo's black Mercedes limousine squeal away into the night. I ran to Kate who stepped off the stepladder just in time to take the beer from me.

"Hot night, thanks for the beer. Can we sneak away now?"

Just at that moment Davide's Maserati squealed to a stop on the roadway.

"No, can't. I gotta do something."

Much to Kate's chagrin, I hurried toward him. "Vincenzo knows. Get out of here."

Davide's handsome face looked panicked and he kept rubbing his hands. "I saw them drive away. Everything's all right."

"Call Carmela, let her know."

"I can't phone her, Gerri. Vincenzo monitors her calls," Davide said. "His bodyguard, he wants to kidnap me, or kill me. But the villagers stayed late to decorate. Too many witnesses." A handful of villagers remained, some busy picking up the litter. "I was to meet her here tonight, but he showed up at the bar."

Davide rubbed away a Rune chalk mark on the bench beside us, except this one had been drawn reversed. "Ah-ha!" I exclaimed. I felt relieved to finally confirm the chalk mark meant a rendezvous signal, in this case, for Davide and Carmela to meet either here or in the olive grove, depending on whether they drew it reversed.

Two villagers were setting up a canvas tent and a rope broke loose. Kate and another local ran over to help out.

I felt a connection to Davide, wanting to help him in a brotherly way, "Davide, I have to tell you—"

"I don't know what to do about Carmela." Davide's voice quivered.

"Go home, get some sleep."

Thinking of Kate, I didn't know what to do either. Distracted, I forgot what I was about to tell him.

"Come home with me. I need you," he purred, coming closer. I had to push him away.

"Davide, you know, we can't be romantic. We're blood relatives."

"Gerri, it's too distant to count, way far away."

"You knew all this time." I slugged his arm. "Carlo is Marcella's father, and Marcella is my mother, so you and I are blood relatives. You're my frickin' uncle. Like, that sounds so weird. And, well..." I bit my lower lip. "It doesn't matter anyway—I'm Gay."

"*Che cosa*? What?"

"Yup, I'm Gay! *Sono lesbico*—I'm a lesbian, gay, queer, whatever you want to call it. I've wanted to say that all my life."

Saying it aloud felt like an undeniable awakening. I glanced over at Kate, helping with the topsy-turvy tent.

Davide followed my gaze, his mouth dropped open, his eyes widened, but he managed to say, "Then, I am happy for you, *cara mia.*"

"Thanks," I sighed, then noticed Kate eyed us suspiciously. "Gotta go. Wait! I forgot. Carmela gave me a message. She said, tell Davide I'll meet him. Tomorrow is the night. Meaning, *tonight* is the night."

Davide froze, an odd expression on his face. His body went stiff, and his beautiful brown eyes stared out into space.

"Are you all right? Do you know what she means?"

He awoke from his trance. "I go now. Please to meet me at the dock, 21:00-hours."

"Nine o'clock at the ferry dock, why?"

"No, the private dock, next by close. To help me, in case. Do you promise, Gerri?"

"In case of what?"

"You and I, we are blood. We help one another."

"Right, sorry. I've never had a sort-of brotherly uncle before. I'll be there."

"Gerri, tonight is the night! You are the light of my eyes, *dolcezza*—sweetheart."

Do all Italian men say that stuff? And what the heck does it mean, if anything? He grabbed me and kissed my cheek, the brat. And of course, Kate happened to look over at that precise moment. Then he jumped into his Maserati and drove away, doing a U-turn and speeding away up the hill onto the main road.

I grabbed Kate's hand, pulling her away from the tent and, seeing Tommaso still in front of the hotel, we jumped back into their taxi. Smiling, they managed to squeeze the cab past the remaining villagers decorating their private boats and setting up market stalls.

At the villa's front gate, we waved to Tommaso as they drove away.

"Sooo…?" Kate paused with a grin and put an arm around me, "Did you want to…? Like, well, actually, I don't know what you want?"

"Meet you in your room. I've got to check on the pups."

"Right," she kissed me, "Hope you're not too long," and went in the front entrance.

I hurried into my apartment. Having asked Isabella to feed the dogs dinner, I let them out for a romp. My phone dinged with a text message from Kate. It read: "Miss you already."

My thumbs paused over the keypad, wondering, should I say it? What would be the consequences if I said it, even to myself? Instead, I thumb-typed: "I miss you, too :-("

Two seconds later I received a reply: "Come to my room."

My heart flipped. I wanted to sprint to her room right then. But I was exhausted. I had barely slept for two nights. I needed time to myself. I poured a glass of water and stood at the Dutch door, keeping an eye on the dogs. My mind mused in the clear still glimmer of dawn, focusing on my inner voice.

I gazed at an early morning fishing trawler that floated on the mist-laden surface. It looked ethereal. On foggy days, the lake fish swim close to the surface, unaware of the point where sky meets water—my problem exactly. Not knowing where my heart met my mind, blurred lines fraught by an overwhelming urge to jump in *headfirst* as opposed to *heart-first*, and pretend to be unafraid to experience loss, once again.

Running away is vital, sometimes. *Hejira*, running away with honor on a journey. But where had I landed? I ran away to Lake Como and, diving deep, had surfaced by loving a woman. I wanted to accept and merge into this new awakening, to regenerate.

My heart told me, *"Life is extraordinary if you choose it to be."*

I am learning to be unafraid to swim through the storms of life. Like a club-footed Lord Byron who dove into the Ligurian Sea, swimming 7.5 km to Lerici from Portovenere across the Golfo dei Poeti—Gulf of Poets, I have become the swimmer. I have become my middle name, Allegra. Like his abandoned illegitimate daughter, Allegra must have been unafraid to use broad strokes to swim through her short little life.

I remembered what we'd talked about at the Milan disco, about loving and losing, and the words that came to me: *"Brave the fear and fall in love ... step onto the dance floor to dance."*

Boldly, I gathered my thoughts as I opened my bedroom door and crept along the villa's upper hallway to the room with the open doorway. Quietly, I slipped into her bed; her bed sheets felt warm, inviting. I snuggled in close to her, putting my arm around her waist.

"I don't want to be anywhere else," I whispered. She hugged me. We both fell sound asleep.

We woke up Saturday morning to the sound of her alarm clock but luxuriated in bed most of the day. We made love. I made her breakfast and coffee; we ate it in bed. We made love again. Her long, smooth legs entwined with mine. We heard noises, movements, as the other women in the villa got ready to go out for the day, to the festival. Someone knocked on our locked door.

"Go away!" we both yelled.

"Are we meeting you in town, at the festival?"

"Yes!"

They left.

We made love until we were both satiated.

CHAPTER 23
Tunnel of Tears

The key is to stay curious and open to all perspectives.
Only then do secrets reveal themselves.

—G. A. McKenna, journal entry

K ate's bedroom wall clock read 5:00 p.m. The day had gone by in a dream. "I want to show you something," I said to Kate, as we both finished dressing to go to the festival.

"Ready? Follow me."

I led her down the main staircase, through the living room, and past the life-size portrait of Angelina, toward the villa's library. Seeing her empty easel against the wall, I stopped.

"Hey, where's your painting?"

"Ah, yes, I had movers ship it off to the Venice art exhibit."

"Too bad, I wanted to see it."

"I'll show you the photos later," she said as we hurried into the library and stood at the bookcase. Kate asked, "Okay, so what are we doing here?"

"Watch."

She watched as I placed my fingers on the brick with the faded Masonic mark and pressed the fake brick. It clicked and popped open like a wooden drawer.

"What the…?"

"Wait for it."

A second later the fake bookcase with the recessed photo shelf creaked open and Kate jumped back.

"Whoa, that's clever." She peeked inside, "A secret doorway, with another door inside. How do we open it?"

"In a minute."

I took a thick book and blocked the door open before it creaked closed. Kate watched me as I grabbed the antique skeleton key from the brick's secret drawer and went to the walnut-veneer writing cabinet.

"Now what are you doing?"

"Checking on a hunch. My adoptive grandmother had one of these cabinets. And…" I held my breath and turned the key in the cabinet's brass keyhole. Sure enough, just like my grandmother's, a piece of wood on the inside flipped open, exposing a concealed hiding place.

"Huh, brilliant!" Kate exclaimed. "What's your hunch, Sherlock?"

I kissed her. Then stuck my hand inside the secret opening. Well hidden, was a plain manila file folder. The white label read: "Allegra."

I smiled, saying, "Allegra's my middle name."

"You're kidding?"

By now my heart raced, wondering, "*Am I about to find an important piece of my history?*"

I opened the folder with trepidation, unsure what I would find. Inside was a copy of a government document. We both read it at the same time.

Kate said, "It's a birth certificate. Allegra Angelina McKenna Ferrario. Born in Milan. Is that…?"

"Yes, it must be the original name of Marcella's daughter."

"*Your* real name. This is your original birth certificate, hidden away. What's your full adopted name?" Kate asked.

"Bianchi is my adoptive surname. They told me my name is Geraldine Allegra McKenna Bianchi. I often wondered where the McKenna came from."

"I thought McKenna was your married name."

"No, Lang is, or would have been if I'd changed it when I got married, but I didn't. McKenna, along with Allegra, is a middle name that came with me from the adoption agency. Before starting to teach, I changed my legal surname to McKenna. It's interesting, now, to remember that I always resonated more with McKenna than my adoptive name of Bianchi."

"Who is McKenna? Middle names are given in honor of someone."

"My adoptive parents didn't know."

I pulled out a sealed manila envelope from inside the folder. "Okay, what's this? Rats. It's sealed, can't open it."

I had my phone in my shoulder purse and snapped a photo of the birth certificate.

"Why isn't it filed with the Registrar of Vital Statistics?" Kate asked. "They must have hidden it because there's no death certificate to go with it."

I tucked the folder and envelope back inside and pressed the cabinet's secret drawer, clicking it back in place. Then I returned the skeleton key to the brick drawer, exchanging it for one of the smaller brass keys, which I held up to Kate.

"Are you game?"

"Did Watson ever stop Holmes?" Kate kissed me and eagerly snapped the key out of my hand. She unlocked the smaller inside door and peered inside the dark tunnel. "Yikes, it's pitch black in there." She turned on her phone's flashlight and I followed her lead. The light shone down three narrow steps going down into nothingness. "Coming?"

"Sure, why not? My life's been way too long anyway. Wait! The door might lock behind us. God, that would be terrible. We'd never get out."

Kate checked the moveable bookcase door, "There's a lever, here, on the inside, to unlock it." She tested it while I stood in the library; I returned the small door key to the brick's secret drawer. "It's okay. Come on, let's do it."

She shut the bookcase door and went down the steps first. Noticing a light switch on the wall, she flipped it and a row of lights that ran along the wall flickered on. But the light bulb above us and another one exploded in a burst of shattered glass.

"Shit!" Kate covered us with her arms. "It's okay, a few lights stayed on."

We still used our phone flashlights as we crept along the narrow tunnel. About twenty-five feet into the tunnel, we emerged into an open space. Timeworn wooden benches lined the perimeter of the square room that had been carved out of the rock and dirt, similar to a bomb shelter.

Kate found a stack of disintegrating newspapers and shone the flashlight on the headlines.

"Dated 1944, some 1943. All during the Second World War."

Empty tin cans, glass bottles, and utensils littered the area, all of them possibly over seventy years old, circa 1940s. And lots of spider webs.

"I hate spiders," Kate said, fighting with a sticky web.

"Don't hurt the spiders."

"Seriously?"

I spotted something on the wall and crept closer to it with my flashlight. "Interesting graffiti." Along with people's initials, I recognized carved Masonic symbols that had now become a familiar sight to me. I heard noises and footsteps.

"Do you hear that?"

Kate froze and listened. "No, nothing. Except the breeze from down the tunnel."

"You don't hear the whispers?" I described to her what I envisioned:

People of all ages huddled together in the dark interior of the hidden underground room. They ate, slept, talked in whispers, read newspapers or books. The whites of their eyes glowed under the dim lights. Most wore traveling coats, caps, and boots, and had a packsack close by, ready to escape at the first alarm. The sweat of fear and panic radiated in the room, and the smell of urine-stained buckets filled the air.

"Let's get out of here," I told Kate.

"Wait a minute. Don't you find all this interesting? It's an escape tunnel—for whom, the war refugees? Carlo told us Angelina helped smuggle persecuted people to escape fascist Italy, right?"

"I believe so." The palm of my hand touched several carved letters on the wall. "Here, shine your light."

We both aimed our flashlights at a section of the wall. The words were scratched into the solid clay, deep and worn. We stepped back in order to read it because it covered half the wall:

Resistere a ogni costa! L'amore trova la strada. Non mollare mai.

Kate asked, "Can you translate?"

"I'll try. First word is 'resist'… *costa*, price…*L'amore*, love… 'never' something… *mollare*, what's 'mollare'? Yes, I see it." I paused, then said, "It says, Resist no matter the price! Love will find a way. Never quit, never give up."

"Wow, pretty amazing," Kate said. "Imagine, all these people, escaping during the war. From the murderous Nazis. And here they sat in the cold and the dark, believing this—to never give up because eventually love will find a way."

"Please, let's get out, can we? Please. I can't breathe," I said, sucking in the rancorous, tight air of past terror.

"Follow the wind," Kate said, taking hold of my hand to lead us into the second part of the carved tunnel, another twenty feet to a set of earthen stairs going uphill. At the top, a wooden door made from planks blocked our way. Half of the planks sagged inward, broken. I recognized them; I'd fallen on them just the other day while hiding in the bushes.

Kate pushed on them and they fell away, rusty nails falling off hinges. The rush of air going down the tunnel was life entering a dead place. I stepped through the entrance into the olive grove, filling my lungs with the oxygenating olive trees and sunlight. The villa stood behind us a mere sixty feet or so, far enough away for anyone to escape into the grove under cover of darkness.

CHAPTER 24
Full Moon Festival

Forgiving everyone releases you; however,
trusting them again is another matter.

—G. A. McKenna, journal entry

A t seven o'clock, as Kate and I walked toward the village, we heard a booming voice on a loudspeaker way down in Argegno's main piazza. The Strawberry Moon Festival was getting underway. We soon stood in the middle of the activity and listened to live music and a woman singing. I had never seen so many people in tiny Argegno. The town buzzed with hundreds of tourists and locals, with more arriving by ferry.

My promised rendezvous with Davide at the dock wasn't until nine o'clock, which left plenty of time to enjoy the festivities. I meant to tell Kate about this commitment but got distracted by the carnival atmosphere. The din of jovial voices filled the air from hawkers shouting to sell crafts and folk art at stalls, excited children shrieking with delight, dogs barking, riders on noisy scooters weaving through the crowds, along with the shrill sound of a cop whistle on the roadway directing traffic.

After texting, we found the Villa Galz at the fountain. We tagged along, walking with them around the festival. Kate and I held hands, both feeling a little intoxicated from our all-day lovemaking, our legs like rubber, our hearts wide open. After being so close for so long, our bodies felt connected by an invisible energy that embraced us. We couldn't let go of one another.

Tommaso ran up to me, excited, yet a little shy, and I introduced them to the Villa Galz, who immediately embraced the timid bird into their flock. With an ear-to-ear grin, Tommaso clung to the sides of the more masculine Erin and Luciana.

The aroma from several food stalls outside the cafes made my hungry stomach rumble. The local dishes included lake perch and risotto, tripe served with polenta, and braised wild boar, plus veggies and salad.

Kate and I filled our plates with fish and salad. We found a spot and huddled in a corner to eat our dinner. I turned my phone on to look at the photograph of my real birth certificate from the library's cabinet. Kate watched me with smiling eyes.

I whispered my birth name into her ear, "Allegra Ferrario."

"Sexy name," Kate whispered back.

"Allegra in Italian means 'joyous.' I'll try to live up to it."

My senses thirsty, I drank of the Italian life, seeing with different eyes and hearing with different ears. I felt pure joy, drinking in the small-town Italian life during *la passeggiata*, the walk or evening stroll. Before dusk, all over Italy in local squares or along boardwalks, residents promenade arm in arm with family and friends, a time to see and be seen. Young people hope for new romances, and the elderly sit on benches sharing the latest gossip. Witnessing this wonderful custom in Argegno, I understood why *passeggiata* strengthened a sense of belonging. However, tonight was special: it became a part of *my* belonging, *my* people, *my* heritage, and *my* birthright. The feeling of belonging precipitated an inner shift, feeling it with all my physical sensations and inner being. It made me realize how tragic it is to forget the magic of life and the connection to others. At long last, their world opened to me and I felt a part of it.

I scanned the crowd and noticed the familiar faces of the villagers, happily selling their wares. An idea struck me to the very core of what we'd witnessed in the library's tunnel. And I said to Kate, "These people, many of them locals, they're the relatives of the refugees who escaped from the Nazis. As in Carlo's story and in the tunnel. They returned to live here."

Kate's beautiful eyes teared up as she watched them intently.

"Yes, I think you're onto something, Professor. Your grand-mother, Angelina, helped their relatives escape the Nazis by hiding them in the villa's tunnel or in the olive grove."

"Right. To await transport to safety out of the country. It makes me shudder to think such a global conflict will ever happen again. Greed and power are hungers that are never quenched. Like the corruption of power and the power of corruption."

Scanning the environs, I recognized Diego at the butcher's cart selling salami sandwiches, along with his old father from Poland. The old man, usually in the back of the butcher's shop, now in his nineties, walked with a cane. I assumed he had escaped from Poland in his youth.

I watched Sofia Valente in front of her hotel, beside her dentist husband Sergio, chatting with friends as their waiter served beer and wine at the outdoor tables. I could easily picture her parents standing beside her, remembering that Alex told me they had been famous Austrian journalists, who must have escaped the Nazi invasion.

I could not imagine what they'd gone through, what they'd experienced, like so many in other countries, fleeing their homes, taking what little they could carry and leaving the rest behind, running from persecution for simply being alive.

No doubt similar stories revolved around Dr. Emilio Leoni's relatives, whose mother had been my midwife. I saw him enjoying the festival near his closed office, visiting with friends. I noticed Johan, the German pharmacist, exit his shop's door, lock it, and then join a few friends. I recalled the story he'd told me about his parents working in Angelina's olive grove when he was a baby. Johan and his friends jumped into a rickety Volkswagen bus and drove up the hill, perhaps to escape the crowds.

I smiled at seeing Carlo's grandson, Roberto, flirting with Lia, the Gelato Girl, while her boss, the big bellied Rocco, tended the hordes of gelato customers. Rocco's T-shirt had a flag of the Romani people, with the words "Gypsy Lives Matter," along with the Muslim star and crescent moon symbol. His family may have also been affected by Hitler's prejudice like so many others from various backgrounds and religions.

Next door, Carlo stood at his bakery cart, busy selling freshly baked goods, the aroma lingering in the air. I waved to him, and he waved back, smiling.

"Angelina helped so many people. All those stories will soon be lost to time," I said to Kate.

"Not lost if we remember," she said.

"I wonder what Marcella thought of having a heroine as a mother? Growing up knowing how well-loved her mother Angelina was. And yet, when Marcella had me, she gave me away like a sack of potatoes."

"Gerri, full stop! You don't know that."

"You're right, of course. Thanks," I reconsidered, then, "Young women have many reasons for giving away their illegitimate baby. They're either too poor, or too emotionally unprepared, or too alone."

"Or too scared."

"Yes. Too scared the villagers might have shamed her for dishonouring Angelina's memory. Or perhaps they wouldn't have."

The sounds and sights of the festival intervened. I leaned into Kate, putting my arm around her, caressing her back. I knew we had to have "our talk" but didn't know how to broach the subject. I bit down on the bullet and blurted it out.

"Is this our last night?" I asked, watching for her reaction.

"You know it is. I have to leave tomorrow for Venice and my art exhibit. And then, as I mentioned, I'm off to London. My art agent called again. She wants to set up an exhibit there. Gerri, you have an open invitation to visit me anywhere. My exhibition schedule's on my website. Come to me anytime."

"I'd love to be with you, but I have school starting in September, unless…"

Kate frowned. "Unless what?"

"Unless one of us uproots themselves to be with the other."

Kate's expression turned sad. "We're from two different countries, two different worlds. An American visual artist and Canadian culinary artist. We fell so fast."

I found the courage to say what we were both thinking. "Long-distance relationships—some work, most don't."

"I hear you. You've got to admit, it's been amazing." Kate whispered sweet and slow, "I'm going to miss your kisses." She kissed me.

She was saying goodbye. I tried to hide my tears. Sadness crept into our celebratory mood.

"We'll keep in touch, won't we? There's always video calling, you know. And Sonoma is only a two-hour flight from Vancouver."

I felt her body go rigid against mine. "That's not good enough for me," Kate whispered, as she clasped my hand in hers. "If there's no hint of being together, of starting a life together, then what's the point?"

I retracted, feeling upset. She'd said it aloud, the inevitable. Kate put her arm around my shoulders and hugged me close. Being near her like this, it felt as if nothing else mattered.

"We shouldn't have started anything," she said.

"Kate, please, don't say that. These past few days have been the happiest I've had in a long time. It's just...My heart has to handle a lot of changes right now."

"I get it, I understand. I do. You've just found out who your biological mother is. Take the time to see what happens, to meet her. I know you're scared."

Out of nowhere, Isabella came running up to us, yelling, "Did you see this?" she asked, flashing the local newspaper. "You famous!"

An advertisement with a huge photograph of me blared on the front page of the local tourist newspaper. I remembered that one of the kiosk owners had taken photos of me at the market with the Villa Galz. My likeness looked frozen in time. The photograph had been digitally altered, putting a chef's hat on my head and a long mixing spoon in my hand. The advertisement read: Famous Chef Teaches Cooking Class in Argegno Hotel. True to her word, Sofia had advertised the cooking class, albeit exaggerating the truth.

"And posters are everywhere," Isabella said, pointing animatedly.

I glanced around and saw a few, but I also saw homemade posters that read, "Davide Vacchini for Mayor."

"Davide's running for Mayor? Does he know?" I chuckled.

Isabella said. "We want him to run. He accepted this morning at our village meeting. He no want the casino, too."

Kate read another article in the newspaper. "Issy, did you see this?" Kate showed her the headline: Casino Building Permit Favored to Pass. "It says the town council will see the plans next week. Ay-yah but, if they haven't seen the plans, why is it favoured to pass?"

Isabella grabbed the newspaper, "Does it say where, where they want to build it?" she asked, walking away to the van, still reading the article. She jumped into the van and quickly drove away, heading out of town.

"Where's she going?"

That's when Alex rushed outside from the bakery and stopped beside Carlo in the front doorway. His new front teeth glinted in the light. He whispered in Carlo's ear. Carlo frowned and shook his head, rather disgusted. Glancing up, I saw a light in the apartment above them.

Liliana, Carlo's wife, the elderly flower-cart lady, caught him and hugged him. After a long lusty moment, she slapped him on the chest, shouting at him. I translated, "What are up to, old man?"

Suddenly, I started to sense a menacing aspect to the night's festivities. I focused on a few local motorcycle *polizia* standing guard, dressed in their tailored police uniforms: a bomber jacket, tight pants, and chopper sunglasses.

Nearby, Mayor Franco Rossetti rode into town in his shiny black limo, like a Black Hat in a western movie. Exiting the limo, Rossetti strutted around in his light blue suit, shaking hands and smiling with gritted teeth, his silver-speckled hair perfectly coiffed. He stopped near me, facing the crowd and waving. His eyes froze on me for a moment. Did he recognize me? Danger dangled in the air. But then he looked past me to one of the posters advocating Davide for mayor. The hostile look on his face warned me that, along with his pal Vincenzo, he also had a strong dislike of Davide becoming mayor.

While Kate bought a flower from the cart, I side-stepped over to Rossetti, "Do you think he'd win? He's against a casino. So are the villagers."

"It's a joke. He'll never be mayor. Stay out of it. Don't make any trouble." He glared.

"Excuse me?"

"We don't need an outsider to make trouble. Too many here owe back taxes. The casino will save them."

Mayor Rossetti's face grew red. He ripped up the poster and stormed away.

Lia, the Gelato Girl, overheard. "What an asshole."

"What did he mean?"

"He tries to convince the council to evict us from our homes for redevelopment. Argegno needs more business, like tonight," Lia said.

"Or start a town business," I muttered to Lia who queried me with a probing look.

But a sinister feeling gnawed at me. Something was about to happen.

Most of the Villa Galz clearly felt festive, with full wine glasses in hand. I joined them at the lakeside promenade, where Kate gave me a rose. Renee had taken to the grinning young Tommaso and kept her arm around Tommaso's shoulder; Tracy didn't seem to mind.

As soon as dusk settled over the lake and the full moon peeked over the mountains, Mayor Rossetti, alongside his bald bodyguard, took to the podium to announce the official opening of the first Strawberry Moon Festival. The drum roll sounded, and, in one snap of the switch, the entire town was illuminated with a thousand strings of tiny white lights. Everyone gasped in delight and applauded.

I gave myself over to the romantic setting, holding Kate's hand as we strolled, two lovers whose inevitable ending felt temporarily pre-empted by tonight's beauty.

Gazing at the rising full moon, Kate said, "It's our first full moon together. I hope it's not our last."

As the crowded piazza and streets buzzed with hundreds of tourists, the locals helped bring out from the cafes and restaurants the huge baskets of strawberries for everyone to help themselves, along with paper bowls and jugs of fresh cream. Bibi told us that June is prime time for strawberries and Italy is the world's fourth-largest exporter of strawberries.

Then I saw them.

Vincenzo Lazzaro stepped out of his limousine, driven by the Asian bodyguard. Then the elegant Carmela exited the limo and hung onto the arm of her entrepreneur husband; I assumed for appearances. Compared to the locals and the tourist crowd in casual summer outfits, the Lazzaros looked like celebrities dressed in all their finery. Some of the locals frowned in disgust as the couple moved toward the Mayor, the bodyguard pushing people out of the way.

I edged closer for a better look, momentarily losing Kate in the crowd when our hands got dislodged from one another's by the pressing crowd.

Mayor Franco Rossetti kissed Carmela's hand—the hand with the big diamond ring—and murmured a few words which made her smile. Then Vincenzo whispered in her ear, no doubt her cue to disappear; the men folk had to talk business. Carmela grabbed her husband with one hand at the back of his neck and kissed him on the lips, a hard, cold kiss. His trophy wife turned on her high heel and hurried away. I tried to keep her in my sightline, but she quickly disappeared into the crowd.

Carmela and Davide had both said: "Tonight is the night." But Davide was nowhere around.

Prior years of lip-reading my students came in handy, but I struggled with the Italian translation. Rossetti said to Vincenzo, "A beautiful wife. I'd kill Davide if he played around with my wife."

As *Signori* Rosetti and Lazzaro turned to walk in my direction, I hid in the crowd. Both of their bodyguards forced a pathway in the crowd and escorted the Mayor and Vincenzo, the richest businessmen in the area, toward a special table. I surmised they were also celebrating the casino deal that was favoured to get permits.

Kate found me, "Whew, thought I'd lost you. Let's go some-where quiet, we need to talk more. To figure things out." She walked us toward the water's edge.

"Of course, but I can't leave just yet."

"Why?"

Just then, Davide's yacht pulled into the reserved spot at the private dock. Wearing a nautical jacket, he looked his usual suave self. However, watching him tie up with his foot on a cleat, I noticed he wore a pair of hiking boots. Odd. Davide had said to meet him at 21:00-hours, ten minutes from now.

Vincenzo had also noticed Davide and glared at him.

"Gerri?" Kate implored, trying to get my attention.

"Sorry, I've got to meet Davide at the dock."

"You're meeting Davide? Not him again!" Her face puffed with emotion. "Then are we done here, to quote you? I'll be with the others," she said, pointing to her friends.

I tugged Kate's arm, not letting her leave. "I don't want you to go."

She smiled at me with a sad expression, saying, "Well, it's inevitable, isn't it?"

"Nothing is inevitable."

Her friends were waving us over, but I hung on to her tight, not letting her move. They were at a stall checking for last-minute souvenirs near Carlo's bakery. I noticed Carlo was busy with customers at the bakery cart. My eyes were drawn upward to the second floor above the bakery, where lights shone in the upstairs window. A shadow moved behind the curtains. The curtain shifted and Carmela peeked out. Interesting.

Kate asked me, "What are you frowning at?"

"I'm not sure. Something's about to go down."

I glanced over at Vincenzo. He stood up, his face twisted in anger. I wasn't expecting him to storm toward me. But he was looking over my shoulder at Davide. The crowd parted and people got out of his way. I froze, standing in his path. Vincenzo stopped right in front of me.

"You again? My wife said you saved our daughter," Vincenzo said. "As a favor I tell you. Get out of here before he hurts you. He wants you out of the way," Vincenzo shouted into my ear, his eyes wild.

"Who? Rossetti?" I glanced at the mayor, still sitting at the special table.

"He knows you're the heir to the villa."

Kate intervened, "Back off. Leave her alone."

"Wait, what?" I said, uncertain what he meant. "Is that where he wants to build the casino, at the Villa della Cantante?"

My phone's alarm rang, reminding me to meet Davide at nine o'clock. The ringtone sounded like a loud Gatling gun. Vincenzo put his hand on his gun in his shoulder holster, thinking the worst, as did his bodyguard.

The young Roberto, as if on cue, jumped into the center of the square wearing a handheld marching snare drum. As he began a loud drum roll, we became immersed in a flash mob of several marching drummers and dancers. The crowd loved it, clapping along. Clearly someone had planned the flash mob as a diversion, but a diversion from what?

The front door of the bakery opened and out walked a cloaked figure, clutching Alex's arm. She wore a Venetian mask, but I knew it must be Carmela, with her big diamond ring, wearing a long coat and a Borsalino fedora pulled down low; forever the fashionista.

It happened so fast. Vincenzo had his eyes on Davide, who jumped off the boat and ran toward Carmela. Vincenzo was about to turn and see Carmela, so I stepped in front of him, grabbed him by his expensive lapels. We were the same height except he was as broad as a barn.

"Signor, tell me! Is it true about the villa?"

I glanced over Vincenzo's shoulder, past the flash mob, to where Davide helped Carmela run through the crowd.

"You saved my daughter's life, I am in your debt," he shouted. "*Sì*, to demolish the villa for the casino. It's the largest property."

I shouted back, "There's no way. We won't allow it," I yelled. The poor man looked stunned. By now the crowd of onlookers overheard, as did his nervous-looking bodyguard.

"You must not be here like this, in the open—an easy target. You the *vedova*, you are Allegra, now he knows what you look like." He pointed to my face on a cook's poster plastered on a shop window. The word "ALLEGRA" had been written across it.

"Gerri, let's go," Kate warned.

Shocked, I pushed him away. In a domino effect, he tripped and fell backward into the arms of a fat woman in a Venetian mask, who bucked him away, and he landed on top of his bodyguard and a few others. Kate tried to help the fallen bystanders.

I hurried toward the water's edge, having figured out what was happening. Davide helped Carmela onto the boat while Alex unhooked the lines. I had to warn him. I turned to watch Vincenzo scramble to his feet and head toward us.

"Go! He's got a gun!" I yelled to Davide from the dock.

Too late. Vincenzo reached the dock and withdrew his handgun, yelling at Carmela, "You run off with that gigolo?" He pointed the gun at Davide.

To my shocked surprise, Kate leapt at Vincenzo from behind, grabbing his gun arm. The bodyguard ran up to them, but Kate elbowed him, causing him to teeter and fall off the narrow dock into the water. Kate hung onto Vincenzo's gun hand and a few shots went off into the air, sounding like loud fireworks. Everyone ducked.

I was trying to get out of the way when Alex pulled me into the boat.

Casting off, Davide yelled, "Drive! Get out of here!"

Alex grabbed the wheel and accelerated, gunning the yacht toward the open water. The dock teetered from the wake and both Kate and Vincenzo almost fell off into the water.

"Kate!" I yelled. I could see her worried expression, not knowing what to do. I yelled at Alex, "I don't want to be here, take me back."

Kate hung onto Vincenzo until a motorcycle cop intervened and she ran off the dock away from them. Vincenzo holstered the gun. He must have told the cop we had kidnapped his wife, or whatever, because the cop requisitioned a speedboat from a man who was docking. They got in and came after us. The chase was on.

Kate watched us decelerate because of all the boats. Beside her, a second *Carabinieri* hopped on his police motorcycle and took off up the winding road that followed the shore. Getting the idea, Kate ran to Alex's Vespa scooter, searched around, and found the keys inside the helmet on the seat, and jumped on, starting the motor. The scooter whined slowly up the hilly road; whereas, the motorcycle cop zoomed along, parallel with our boat.

Fireworks shot off a floating barge and lit up the entire area as Davide's yacht zoomed past. We passed a large cruiser, and I spotted Como's Police Chief Niklaus Koehl as he partied, wearing a tacky Hawaiian sport shirt and sucking on a cigar. When he witnessed the chase by one of his policemen, Koehl jumped into his small powerboat tied alongside and also gave chase.

In our boat, Carmela cried, and Davide tried to comfort her, but Alex's swerving style of steering made everyone seasick. I grabbed the wheel. Alex watched me steer us between party boats and the fireworks barge, trying to avoid collateral damage.

"You drive boat, too?" Alex yelled over the noisy party boats.

And here I was driving a boat at night on an Italian lake and feeling unafraid.

"Where to?"

Alex pointed up the lake, his hand shaking, "That way." And then he pointed to the motorcycle cop who zoomed along the lakeside road parallel with our boat, Kate riding a distance behind him.

"Alex, why are you involved in this? If you're caught, they'll deport you, or worse."

"I owe a favor to Davide."

"Yeah, well, this is a harebrained scheme," I said, glancing at Davide who still fawned over Carmela. "And what the heck am I doing here? I need to be with my girlfriend." Alex's eyebrows shot up and he grinned at me. "Do you hear that, world?" I shouted, exultant, "I need to be with my girlfriend!"

I had gained some distance from Vincenzo and the cop's speedboat when I rounded Comacina Island where Davide and I had picnicked in the ruins. Then I drove us past the Villa del Balbianello where I kissed Kate and, then, past Lenno where I bought my orange bra. From there, I could see Bellagio on the right, with Davide's hotel and, across the lake, the castle in Varenna, where I had my emotional meltdown with Artù the owl and met the old vedova. Finally, we reached Menaggio.

"Why Menaggio? Isn't this Vincenzo's town?" I asked. His casino gleamed under its neon lights. It seemed so foreign in such a serene location.

As we reached Menaggio's dock, I saw why we'd gone there. On the roadway, Isabella waited, standing in front of the idling van, headlights on, suitcases inside, along with three little girls, the Lazzaro daughters. This was a kidnapping of a different kind. Carmela was fleeing her husband and taking their daughters.

After stuffing us all into the van, Isabella waved goodbye as Alex pulled out like a maniac, driving on the twisting road out of Menaggio onto the SS340 mountain road. I bounced around beside him in the front seat. Davide sat in the back of the van, his arms around Carmela and her three girls, as we all rocked from side to side, leaning into the switchback curves.

"Vincenzo and the cops, they took someone's car. They follow us," Alex yelled, looking over the edge of the road onto the town below.

I couldn't help myself and yelled to Carmela, "Are you sure about this?"

"He threatened to take our daughters if I divorce. So, I leave him."

"Where will you go?"

"We go to Switzerland." She leaned to one side as Alex swerved around a hairpin curve, headlights beaming onto the moonlit road.

"And do what?"

With her long, painted fingernails, I couldn't imagine how she'd make a living or what she had in mind. She raised both hands as if to say she didn't know.

"If you leave, you'll lose everything. And no alimony."

"No alimony?" Carmela went quiet, her eyes downcast. She hugged her youngest daughter to her breast. Then stared at Davide whose blank expression did not comfort her.

"Hey, nothing's impossible, so everything's possible. Just be sure it's what you want," I said, biting my tongue.

Alex glanced out the van's side window. The curve in the road overlooked the well-lit town below. "*Commissario* Koehl drives the car behind Vincenzo's. This is not good." He broke out in a visible sweat, gripping the steering wheel.

"Alex," I whispered to him, "You shouldn't be here. Vincenzo's now your enemy. And Koehl, he'll want your identity papers. Let me drive."

"You do that for me?"

"If you tell me what your job was for Vincenzo."

"Now? You are crazy woman. Okay-okay." He scrunched his face and whispered, "Ice." I didn't understand, so he yelled, "Diamonds! Vincenzo and the Mayor smuggle diamonds," and everyone heard. "Shaun, the *Americano*, was the hiker. I would drive him into the mountains, and he would hike on the trail into Switzerland. That's all I did."

"Okay, don't say any more."

"I had to, or he would get me deported. I didn't want to."

"I understand. Enough now, say no more!"

Too late, Carmela overheard us and waved her hand with the

big flashy diamond wedding ring, "That bastard didn't even pay for my ring?" she sobbed.

"Mommy, don't cry!" wailed one of her little girls.

Davide looked petrified, "Maybe this isn't such a good idea," he said.

"Ya' *THINK*?—Alex, get out!" I demanded.

He skidded the van to a stop and jumped out. I slid over into the driver's seat.

Davide screamed at us, "They're coming!" which made the girls cry louder.

"I owe you, Miss Gerri," Alex's voice cracked.

"By the way, nice teeth," I said. He smiled, Cheshire Cat-style. "Now hide." I put pedal to the metal, rocks spitting as Alex dove into the bushes.

Vincenzo and Koehl were one switchback behind us. Behind them, the motorcycle cop, then Kate on the Vespa.

Davide muttered, "Mother Mary, what have I done?"

"Geesus, Davide, why did you want me here?" He looked at me with a blank stare, sitting in the back of the van hugging a child, but I didn't have a clue why he had asked me to meet him at the dock.

"Because you are brave Canadian woman, and..." he stuttered. I did a double take over my shoulder to see if he was joking. He wasn't. "Because everyone knows you now, La Cantante's granddaughter. You will keep us safe. They love you," he said in all seriousness.

I shook my head, "Great, just great," and then looked at Davide in the rear-view mirror, "Are you leaving with Carmela?" That shut everyone up.

Davide and Carmela stared at one another. A soft smile came to her lips. "What will you do, my darling? How can you leave your father to be with me in Switzerland?"

"Carmela, I love you, I'll find a way, but...," he couldn't finish. She held his hand.

"You didn't figure all this out beforehand, did you? You're both nuts! Sorry, had to say it."

Thinking again about Kate and me, what will we do? How can we keep seeing one another? We can't. It's over. I heard my heart shatter as if someone had thrown a rock into a glass window. "It'll never work." Davide blanched, thinking I meant the two of them.

Vincenzo and the police kept gaining on us. Several minutes later, after passing three small villages, the road ended at another lake, and I drove slowly into a small town.

CHAPTER 25
The Pirate's Secrets

Sei il mio incantesimo:
You are my enchantment.

—G. A. McKenna, journal entry

"Now what? Where are we?" I asked.

"Porlezza on Lake Lugano, the border between Switzerland and Italy. Hurry, drive to the dock. It's an old escape route." I heard the desperation in Davide's voice.

I pulled up to a wharf. Halfway down the dock, an old boat waited, the word "TAXI" painted on its side. The boat's scruffy captain-for-hire waited patiently for us; the smoke from his rolled cigarette wafted upward, its snapping sparks threatening to light his shaggy beard on fire. His wooden boat idled, the motor sputtering. The boat lights and overhead streetlamps on the wharf lit the area, but the full moon shone the brightest, the water glistening with reflected light.

At this hour, the waterfront street of Porlezza was deserted except for a roadside cafe bar across the street, full of patrons. After opening the van's back doors and letting everyone out, suitcases and all, Davide pulled me aside.

"Wait in the cafe. I don't want you *implied-ed*. Go," he said, nudging me.

"*Implicated*," I corrected him, and hurried past a rickety old bus parked in front of the cafe bar. On closer inspection, the bar resembled an old-fashioned saloon. The overhead sign showed a swashbuckling pirate and read, "*Taverna Pirata*"—Pirate Bar.

Medieval bard or pirate music wafted outside onto the open part of the deck. The taverna's proprietor, a hunched old man with wire-rimmed glasses, sat me at a table on the wobbly porch. He snapped his fingers at an elderly white-haired woman inside.

The patrons seated on the wooden porch watched us with interest; several huddled to whisper. After all, we're at the Swiss border and, I guessed, on a well-known smuggler's route. Those seated inside, were elderly men and women who sat four to a table playing a lively card game. I recognized some of the patrons from Argegno, like Johan the pharmacist, who perhaps escaped the din of the festival on purpose, to come here on the bus for what seemed like a tournament.

"*Buona sera*," I offered politely, and several people nodded.

Together, we watched Davide lug suitcases up the wharf, as Queen Carmela and her three little princesses tried to help.

An elderly woman with a humpback, presumably the proprietor's wife, brought me a glass of honey-colored draft beer without asking. She wore a silver Star of David necklace, and I assumed she might be German because of the two small country flags on the porch that waved in the breeze. She said in Italian with a guttural accent, "*Buona sera*, Signora Allegra."

Allegra? I felt panicked. "How do you know me?" I heard the sound of my pumping heartbeat in my ears.

From her pocket, the old woman unfolded a cooking class poster with my photo and Allegra written on it. "I had faith you would return one day," she smiled. "You have her eyes."

"You knew Marcella's baby lived?"

"A few elders knew. There are no secrets, except—"

"Except what is secret. Yeah, got it."

Carmela screamed! We all turned to see her keep her littlest daughter from falling into the water. Still sweating from the escapade, I drank a gulp of the refreshing cold beer, while watching Carmela herd her daughters down the wharf and Davide, struggling behind, with their suitcases. The boatman helped them into the boat.

Everyone in the taverna watched as two cars came to a screeching stop. Having "borrowed" the two cars in Menaggio, Vincenzo and the cop, and Kohl jumped out of their vehicles. Vincenzo ran down the wharf and grabbed Davide, but only to shove him aside.

"Carmela, don't leave me! I love you, you are my world," Vincenzo cried, reaching for the boat's gunwale, half slipping between the dock and the boat, falling to his knees, crying. Embarrassed, the motorcycle cop tried to get Vincenzo back on his feet.

"You smuggle diamonds? There is blood on my wedding ring," she screamed at him, her words echoing over the water. "You and that Rossetti are smugglers?"

Police Chief Koehl's interest piqued.

"I'll change, I promise. I am a man reborn. Don't take my daughters, my life. You will break my heart." It went on and on until even Koehl was rolling his eyes."

I'd lost my ability to translate and asked the tiny proprietor to elaborate, "What's he saying?"

"Yes-yes, it opens the heart," the old German woman cooed. "He says to her, you're the only one for me. *Non posso vivere senza di te*—I can't live without you."

"Tell that to your mistress!" Carmela exclaimed to him.

I nodded my head, "Right on."

"You're everything I need, he says to the beautiful Carmela," the old woman translated as she sat down on the chair beside me, munching the cocktail nuts; this was better than a soap opera.

Davide hollered at her: "Carmela, please! Tell the captain to leave."

The third cop, on a motorcycle, having taken the entire highway from Argegno, skidded to a stop in front of the dock. And not far behind him came Kate on the Vespa, but she stopped on the hilltop overlooking the scene. Alex sat behind her on the scooter, which meant she wouldn't be coming closer.

She removed the helmet and visor to expose her beautiful face. I melted. I wanted to run to Kate and say to her all the things Vincenzo told Carmela, like: "I too am reborn. I can't live without you. You're everything I need. So now what, Kate?"

A man sitting at the table beside me, said, "That Vinnie, he's such a liar and a flirt. Why doesn't the boat take off? What's Carmela waiting for?" I didn't recognize him at first: his big dirty hands were clean, his bushy moustache combed, and his scruffy beard trimmed. But then he slapped on his Greek cap.

"Gianrico, hello! It's me, the crazy lady on the ferry." He all but hugged me, much to the displeasure of his plump wife, who gave me the evil eye until he introduced us and told her who I was. We clinked beer glasses.

Police Chief Koehl gave up listening to Vinnie and sauntered over to me. He leaned on the balcony railing at my table. Off duty, Koehl still wore his badge and a leather gun holster on the back of his blue jeans.

"*Buona sera,* Niklaus. Your usual?" This time the old lady snapped her fingers for her old husband to get the beer.

Niklaus Koehl nodded and turned to me, leaning over the railing. He grabbed a napkin off my table to wipe his sweaty neck. "*Buona sera,* Signora McKenna. You sit here in this place, so far from Villa della Cantante? And so late at night? Of course, you're not involved in this love fest?"

"Love fest? Is that what you call it?" I smiled, knowing full well he knew I wasn't an innocent bystander.

"You know how it is?" Koehl said. His inflection sounded like an apology. The elderly pub owner brought him a draft beer. Thirsty in the hot and sticky night air, the chief of police gulped down a third of it.

"*Sei il mio incantesimo*—you're my enchantment," translated the white-haired woman as Vincenzo continued his "love fest," putting real effort into wooing his wife.

I repeated the words to myself, "You're my enchantment," and glanced up to Kate on the hill, wondering, "Do we love one another enough to make it work? Or is it easier to walk away now?" Kate looked at me, probably wondering the same.

"Now he gets serious," the old woman said. "He tells her not to leave, to stay with him forever. He'll treat her good."

It's crazy, but I yearned to say that to Kate, "Don't leave, stay with me. I'll treat you good." But then, as if already knowing, "It's impossible to put our lives on hold for one another."

Chief Koehl watched me gazing at Kate. "Friends of yours?" he asked, noticing Kate and Alex on the hill. I nodded. Then he surprised me by saying, "Signora McKenna, I've wanted to tell you that I am beholden to your family. My grandparents are dead now, but I remember as a boy the stories." Koehl stopped.

"Tell me more, I'm all ears," I said, sipping my beer. It had become a familiar story.

He nodded to the old couple then said, "Drink up, the beer is homemade, German-style."

"Is that a secret clue? Oh, but I forgot, there are no secrets, everyone knows. Everyone except the one person who needs to know—me."

"Now is a good time, I think? There are those who say the ghosts of Angelina's refugees haunt her olive grove. There are many stories." He waited for me to react.

"Yes, I've seen the ghosts. Go on, please."

His bushy eyebrows wavered up and down in acknowledgement.

"Our Angelina and the local *contrabbandieri* or smugglers hid many people, Jews and non-Jews. We now know it was not all about the Jewish question; it was to eventually control the world. You see, of the 400,000 prisoners at Auschwitz, half were Jews and half were other religions, mostly Catholics, including also Protestants, Eastern Orthodox, and so on, and some Muslims. It didn't matter to Hitler, anyone who rebelled against the Nazi and Fascist regime was persecuted. Including free thinkers, agitators, journalists, poets, homosexuals, even artists, and many others." Niklaus sipped his beer to refresh his throat.

"Even artists?" I asked.

"Yes, yes. I recall a story about a refugee artist who hid with the others in Angelina's grove. Whether it's true, I don't know."

That caught my interest, thinking of her portrait in the villa's living room.

The elderly people sitting inside the taverna stopped playing cards and hobbled outside onto the patio to join us, their eyes and ears intent on Police Chief Koehl and his story. They gathered around me like sentinels in a ring of protection. The drama of Vincenzo and Carmela became a mere backdrop, now given less attention than a radio playing in the distance.

Koehl turned to the elders in the crowd, their wrinkled lines, pages of a history book. They nodded, knowing exactly what he was talking about, but no one spoke, so he continued. "With her help and the help of Carlo and his father, they created a secret underground network to transport the refugees to safety, many Italians who were Jewish or Catholic or on the Nazi-Fascist hit list. The escapees hid in her villa, to be transported when no Nazis were in the hills."

"Yes, I've seen the tunnel," I said, to his surprise.

"They hiked through her olive grove and went over the mountain to here, right here in this taverna, then onto the boats and to safety into Switzerland's refugee camps. And also, over the Brenner Pass on the Austria-Italy border. Here, even among us now, are some of Angelina's refugees. As you see."

I looked around at the crowd that had gathered. One by one, they nodded their heads and smiled at me. I said to Koehl, "As I understand it, these people, and more in Argegno, are the children and grandchildren of the refugees Angelina hid from the Nazis, right?"

Koehl nodded.

Gianrico said, "Signora Angelina saved many from being sent to one of the four hundred concentration camps in Italy."

Johan, the German pharmacist, who had left Argegno's festival for the card tournament, stepped forward from behind me and said, "Many of her refugees were Masons, members of secret guilds that Hitler wanted to enslave to build his great monuments to the Master Race. As they passed through Angelina's olive grove, they left their secret marks on the church and on the ruins of Comacina Island."

"Yes, I've seen their secret marks."

I recalled the vision I'd had while sitting in the island's ruins with Davide, of souls rising out of the ground, hiding behind dark clothing and hoods, and each one carving their mark into the stone. I also remembered the visions in the olive grove, of travellers escaping with their suitcases. I knew now that, at one time, these visions had been real. Then, a new vision unfolded.

Angelina in a black hood and cloak, standing in the ruins of Comacina Island, spoke with the partisans and a few refugees and planned their escape. Beautiful in the moonlight, serious in her intent, surrounded by protective Masons, she knew the conse-

quences of her actions but refused to be deterred. Suddenly, she turned her face toward me, a brief moment, a half-smile. ...

We were momentarily interrupted by Vincenzo's tormented cries, "We can work it out. Please, Carmela, you don't need to go. You are my only one. The love of my life!"

I wished I'd said that one to Kate.

I heard the faint sound of a motorcycle and saw Kate on the scooter driving toward us. She zoomed down the hill, leaving Alex on the hilltop, then stopped in front of the porch where I sat.

Without turning the motor off she yelled, "Gerri, jump on. Come with me."

"Can you wait? They're telling Angelina stories. Come and listen, that is, if you want. I want to share it with you. Please?"

Kate turned the motor off. "Good. I'd like to ask a few questions myself."

I got her a chair next to me and gave her the rest of my beer which she drank down, thirsty.

Touching her knee, I said, "Sorry for all this. It's all so unexpected." I was well aware that time was running out with Kate, so I risked asking Koehl, "Then it's true, in order to help the refugees escape, Angelina conspired with the partisans, working against Hitler and Mussolini?"

After nodding to the proprietor for a fresh beer, Kate turned to the police chief, adding, "Can you verify she was a double agent?"

Noticing Niklaus Koehl's apprehension, I said, "My friend Kate here, she's an ex-cop."

Koehl acquiesced eye to eye with her, and replied, "We don't like to use the word double agent, but...Yes, we can verify that. Nothing was proven, but there were also rumors she had even helped plan the assassination of Benito Mussolini and his mistress. They were shot by partisans in the town of Giulino di Mezzegra, in front of Villa Belmonte. You can see, there is a sign for the murders."

"Yes, I went there to see it," Kate said.

Chief Koehl quickly leaned forward to whisper, "Clandestine meetings were held in the tunnel. Carlo's father built a tunnel from the villa's library. It leads way into the olive grove. But no one knows—"

"Except those who know. Got it." I nodded. I had been led, on purpose, to the library's brick and the secret door that opened into a tunnel. Everything made sense now.

Kate leaned forward onto the table, "What I'd like to know is, if you don't mind…"

"Go ahead," Niklaus Koehl said.

"Why would Angelina risk it? Risk endangering her nine-month pregnancy and then risk her newborn baby Marcella, just before the war ended?"

Johan answered, "It was a worthy risk. After my parents escaped Germany, our relatives would call and tell us horror stories. Too many people had been murdered by the Nazis, even here in Italy, especially in Rome. Neighbours, friends, relatives—disappeared in the middle of the night just for speaking up, some right off the street. Horrific times. It's hard for us to imagine people doing that to people. It's not the first time, nor will it be the last, that people are locked down and locked up to silence them, to make them disappear because they disagree with those in power."

"As the world watched," I added. "Except the world was blind, because Hitler took over the media with propaganda."

Kate said, "Let's hope we never find out what it was like."

I gazed over at the small crowd: Niklaus Koehl, Gianrico the ferryman, Johan the pharmacist, the old German couple, and the others who watched me with interest.

"Tell me about the night she died. Please."

Koehl placed his hand over his heart. "Your grandmother, Signora Angelina and her husband, Max, sometimes entertained the area's Nazi General in their home, to keep him unsuspecting, *si*?" I nodded to him. "Eventually, the Nazi discovered the ruse but not until two years had passed, by then many had escaped through her grove to freedom." Overcome with emotion, Koehl paused, struggling to hold it together.

Johan said, "For her bravery, we believe the General—Otto Weber's superior officer—forced him to kill her." He looked at Niklaus, saying, "The rumor is not true, about the artist in the grove. He did not paint the portrait. Weber had spent many evenings with Angelina, painting her portrait."

"Excuse me, what? But, so it wasn't painted by a refugee

artist?" I asked.

Koehl's voice broke and he blustered at Johan, "Why tell her? It's monstrous!"

"Please, I want to know everything."

Johan continued, "Otto Weber, before the war, had studied at the university in Berlin. Just another student. He studied art and was an award-winning German art student who graduated as an art teacher."

Realizing I was stunned into silence, Kate said, "I can't believe it. A Nazi, her murderer, painted that incredible portrait. But, of course, in a bizarre way, his love for her makes it come alive."

"If I were Max, I would have destroyed it," Koehl said, then continued the story and I envisioned the scene while he spoke:

One night, Angelina with a small group of partisans and refugees huddled in the villa's library. She gave them instructions, handed out their fake traveling papers, and introduced them to their guide. Afterward, she pushed the secret brick on the wall, it clicked open. She grabbed the key from inside the secret drawer, and waited for a section of the bookcase to slowly slide open. She entered and quickly unlocked the small door inside. Everyone ducked into the tunnel. Each family hugged Angelina before following the others. Going through the tunnel, they grabbed their travel belongings from where they'd been hiding; continuing along the tunnel, they eventually came out into the darkness of the olive grove, away from the villa. Their partisan guides then led them into the woods and to their escape.

Angelina stayed behind in the library. The door to the secret escape tunnel stood open and she locked the small inside door. She returned the key and pushed the secret brick on the wall, it clicked, and the bookcase slowly slid, about to close—but not fast enough. Otto Weber, in his Nazi uniform, entered the library. She tried to block him from entering the tunnel, but Weber pushed her out of the way. With his heavy German boot, he kicked in the small door to expose the tunnel. Angelina grabbed him in an attempt to stop him. Overcome, his face twisted in a confused rage, he held her in a tight grip. He snapped, tried to kiss her, ripping her dress.

Just then, Weber's Commanding Officer entered the room. The black uniformed Nazi General glanced at the fake transport papers on the table, saw the open tunnel and removed his handgun, about to shoot Angelina, no questions asked.

Weber grabbed the gun, yelling at him, "Leave her to me!" The Nazi General ordered him to "Kill her!" and, then, left, leaving Weber to do the deed. Otto Weber withdrew his handgun. Angelina pleaded with him. With his hand shaking, he aimed the gun at her head, but he couldn't pull the trigger.

Angelina got away, running into the living room to where baby Marcella lay in a bassinette on the floor. But Weber caught her. They struggled, she fell backward, and hitting her head on the fireplace, she fell to the floor unconscious. Above her was the portrait hanging on the wall. Weber knelt beside her, taking her in his arms.

A young woman in a maid's uniform watched it happen, frozen in fear, watching through the living room's glass patio doors.

With his hands, Weber grabbed Angelina around the throat, and with the eyes of a madman, he choked her. Amazingly, she woke up when he started to strangle her. Her hand reached out toward her baby in the bassinet. At the last gasp of air before she went limp, Weber watched her with a loving gaze.

A stifled scream came from the maid, who then ran away, having witnessed the murder.

Once Angelina stopped breathing, Weber carefully laid her onto a chaise lounge. He gently kissed her forehead.

Baby Marcella, with wisps of light brown hair, crawled out of the bassinet to her mother, and pulled herself up to try to wake her. Otto Weber picked up the baby. The child became inconsolable. He couldn't stop her crying. He covered his hand over her mouth and nose, about to suffocate her. Tears streaked his face, his shoulders shaking. He couldn't do it.

Hysterical with grief, he put the crying child next to her mother. He withdrew his handgun. He placed the gun's barrel in his mouth and pulled the trigger. His lifeless body fell on the floor next to Angelina. The vision darkened when a gust of wind closed the library's secret passage with a hollow clang.

Police Chief Koehl placed a hand on my shoulder, and I jumped. He said, "Weber loved her, but she rejected him. Love and rage. They say he went mad at the end."

By now my cheeks were wet with the tears from many people's memories. "How horrible."

The old Jewish woman said, "Angelina's bravery, like so many others, is unwritten in the books of time, but not in our hearts." The elderly woman said to me, "Signora, Isabella's grandmother, the live-in housekeeper and nanny, witnessed Weber kill Angelina and ran to get help. It happened so fast, there was nothing she could do, she said, she feared for her own life. Then she heard the gunshot and went back for baby Marcella."

Unable to speak, Kate said the words I wanted to say, "Amazing. We have no idea. Baby Marcella was too young to remember anything, thank goodness."

Johan spoke to me in a hushed tone, "I grew up with Marcella. Your mother and I went to the same school together. Giving you up was the hardest thing she did. But it is not *our* place to tell you *her* story."

A loud boat whistle echoed off the mountains and lake, distracting us. The boat's captain grew restless as Carmela and Vincenzo still argued on the dock. The boat taxi idled, smoking and sputtering; the captain scratched his beard and took off his cap to wipe a sweaty brow. The three little daughters cried for their father.

Davide paced up and down alongside the young motorcycle cop who kept shrugging, not knowing what to do. After all, no actual law had been broken, unless you count speeding.

Carmela yelled at Vincenzo, "You'll even give up your mistress?"

"But of course! I only keep her around because she reminds me of you," he pleaded. "And you, you'll give up Davide?"

"But of course," she said, exactly as he had. I doubt anyone believed them.

The sweet proprietor woman placed her hand on her frail husband's chest, saying, "Abe, *Ba'al Shem*, turn evil into good. Forgive. And forgive *us*. All of us."

I stared in disbelief at the old Jewish couple, and, then, at Police Chief Koehl. Then it dawned on me. "Carmela's not going to leave, is she? Fffffrickin' hell!"

We watched as Carmela and Vincenzo did the typical Italian thing: make love, not war; or at least, make up, not fight. I figured Carmela and Davide were too scared to make their long-distance relationship work, she in Switzerland and he in Lake Como. Am I also too scared to even try to make it work with Kate? It infuriated me.

I'd had enough and yelled, "Davide, I'm leaving." Thanking everyone, I took a hefty bundle of Euros from my back pocket and left them on the table, then stood beside Kate, ready to leave.

Dejected, Davide headed toward us. As he crossed the road, a speeding black Lamborghini swerved to miss him. It parked several meters away from the dock. Someone kept the motor running. I didn't see the driver.

Right away Koehl noticed the Lamborghini. "Good time for a speeding ticket."

"Niklaus, thanks for telling me everything. I'll never forget this night," I said.

Niklaus Koehl nodded, "My pleasure, Signora Allegra Ferrario, our hope is your happiness." Then he pulled out his badge and ambled over to the Lamborghini.

The black Lamborghini with the motor running suddenly gunned it and roared toward me, straight toward me! Kate pulled both of us out of the way as he swerved and squealed past. This time we saw the driver: Mayor Franco Rossetti with his middle finger up. Pissed off there were too many people around for another hit and run?

CHAPTER 26
Slamming Doors

Love can drown you or free you.
It's our choice.

—G. A. McKenna, journal entry

*M*y Third Eye opened and I saw the dock, the same
wooden dock on Lake Lugano. The old taxi boat
waited, swaying on the sparkling waters. The salty
captain glowed in an aura of light. Paul and I stood together on
the sunlit dock, as the sun peeked over the Swiss mountaintops.
We held one another's hands. A voice echoed whispers into my
dream and went through my physical body like a wave of
energy, the vibration said, "Forgive." Paul's spirit let go of my
hand. He walked to the end of the dock and then disappeared,
along with the boat, melting into the magical sunlight.

A bump. I hit my head on the car window and awoke in the
van. Davide was driving.

"She wakes, my sleeping beauty."

Disorientated, I yelled, "Where's Kate?"

He looked in the rear-view mirror, "Sleeping in the back. Your
new girlfriend, she's pretty."

I turned to make sure of her, and she moaned in her sleep. "Yes,
she is." Then I saw Alex driving his Vespa scooter behind us.
Davide swerved around a bend that overlooked Argegno. The

festival had ended but we could still hear a smattering of music.

"What a night! You know that Rossetti almost ran us down back there. Just like he ran down Giorgio Romano years ago, Marcella's first husband. A hit and run, right? I'll bet Vincenzo knows and is blackmailing Rossetti to pass the casino development permits," I offered. "Time you ran for mayor, Davide."

He smiled and said, "There's no proof. But, you're not just a pretty face." He ducked when I swatted him on the arm. "Ouch! What was that for?"

"For not telling me everything. I had to hear it from your dad and Koehl. Why is everyone so secretive about Angelina and her refugees? Still to this day."

"There are bad people with long reaches."

"Huh?"

"Angelina protected many people. Now we protect Angelina's daughter and legacy. And we protect you. It's as simple as that."

The long night ended with Davide giving me a brotherly kiss on both cheeks as he dropped us off at the villa. Kate yawned a goodbye, but still had not warmed to him. Poor Davide, Carmela had rejected him again. I knew their future included continuing their affair behind her husband's back. Davide drove away, tooting the van's horn. I wished him the best.

I held Kate's hand, saying, "I've got to check on the dogs. Meet you in your room? I hope."

Sleepy-eyed, Kate nodded and stumbled up the well-lit entrance steps.

After checking on the dogs, I tiptoed along the Villa's upper hallway to her room and knocked quietly before opening her bedroom door. She stood by her bed, packing a suitcase.

"You really are leaving."

"In a few hours."

"Right, I knew that."

"You're the one who didn't want to talk about leaving, remember."

I came up behind to hug her; she stiffened. I hugged her harder, not letting go.

"We can work it out, please, you don't need to go," I said, remembering what Vincenzo had told Carmela. But the rest of what he said stopped at my lips. "I'm lousy at goodbyes, sorry."

Kate shook her head, saying, "What a weird night. You took off without me. I got worried. I hated it. And then you wouldn't come with me. But I understand why."

"You're right, and I'm sorry. Our last night and I get pulled into some crazy Italian drama. But I learned a lot about Angelina and the refugees."

"You took off with that guy, Davide. Are you into him or something?"

"No way! He's feels like a brother to me, and a friend. My beautiful artist, are you jealous?"

"You drive me crazy."

"Thank goodness, I thought you'd banish me. Let's not waste all that passion."

Slowly, I undressed Kate, pausing to gaze at her and to kiss the parts I unveiled.

"Does this mean you don't want to have *the talk?*"

"Let's talk after. Simply enjoy the moment," I deflected, smiling, holding back tears. Realizing this was our last time at lovemaking, I couldn't talk about it further, and I felt a door silently close—another loss.

With each article of clothing she melted more. I stopped at her underwear and jumped into her luxurious bed, under the sheets, and then threw off my orange bra. It made her laugh.

Later, at some point in the night, I woke up, wide awake. I didn't want to disturb Kate. While she slept soundly, I tiptoed to my own room to write in my journal and tried to remember everything Koehl had said.

At 9:00 a.m., I awoke, having fallen asleep at the desk. My entire body ached as if I'd been in a battle. I stretched my back, remembering the old couple at the Pirate Bar and the word "Forgive," letting it roll off my tongue. I realized what they had meant, that forgiveness is compassion, and feeling compassionate is the only way to move on. Forgiving is not forgetting; it's remembering without anger.

I heard car doors slamming. Shit! Throwing on some clothes, I rushed down the enclosed spiral staircase into the villa's kitchen. Then I slowed to a crawl, feeling oddly apprehensive to go outside. I took a quick glance out the window to see all the Villa

Galz packing up their cars, some of them swearing as they tried to stuff the suitcases inside. But where's Kate?

"Good morning." I spun around to see Isabella who had greeted me in English. She held a broom and a dustbin, busy cleaning the villa.

"Thanks, Issy, for feeding the dogs. I owe you."

Isabella shook her head, "*Tu sei una cara amica*," she said, meaning, you are a dear friend.

"The house feels empty already."

"Neh, full of much good memories." Then she pointed out the kitchen window, "They are outside, leaving. And Kate too, she goes, there, with her suitcase."

"Where?" I leapt to the window.

We both peeked out the window and watched Kate stuff her suitcase into a car's trunk. Then Kate looked around, stalling beside the car, not getting in. I jumped back, my heart pounding.

"You not say goodbye? Kate, she goes with the others."

We both heard the slamming of a car's trunk and swear words.

"Yup, she's really leaving without saying goodbye. Maybe she hates goodbyes, like me?"

"You crazy? Go! She waits!" Isabella pushed me out the door, the dogs escorting me.

All thirteen women greeted me alongside the four rental cars. They teased Bibi who had bought too many souvenirs and had to buy an extra suitcase, which she stuffed into a backseat.

"Goodbye, everyone. I'll miss you, you lovely American Villa Galz," I said as bravely as I could muster.

They encircled me with hugs and kisses and took turns adding their contact info into my phone. "Come visit us!" they chorused. Kate stood off to the side, waiting. How could I say goodbye?

"Can I talk to you?" She followed me to the arbor, our favorite spot.

"I'm not going to say it," Kate said, distant, unsmiling.

"Say what? Say goodbye, say I'll miss you, say…?" I hugged her tight. "Don't be too long gone," I whispered.

"Not sure what you mean?"

"I mean, I want to see you again, sometime, somewhere."

"You know my schedule. After the art exhibits and England, I'm home to California." Kate handed me her business card; on the back she'd written her address and contact info. "I'll keep a bottle of Prosecco on ice for you, in case."

"I wish things were different. I wish—I don't know."

"Gerri, a person might be madly in love with someone but still not be ready. And I don't want to have to convince you that you're ready."

That blew me away. I fell silent. We hugged one another and I didn't want to let her go.

"I'm missing you already," I whispered.

Erin slammed her car door, as did the others, and they all revved their motors on purpose.

Erin yelled, "Have a great cooking class, Chef!"

"Oh my god, Sofia's cooking class!" I couldn't stand there looking into Kate's eyes and waiting to break down. I tore myself away as Kate squeezed into the convertible's backseat.

I waved as they honked and drove down the road. My heart ached. My body felt weakened, as it already began to withdraw from her energy. I couldn't stand it. I ran to the hill at the end of the property with the dogs at my heels, and I waved madly. They honked. And Kate kneeled on the backseat of the convertible and raised both arms to me, showing me a big wide hug.

I broke down in sobs, whispering what I'd meant to say to her, "You're the love of my life."

CHAPTER 27
The Shift

Oh, dear Italy, you gave me the heavens
yet took away the stars.

—G. A. McKenna, journal entry

Watching Kate drive away was devastating, heartrending. But I had to force myself to get ready for cooking class number two, find a mask to resemble a "famous chef" and pretend to be one. The morning went by like a bullet, and before I knew it, I stood in the restaurant of Argegno's "famous" hotel. My helpmate Isabella and I started the cooking class in front of thirty people, tourists from all over the world. An overflow of local busybodies and village shop owners spilled out onto the piazza, and even included a two-person television crew from the local station. I couldn't think why.

Sofia Valente had set up her restaurant with a roll-in stove and kitchen island. Impressive. I'd emailed her my market list, and she had all the fresh ingredients ready. For my main dish this time, I had chosen lake fish: perch (*persico*) and pike (*luccio*), giving the fishermen of Lake Como well-earned business.

Happily, everyone enjoyed the two-hour class, watching me cook up a storm. I had no time to agonize over Kate or anything else. The time then came for Isabella and me to pass out small dishes for everyone to taste the meal. I also served a pot of special tea that I'd made. Over the din of clattering plates, I overheard a murmur at the back of the class.

The local villagers who stood at the entrance, opened like the petals of a flower to allow someone through. I couldn't see who, so I carried on being busy. However, my inner sense felt alive, on alert to something important.

The skin on my arms had goosebumps, the room became unusually vivid, and I experienced a shift in the air. The Shift is real, that feeling you're about to step into the raging flow of life. I'd heard that once we make this choice, we move through the universe like moving through water, it moves with us, flowing as long as our choices follow our spiritual path.

I recognized Rosie, all smiles, and wanted to run to her. I didn't recognize the elegant older woman alongside her, although I guessed her name. She was imbued with an inner and outer beauty: long silver-white hair kept loose like hippie chic, a free spirit; her soft, wrinkle-free face blushed with rosy-orange tones; her strong, slender body; and she wore gemstone jewelry. She stood with Rosie, watching me, her arms wrapped around her own body, an unconscious protection.

As the class enjoyed their meal and tea, Isabella, who had already quietly cleaned up, ran over to the older woman and they hugged like family friends. Nervous, I rambled on to the class about olive oil and the olive tree leaf, and how impressed I was by Villa della Cantante's olive oil.

"I hope everyone enjoys the tea. It's made from olive tree leaves. An idea came to me recently. Because of the olive leaf's amazing medicinal properties, it's getting international attention," I said. "Argegno's ancient olive trees can bring in even more profit when its leaves are exported to herbal companies. And, if done legally as a village business, where those families who work the olive grove get a profit share, it means you won't need a casino." The ears of the locals perked up. "But I have a question. Would taking the leaves kill the olive tree or affect Argegno's olive oil production?"

Several locals conferred a bit, but the older elegant lady answered. Everyone hushed to listen.

"*Buona sera,* Signora McKenna. The taking of olive leaves never destroys the tree. It is a simple procedure. You have—how do you say?—a freakin' good idea."

Laughter from the crowd made me snicker as well. She sounded like me.

She said, "I take olive leaf extract myself, as an antioxidant. Shall we talk, you and I, over a glass of wine?" The elegant woman smiled, but her arm across her waist gripped the opposite arm; the movement revealed her nervousness, anticipating my answer.

"More like a few bottles of wine, Signora Marcella Eaton," I smiled, needing to say her name aloud. While listening to her, I had looked into her eyes and recognized Marcella Angelina Ferrario-Eaton, my feisty birth mother as Soul.

Marcella smiled and nodded. I felt delirious but had to keep it together, standing in front of the class. I collected my notes, trying to stay conscious. My knees felt like rubber.

"Thank you all for coming. It's been a magnificent pleasure," I said, grateful. "I hope we see you all again next year." These words surprised even me.

I made a beeline toward Marcella and my friend Rosie. While the villagers surrounded Marcella to hug and greet her, Rosie grabbed me and gave me a teary-eyed hug.

"Forgive me someday?"

"We'll see about that," I said, smiling and hugging her. Then, my heart pounding, I faced Marcella, my birth mother.

Marcella and I were the exact same height. I wanted to know everything about her. Rosemary and lavender, the essence of her feisty yet sweet energy. I recognized myself in her features: high cheekbones, full pink lips, long rounded nose, and her sparkling bright brown eyes. Brown?

"Where did I get my blue eyes?" I asked her, feeling a wide smile release all of my sadness.

"Your Grandmother Angelina had blue eyes."

"Yes, of course."

"Your necklace—Is it the one?" She eyed my gold pendant. "The mason symbols for rebirth and protection. I placed it around your neck before I let you go."

"My adoptive mother found it in my swaddling clothes and saved it for my sixteenth birthday. She said it was a special gift from you. And that's when she told me I'd been adopted."

Tears filled Marcella's eyes. "Forgive me, Allegra. You have been in my heart forever. May I call you Allegra?"

I nodded, unable to speak.

Finally, she hugged me, holding on for dear life. My entire body quaked, feeling her arms around me. I barely got out the words, "There is nothing to forgive. You did what you had to do."

I embraced someone whose womb had carried and loved me, but who could not, for reasons only she knew, keep me. At no time did these feelings ever diminish the love of my adoptive parents, the Bianchi couple. The difference was worlds beyond rationalization. In that moment, I knew that DNA isn't a requirement to be family, love is.

Marcella and I walked outside onto the piazza, clinging together, afraid, if we let go, we'd disappear from one another again. By now, the entire village had heard that Signora Marcella was here to greet her only daughter. On the sunny piazza, everyone clapped their hands, acknowledging the special event. I moved inside the circle of well-wishers to stand next to my birth mother, filling me with emotions I no longer needed to keep inside. Feeling her hand on my back gave me strength to withstand the vibratory deluge of emotions from everyone in the square.

Rosie stood on the other side of me and asked, "Who are all these people?"

"I'll explain later. Suffice it to say, they're the children and grandchildren of refugees whom Marcella's mother, my grandmother, saved during the war."

Outside Sofia Valente's hotel and trattoria-bar, standing on the piazza and seated in the chairs under the cafe umbrellas, people waited for us. These villagers, whose families and homes had been taken from them by the riptide of history, greeted us with open arms. A group of elderly villagers, along with the familiar *vedovas* dressed in all black, rested on the cafe chairs, too old to join the others. Surprised, I noticed my toothless *vedova*, the cat lady of Varenna. She had ripped off the shackles of black and, instead, wore a colorful summer dress befitting a stylish older woman. She looked radiant. The others fussed over her dress.

Carlo Vacchini greeted Marcella, kissing her cheeks several times and hugging her. Then Carlo said to me, "Signora McKenna, it is a day of celebration for all of us. Niklaus Koehl called me this morning and told me about your conversation. Now you know everything."

"For now," I said.

Marcella drew in a deep breath and announced, "Now, it's time to celebrate."

Carlo whispered to Marcella, "Are you all right?" She looked wide-eyed and frightened for a moment, but she nodded and turned to greet a few young village friends like Lia and Roberto.

Her lilting voice made a forceful pronouncement: "*In gioia e in lutto la casa è tutto.*"

The villagers agreed with nods. Marcella said to me, "An Italian proverb, it means, *in joy and in grief, home is everything.*" Marcella wrapped a loving arm around my arm.

Single file, with expressions of fondness, Angelina's refugees walked past to pay their respects. Then, they helped themselves to the refreshments that the servers brought outside. Later, everyone dispersed to their respective homes, no doubt with a year's worth of gossip.

I drove the van uphill toward the villa with Marcella in the front seat and Rosie in the back. The squawky loudspeakers from down in Argegno echoed from the main square.

"What are they saying?"

"It's official. Davide Vacchini is running for mayor," Marcella announced. "He'll win."

I laughed aloud, "Well, that'll keep his mind off Carmela Lazzaro."

On the drive to the villa, I still needed some answers.

"Soooo, Rosie," I yelled into the backseat. She jumped. "I'm pissed at you. Why didn't you tell me? Why all the deception?"

"Not my idea. Your children suggested we tell you gradually, because of your emotional state. You were such a mess after Paul died." I looked into the rear-view mirror; my mouth dropped open as I listened to Rosie's explanation. "A year ago in Devon, I finally met our neighbour Marcella and her husband. One day while visiting her, we were in her den and, by coincidence, I recognized the framed baby photograph on her mantle and asked her about it. She told me the story of giving away her baby. I took a snap and sent it to your daughter. As I suspected, Julie said it's similar to your black and white baby photo."

"Okay, yeah. Then?"

Rosie said, "That's when I approached Marcella and she told me the entire story. She told me she'd hired a private detective to search for you, but by then, years later—"

Marcella continued, "I lost contact with your adopted parents and, of course, no registered paper trail. Too late I waited. I never gave up hope. Each life has miracles of love," Marcella said in a hushed, reverent tone. She reached over to touch my hand. "You are my miracle." She hung onto my hand with tears in her eyes.

From the van's backseat, Rosie poked her head closer, like an inquisitive child. "What now, old friend? What will you do?"

I didn't know how to respond and deflected. "I'm still mad at you for not telling me."

"I meant to join you and help out, honest, but then Bill got sick, yeah," Rosie said, sheepish.

"Did one of you hire Kate Bradshaw to watch over me? She's an ex-cop."

"No dear, no one hired her," Marcella said.

Rosie asked, "Where is Kate? Aren't you and she, you know, getting along quite well?"

"Kate left. She's gone," I blurted out, unexpectedly exasperated. Truth was, my heart's withdrawal from her wasn't going well. I deflected, saying, "Besides, what would my children think if their mother *came out*?"

"They love you. Don't hesitate," Rosie said in the back seat. "Why save up love like you're going to retire on it? Give it away. So. What now?"

Marcella offered, "Stay with me as long as you wish, my dear. There's no hurry to rush back to Canada, is there? This is your home, too." I felt her words rang true for me.

With my wish of meeting my birth mother fulfilled, although it happened in the strangest way, I felt my clenched heart release and open wide, no longer afraid to accept love, finally ready to accept whatever comes into my life.

I honestly didn't know how to respond to Rosie's question. What now, indeed? Do I go home in September to continue teaching, or take a Leave of Absence, and stay with Marcella for a while? Do I work as a chef for Sophia or Davide in their hotels, or continue to house-sit around the world? And most of all, what about Kate? Life is, indeed, full of miracles and choices.

Later that night when we were alone, Marcella took me into the library and opened the secret brick drawer over the fake fireplace to get the key and, then, she unlocked the compartment in the walnut-veneered writing cabinet. She removed the file folder.

"Allegra Angelina McKenna Ferrario, this belongs to you." Marcella opened the plain manila file folder labelled "Allegra," the same folder I'd seen in the cabinet, and she handed me my official birth certificate.

"Thank you," I said, barely able to speak.

"And this…" She held the sealed envelope, "This is my Will. I'll keep it here in the cabinet for when you need it. The drawer's key is in the hidden brick drawer."

"Yes, I know."

She smiled, realizing I'd found the skeleton key in the brick's pop-out drawer. One skeleton key to open the cabinet's secret drawer, one smaller brass key to open the secret escape tunnel's inner door, but what of the third key? Perhaps a key to open yet another secret?

"Who's McKenna?" I asked.

Marcella paused, and then said, "A lost friend."

"Just as I figured. McKenna, I'll bet he was a young olive picker from Scotland? Lust in the olive grove, perhaps?"

With raised eyebrows and a half-smile, she said, "A story for another time." She wrapped her hands in mine. "*Ti voglio bene.* It means 'I love you,' but it is meant for family. You're the rightful heir to the Villa della Cantante. Let's hope not for a long while," she smiled, "I'd like to stick around to see what you do next with your life."

CHAPTER 28
Surfacing

Remember the Villa, the tranquility of space,
the lushness of greens and golds,
the open window, your open heart,
the feeling of being free.

—G. A. McKenna, last journal entry

A fter a week of food, wine, and endless conversation, Rosie left for England and home. I eventually forgave her for all the subterfuge. Rosie's leaving gave Marcella and me a further chance to talk openly and to grow closer. Over the week we spoke about many things, and she told me her story.

"Having an illegitimate baby in the mid-1960s was a big deal to an Italian Catholic girl in a small village. Abortion was out of the question then. When I was six months pregnant, my father Max, along with Carlo, convinced me to give the baby up to the nuns for adoption. But I refused. I was, how you say, a child with a mind of her own." Marcella smiled at me. "One of the nuns connected my father with a young Italian couple in Milan who was unable to have children. They wanted to adopt you right after your birth. I met them and agreed. My father's lawyer did the transaction, all legal, with no government involvement. A few months after the adoption, I changed my mind, but it was too late. They had immigrated to Canada and we lost touch."

Marcella paused, closing her eyes for a moment. Then she said,

"I gave you up so you could have a devoted family. I was young, reckless, and selfish. I wanted to be free. It took me years to forgive myself. I hope you are able to forgive me."

I squeezed Marcella's hand, "Well, I got confused when told, at age sixteen, that I'd been adopted. I went through an angry stage, mad at you for leaving me, for making me feel separated from my lineage, from my sense of belonging. I didn't want to feel lost as if I was an orphan." I paused, watching Marcella's sad eyes. "I'm no longer angry. I'll always love my mom and dad who adopted me. I like my life. I've worked as a teacher for twenty-five-years, raised two wonderful children, been married to a good man who turned out to be not so good, but it didn't break me, and he didn't make me who I am—I did. And, there is nothing to forgive."

"I'll be right here, for whatever you need," she promised me.

And that's my birth story. Like thousands of adopted babies, mine had a happy ending. I felt complete. I had no more questions, well, except the McKenna-question; for another time.

It was time to call my adoptive mother to let her know; which I did. I told her I'd met my birth mother, then I said, "Marcella might be the woman who brought me into this world. But you'll always be my mom. Nothing is ever going to change that, ever."

While Marcella prepared for her husband's arrival in a few days, I grew restless. I emailed Kate that I'd met Marcella and received an immediate reply from her: Kate wrote back that she was happy for me. After that, not one word, even though I'd texted and emailed her several times; yet, I never phoned her. I figured she wanted to distance herself from me for her own heart's protection. I let her be.

Early one morning, not wanting to wake Marcella, I tiptoed outside. My usual morning walk with the dogs ended at the villa's rickety dock. Lake Como shimmered with calm transparency, reflecting my mood. I took a photograph with the new phone I'd bought. Then I swapped it into my back pocket for Paul's phone.

I held onto Paul's cell phone like the ending of a good yet disturbing book, one you didn't want to put down but knew the time had come. I opened the back cover and removed the battery to get to the SIM card and the SD memory card. I slipped them out and broke them in half. I felt no regret. All the anger, anguish, hateful slings at him and the Freighter Girl, all of it, had withered away. It no longer served me to hang on to those feelings, nor his text messages and photos, plus the contacts. By releasing Paul's SIM card, I released the bad memories, keeping only the good; feeling no sadness, no grief, just a willingness to move forward.

I threw the broken pieces along with his phone into the lake and witnessed them splash on top of the lake's surface like tiny skipping stones. As the pieces sunk below surface, they became yet another secret at the bottom of Lake Como. Watching them disappear, I realized how much this Italian adventure had changed me. It had not always been kind, but it was life-changing, making me realize I have a choice between being a victim or being free. My world had shifted from an enclosed, almost suicidal sadness—thinking myself unworthy—to a grateful and joyful expansiveness. It had happened in such a short time. Love, sex, and secrets in an Italian villa. Who would have believed it?

"No one. It's impossible," I answered aloud.

I heard hollow footsteps behind me and the dogs whining.

"Nothing's impossible," said a familiar voice. Of all people, Alex joined me on the dock. "You told me that." He wore a knapsack on his back and carried his toolbox from the villa. He put them into the runabout. "They're my tools. I need them where I'm going," he said.

"After everything, you get your immigration papers, and you leave her? You said goodbye?"

"I can't."

"Alex, don't be a *culaccino!*"

There's no English translation for *culaccino* except to say, he's like a water mark left on a table from a cold glass that slowly disappears in the hot sun. Or, he's the butt end of a salami.

"Don't let Isabella think it's something *she* did. She'll always wonder, and it'll kill her the most."

"It's not forever."

"Be a man Alex, tell her the truth."

"What is truth? To say goodbye but say I love her? Better to be a shithead."

I understood and wondered if I should have played the shithead with Kate, to make it easier for her.

Alex got into the boat and turned on the ignition. "I'll never forget you Miss Gerri," he yelled driving away, staying clear of an approaching ferry. Over the roar of the boat's engine I heard him yell, "*Rocambolesco!*" standing arms akimbo in a swash-buckler's stance as he left on his incredible, fantastic adventure.

I recalled how Rosie had said it to me before I set out on my Italian adventure. I waved goodbye and yelled, "We'll miss you!" but he couldn't hear me. I figured he'd crave Isabella's cooking and return soon enough.

The lake ferry passed by. Startled, I felt a *WHOOSH* over my head and looked skyward to see Artù the owl, circling only a few metres above, and I sensed he recognized me. Smiling, I watched as the incredible owl flew back toward the ferry, where the Scottish falconer waited on the top deck with his arm ready. I got the message. Finalities are like great big wings that fly you away. In that moment, I opened my wings, ready and open to life and to love.

Love is there in every step we take, but blind I had been for far too long. I had healed from a painful wound through meeting the frolicking and lovely Villa Galz, Davide the lake's infamous walking groin, the secretive and curious villagers, and the enigmatic Marcella, who welcomed me with open arms. Their love changed me and opened my heart. Still, I felt an aching, an inner yearning. I missed her. The One. I needed to call.

My hands trembled as I dialed. Hearing it ring, I almost hung up. It kept ringing and with each ring my heart expanded. What am I going to say? Let go…

"Hello?"

"Kate, hiya! It's me, Gerri."

"Yes, I know it's you. How's your world? Mine is like, busy. I'm in the middle of the Venice exhibition. It's crazy here at the Guggenheim." A cool response and I could barely hear her amid all the background noise. Afraid this would all go badly, I took a deep breath.

"What are you wearing?"

"Huh? My agent made me wear a tailored suit. Why?"

"I meant underneath," I said in a sexy voice.

"My black G-string. You want to do phone sex in the middle of the Guggenheim gallery?" Kate laughed, then her voice turned despondent. "Not fair, Professor."

"That painting you did of me is attracting a lot of attention, a big crowd."

"Yeah it is…. How do you know?"

Holding a bouquet of Forget-Me-Not flowers, I stepped around the corner, into full view. "I'm here!" I yelled into the phone and clicked it off. I prayed Kate would be pleased to see me, but where was she? I couldn't see her in the crowd.

That particular room in the Peggy Guggenheim art gallery was crowded with patrons, clustered around both of Kate's distinctive paintings, especially around the one of me. Her other painting was darker, of a woman surrounded in brooding light; whereas her new painting was full of magical light. I walked toward it, thinking she might be there. The enormous canvas glowed under spotlights and held the room's attention. Set against the backdrop of a surreal Lake Como, the figure was comparable to the portrait of Angelina except with my face and my blue eyes. Instead of an opera gown, I wore a satiny silk robe off one shoulder, also revealing a bare thigh. The two dogs, Pucci and Goldie, were painted curled at my feet, and my gold necklace had a sparkle of light on the pendant.

Then I heard a shriek, almost a hollered sob. Kate ran toward me, squeezing past people to close the distance between us. I dropped my packsack and opened my arms. She swept me into a kiss, holding me tight. Home at last, I melted into her arms.

"Am I dreaming?" Kate gasped, squeezing me tighter. I drew back long enough to hold out the flowers to her and she accepted them, saying, "Forget-Me-Nots. No way I can forget you."

Her beauty filling me, I barely got the words out, "I needed to see you. I knew your opening was today—" before she kissed me again.

"I want to hear what happened. Everything. Between you and Marcella."

"Not here. This is your day."

"To hell with that, I've had enough. Let's escape."

Without another word to any of her important guests, Kate pulled me out a side exit and we ended up in the front lobby of the museum. On our way out, she tossed my travel packsack and the bouquet to an attractive woman in a dark suit, I presumed her art agent, who said, "Kate, where are you going?" as Kate grabbed a champagne bottle and two glasses.

Motorboats and gondolas waited outside along the Guggenheim's front dock on the Grand Canal of Venice. Located between the Accademia Bridge and the Church of Santa Maria della Salute, the easiest way to get around was to take either a *vaporetto* ferry, or a gondola. She chose the more romantic way.

Kate whistled at a gondolier. Upon its speedy arrival, we stepped aboard the floating gondola, a traditional, flat-bottomed Venetian rowing boat; piloted by one gondolier in a striped shirt, black pants, wide-brimmed hat, and one long rowing oar. Although usually a man, our pilot happened to be one of the few licensed women gondoliers. It only took Giorgia 900-years to break the patriarchy of gondoliers, or so she later informed us. We were delighted.

As the gondola skimmed the surface along the Grand Canal, we settled into the cozy seats by lying down next to one another. Kate tried to get the cork out of the champagne bottle.

"I wish they made corks easier."

"And you're a sommelier?" I said with a chuckle.

"Never been good with champagne."

"Here, let me do it." Placing my two thumbs on each side of the cork, I put on the pressure. "I've always wanted to ride in a gondola with someone I love. And here I am," I blurted out.

"Did you just tell me you love me?"

"Shut up. Yes, I did—I do. I love you, Kate." And then I said the words I'd been longing to say to her, "You are the love of my life."

In saying this to her, with all my heart, I heard within:

I found the one my soul loves.

As we were about to kiss, POP, went the champagne cork! Quickly, Kate held the two glasses out to catch the bubbling liquid.

Before we clinked glasses, she said, "I want to hear all about your meet up with Marcella. What was it like meeting your birth mother? It must have felt like a homecoming, in a way."

"Later, I'll tell you everything. I've taken a year's leave of absence from teaching, effective immediately. And I plan on spending time with Marcella. But I want to be with you, Kate. I'm ready. I'm so ready to be with you. You are *home* for me."

Kate, teary-eyed, said tenderly, "I'll never give up on us. We'll make it work. Remember, love will find a way."

Lying next to one another in the gondola, our bodies touching, I felt comfortable with her, with who I am, and with the new life opening to me. In that moment, I realized that my husband gave up on me and went with another; my birth mother gave me away to another; I almost gave up on myself; but I knew in my heart that Kate won't give up on me.

I said to Kate, "One thing I'll tell you, when Marcella drove me to the Como train station to come here to Venice, she said to me, 'I feel I've known you all my life.' And then Marcella hugged me like she never wanted to let me go."

Kate said, "You mean like this?" And Kate took me in her arms. "I never want to let you go, ever again."

Before we kissed, I held up my glass.

"To our new adventure. Rock-am-bow-*lets-go!*"

Author's Note & Acknowledgements

Writing a romance novel came out of nowhere, born out of a brief conversation with my sister Anastasia. In 2014, we were sitting in Florence at a restaurant half a block from the famous cathedral. I was still reeling from my 20-year relationship breakup. I said to my sister, "I can't get back to writing," and she looked around at the Florentine surroundings and said, "Why not write an Italian novel?" and my answer was, "Okay," which surprised me. So, a profound thank you to my sister Anastasia because I returned home and started to write about the aftermath of my breakup, about staying in an Italian villa with twelve joyful friends in 2011 (thanks for liberating me!), and about falling in love with life again. It evolved into a story of release and resurrection. I hope that you will find solace and inspiration, or if all else fails, a tasty recipe or two.

Special thanks to all of you who have been a part of this incredible journey, so many great hearts showed up to help, including my dearest family and friends. I am deeply grateful to Tanya A., Elizabeth C., Denise K., Rae A., Jocelyn P., Jodi S., Babe G., Linda S., Marilyn B., Joan H., and Liz C., all of whom read various drafts and made important suggestions. Thank you to musician Babe Gurr for the book trailer; to graphic designer Jerry Leonard for the book cover; and John Pritchard of Pritchard Digital Arts for the website. And a special thanks to editor, Karla Joy McMechan.

Thanks to everyone, for all you did because I couldn't have done it without you. Here's to our futures and lots more wonderful adventures!

About the Author

[Photo by Michael O'Shea]

M. J. Milne is an artist, author, and scriptwriter, born and raised in Vancouver, B.C., Canada. "MJ" studied at the Vancouver School of Art, SFU, and UBC.; she has traveled extensively; produced and directed music events; and loved being a city bus driver. She has written feature film screenplays; published the revolutionary new-age / science-fiction novel, *Universal Tides*; the inspirational nonfiction book, *12 Golden Keys for a New World: Change your Life, Change Your Planet*; and the romance novel, *Secrets of the Italian Villa*.

Discover more at: www.mjmilne.com

Printed in Great Britain
by Amazon

46430225R00165